AF521163

Clarissa Harlowe

Or The History Of A Young Lady

Vol. I

by

Samuel Richardson

Double9 BOOKS

Clarissa Harlowe

Or The History Of A Young Lady

Vol. I

by Samuel Richardson

Copyright © 2025

All Rights reserved.

No part of this publication may be reproduced, stored in a retrieval system, or transmitted in any form or by any means, electronic, mechanical, photocopying or Otherwise, without the written permission of the publisher.
The author/editor asserts the moral right to be identified as the author/editor of this work.

ISBN: 978-93-70819-05-4

Published by

DOUBLE 9 BOOKS

2/13-B, Ansari Road
Daryaganj, New Delhi – 110002
info@double9books.com
www.double9books.com
Tel. 011-40042856

This book is under public domain

ABOUT THE AUTHOR

Samuel Richardson was an English novelist and printer, widely recognized for his contributions to the epistolary novel form. Born on August 19, 1689, in Mackworth, United Kingdom, Richardson is best known for his three major works: Pamela; or, Virtue Rewarded, Clarissa: Or the History of a Young Lady, and The History of Sir Charles Grandison. His novels explored complex human emotions, societal norms, and the relationships between individuals, often emphasizing the virtues of morality and virtue. Richardson's innovative use of the epistolary format, telling stories through letters, was groundbreaking and greatly influenced the development of the novel as a literary genre. He was married to Elizabeth Leake in 1733 and had a previous marriage with Martha Wilde, which ended in 1731. Educated at Christ's Hospital, Richardson initially worked as a printer before achieving fame as a writer. His works, which delved into themes of virtue, social class, and moral dilemmas, were immensely popular in their time and remain important contributions to English literature. Samuel Richardson passed away on July 4, 1761, at the age of 71 in London.

CONTENTS

PREFACE.......7

THE HISTORY OF CLARISSA HARLOWE

LETTER I.......10
LETTER II.......13
LETTER III.......18
LETTER IV.......24
LETTER V.......32
LETTER VI.......35
LETTER VII.......39
LETTER VIII.......44
LETTER IX.......50
LETTER X.......53
LETTER XI.......60
LETTER XII.......63
LETTER XIII.......68
LETTER XIV.......78
LETTER XV.......80
LETTER XVI.......84
LETTER XVII.......94
LETTER XVIII.......105
LETTER XIX.......108
LETTER XX.......113
LETTER XXI.......122
LETTER XXII.......127

LETTER XXIII 131
LETTER XXIV 133
LETTER XXV 135
LETTER XXVI 141
LETTER XXVII 145
LETTER XXVIII 153
LETTER XXIX 156
LETTER XXX 162
LETTER XXXI 165
LETTER XXXII 173
LETTER XXXIII 187
LETTER XXXIV 191
LETTER XXXV 195
LETTER XXXVI 198
LETTER XXXVII 208
LETTER XXXVIII 212
LETTER XXXIX 214
LETTER XL 221
LETTER XLI 230
LETTER XLII 236
LETTER XLIII 246
LETTER XLIV 252

PREFACE

The following History is given in a series of letters, written Principally in a double yet separate correspondence;

Between two young ladies of virtue and honor, bearing an inviolable friendship for each other, and writing not merely for amusement, but upon the most interesting subjects; in which every private family, more or less, may find itself concerned; and,

Between two gentlemen of free lives; one of them glorying in his talents for stratagem and invention, and communicating to the other, in confidence, all the secret purposes of an intriguing head and resolute heart.

But here it will be proper to observe, for the sake of such as may apprehend hurt to the morals of youth, from the more freely-written letters, that the gentlemen, though professed libertines as to the female sex, and making it one of their wicked maxims, to keep no faith with any of the individuals of it, who are thrown into their power, are not, however, either infidels or scoffers; nor yet such as think themselves freed from the observance of those other moral duties which bind man to man.

On the contrary, it will be found, in the progress of the work, that they very often make such reflections upon each other, and each upon himself and his own actions, as reasonable beings must make, who disbelieve not a future state of rewards and punishments, and who one day propose to reform—one of them actually reforming, and by that means giving an opportunity to censure the freedoms which fall from the gayer pen and lighter heart of the other.

And yet that other, although in unbosoming himself to a select friend, he discovers wickedness enough to entitle him to general detestation, preserves a decency, as well in his images as in his language, which is not always to be found in the works of some of the most celebrated modern writers, whose subjects and characters have less warranted the liberties they have taken.

In the letters of the two young ladies, it is presumed, will be found not only the highest exercise of a reasonable and practicable friendship, between minds endowed with the noblest principles of virtue and religion, but occasionally interspersed, such delicacy of sentiments, particularly with regard to the other sex; such instances of impartiality, each freely, as a fundamental principle of their friendship, blaming, praising, and setting right the other, as are strongly to be recommended to the observation of the younger part (more specially) of female readers.

The principle of these two young ladies is proposed as an exemplar to her sex. Nor is it any objection to her being so, that she is not in all respects a perfect character. It was not only natural, but it was necessary, that she should have some faults, were it only to show the reader how laudably she could mistrust and blame herself, and carry to her own heart, divested of self-partiality, the censure which arose from her own convictions, and that even to the acquittal of those, because revered characters, whom no one else would acquit, and to whose much greater faults her errors were owing, and not to a weak or reproachable heart. As far as it is consistent with human frailty, and as far as she could be perfect, considering the people she had to deal with, and those with whom she was inseparably connected, she is perfect. To have been impeccable, must have left nothing for the Divine Grace and a purified state to do, and carried our idea of her from woman to angel. As such is she often esteemed by the man whose heart was so corrupt that he could hardly believe human nature capable of the purity, which, on every trial or temptation, shone out in her's [sic].

Besides the four principal person, several others are introduced, whose letters are characteristic: and it is presumed that there will be found in some of them, but more especially in those of the chief character among the men, and the second character among the women, such strokes of gayety, fancy, and humour, as will entertain and divert, and at the same time both warn and instruct.

All the letters are written while the hearts of the writers must be supposed to be wholly engaged in their subjects (the events at the time generally dubious): so that they abound not only in critical situations, but with what may be called instantaneous descriptions and reflections (proper to be brought home to the breast of the youthful reader;) as also with affecting conversations; many of them written in the dialogue or dramatic way.

'Much more lively and affecting,' says one of the principal character, 'must be the style of those who write in the height of a present distress; the mind tortured by the pangs of uncertainty (the events then hidden in the womb of fate;) than the dry, narrative, unanimated style of a person relating difficulties and danger surmounted, can be; the relater perfectly at ease; and if himself unmoved by his own story, not likely greatly to affect the reader.'

What will be found to be more particularly aimed at in the following work is—to warn the inconsiderate and thoughtless of the one sex, against the base arts and designs of specious contrivers of the other—to caution parents against the undue exercise of their natural authority over their children in the great article of marriage—to warn children against preferring a man of pleasure to a man of probity upon that dangerous but too-commonly-received notion, that a reformed rake makes the best husband—but above all, to investigate the highest and most important doctrines not only of morality, but of Christianity, by showing them thrown into action in the conduct of the worthy characters; while the unworthy, who set those doctrines at defiance, are condignly, and, as may be said, consequentially punished.

From what has been said, considerate readers will not enter upon the perusal of the piece before them as if it were designed only to divert and amuse. It will probably be thought tedious to all such as dip into it, expecting a light novel, or transitory romance; and look upon story in it (interesting as that is generally allowed to be) as its sole end, rather than as a vehicle to the instruction.

Different persons, as might be expected, have been of different opinions, in relation to the conduct of the Heroine in particular situations; and several worthy persons have objected to the general catastrophe, and other parts of the history. Whatever is thought material of these shall be taken notice of by way of Postscript, at the conclusion of the History; for this work being addressed to the public as a history of life and manners, those parts of it which are proposed to carry with them the force of an example, ought to be as unobjectionable as is consistent with the design of the whole, and with human nature.

THE HISTORY OF CLARISSA HARLOWE

LETTER I

MISS ANNA HOWE, TO MISS CLARISSA HARLOWE JAN 10

I am extremely concerned, my dearest friend, for the disturbances that have happened in your family. I know how it must hurt you to become the subject of the public talk: and yet, upon an occasion so generally known, it is impossible but that whatever relates to a young lady, whose distinguished merits have made her the public care, should engage every body's attention. I long to have the particulars from yourself; and of the usage I am told you receive upon an accident you could not help; and in which, as far as I can learn, the sufferer was the aggressor.

Mr. Diggs, the surgeon, whom I sent for at the first hearing of the rencounter, to inquire, for your sake, how your brother was, told me, that there was no danger from the wound, if there were none from the fever; which it seems has been increased by the perturbation of his spirits.

Mr. Wyerley drank tea with us yesterday; and though he is far from being partial to Mr. Lovelace, as it may well be supposed, yet both he and Mr. Symmes blame your family for the treatment they gave him when he went in person to inquire after your brother's health, and to express his concern for what had happened.

They say, that Mr. Lovelace could not avoid drawing his sword: and that either your brother's unskilfulness or passion left him from the very first pass entirely in his power.

This, I am told, was what Mr. Lovelace said upon it; retreating as he spoke: 'Have a care, Mr. Harlowe—your violence puts you out of your defence. You give me too much advantage. For your sister's sake, I will pass by every thing:—if—'

But this the more provoked his rashness, to lay himself open to the advantage of his adversary—who, after a slight wound given him in the arm, took away his sword.

There are people who love not your brother, because of his natural imperiousness and fierce and uncontroulable temper: these say, that the young gentleman's passion was abated on seeing his blood gush plentifully down his arm; and that he received the generous offices of his adversary (who helped him off with his coat and waistcoat, and bound up his arm, till the surgeon could come,) with such patience, as was far from making a visit afterwards from that adversary, to inquire after his health, appear either insulting or improper.

Be this as it may, every body pities you. So steady, so uniform in your conduct: so desirous, as you always said, of sliding through life to the end of it unnoted; and, as I may add, not wishing to be observed even for your silent benevolence; sufficiently happy in the noble consciousness which attends it: Rather useful than glaring, your deserved motto; though now, to your regret, pushed into blaze, as I may say: and yet blamed at home for the faults of others—how must such a virtue suffer on every hand!—yet it must be allowed, that your present trial is but proportioned to your prudence.

As all your friends without doors are apprehensive that some other unhappy event may result from so violent a contention, in which it seems the families on both sides are now engaged, I must desire you to enable me, on the authority of your own information, to do you occasional justice.

My mother, and all of us, like the rest of the world, talk of nobody but you on this occasion, and of the consequences which may follow from the resentments of a man of Mr. Lovelace's spirit; who, as he gives out, has been treated with high indignity by your uncles. My mother will have it, that you cannot now, with any decency, either see him, or correspond with him. She is a good deal prepossessed by your uncle Antony; who occasionally calls upon us, as you know; and, on this rencounter, has represented to her the crime which it would be in a sister to encourage a man who is to wade into her favour (this was his expression) through the blood of her brother.

Write to me therefore, my dear, the whole of your story from the time that Mr. Lovelace was first introduced into your family; and particularly an account of all that passed between him and your sister; about which there are different reports; some people scrupling not to insinuate that the younger sister has stolen a lover from the elder: and pray write in so full a manner as may satisfy those who know not so much of your affairs as I do. If anything unhappy should fall out from the violence of such spirits as you have to deal with, your account of all things previous to it will be your best justification.

You see what you draw upon yourself by excelling all your sex. Every individual of it who knows you, or has heard of you, seems to think you answerable to her for your conduct in points so very delicate and concerning.

Every eye, in short, is upon you with the expectation of an example. I wish to heaven you were at liberty to pursue your own methods: all would then, I dare say, be easy, and honourably ended. But I dread your directors and directresses; for your mother, admirably well qualified as she is to lead, must submit to be led. Your sister and brother will certainly put you out of your course.

But this is a point you will not permit me to expatiate upon: pardon me therefore, and I have done.—Yet, why should I say, pardon me? when your concerns are my concerns? when your honour is my honour? when I love you, as never woman loved another? and when you have allowed of that concern and of that love; and have for years, which in persons so young may be called many, ranked in the first class of your friends,

Your ever grateful and affectionate, ANNA HOWE.

Will you oblige me with a copy of the preamble to the clauses in your grandfather's will in your favour; and allow me to send it to my aunt Harman?—She is very desirous to see it. Yet your character has so charmed her, that, though a stranger to you personally, she assents to the preference given you in that will, before she knows the testator's reasons for giving you that preference.

LETTER II

MISS CLARISSA HARLOWE, TO MISS HOWE HAR-LOWE-PLACE, JAN. 13

How you oppress me, my dearest friend, with your politeness! I cannot doubt your sincerity; but you should take care, that you give me not reason from your kind partiality to call in question your judgment. You do not distinguish that I take many admirable hints from you, and have the art to pass them upon you for my own: for in all you do, in all you say, nay, in your very looks (so animated!) you give lessons to one who loves you and observes you as I love you and observe you, without knowing that you do—So pray, my dear, be more sparing of your praise for the future, lest after this confession we should suspect that you secretly intend to praise yourself, while you would be thought only to commend another.

Our family has indeed been strangely discomposed.—Discomposed!—It has been in tumults, ever since the unhappy transaction; and I have borne all the blame; yet should have had too much concern from myself, had I been more justly spared by every one else.

For, whether it be owing to a faulty impatience, having been too indulgently treated to be inured to blame, or to the regret I have to hear those censured on my account, whom it is my duty to vindicate; I have sometimes wished, that it had pleased God to have taken me in my last fever, when I had every body's love and good opinion; but oftener that I had never been distinguished by my grandfather as I was: since that distinction has estranged from me my brother's and sister's affections; at least, has raised a jealousy with regard to the apprehended favour of my two uncles, that now-and-then overshadows their love.

My brother being happily recovered of his fever, and his wound in a hopeful way, although he has not yet ventured abroad, I will be as particular as you desire in the little history you demand of me. But heaven forbid that any thing should ever happen which may require it to be produced for the purpose you mention!

I will begin, as you command, with Mr. Lovelace's address to my sister; and be as brief as possible. I will recite facts only; and leave you to judge of the truth of the report raised, that the younger sister has robbed the elder.

It was in pursuance of a conference between Lord M. and my uncle Antony, that Mr. Lovelace [my father and mother not forbidding] paid his respect to my sister Arabella. My brother was then in Scotland, busying himself in viewing the condition of the considerable estate which was left him there by his generous godmother, together with one as considerable in Yorkshire. I was also absent at my Dairy-house, as it is called,* busied in the accounts relating to the estate which my grandfather had the goodness to devise to me; and which once a year was left to my inspection, although I have given the whole into my father's power.

> * *Her grandfather, in order to invite her to him as often as her other friends would spare her, indulged her in erecting and fitting up a dairy-house in her own taste. When finished, it was so much admired for its elegant simplicity and convenience, that the whole seat (before, of old time, from its situation, called The Grove) was generally known by the name of The Dairy-house. Her grandfather in particular was fond of having it so called.*

My sister made me a visit there the day after Mr. Lovelace had been introduced; and seemed highly pleased with the gentleman. His birth, his fortune in possession, a clear 2000L. a year, as Lord M. had assured my uncle; presumptive heir to that nobleman's large estate: his great expectations from Lady Sarah Sadleir and Lady Betty Lawrence; who with his uncle interested themselves very warmly (he being the last of his line) to see him married.

'So handsome a man!—O her beloved Clary!' (for then she was ready to love me dearly, from the overflowings of her good humour on his account!) 'He was but too handsome a man for her!—Were she but as amiable as somebody, there would be a probability of holding his affections!—For he was wild, she heard; very wild, very gay; loved intrigue—but he was young; a man of sense: would see his error, could she but have patience with his faults, if his faults were not cured by marriage!'

Thus she ran on; and then wanted me 'to see the charming man,' as she called him.—Again concerned, 'that she was not handsome enough for him;' with, 'a sad thing, that the man should have the advantage of the woman in that particular!'—But then, stepping to the glass, she complimented herself, 'That she was very well: that there were many women deemed passable who were inferior to herself: that she was always thought comely; and comeliness, let her tell me, having not so much to lose as beauty had, would hold, when that would evaporate or fly off:—nay, for that matter,' [and again she turned to the glass] 'her features were not irregular; her eyes not at all amiss.' And I remember they were more than usually brilliant at that time.—'Nothing, in short, to be found fault with, though nothing very engaging she doubted—was there, Clary.'

Excuse me, my dear, I never was thus particular before; no, not to you. Nor would I now have written thus freely of a sister, but that she makes a merit to my brother of disowning that she ever liked him; as I shall mention hereafter: and then you will always have me give you minute descriptions, nor suffer me to pass by the air and manner in which things are spoken that are to be taken notice of; rightly observing, that air and manner often express more than the accompanying words.

I congratulated her upon her prospects. She received my compliments with a great deal of self-complacency.

She liked the gentleman still more at his next visit; and yet he made no particular address to her, although an opportunity was given him for it. This was wondered at, as my uncle has introduced him into our family declaredly as a visitor to my sister. But as we are ever ready to make excuses when in good humour with ourselves for the perhaps not unwilful slights of those whose approbation we wish to engage; so my sister found out a reason much to Mr. Lovelace's advantage for his not improving the opportunity that was given him.—It was bashfulness, truly, in him. [Bashfulness in Mr. Lovelace, my dear!]—Indeed, gay and lively as he is, he has not the look of an impudent man. But, I fancy, it is many, many years ago since he was bashful.

Thus, however, could my sister make it out—'Upon her word, she believed Mr. Lovelace deserved not the bad character he had as to women.—He was really, to her thinking, a modest man. He would have spoken out, she believed; but once or twice as he seemed to intend to do so, he was under so agreeable a confusion! Such a profound respect he seemed to shew her! A perfect reverence, she thought: she loved dearly that a man in courtship should shew a reverence to his mistress'—So indeed we all do, I believe: and with reason; since, if I may judge from what I have seen in many families, there is little enough of it shewn afterwards.—And she told my aunt Hervey, that she would be a little less upon the reserve next time he came: 'She was not one of those flirts, not she, who would give pain to a person that deserved to be well-treated; and the more pain for the greatness of his value for her.'—I wish she had not somebody whom I love in her eye.

In his third visit, Bella governed herself by this kind and considerate principle: so that, according to her own account of the matter, the man might have spoken out.—But he was still bashful: he was not able to overcome this unseasonable reverence. So this visit went off as the former.

But now she began to be dissatisfied with him. She compared his general character with this his particular behaviour to her; and having never been courted before, owned herself puzzled how to deal with so odd a lover. 'What did the man mean, she wondered? Had not her uncle brought him declaredly as a suitor to her?—It could not be bashfulness (now she thought of it) since he might have opened his mind to her uncle, if he wanted courage to speak directly to her.—Not that she cared much for the man neither: but it was right, surely, that a woman should be put out of doubt early as to a man's intentions in such a case as this, from his own mouth.—But, truly, she had begun to think, that he was more solicitous to cultivate her mamma's good opinion, than hers!—Every body, she owned, admired her mother's conversation; but he was mistaken if he thought respect to her mother only would do with her. And then, for his own sake, surely he should put it into her power to be complaisant to him, if he gave her reason to approve of him. This distant behaviour, she must take upon herself to say, was the more extraordinary, as he continued his visits, and declared himself extremely desirous to cultivate a friendship with the whole family; and as he could have no doubt about her sense, if she might take upon her to join her own with the general opinion; he having taken great notice of, and admired many of her good things as they fell from her lips. Reserves were painful, she must needs say, to open and free spirits, like hers: and yet she must tell my aunt,' (to whom all this was directed) 'that she should never forget what she owed to her sex, and to herself, were Mr. Lovelace as unexceptionable in his morals as in his figure, and were he to urge his suit ever so warmly.'

I was not of her council. I was still absent. And it was agreed upon between my aunt Hervey and her, that she was to be quite solemn and shy in his next visit, if there were not a peculiarity in his address to her.

But my sister it seems had not considered the matter well. This was not the way, as it proved, to be taken for matters of mere omission, with a man of Mr. Lovelace's penetration. Nor with any man; since if love has not taken root deep enough to cause it to shoot out into declaration, if an opportunity be fairly given for it, there is little room to expect, that the blighting winds of anger or resentment will bring it forward. Then my poor sister is not naturally good-humoured. This is too well-known a truth for me to endeavor to conceal it, especially from you. She must therefore, I doubt, have appeared to great disadvantages when she aimed to be worse tempered than ordinary.

How they managed it in their next conversation I know not. One would be tempted to think by the issue, that Mr. Lovelace was ungenerous enough to seek the occasion given,* and to improve it. Yet he thought fit to put the question too:—But, she says, it was not till, by some means or other (she knew not how) he had wrought her up to such a pitch of displeasure with him, that it was impossible for her to recover herself at the instant. Nevertheless he re-urged his question, as expecting a definitive answer, without waiting for the return of her temper, or endeavouring to mollify her; so that she was under a necessity of persisting in her denial: yet gave him reason to think she did not dislike his address, only the manner of it; his court being rather made to her mother than to herself, as if he was sure of her consent at any time.

** See Mr. Lovelace's Letter, No. XXXI, in which he briefly accounts for his conduct in this affair.*

A good encouraging denial, I must own: as was the rest of her plea; to wit, 'A disinclination to change her state. Exceedingly happy as she was: she never could be happier!' And such-like consenting negatives, as I may call them, and yet not intend a reflection upon my sister: for what can any young creature in the like circumstances say, when she is not sure but a too-ready consent may subject her to the slights of a sex that generally values a blessing either more or less as it is obtained with difficulty or ease? Miss Biddulph's answer to a copy of verse from a gentleman, reproaching our sex as acting in disguise, is not a bad one, although you may perhaps think it too acknowledging for the female character.

Ungen'rous Sex!—To scorn us if we're kind;
And yet upbraid us if we seem severe!
Do you, t' encourage us to tell our mind,
Yourselves put off disguise, and be sincere.
You talk of coquetry!—Your own false hearts
Compel our sex to act dissembling parts.

Here I am obliged to lay down my pen. I will soon resume it.

LETTER III

MISS CLARISSA HARLOWE, TO MISS HOWE JAN. 13, 14

And thus, as Mr. Lovelace thought fit to take it, had he his answer from my sister. It was with very great regret, as he pretended, [I doubt the man is an hypocrite, my dear] that he acquiesced in it. 'So much determinedness; such a noble firmness in my sister, that there was no hope of prevailing upon her to alter sentiments she had adopted on full consideration.' He sighed, as Bella told us, when he took his leave of her: 'Profoundly sighed; grasped her hand, and kissed it with such an ardour—Withdrew with such an air of solemn respect—She could almost find it in her heart, although he had vexed her, to pity him.' A good intentional preparative to love, this pity; since, at the time, she little thought that he would not renew his offer.

He waited on my mother after he had taken leave of Bella, and reported his ill success in so respectful a manner, as well with regard to my sister, as to the whole family, and with so much concern that he was not accepted as a relation to it, that it left upon them all (my brother being then, as I have said, in Scotland) impressions in his favour, and a belief that this matter would certainly be brought on again. But Mr. Lovelace going up directly to town, where he staid a whole fortnight, and meeting there with my uncle Antony, to whom he regretted his niece's cruel resolution not to change her state; it was seen that there was a total end of the affair.

My sister was not wanting to herself on this occasion. She made a virtue of necessity; and the man was quite another man with her. 'A vain creature! Too well knowing his advantages: yet those not what she had conceived them to be!—Cool and warm by fits and starts; an ague-like lover. A steady man, a man of virtue, a man of morals, was worth a thousand of such gay flutterers. Her sister Clary might think it worth her while perhaps to try to engage such a man: she had patience: she was mistress of persuasion: and indeed, to do the girl justice, had something of a person: But as for her, she would not have a man of whose heart she could not be sure for one moment; no, not for the world: and most sincerely glad was she that she had rejected him.'

But when Mr. Lovelace returned into the country, he thought fit to visit my father and mother; hoping, as he told them, that, however unhappy he had been in the rejection of the wished-for alliance, he might be allowed to keep up an acquaintance and friendship with a family which he should always respect. And then unhappily, as I may say, was I at home and present.

It was immediately observed, that his attention was fixed on me. My sister, as soon as he was gone, in a spirit of bravery, seemed desirous to promote his address, should it be tendered.

My aunt Hervey was there; and was pleased to say, we should make the finest couple in England—if my sister had no objection.—No, indeed! with a haughty toss, was my sister's reply—it would be strange if she had, after the denial she had given him upon full deliberation.

My mother declared, that her only dislike of his alliance with either daughter, was on account of his reputed faulty morals.

My uncle Harlowe, that his daughter Clary, as he delighted to call me from childhood, would reform him if any woman in the world could.

My uncle Antony gave his approbation in high terms: but referred, as my aunt had done, to my sister.

She repeated her contempt of him; and declared, that, were there not another man in England, she would not have him. She was ready, on the contrary, she could assure them, to resign her pretensions under hand and seal, if Miss Clary were taken with his tinsel, and if every one else approved of his address to the girl.

My father indeed, after a long silence, being urged by my uncle Antony to speak his mind, said, that he had a letter from his son, on his hearing of Mr. Lovelace's visits to his daughter Arabella; which he had not shewn to any body but my mother; that treaty being at an end when he received it: that in this letter he expressed great dislike to an alliance with Mr. Lovelace on the score of his immoralities: that he knew, indeed, there was an old grudge between them; but that, being desirous to prevent all occasions of disunion and animosity in his family, he would suspend the declaration of his own mind till his son arrived, and till he had heard his further objections: that he was the more inclined to make his son this compliment, as Mr. Lovelace's general character gave but too much ground for his son's dislike of him; adding, that he had hear (so, he supposed, had every one,) that he was a very extravagant man; that he had contracted debts in his travels: and indeed, he was pleased to say, he had the air of a spendthrift.

These particulars I had partly from my aunt Hervey, and partly from my sister; for I was called out as soon as the subject was entered upon. When I returned, my uncle Antony asked me, how I should like Mr. Lovelace? Every body saw, he was pleased to say, that I had made a conquest.

I immediately answered, that I did not like him at all: he seemed to have too good an opinion both on his person and parts, to have any regard to his wife, let him marry whom he would.

My sister particularly was pleased with this answer, and confirmed it to be just; with a compliment to my judgment.—For it was hers.

But the very next day Lord M. came to Harlowe-Place [I was then absent]; and in his nephew's name made a proposal in form; declaring, that it was the ambition of all his family to be related to ours: and he hoped his kinsman would not have such an answer on the part of the younger sister, as he had on that of the elder.

In short, Mr. Lovelace's visits were admitted as those of a man who had not deserved disrespect from our family; but as to his address to me, with a reservation, as above, on my father's part, that he would determine nothing without his son. My discretion as to the rest was confided in: for still I had the same objections as to the man: nor would I, when we were better acquainted, hear any thing but general talk from him; giving him no opportunity of conversing with me in private.

He bore this with a resignation little expected from his natural temper, which is generally reported to be quick and hasty; unused it seems from childhood to check or controul. A case too common in considerable families where there is an only son: and his mother never had any other child. But, as I have heretofore told you, I could perceive, notwithstanding this resignation, that he had so good an opinion of himself, as not to doubt, that his person and accomplishments would insensibly engage me: And could that be once done, he told my aunt Hervey, he should hope, from so steady a temper, that his hold in my affections would be durable: While my sister accounted for his patience in another manner, which would perhaps have had more force if it had come from a person less prejudiced: 'That the man was not fond of marrying at all: that he might perhaps have half a score mistresses: and that delay might be as convenient for his roving, as for my well-acted indifference.' That was her kind expression.

Whatever was his motive for a patience so generally believed to be out of his usual character, and where the object of his address was supposed to be of fortune considerable enough to engage his warmest attention, he certainly escaped many mortifications by it: for while my father suspended his approbation till my brother's arrival, Mr. Lovelace received from every one those civilities which were due to his birth: and although we heard from time to time reports to his disadvantage with regard to morals, yet could we not question him upon them without giving him greater advantages in his own opinion than the situation he was in with us would justify to prudence; since it was much more likely that his address would not be allowed of, than that it would.

And thus was he admitted to converse with our family almost upon his own terms; for while my friends saw nothing in his behaviour but what was extremely respectful, and observed in him no violent importunity, they seemed to have taken a great liking to his conversation: While I considered him only as a common guest when he came; and thought myself no more concerned in his visits, not at his entrance and departure, than any other of the family.

But this indifference on my side was the means of procuring him one very great advantage; since upon it was grounded that correspondence by letters which succeeded;—and which, had it been to be begun when the family animosity broke out, would never have been entered into on my part. The occasion was this:

My uncle Hervey has a young gentleman intrusted to his care, whom he has thoughts of sending abroad a year or two hence, to make the Grand Tour, as it is called; and finding Mr. Lovelace could give a good account of every thing necessary for a young traveller to observe upon such an occasion, he desired him to write down a description of the courts and countries he had visited, and what was most worthy of curiosity in them.

He consented, on condition that I would direct his subjects, as he called it: and as every one had heard his manner of writing commended; and thought his narratives might be agreeable amusements in winter evenings; and that he could have no opportunity particularly to address me directly in them, since they were to be read in full assembly before they were given to the young gentleman, I made the less scruple to write, and to make observations, and put questions for our further information—Still the less perhaps as I love writing; and those who do, are fond, you know, of occasions to use the pen: And then, having ever one's consent, and my uncle Hervey's desire that I would write, I thought that if I had been the only scrupulous person, it would have shewn a particularity that a vain man might construe to his advantage; and which my sister would not fail to animadvert upon.

You have seen some of these letters; and have been pleased with this account of persons, places, and things; and we have both agreed, that he was no common observer upon what he had seen.

My sister allowed that the man had a tolerable knack of writing and describing: And my father, who had been abroad in his youth, said, that his remarks were curious, and shewed him to be a person of reading, judgment and taste.

Thus was a kind of correspondence begun between him and me, with general approbation; while every one wondered at, and was pleased with, his patient veneration of me; for so they called it. However, it was not doubted but he would soon be more importunate, since his visits were more frequent, and he acknowledged to my aunt Hervey a passion for me, accompanied with an awe that he had never known before; to which he attributed what he called his but seeming acquiescence with my father's pleasure, and the distance I kept him at. And yet, my dear, this may be his usual manner of behaviour to our sex; for had not my sister at first all his reverence?

Mean time, my father, expecting his importunity, kept in readiness the reports he had heard in his disfavour, to charge them upon him then, as so many objections to address. And it was highly agreeable to me that he did so: it would have been strange if it were not; since the person who could reject Mr. Wyerley's address for the sake of his free opinions, must have been inexcusable, had she not rejected another's for his freer practices.

But I should own, that in the letters he sent me upon the general subject, he more than once inclosed a particular one, declaring his passionate regards for me, and complaining with fervour enough, of my reserves. But of these I took not the least notice: for, as I had not written to him at all, but upon a subject so general, I thought it was but right to let what he wrote upon one so particular pass off as if I had never seen it; and the rather, as I was not then at liberty (from the approbation his letters met with) to break off the correspondence, unless I had assigned the true reason for doing so. Besides, with all his respectful assiduities, it was easy to observe, (if it had not been his general character) that his temper is naturally haughty and violent; and I had seen too much of that untractable spirit in my brother to like it in one who hoped to be still more nearly related to me.

I had a little specimen of this temper of his upon the very occasion I have mentioned: For after he had sent me a third particular letter with the general one, he asked me the next time he came to Harlowe-Place, if I had not received such a one from him?—I told him I should never answer one so sent; and that I had waited for such an occasion as he had now given me, to tell him so: I desired him therefore not to write again on the subject; assuring him, that if he did, I would return both, and never write another line to him.

You can't imagine how saucily the man looked; as if, in short, he was disappointed that he had not made a more sensible impression upon me: nor, when he recollected himself (as he did immediately), what a visible struggle it cost him to change his haughty airs for more placid ones. But I took no notice of either; for I thought it best to convince him, by the coolness and indifference with which I repulsed his forward hopes (at the same time intending to avoid the affectation of pride or vanity) that he was not considerable enough in my eyes to make me take over-ready offence at what he said, or at his haughty looks: in other words, that I had not value enough for him to treat him with peculiarity either by smiles or frowns. Indeed he had cunning enough to give me, undesignedly, a piece of instruction which taught me this caution; for he had said in conversation once, 'That if a man could not make a woman in courtship own herself pleased with him, it was as much and oftentimes more to his purpose to make her angry with him.'

I must break off here, but will continue the subject the very first opportunity. Mean time, I am

Your most affectionate friend and servant, CL. HARLOWE.

LETTER IV

MISS CLARISSA HARLOWE, TO MISS HOWE JAN. 15

Such, my dear, was the situation Mr. Lovelace and I were in when my brother arrived from Scotland.

The moment Mr. Lovelace's visits were mentioned to him, he, without either hesitation or apology, expressed his disapprobation of them. He found great flaws in his character; and took the liberty to say in so many words, that he wondered how it came into the heads of his uncles to encourage such a man for either of his sisters: At the same time returning his thanks to my father for declining his consent till he arrived, in such a manner, I thought, as a superior would do, when he commended an inferior for having well performed his duty in his absence.

He justified his avowed inveteracy by common fame, and by what he had known of him at college; declaring, that he had ever hated him; ever should hate him; and would never own him for a brother, or me for a sister, if I married him.

That early antipathy I have heard accounted for in this manner:

Mr. Lovelace was always noted for his vivacity and courage; and no less, it seems, for the swift and surprising progress he made in all parts of literature: for diligence in his studies in the hours of study, he had hardly his equal. This it seems was his general character at the university; and it gained him many friends among the more learned; while those who did not love him, feared him, by reason of the offence his vivacity made him too ready to give, and of the courage he shewed in supporting the offence when given; which procured him as many followers as he pleased among the mischievous sort.—No very amiable character, you'll say, upon the whole.

But my brother's temper was not more happy. His native haughtiness could not bear a superiority so visible; and whom we fear more than love, we are not far from hating: and having less command of his passions than the other, he was evermore the subject of his perhaps indecent ridicule: so that every body, either from love or fear, siding with his antagonist, he had a most uneasy time of it while both continued in the same college.—It was the less wonder therefore that a young man who is not noted for the gentleness of his temper, should resume an antipathy early begun, and so deeply rooted.

He found my sister, who waited but for the occasion, ready to join him in his resentments against the man he hated. She utterly disclaimed all manner of regard for him: 'Never liked him at all:—His estate was certainly much incumbered: it was impossible it should be otherwise; so entirely devoted as he was to his pleasures. He kept no house; had no equipage: Nobody pretended that he wanted pride: the reason therefore was easy to be guessed at.' And then did she boast of, and my brother praised her for, refusing him: and both joined on all occasions to depreciate him, and not seldom made the occasions; their displeasure against him causing every subject to run into this, if it began not with it.

I was not solicitous to vindicate him when I was not joined in their reflection. I told them I did not value him enough to make a difference in the family on his account: and as he was supposed to have given much cause for their ill opinion of him, I thought he ought to take the consequence of his own faults.

Now and then indeed, when I observed that their vehemence carried them beyond all bounds of probability in their charges against him, I thought it but justice to put in a word for him. But this only subjected me to reproach, as having a prepossession in his favour which I would not own.—So that, when I could not change the subject, I used to retire either to my music, or to my closet.

Their behaviour to him, when they could not help seeing him, was very cold and disobliging; but as yet not directly affrontive. For they were in hopes of prevailing upon my father to forbid his visits. But as there was nothing in his behaviour, that might warrant such a treatment of a man of his birth and fortune, they succeeded not: And then they were very earnest with me to forbid them. I asked, what authority I had to take such a step in my father's house; and when my behaviour to him was so distant, that he seemed to be as much the guest of any other person of the family, themselves excepted, as mine?—In revenge, they told me, that it was cunning management between us; and that we both understood one another better than we pretended to do. And at last they gave such a loose to their passions, all of a sudden* as I may say, that instead of withdrawing, as they used to do when he came, they threw themselves in his way purposely to affront him.

* *The reason of this their more openly shown animosity is given in Letter XIII.*

Mr. Lovelace, you may believe, very ill brooked this: but nevertheless contented himself to complain of it to me: in high terms, however, telling me, that but for my sake my brother's treatment of him was not to be borne.

I was sorry for the merit this gave him in his own opinion with me: and the more, as some of the affronts he received were too flagrant to be excused: But I told him, that I was determined not to fall out with my brother, if I could help it, whatever faults he had: and since they could not see one another with temper, should be glad that he would not throw himself in my brother's way; and I was sure my brother would not seek him.

He was very much nettled at this answer: But said, he must bear his affronts if I would have it so. He had been accused himself of violence in his temper; but he hoped to shew on this occasion that he had a command of his passions which few young men, so highly provoked, would be able to shew; and doubted not but it would be attributed to a proper motive by a person of my generosity and penetration.

My brother had just before, with the approbation of my uncles, employed a person related to a discharged bailiff or steward of Lord M. who had had the management of some part of Mr. Lovelace's affairs (from which he was also dismissed by him) to inquire into his debts, after his companions, into his amours, and the like.

My aunt Hervey, in confidence, gave me the following particulars of what the man had said of him.

'That he was a generous landlord: that he spared nothing for solid and lasting improvements upon his estate; and that he looked into his own affairs, and understood them: that he had been very expensive when abroad; and contracted a large debt (for he made no secret of his affairs); yet chose to limit himself to an annual sum, and to decline equipage, in order to avoid being obliged to his uncle and aunts; from whom he might have what money he pleased; but that he was very jealous of their controul; had often quarrels with them; and treated them so freely, that they were all afraid of him. However, that his estate was never mortgaged, as my brother had heard it was; his credit was always high; and the man believed, he was by this time near upon, if not quite, clear of the world.

'He was a sad gentleman, he said, as to women:—If his tenants had pretty daughters, they chose to keep them out of his sight. He believed he kept no particular mistress; for he had heard newelty, that was the man's word, was every thing with him. But for his uncle's and aunt's teazings, the man fancied he would not think of marriage: he was never known to be disguised with liquor; but was a great plotter, and a great writer: That he lived a wild life in town, by what he had heard: had six or seven companions as bad as himself; whom now and then he brought down with him; and the country was always glad when they went up again. He would have it, that although passionate, he was good-humoured; loved as well to take a jest as to give one; and would rally himself upon occasion the freest of any man he ever knew.'

This was his character from an enemy; for, as my aunt observed, every thing the man said commendably of him came grudgingly, with a must needs say—to do him justice, &c. while the contrary was delivered with a free good-will. And this character, as a worse was expected, though this was bad enough, not answering the end of inquiring after it, my brother and sister were more apprehensive than before, that his address would be encouraged, since the worst part of it was known, or supposed, when he was first introduced to my sister.

But, with regard to myself, I must observe in his disfavour, that, notwithstanding the merit he wanted to make with me for his patience upon my brother's ill-treatment of him, I owed him no compliments for trying to conciliate with him. Not that I believe it would have signified any thing if he had made ever such court either to him or to my sister: yet one might have expected from a man of his politeness, and from his pretensions, you know, that he would have been willing to try. Instead of which, he shewed such a contempt both of my brother and my sister, especially my brother, as was construed into a defiance of them. And for me to have hinted at an alteration in his behaviour to my brother, was an advantage I knew he would have been proud of; and which therefore I had no mind to give him. But I doubted not that having so very little encouragement from any body, his pride would soon take fire, and he would of himself discontinue his visits, or go to town; where, till he came acquainted with our family, he used chiefly to reside: And in this latter case he had no reason to expect, that I would receive, much less answer, his Letters: the occasions which had led me to receive any of his, being by this time over.

But my brother's antipathy would not permit him to wait for such an event; and after several excesses, which Mr. Lovelace still returned with contempt, and a haughtiness too much like that of the aggressor, my brother took upon himself to fill up the door-way once when he came, as if to oppose his entrance: And upon his asking for me, demanded, what his business was with his sister?

The other, with a challenging air, as my brother says, told him, he would answer a gentleman any question; but he wished that Mr. James Harlowe, who had of late given himself high airs, would remember that he was not now at college.

Just then the good Dr. Lewen, who frequently honours me with a visit of conversation, as he is pleased to call it, and had parted with me in my own parlour, came to the door: and hearing the words, interposed; both having their hands upon their swords: and telling Mr. Lovelace where I was, he burst by my brother, to come to me; leaving him chafing, he said, like a hunted boar at bay.

This alarmed us all. My father was pleased to hint to Mr. Lovelace, that he wished he would discontinue his visits for the peace-sake of the family: And I, by his command, spoke a great deal plainer.

But Mr. Lovelace is a man not easily brought to give up his purpose, especially in a point wherein he pretends his heart is so much engaged: and no absolute prohibition having been given, things went on for a little while as before: for I saw plainly, that to have denied myself to his visits (which however I declined receiving as often as I could) was to bring forward some desperate issue between the two; since the offence so readily given on one side was brooked by the other only out of consideration to me.

And thus did my brother's rashness lay me under an obligation where I would least have owed it.

The intermediate proposals of Mr. Symmes and Mr. Mullins, both (in turn) encouraged by my brother, induced him to be more patient for a while, as nobody thought me over-forward in Mr. Lovelace's favour; for he hoped that he should engage my father and uncles to approve of the one or the other in opposition to the man he hated. But when he found that I had interest enough to disengage myself from the addresses of those gentlemen, as I had (before he went to Scotland, and before Mr. Lovelace visited here) of Mr. Wyerley's, he then kept no measures: and first set himself to upbraid me for supposed prepossession, which he treated as if it were criminal; and then to insult Mr. Lovelace in person, at Mr. Edward Symmes's, the brother of the other Symmes, two miles off; and no good Dr. Lewen being there to interpose, the unhappy rencounter followed. My brother was disarmed, as you have heard; and on being brought home, and giving us ground to suppose he was much worse hurt than he really was, and a fever ensuing, every one flamed out; and all was laid at my door.

Mr. Lovelace for three days together sent twice each day to inquire after my brother's health; and although he received rude and even shocking returns, he thought fit on the fourth day to make in person the same inquiries; and received still greater incivilities from my two uncles, who happened to be both there. My father also was held by force from going to him with his sword in his hand, although he had the gout upon him.

I fainted away with terror, seeing every one so violent, and hearing Mr. Lovelace swear that he would not depart till he had made my uncles ask his pardon for the indignities he had received at their hands; a door being held fast locked between him and them. My mother all the time was praying and struggling to with-hold my father in the great parlour. Meanwhile my sister, who had treated Mr. Lovelace with virulence, came in to me, and insulted me as fast as I recovered. But when Mr. Lovelace was told how ill I was, he departed; nevertheless vowing revenge.

He was ever a favourite with our domestics. His bounty to them, and having always something facetious to say to each, had made them all of his party: and on this occasion they privately blamed every body else, and reported his calm and gentlemanly behaviour (till the provocations given him ran very high) in such favourable terms, that those reports, and my apprehensions of the consequence of this treatment, induced me to read a letter he sent me that night; and, it being written in the most respectful terms (offering to submit the whole to my decision, and to govern himself entirely by my will) to answer it some days after.

To this unhappy necessity was owing our renewed correspondence, as I may call it; yet I did not write till I had informed myself from Mr. Symmes's brother, that he was really insulted into the act of drawing his sword by my brother's repeatedly threatening (upon his excusing himself out of regard to me) to brand me ir he did not; and, by all the inquiry I could make, that he was again the sufferer from my uncles in a more violent manner than I have related.

The same circumstances were related to my father and other relations by Mr. Symmes; but they had gone too far in making themselves parties to the quarrel either to retract or forgive; and I was forbidden to correspond with him, or to be seen a moment in his company.

One thing however I can say, but that in confidence, because my mother commanded me not to mention it:—That, expressing her apprehension of the consequences of the indignities offered to Mr. Lovelace, she told me, she would leave it to my prudence to do all I could to prevent the impending mischief on one side.

I am obliged to break off. But I believe I have written enough to answer very fully all that you have required of me. It is not for a child to seek to clear her own character, or to justify her actions, at the expense of the most revered ones: yet, as I know that the account of all those further proceedings by which I may be affected, will be interesting to so dear a friend (who will communicate to others no more than what is fitting) I will continue to write, as I have opportunity, as minutely as we are used to write to each other.

Indeed I have no delight, as I have often told you, equal to that which I take in conversing with you by letter, when I cannot in person.

Mean time, I cannot help saying, that I am exceedingly concerned to find, that I am become so much the public talk as you tell me I am. Your kind, your precautionary regard for my fame, and the opportunity you have given me to tell my own story previous to any new accident (which heaven avert!) is so like the warm friend I have ever found in my dear Miss Howe, that, with redoubled obligation, you bind me to be

Your ever grateful and affectionate, CLARISSA HARLOWE.

Copy of the requested Preamble to the clauses in her Grandfather's Will: inclosed in the preceding Letter.

As the particular estate I have mentioned and described above, is principally of my own raising: as my three sons have been uncommonly prosperous; and are very rich: the eldest by means of the unexpected benefits he reaps from his new found mines; the second, by what has, as unexpectedly, fallen in to him on the deaths of several relations of his present wife, the worthy daughter by both sides of very honourable families; over and above the very large portion which he received with her in marriage: my son Antony by his East-India traffic, and successful voyages: as furthermore my grandson James will be sufficiently provided for by his grandmother Lovell's kindness to him; who, having no near relations, hath assured me, that she hath, as well by deed of gift as by will, left him both her Scottish and English estates: for never was there a family more prosperous in all its branches, blessed be God therefore: and as my said son James will very probably make it up to my grand-daughter Arabella; to whom I intend no disrespect; nor have reason; for she is a very hopeful and dutiful child: and as my sons, John and Antony, seem not inclined to a married life; so that my son James is the only one who has children, or is likely to have any. For all these reasons; and because my dearest and beloved grand-daughter Clarissa hath been from her infancy a matchless young creature in her duty to me, and admired by all who knew her, as a very extraordinary child; I must therefore take the pleasure of considering her as my own peculiar child; and this without intending offence; and I hope it will not be taken as any, since my son James can bestow his favours accordingly, and in greater proportion, upon his son James, and upon his daughter Arabella.—

These, I say, are the reasons which move me to dispose of the above-described estate in the precious child's favour; who is the delight of my old age: and, I verily think, has contributed, by her amiable duty and kind and tender regards, to prolong my life.

Wherefore it is my express will and commandment, and I enjoin my said three sons, John, James, and Antony, and my grandson James, and my grand-daughter Arabella, as they value my blessing, and will regard my memory, and would wish their own last wills and desires to be fulfilled by their survivors, that they will not impugn or contest the following bequests and devises in favour of my said grand-daughter Clarissa, although they should not be strictly conformable to law or to the forms thereof; nor suffer them to be controverted or disputed on any pretence whatsoever.

And in this confidence, &c. &c. &c.

LETTER V

MISS CLARISSA HARLOWE, TO MISS HOWE JAN. 20

I have been hindered from prosecuting my intention. Neither nights nor mornings have been my own. My mother has been very ill; and would have no other nurse but me. I have not stirred from her bedside (for she kept her bed); and two nights I had the honour of sharing it with her.

Her disorder was a very violet colic. The contentions of these fierce, these masculine spirits, and the apprehension of mischiefs that may arise from the increasing animosity which all here have against Mr. Lovelace, and his too well known resenting and intrepid character, she cannot bear. Then the foundations laid, as she dreads, for jealousy and heart-burnings in her own family, late so happy and so united, afflict exceedingly a gentle and sensible mind, which has from the beginning, on all occasions, sacrificed its own inward satisfaction to outward peace. My brother and sister, who used very often to jar, are now so entirely one, and are so much together, (caballing was the word that dropt from my mother's lips, as if at unawares,) that she is very fearful of the consequences that may follow;—to my prejudice, perhaps, is her kind concern; since she sees that they behave to me every hour with more and more shyness and reserve: yet, would she but exert that authority which the superiority of her fine talents gives her, all these family feuds might perhaps be extinguished in their but yet beginnings; especially as she may be assured that all fitting concessions shall be made by me, not only as my brother and sister are my elders, but for the sake of so excellent and so indulgent a mother.

For, if I may say to you, my dear, what I would not to any other person living, it is my opinion, that had she been of a temper that would have borne less, she would have had ten times less to bear, than she has had. No commendation, you'll say, of the generosity of those spirits which can turn to its own disquiet so much condescending goodness.

Upon my word I am sometimes tempted to think that we may make the world allow for and respect us as we please, if we can but be sturdy in our wills, and set out accordingly. It is but being the less beloved for it, that's all: and if we have power to oblige those we have to do with, it will not appear to us that we are. Our flatterers will tell us any thing sooner than our faults, or what they know we do not like to hear.

Were there not truth in this observation, is it possible that my brother and sister could make their very failings, their vehemences, of such importance to all the family? 'How will my son, how will my nephew, take this or that measure? What will he say to it? Let us consult him about it;' are references always previous to every resolution taken by his superiors, whose will ought to be his. Well may he expect to be treated with this deference by every other person, when my father himself, generally so absolute, constantly pays it to him; and the more since his godmother's bounty has given independence to a spirit that was before under too little restraint.—But whither may these reflections lead me!—I know you do not love any of us but my mother and me; and, being above all disguises, make me sensible that you do not oftener than I wish.—Ought I then to add force to your dislikes of those whom I wish you to like?—of my father especially; for he, alas! has some excuse for his impatience of contradiction. He is not naturally an ill-tempered man; and in his person and air, and in his conversation too, when not under the torture of a gouty paroxysm, every body distinguishes the gentleman born and educated.

Our sex perhaps must expect to bear a little—uncourtliness shall I call it?—from the husband whom as the lover they let know the preference their hearts gave him to all other men.—Say what they will of generosity being a manly virtue; but upon my word, my dear, I have ever yet observed, that it is not to be met with in that sex one time in ten that it is to be found in ours.—But my father was soured by the cruel distemper I have named; which seized him all at once in the very prime of life, in so violent a manner as to take from the most active of minds, as his was, all power of activity, and that in all appearance for life.—It imprisoned, as I may say, his lively spirits in himself, and turned the edge of them against his own peace; his extraordinary prosperity adding to his impatiency. Those, I believe, who want the fewest earthly blessings, most regret that they want any.

But my brother! What excuse can be made for his haughty and morose temper? He is really, my dear, I am sorry to have occasion to say it, an ill-temper'd young man; and treats my mother sometimes—Indeed he is not dutiful.—But, possessing every thing, he has the vice of age, mingled with the ambition of youth, and enjoys nothing—but his own haughtiness and ill-temper, I was going to say.—Yet again am I adding force to your dislikes of some of us.—Once, my dear, it was perhaps in your power to have moulded him as you pleased.—Could you have been my sister!—Then had I friend in a sister.—But no wonder that he does not love you now; who could nip in the bud, and that with a disdain, let me say, too much of kin to his haughtiness, a passion that would not have wanted a fervour worthy of the object; and which possibly would have made him worthy.

But no more of this. I will prosecute my former intention in my next; which I will sit down to as soon as breakfast is over; dispatching this by the messenger whom you have so kindly sent to inquire after us on my silence. Mean time, I am,

Your most affectionate and obliged friend and servant, CL. HARLOWE.

LETTER VI

MISS CLARISSA HARLOWE, TO MISS HOWE HARLOWE-PLACE, JAN. 20

I will now resume my narrative of proceedings here.—My brother being in a good way, although you may be sure that his resentments are rather heightened than abated by the galling disgrace he has received, my friends (my father and uncles, however, if not my brother and sister) begin to think that I have been treated unkindly. My mother been so good as to tell me this since I sent away my last.

Nevertheless I believe they all think that I receive letters from Mr. Lovelace. But Lord M. being inclined rather to support than to blame his nephew, they seem to be so much afraid of Mr. Lovelace, that they do not put it to me whether I do or not; conniving on the contrary, as it should seem, at the only method left to allay the vehemence of a spirit which they have so much provoked: For he still insists upon satisfaction from my uncles; and this possibly (for he wants not art) as the best way to be introduced again with some advantage into our family. And indeed my aunt Hervey has put it to my mother, whether it were not best to prevail upon my brother to take a turn to his Yorkshire estate (which he was intending to do before) and to stay there till all is blown over.

But this is very far from being his intention: For he has already began to hint again, that he shall never be easy or satisfied till I am married; and, finding neither Mr. Symmes nor Mr. Mullins will be accepted, has proposed Mr. Wyerley once more, on the score of his great passion for me. This I have again rejected; and but yesterday he mentioned one who has applied to him by letter, making high offers. This is Mr. Solmes; Rich Solmes you know they call him. But this application has not met with the attention of one single soul.

If none of his schemes of getting me married take effect, he has thoughts, I am told, of proposing to me to go to Scotland, that as the compliment is, I may put his house there in such order as our own is in. But this my mother intends to oppose for her own sake; because having relieved her, as she is pleased to say, of the household cares (for which my sister, you know, has no turn) they must again devolve upon her if I go. And if she did not oppose it, I should; for, believe me, I have no mind to be his housekeeper; and I am sure, were I to go with him, I should be treated rather as a servant than a sister:—perhaps, not the better because I am his sister. And if Mr. Lovelace should follow me, things might be worse than they are now.

But I have besought my mother, who is apprehensive of Mr. Lovelace's visits, and for fear of whom my uncles never stir out without arms and armed servants (my brother also being near well enough to go abroad), to procure me permission to be your guest for a fortnight, or so.—Will your mother, think you, my dear, give me leave?

I dare not ask to go to my dairy-house, as my good grandfather would call it: for I am now afraid of being thought to have a wish to enjoy that independence to which his will has entitled me: and as matter are situated, such a wish would be imputed to my regard to the man to whom they have now so great an antipathy. And indeed could I be as easy and happy here as I used to be, I would defy that man and all his sex; and never repent that I have given the power of my fortune into my father's hands.

Just now, my mother has rejoiced me with the news that my requested permission is granted. Every one thinks it best that I should go to you, except my brother. But he was told, that he must not expect to rule in every thing. I am to be sent for into the great parlour, where are my two uncles and my aunt Hervey, and to be acquainted with this concession in form.

You know, my dear, that there is a good deal of solemnity among us. But never was there a family more united in its different branches than ours. Our uncles consider us as their own children, and declare that it is for our sakes that they live single. So that they are advised with upon every article relating to us, or that may affect us. It is therefore the less wonder, at a time when they understand that Mr. Lovelace is determined to pay us an amicable visit, as he calls it, (but which I am sure cannot end amicably,) that they should both be consulted upon the permission I had desired to attend you.

I will acquaint you with what passed at the general leave given me to be your guest. And yet I know that you will not love my brother the better for my communication. But I am angry with him myself, and cannot help it. And besides, it is proper to let you know the terms I go upon, and their motives for permitting me to go.

Clary, said my mother, as soon as I entered the great parlour, your request to go to Miss Howe's for a few days has been taken into consideration, and granted—

Much against my liking, I assure you, said my brother, rudely interrupting her.

Son James! said my father, and knit his brows.

He was not daunted. His arm was in a sling. He often has the mean art to look upon that, when any thing is hinted that may be supposed to lead toward the least favour to or reconciliation with Mr. Lovelace.—Let the girl then [I am often the girl with him] be prohibited seeing that vile libertine.

Nobody spoke.

Do you hear, sister Clary? taking their silence for approbation of what he had dictated; you are not to receive visits from Lord M.'s nephew.

Every one still remained silent.

Do you so understand the license you have, Miss? interrogated he.

I would be glad, Sir, said I, to understand that you are my brother;—and that you would understand that you are only my brother.

O the fond, fond heart! with a sneer of insult, lifting up his hands.

Sir, said I, to my father, to your justice I appeal: If I have deserved reflection, let me be not spared. But if I am to be answerable for the rashness—

No more!—No more of either side, said my father. You are not to receive the visits of that Lovelace, though.—Nor are you, son James, to reflect upon your sister. She is a worthy child.

Sir, I have done, replied he:—and yet I have her honour at heart, as much as the honour of the rest of the family.

And hence, Sir, retorted I, your unbrotherly reflections upon me?

Well, but you observe, Miss, said he, that it is not I, but your father, that tells you, that you are not to receive the visits of that Lovelace.

Cousin Harlowe, said my aunt Hervey, allow me to say, that my cousin Clary's prudence may be confided in.

I am convinced it may, joined my mother.

But, aunt, but, madam (put in my sister) there is no hurt, I presume, in letting my sister know the condition she goes to Miss Howe upon; since, if he gets a nack of visiting her there—

You may be sure, interrupted my uncle Harlowe, he will endeavour to see her there.

So would such an impudent man here, said my uncle Antony: and 'tis better done there than here.

Better no where, said my father.—I command you (turning to me) on pain of displeasure, that you see him not at all.

I will not, Sir, in any way of encouragement, I do assure you: not at all, if I can properly avoid it.

You know with what indifference, said my mother, she has hitherto seen him.—Her prudence may be trusted to, as my sister Hervey says.

With what appa—rent indifference, drawled my brother.

Son James! said my father sternly.

I have done, Sir, said he. But again, in a provoking manner, he reminded me of the prohibition.

Thus ended the conference.

Will you engage, my dear, that the hated man shall not come near your house?—But what an inconsistence is this, when they consent to my going, thinking his visits here no otherwise to be avoided!—But if he does come, I charge you never to leave us alone together.

As I have no reason to doubt a welcome from your good mother, I will put every thing in order here, and be with you in two or three days.

Mean time, I am Your most affectionate and obliged, CLARISSA HARLOWE.

LETTER VII

MISS CLARISSA HARLOWE, TO MISS HOWE [AFTER HER RETURN FROM HER.] HARLOWE-PLACE, FEB. 20

I beg your excuse for not writing sooner. Alas! my dear, I have sad prospects before me! My brother and sister have succeeded in all their views. They have found out another lover for me; an hideous one!—Yet he is encouraged by every body. No wonder that I was ordered home so suddenly. At an hour's warning!—No other notice, you know, than what was brought with the chariot that was to carry me back.—It was for fear, as I have been informed [an unworthy fear!] that I should have entered into any concert with Mr. Lovelace had I known their motive for commanding me home; apprehending, 'tis evident, that I should dislike the man they had to propose to me.

And well might they apprehend so:—For who do you think he is?—No other than that Solmes—Could you have believed it?—And they are all determined too; my mother with the rest!—Dear, dear excellence! how could she be thus brought over, when I am assured, that on his first being proposed she was pleased to say, That had Mr. Solmes the Indies in possession, and would endow me with them, she should not think him deserving of her Clarissa!

The reception I met with at my return, so different from what I used to meet with on every little absence [and now I had been from them three weeks], convinced me that I was to suffer for the happiness I had had in your company and conversation for that most agreeable period. I will give you an account of it.

My brother met me at the door, and gave me his hand when I stepped out of the chariot. He bowed very low: pray, Miss, favour me.—I thought it in good humour; but found it afterwards mock respect: and so he led me in great form, I prattling all the way, inquiring of every body's health, (although I was so soon to see them, and there was hardly time for answers,) into the great parlour; where were my father, mother, my two uncles, and sister.

I was struck all of a heap as soon as I entered, to see a solemnity which I had been so little used to on the like occasions in the countenance of every dear relation. They all kept their seats. I ran to my father, and kneeled: then to my mother: and met from both a cold salute: From my father a blessing but half pronounced: My mother indeed called me child; but embraced me not with her usual indulgent ardour.

After I had paid my duty to my uncles, and my compliments to my sister, which she received with solemn and stiff form, I was bid to sit down. But my heart was full: and I said it became me to stand, if I could stand, upon a reception so awful and unusual. I was forced to turn my face from them, and pull out my handkerchief.

My unbrotherly accuser hereupon stood forth, and charged me with having received no less than five or six visits at Miss Howe's from the man they had all so much reason to hate [that was the expression]; notwithstanding the commands I had had to the contrary. And he bid me deny it if I could.

I had never been used, I said, to deny the truth, nor would I now. I owned I had in the three weeks passed seen the person I presumed he meant oftener than five or six times [Pray hear me, brother, said I; for he was going to flame out], but he always asked for Mrs. or Miss Howe, when he came.

I proceeded, that I had reason to believe, that both Mrs. Howe and Miss, as matters stood, would much rather have excused his visits; but they had more than once apologized, that having not the same reason my papa had to forbid him their house, his rank and fortune entitled him to civility.

You see, my dear, I made not the pleas I might have made.

My brother seemed ready to give a loose to his passion: My father put on the countenance which always portends a gathering storm: My uncles mutteringly whispered: And my sister aggravatingly held up her hands. While I begged to be heard out:—And my mother said, let the child, that was her kind word, be heard.

I hoped, I said, there was no harm done: that it became not me to prescribe to Mrs. or Miss Howe who should be their visitors: that Mrs. Howe was always diverted with the raillery that passed between Miss and him: that I had no reason to challenge her guest for my visitor, as I should seem to have done had I refused to go into their company when he was with them: that I had never seen him out of the presence of one or both of those ladies; and had signified to him once, on his urging a few moments' private conversation with me, that, unless a reconciliation were effected between my family and his, he must not expect that I would countenance his visits, much less give him an opportunity of that sort.

I told him further, that Miss Howe so well understood my mind, that she never left me a moment while Mr. Lovelace was there: that when he came, if I was not below in the parlour, I would not suffer myself to be called to him: although I thought it would be an affectation which would give him an advantage rather than the contrary, if I had left company when he came in; or refused to enter into it when I found he would stay any time.

My brother heard me out with such a kind of impatience as shewed he was resolved to be dissatisfied with me, say what I would. The rest, as the event has proved, behaved as if they would have been satisfied, had they not further points to carry by intimidating me. All this made it evident, as I mentioned above, that they themselves expected not my voluntary compliance; and was a tacit confession of the disagreeableness of the person they had to propose.

I was no sooner silent than my brother swore, although in my father's presence, (swore, unchecked either by eye or countenance,) That for his part, he would never be reconciled to that libertine: and that he would renounce me for a sister, if I encouraged the addresses of a man so obnoxious to them all.

A man who had like to have been my brother's murderer, my sister said, with a face even bursting with restraint of passion.

The poor Bella has, you know, a plump high-fed face, if I may be allowed the expression. You, I know, will forgive me for this liberty of speech sooner than I can forgive myself: Yet how can one be such a reptile as not to turn when trampled upon!

My father, with vehemence both of action and voice [my father has, you know, a terrible voice when he is angry] told me that I had met with too much indulgence in being allowed to refuse this gentleman, and the other gentleman,; and it was now his turn to be obeyed!

Very true, my mother said:—and hoped his will would not now be disputed by a child so favoured.

To shew they were all of a sentiment, my uncle Harlowe said, he hoped his beloved niece only wanted to know her father's will, to obey it.

And my uncle Antony, in his rougher manner, added, that surely I would not give them reason to apprehend, that I thought my grandfather's favour to me had made me independent of them all.—If I did, he would tell me, the will could be set aside, and should.

I was astonished, you must needs think.—Whose addresses now, thought I, is this treatment preparative to?—Mr. Wyerley's again?—or whose? And then, as high comparisons, where self is concerned, sooner than low, come into young people's heads; be it for whom it will, this is wooing as the English did for the heiress of Scotland in the time of Edward the Sixth. But that it could be for Solmes, how should it enter into my head?

I did not know, I said, that I had given occasion for this harshness. I hoped I should always have a just sense of every one's favour to me, superadded to the duty I owed as a daughter and a niece: but that I was so much surprised at a reception so unusual and unexpected, that I hoped my papa and mamma would give me leave to retire, in order to recollect myself.

No one gainsaying, I made my silent compliments, and withdrew;—leaving my brother and sister, as I thought, pleased; and as if they wanted to congratulate each other on having occasioned so severe a beginning to be made with me.

I went up to my chamber, and there with my faithful Hannah deplored the determined face which the new proposal it was plain they had to make me wore.

I had not recovered myself when I was sent for down to tea. I begged my maid to be excused attending; but on the repeated command, went down with as much cheerfulness as I could assume; and had a new fault to clear myself of: for my brother, so pregnant a thing is determined ill-will, by intimations equally rude and intelligible, charged my desire of being excused coming down, to sullens, because a certain person had been spoken against, upon whom, as he supposed, my fancy ran.

I could easily answer you, Sir, said I, as such a reflection deserves: but I forbear. If I do not find a brother in you, you shall have a sister in me.

Pretty meekness! Bella whisperingly said; looking at my brother, and lifting up her lip in contempt.

He, with an imperious air, bid me deserve his love, and I should be sure to have it.

As we sat, my mother, in her admirable manner, expatiated upon brotherly and sisterly love; indulgently blamed my brother and sister for having taken up displeasure too lightly against me; and politically, if I may say so, answered for my obedience to my father's will.—The it would be all well, my father was pleased to say: Then they should dote upon me, was my brother's expression: Love me as well as ever, was my sister's: And my uncles, That I then should be the pride of their hearts.—But, alas! what a forfeiture of all these must I make!

This was the reception I had on my return from you.

Mr. Solmes came in before we had done tea. My uncle Antony presented him to me, as a gentleman he had a particular friendship for. My uncle Harlowe in terms equally favourable for him. My father said, Mr. Solmes is my friend, Clarissa Harlowe. My mother looked at him, and looked at me, now-and-then, as he sat near me, I thought with concern.—I at her, with eyes appealing for pity. At him, when I could glance at him, with disgust little short of affrightment. While my brother and sister Mr. Solmes'd him, and Sirr'd—yet such a wretch!—But I will at present only add, My humble thanks and duty to your honoured mother (to whom I will particularly write, to express the grateful sense I have of her goodness to me); and that I am

Your ever obliged, CL. HARLOWE.

LETTER VIII

MISS CLARISSA HARLOWE, TO MISS HOWE FEB. 24

They drive on here at a furious rate. The man lives here, I think. He courts them, and is more and more a favourite. Such terms, such settlements! That's the cry.

O my dear, that I had not reason to deplore the family fault, immensely rich as they all are! But this I may the more unreservedly say to you, as we have often joined in the same concern: I, for a father and uncles; you, for a mother; in every other respect, faultless.

Hitherto, I seem to be delivered over to my brother, who pretends as great a love to me as ever.

You may believe I have been very sincere with him. But he affects to rally me, and not to believe it possible, that one so dutiful and discreet as his sister Clary can resolve to disoblige all her friends.

Indeed, I tremble at the prospect before me; for it is evident that they are strangely determined.

My father and mother industriously avoid giving me opportunity of speaking to them alone. They ask not for my approbation, intended, as it should seem, to suppose me into their will. And with them I shall hope to prevail, or with nobody. They have not the interest in compelling me, as my brother and sister have: I say less therefore to them, reserving my whole force for an audience of my father, if he will permit me a patient ear. How difficult is it, my dear, to give a negative where both duty and inclination join to make one wish to oblige!

I have already stood the shock of three of this man's particular visits, besides my share in his more general ones; and find it is impossible I should ever endure him. He has but a very ordinary share of understanding; is very illiterate; knows nothing but the value of estates, and how to improve them, and what belongs to land-jobbing and husbandry. Yet I am as one stupid, I think. They have begun so cruelly with me, that I have not spirit enough to assert my own negative.

They had endeavoured it seems to influence my good Mrs. Norton before I came home—so intent are they to carry their point! And her opinion not being to their liking, she has been told that she would do well to decline visiting here for the present: yet she is the person of all the world, next to my mother, the most likely to prevail upon me, were the measures they are engaged in reasonable measures, or such as she could think so.

My aunt likewise having said that she did not think her niece could ever be brought to like Mr. Solmes, has been obliged to learn another lesson.

I am to have a visit from her to-morrow. And, since I have refused so much as to hear from my brother and sister what the noble settlements are to be, she is to acquaint me with the particulars; and to receive from me my determination: for my father, I am told, will not have patience but to suppose that I shall stand in opposition to his will.

Mean time it has been signified to me, that it will be acceptable if I do not think of going to church next Sunday.

The same signification was made for me last Sunday; and I obeyed. They are apprehensive that Mr. Lovelace will be there with design to come home with me.

Help me, dear Miss Howe, to a little of your charming spirit: I never more wanted it.

The man, this Solmes, you may suppose, has no reason to boast of his progress with me. He has not the sense to say any thing to the purpose. His courtship indeed is to them; and my brother pretends to court me as his proxy, truly!—I utterly, to my brother, reject his address; but thinking a person, so well received and recommended by all my family, entitled to good manners, all I say against him is affectedly attributed to coyness: and he, not being sensible of his own imperfections, believes that my avoiding him when I can, and the reserves I express, are owing to nothing else: for, as I said, all his courtship is to them; and I have no opportunity of saying no, to one who asks me not the question. And so, with an air of mannish superiority, he seems rather to pity the bashful girl, than to apprehend that he shall not succeed.

FEBRUARY 25.

I have had the expected conference with my aunt.

I have been obliged to hear the man's proposals from her; and have been told also what their motives are for espousing his interest with so much warmth. I am even loth to mention how equally unjust it is for him to make such offers, or for those I am bound to reverence to accept of them.

I hate him more than before. One great estate is already obtained at the expense of the relations to it, though distant relations; my brother's, I mean, by his godmother: and this has given the hope, however chimerical that hope, of procuring others; and that my own at least may revert to the family. And yet, in my opinion, the world is but one great family. Originally it was so. What then is this narrow selfishness that reigns in us, but relationship remembered against relationship forgot?

But here, upon my absolute refusal of him upon any terms, have I had a signification made me that wounds me to the heart. How can I tell it you? Yet I must. It is, my dear, that I must not for a month to come, or till license obtained, correspond with any body out of the house.

My brother, upon my aunt's report, (made, however, as I am informed, in the gentlest manner, and even giving remote hopes, which she had no commission from me to give,) brought me, in authoritative terms, the prohibition.

Not to Miss Howe? said I.

No, not to Miss Howe, Madam, tauntingly: for have you not acknowledged, that Lovelace is a favourite there?

See, my dear Miss Howe—!

And do you think, Brother, this is the way—

Do you look to that.—But your letters will be stopt, I can tell you.—And away he flung.

My sister came to me soon after—Sister Clary, you are going on in a fine way, I understand. But as there are people who are supposed to harden you against your duty, I am to tell you, that it will be taken well if you avoid visits or visitings for a week or two till further order.

Can this be from those who have authority—

Ask them; ask them, child, with a twirl of her finger.—I have delivered my message. Your father will be obeyed. He is willing to hope you to be all obedience, and would prevent all incitements to refractoriness.

I know my duty, said I; and hope I shall not find impossible condition annexed to it.

A pert young creature, vain and conceited, she called me. I was the only judge, in my own wise opinion, of what was right and fit. She, for her part, had long seen into my specious ways: and now I should shew every body what I was at bottom.

Dear Bella! said I, hands and eyes lifted up—why all this?—Dear, dear Bella, why—

None of your dear, dear Bella's to me.—I tell you, I see through your witchcrafts [that was her strange word]. And away she flung; adding, as she went, and so will every body else very quickly, I dare say.

Bless me, said I to myself, what a sister have I!—How have I deserved this?

Then I again regretted my grandfather's too distinguishing goodness to me.

FEB. 25, IN THE EVENING.

What my brother and sister have said against me I cannot tell:—but I am in heavy disgrace with my father.

I was sent for down to tea. I went with a very cheerful aspect: but had occasion soon to change it.

Such a solemnity in every body's countenance!—My mother's eyes were fixed upon the tea-cups; and when she looked up, it was heavily, as if her eye-lids had weights upon them; and then not to me. My father sat half-aside in his elbow-chair, that his head might be turned from me: his hands clasped, and waving, as it were, up and down; his fingers, poor dear gentleman! in motion, as if angry to the very ends of them. My sister was swelling. My brother looked at me with scorn, having measured me, as I may say, with his eyes as I entered, from head to foot. My aunt was there, and looked upon me as if with kindness restrained, bending coldly to my compliment to her as she sat; and then cast an eye first on my brother, then on my sister, as if to give the reason [so I am willing to construe it] of her unusual stiffness.—Bless me, my dear! that they should choose to intimidate rather than invite a mind, till now, not thought either unpersuadable or ungenerous!

I took my seat. Shall I make tea, Madam, to my mother?—I always used, you know, my dear, to make tea.

No! a very short sentence, in one very short word, was the expressive answer. And she was pleased to take the canister in her own hand.

My brother bid the footman, who attended, leave the room—I, he said, will pour out the water.

My heart was up in my mouth. I did not know what to do with myself. What is to follow? thought I.

Just after the second dish, out stept my mother—A word with you, sister Hervey! taking her in her hand. Presently my sister dropt away. Then my brother. So I was left alone with my father.

He looked so very sternly, that my heart failed me as twice or thrice I would have addressed myself to him: nothing but solemn silence on all hands having passed before.

At last, I asked, if it were his pleasure that I should pour him out another dish?

He answered me with the same angry monosyllable, which I had received from my mother before; and then arose, and walked about the room. I arose too, with intent to throw myself at his feet; but was too much overawed by his sternness, even to make such an expression of my duty to him as my heart overflowed with.

At last, as he supported himself, because of his gout, on the back of a chair, I took a little more courage; and approaching him, besought him to acquaint me in what I had offended him?

He turned from me, and in a strong voice, Clarissa Harlowe, said he, know that I will be obeyed.

God forbid, Sir, that you should not!—I have never yet opposed your will—

Nor I your whimsies, Clarissa Harlowe, interrupted he.—Don't let me run the fate of all who shew indulgence to your sex; to be the more contradicted for mine to you.

My father, you know, my dear, has not (any more than my brother) a kind opinion of our sex; although there is not a more condescending wife in the world than my mother.

I was going to make protestations of duty—No protestations, girl! No words! I will not be prated to! I will be obeyed! I have no child, I will have no child, but an obedient one.

Sir, you never had reason, I hope—

Tell me not what I never had, but what I have, and what I shall have.

Good Sir, be pleased to hear me—My brother and sister, I fear—

Your brother and sister shall not be spoken against, girl!—They have a just concern for the honour of my family.

And I hope, Sir—

Hope nothing.—Tell me not of hopes, but of facts. I ask nothing of you but what is in your power to comply with, and what it is your duty to comply with.

Then, Sir, I will comply with it—But yet I hope from your goodness—

No expostulations! No but's, girl! No qualifyings! I will be obeyed, I tell you; and cheerfully too!—or you are no child of mine!

I wept.

Let me beseech you, my dear and ever-honoured Papa, (and I dropt down on my knees,) that I may have only yours and my mamma's will, and not my brother's, to obey.

I was going on; but he was pleased to withdraw, leaving me on the floor; saying, That he would not hear me thus by subtilty and cunning aiming to distinguish away my duty: repeating, that he would be obeyed.

My heart is too full;—so full, that it may endanger my duty, were I to try to unburden it to you on this occasion: so I will lay down my pen.—But can—Yet positively, I will lay down my pen—!

LETTER IX

MISS CLARISSA HARLOWE, TO MISS HOWE FEB. 26, IN THE MORNING

My aunt, who staid here last night, made me a visit this morning as soon as it was light. She tells me, that I was left alone with my father yesterday on purpose that he might talk with me on my expected obedience; but that he owned he was put beside his purpose by reflecting on something my brother had told him in my disfavour, and by his impatience but to suppose, that such a gentle spirit as mine had hitherto seemed to be, should presume to dispute his will in a point where the advantage of the whole family was to be so greatly promoted by my compliance.

I find, by a few words which dropt unawares from my aunt, that they have all an absolute dependence upon what they suppose to be meekness in my temper. But in this they may be mistaken; for I verily think, upon a strict examination of myself, that I have almost as much in me of my father's as of my mother's family.

My uncle Harlowe it seems is against driving me upon extremities: But my brother has engaged, that the regard I have for my reputation, and my principles, will bring me round to my duty; that's the expression. Perhaps I shall have reason to wish I had not known this.

My aunt advises me to submit for the present to the interdicts they have laid me under; and indeed to encourage Mr. Solmes's address. I have absolutely refused the latter, let what will (as I have told her) be the consequence. The visiting prohibition I will conform to. But as to that of not corresponding with you, nothing but the menace that our letters shall be intercepted, can engage my observation of it.

She believes that this order is from my father, and that my mother has not been consulted upon it. She says, that it is given, as she has reason think, purely in consideration to me, lest I should mortally offend him; and this from the incitements of other people (meaning you and Miss Lloyd, I make no doubt) rather than by my own will. For still, as she tells me, he speaks kind and praiseful things of me.

Here is clemency! Here is indulgence!—And so it is, to prevent a headstrong child, as a good prince would wish to deter disaffected subjects, from running into rebellion, and so forfeiting every thing! But this is allowing to the young-man's wisdom of my brother; a plotter without a head, and a brother without a heart!

How happy might I have been with any other brother in the world but James Harlowe; and with any other sister but his sister! Wonder not, my dear, that I, who used to chide you for these sort of liberties with my relations, now am more undutiful than you ever was unkind. I cannot bear the thought of being deprived of the principal pleasure of my life; for such is your conversation by person and by letter. And who, besides, can bear to be made the dupe of such low cunning, operating with such high and arrogant passions?

But can you, my dear Miss Howe, condescend to carry on a private correspondence with me?—If you can, there is one way I have thought of, by which it may be done.

You must remember the Green Lane, as we call it, that runs by the side of the wood-house and poultry-yard where I keep my bantams, pheasants, and pea-hens, which generally engage my notice twice a day; the more my favourites because they were my grandfather's, and recommended to my care by him; and therefore brought hither from my Dairy-house since his death.

The lane is lower than the floor of the wood-house; and, in the side of the wood-house, the boards are rotted away down to the floor for half an ell together in several places. Hannah can step into the lane, and make a mark with chalk where a letter or parcel may be pushed in, under some sticks; which may be so managed as to be an unsuspected cover for the written deposits from either.

I have been just now to look at the place, and find it will answer. So your faithful Robert may, without coming near the house, and as only passing through the Green Lame which leads to two or three farm-houses [out of livery if you please] very easily take from thence my letters and deposit yours.

This place is the more convenient, because it is seldom resorted to but by myself or Hannah, on the above-mentioned account; for it is the general store-house for firing; the wood for constant use being nearer the house.

One corner of this being separated off for the roosting-place of my little poultry, either she or I shall never want a pretence to go thither.

Try, my dear, the success of a letter this way; and give me your opinion and advice what to do in this disgraceful situation, as I cannot but call it; and what you think of my prospects; and what you would do in my case.

But before-hand I will tell you, that your advice must not run in favour of this Solmes: and yet it is very likely they will endeavour to engage your mother, in order to induce you, who have such an influence over me, to favour him.

Yet, on second thoughts, if you incline to that side of the question, I would have you write your whole mind. Determined as I think I am, and cannot help it, I would at least give a patient hearing to what may be said on the other side. For my regards are not so much engaged [upon my word they are not; I know not myself if they be] to another person as some of my friends suppose; and as you, giving way to your lively vein, upon his last visits, affected to suppose. What preferable favour I may have for him to any other person, is owing more to the usage he has received, and for my sake borne, than to any personal consideration.

I write a few lines of grateful acknowledgement to your good mother for her favours to me in the late happy period. I fear I shall never know such another. I hope she will forgive me, that I did not write sooner.

The bearer, if suspected and examined, is to produce that as the only one he carries.

How do needless watchfulness and undue restraint produce artifice and contrivance! I should abhor these clandestine correspondences, were they not forced upon me. They have so mean, so low an appearance to myself, that I think I ought not to expect that you should take part in them.

But why (as I have also expostulated with my aunt) must I be pushed into a state, which I have no wish to enter into, although I reverence it?—Why should not my brother, so many years older, and so earnest to see me engaged, be first engaged?—And why should not my sister be first provided for?

But here I conclude these unavailing expostulations, with the assurance, that I am, and ever will be,

Your affectionate, CLARISSA HARLOWE.

LETTER X

MISS HOWE, TO MISS CLARISSA HARLOWE FEB. 27

What odd heads some people have!—Miss Clarissa Harlowe to be sacrificed in marriage to Mr. Roger Solmes!—Astonishing!

I must not, you say, give my advice in favour of this man!—You now convince me, my dear, that you are nearer of kin than I thought you, to the family that could think of so preposterous a match, or you would never have had the least notion of my advising in his favour.

Ask for his picture. You know I have a good hand at drawing an ugly likeness. But I'll see a little further first: for who knows what may happen, since matters are in such a train; and since you have not the courage to oppose so overwhelming a torrent?

You ask me to help you to a little of my spirit. Are you in earnest? But it will not now, I doubt, do you service.—It will not sit naturally upon you. You are your mother's girl, think what you will; and have violent spirits to contend with. Alas! my dear, you should have borrowed some of mine a little sooner;—that is to say, before you had given the management of your estate into the hands of those who think they have a prior claim to it. What though a father's!—Has not the father two elder children?—And do they not both bear more of his stamp and image than you do?—Pray, my dear, call me not to account for this free question; lest your application of my meaning, on examination, prove to be as severe as that.

Now I have launched out a little, indulge me one word more in the same strain—I will be decent, I promise you. I think you might have know, that Avarice and Envy are two passions that are not to be satisfied, the one by giving, the other by the envied person's continuing to deserve and excel.—Fuel, fuel both, all the world over, to flames insatiate and devouring.

But since you ask for my opinion, you must tell me all you know or surmise of their inducements. And if you will not forbid me to make extracts from your letters for the entertainment of my aunt and cousin in the little island, who long to hear more of your affairs, it will be very obliging.

But you are so tender of some people who have no tenderness for any body but themselves, that I must conjure you to speak out. Remember, that a friendship like ours admits of no reserves. You may trust my impartiality. It would be an affront to your own judgment, if you did not: For do you not ask my advice? And have you not taught me that friendship should never give a bias against justice?—Justify them, therefore, if you can. Let us see if there be any sense, whether sufficient reason or not in their choice. At present I cannot (and yet I know a good deal of your family) have any conception how all of them, your mother and your aunt Hervey in particular, can join with the rest against judgments given. As to some of the others, I cannot wonder at any thing they do, or attempt to do, where self is concerned.

You ask, Why may not your brother be first engaged in wedlock? I'll tell you why: His temper and his arrogance are too well known to induce women he would aspire to, to receive his addresses, notwithstanding his great independent acquisitions, and still greater prospects. Let me tell you, my dear, those acquisitions have given him more pride than reputation. To me he is the most intolerable creature that I ever conversed with. The treatment you blame, he merited from one whom he addressed with the air of a person who presumes that he is about to confer a favour, rather than to receive one. I ever loved to mortify proud and insolent spirits. What, think you, makes me bear Hickman near me, but that the man is humble, and knows and keeps his distance?

As to your question, Why your elder sister may not be first provided for? I answer, Because she must have no man, but one who has a great and clear estate; that's one thing. Another is, Because she has a younger sister. Pray, my dear, be so good as to tell me, What man of a great and clear estate would think of that eldest sister, while the younger were single?

You are all too rich to be happy, child. For must not each of you, by the constitutions of your family, marry to be still richer? People who know in what their main excellence consists, are not to be blamed (are they) for cultivating and improving what they think most valuable?—Is true happiness any part of your family view?—So far from it, that none of your family but yourself could be happy were they not rich. So let them fret on, grumble and grudge, and accumulate; and wondering what ails them that they have not happiness when they have riches, think the cause is want of more; and so go on heaping up, till Death, as greedy an accumulator as themselves, gathers them into his garner.

Well then once more I say, do you, my dear, tell me what you know of their avowed and general motives; and I will tell you more than you will tell me of their failings! Your aunt Hervey, you say,* has told you: Why must

I ask you to let me know them, when you condescend to ask my advice on the occasion?

* *See Letter VIII.*

That they prohibit your corresponding with me, is a wisdom I neither wonder at, nor blame them for: since it is an evidence to me, that they know their own folly: And if they do, is it strange that they should be afraid to trust one another's judgment upon it?

I am glad you have found out a way to correspond with me. I approve it much. I shall more, if this first trial of it prove successful. But should it not, and should it fall into their hands, it would not concern me but for your sake.

We have heard before you wrote, that all was not right between your relations and you at your coming home: that Mr. Solmes visited you, and that with a prospect of success. But I concluded the mistake lay in the person; and that his address was to Miss Arabella. And indeed had she been as good-natured as your plump ones generally are, I should have thought her too good for him by half. This must certainly be the thing, thought I; and my beloved friend is sent for to advise and assist in her nuptial preparations. Who knows, said I to my mother, but that when the man has thrown aside his yellow full-buckled peruke, and his broad-brimmed beaver (both of which I suppose were Sir Oliver's best of long standing) he may cut a tolerable figure dangling to church with Miss Bell!—The woman, as she observes, should excel the man in features: and where can she match so well for a foil?

I indulged this surmise against rumour, because I could not believe that the absurdest people in England could be so very absurd as to think of this man for you.

We heard, moreover, that you received no visiters. I could assign no reason for this, except that the preparations for your sister were to be private, and the ceremony sudden, for fear this man should, as another man did, change his mind. Miss Lloyd and Miss Biddulph were with me to inquire what I knew of this; and of your not being in church, either morning or afternoon, the Sunday after your return from us; to the disappointment of a little hundred of your admirers, to use their words. It was easy for me to guess the reason to be what you confirm—their apprehensions that Lovelace would be there, and attempt to wait on you home.

My mother takes very kindly your compliments in your letter to her. Her words upon reading it were, 'Miss Clarissa Harlowe is an admirable young lady: wherever she goes, she confers a favour: whomever she leaves, she fills with regret.'—And then a little comparative reflection—'O my Nancy, that you had a little of her sweet obligingness!'

No matter. The praise was yours. You are me; and I enjoyed it. The more enjoyed it, because—Shall I tell you the truth?—Because I think myself as well as I am—were it but for this reason, that had I twenty brother James's, and twenty sister Bell's, not one of them, nor all of them joined together, would dare to treat me as yours presume to treat you. The person who will bear much shall have much to bear all the world through; it is your own sentiment,* grounded upon the strongest instance that can be given in your own family; though you have so little improved by it.

* *Letter V.*

The result is this, that I am fitter for this world than you; you for the next than me:—that is the difference.—But long, long, for my sake, and for hundreds of sakes, may it be before you quit us for company more congenial to you and more worthy of you!

I communicated to my mother the account you give of your strange reception; also what a horrid wretch they have found out for you; and the compulsory treatment they give you. It only set her on magnifying her lenity to me, on my tyrannical behaviour, as she will call it [mothers must have their way, you know, my dear] to the man whom she so warmly recommends, against whom it seems there can be no just exception; and expatiating upon the complaisance I owe her for her indulgence. So I believe I must communicate to her nothing farther—especially as I know she would condemn the correspondence between us, and that between you and Lovelace, as clandestine and undutiful proceedings, and divulge our secret besides; for duty implicit is her cry. And moreover she lends a pretty open ear to the preachments of that starch old bachelor your uncle Antony; and for an example to her daughter would be more careful how she takes your part, be the cause ever so just.

Yet is this not the right policy neither. For people who allow nothing will be granted nothing: in other words, those who aim at carrying too many points will not be able to carry any.

But can you divine, my dear, what the old preachment-making, plump-hearted soul, your uncle Antony, means by his frequent amblings hither?—There is such smirking and smiling between my mother and him! Such mutual praises of economy; and 'that is my way!'—and 'this I do!'—and 'I am glad it has your approbation, Sir!'—and 'you look into every thing, Madam!'—'Nothing would be done, if I did not!'—

Such exclamations against servants! Such exaltings of self! And dear heart, and good lack!—and 'las a-day!—And now-and-then their conversation sinking into a whispering accent, if I come across them!—I'll tell you, my dear, I don't above half like it.

Only that these old bachelors usually take as many years to resolve upon matrimony as they can reasonably expect to live, or I should be ready to fire upon his visits; and to recommend Mr. Hickman to my mother's acceptance, as a much more eligible man: for what he wants in years, he makes up in gravity; and if you will not chide me, I will say, that there is a primness in both (especially when the man has presumed too much with me upon my mother's favour for him, and is under discipline on that account) as make them seem near of kin: and then in contemplation of my sauciness, and what they both fear from it, they sigh away! and seem so mightily to compassionate each other, that if pity be but one remove from love, I am in no danger, while they are both in a great deal, and don't know it.

Now, my dear, I know you will be upon me with your grave airs: so in for the lamb, as the saying is, in for the sheep; and do you yourself look about you; for I'll have a pull with you by way of being aforehand. Hannibal, we read, always advised to attack the Romans upon their own territories.

You are pleased to say, and upon your word too! that your regards (a mighty quaint word for affections) are not so much engaged, as some of your friends suppose, to another person. What need you give one to imagine, my dear, that the last month or two has been a period extremely favourable to that other person, whom it has made an obliger of the niece for his patience with the uncles.

But, to pass that by—so much engaged!—How much, my dear?—Shall I infer? Some of your friends suppose a great deal. You seem to own a little.

Don't be angry. It is all fair: because you have not acknowledged to me that little. People I have heard you say, who affect secrets, always excite curiosity.

But you proceed with a kind of drawback upon your averment, as if recollection had given you a doubt—you know not yourself, if they be [so much engaged]. Was it necessary to say this to me?—and to say it upon your word too?—But you know best.—Yet you don't neither, I believe. For a beginning love is acted by a subtle spirit; and oftentimes discovers itself to a by-stander, when the person possessed (why should I not call it possessed?) knows not it has such a demon.

But further you say, what preferable favour you may have for him to any other person, is owing more to the usage he has received, and for your sake borne, than to any personal consideration.

This is generously said. It is in character. But, O my friend, depend upon it, you are in danger. Depend upon it, whether you know it or not, you are a little in for't. Your native generosity and greatness of mind endanger you: all your friends, by fighting against him with impolitic violence, fight for him. And Lovelace, my life for yours, notwithstanding all his veneration and assiduities, has seen further than that veneration and those assiduities (so well calculated to your meridian) will let him own he has seen—has seen, in short, that his work is doing for him more effectually than he could do it for himself. And have you not before now said, that nothing is so penetrating as the eye of a lover who has vanity? And who says Lovelace wants vanity?

In short, my dear, it is my opinion, and that from the easiness of his heart and behaviour, that he has seen more than I have seen; more than you think could be seen—more than I believe you yourself know, or else you would let me know it.

Already, in order to restrain him from resenting the indignities he has received, and which are daily offered him, he has prevailed upon you to correspond with him privately. I know he has nothing to boast of from what you have written: but is not his inducing you to receive his letters, and to answer them, a great point gained? By your insisting that he should keep the correspondence private, it appears there is one secret which you do not wish the world should know: and he is master of that secret. He is indeed himself, as I may say, that secret! What an intimacy does this beget for the lover! How is it distancing the parent!

Yet who, as things are situated, can blame you?—Your condescension has no doubt hitherto prevented great mischiefs. It must be continued, for the same reasons, while the cause remains. You are drawn in by a perverse fate against inclination: but custom, with such laudable purposes, will reconcile the inconveniency, and make an inclination.—And I would advise you (as you would wish to manage on an occasion so critical with that prudence which governs all your actions) not to be afraid of entering upon a close examination into the true springs and grounds of this your generosity to that happy man.

It is my humble opinion, I tell you frankly, that on inquiry it will come out to be LOVE—don't start, my dear!—Has not your man himself had natural philosophy enough to observe already to your aunt Hervey, that love takes the deepest root in the steadiest minds? The deuce take his sly penetration, I was going to say; for this was six or seven weeks ago.

I have been tinctured, you know. Nor on the coolest reflection, could I account how and when the jaundice began: but had been over head and ears, as the saying is, but for some of that advice from you, which I now return you. Yet my man was not half so—so what, my dear—to be sure Lovelace is a charming fellow. And were he only—but I will not make you glow, as you read—upon my word I will not.—Yet, my dear, don't you find at your heart somewhat unusual make it go throb, throb, throb, as you read just here?—If you do, don't be ashamed to own it—it is your generosity, my love, that's all.—But as the Roman augur said, Caesar, beware of the Ides of March!

Adieu, my dearest friend.—Forgive, and very speedily, by the new found expedient, tell me that you forgive,

Your ever-affectionate, ANNA HOWE.

LETTER XI

MISS CLARISSA HARLOWE, TO MISS HOWE WEDNESDAY, MARCH 1

You both nettled and alarmed me, my dearest Miss Howe, by the concluding part of your last. At first reading it, I did not think it necessary, said I to myself, to guard against a critic, when I was writing to so dear a friend. But then recollecting myself, is there not more in it, said I, than the result of a vein so naturally lively? Surely I must have been guilty of an inadvertence. Let me enter into the close examination of myself which my beloved friend advises.

I do so; and cannot own any of the glow, any of the throbs you mention.—Upon my word I will repeat, I cannot. And yet the passages in my letter, upon which you are so humourously severe, lay me fairly open to your agreeable raillery. I own they do. And I cannot tell what turn my mind had taken to dictate so oddly to my pen.

But, pray now—is it saying so much, when one, who has no very particular regard to any man, says, there are some who are preferable to others? And is it blamable to say, they are the preferable, who are not well used by one's relations; yet dispense with that usage out of regard to one's self which they would otherwise resent? Mr. Lovelace, for instance, I may be allowed to say, is a man to be preferred to Mr. Solmes; and that I do prefer him to that man: but, surely, this may be said without its being a necessary consequence that I must be in love with him.

Indeed I would not be in love with him, as it is called, for the world: First, because I have no opinion of his morals; and think it a fault in which our whole family (my brother excepted) has had a share, that he was permitted to visit us with a hope, which, however, being distant, did not, as I have observed heretofore,* entitle any of us to call him to account for such of his immoralities as came to our ears. Next, because I think him to be a vain man, capable of triumphing (secretly at least) over a person whose heart he thinks he has engaged. And, thirdly, because the assiduities and veneration which you impute to him, seem to carry an haughtiness in them, as if he thought his address had a merit in it, that would be more than an equivalent to a woman's love. In short, his very politeness, notwithstanding the advantages he must have had from his birth and education, appear to be constrained; and, with the most remarkable easy and genteel person, something, at times, seems to be behind in his manner that is too studiously kept in. Then, good-humoured as he is thought to be in the main to other people's servants, and this even to familiarity (although, as you have observed, a familiarity that has dignity in it not unbecoming to a man of quality) he is apt sometimes to break out into a passion with his own: An oath or a curse follows, and such looks from those servants as plainly shew terror, and that they should have fared worse had they not been in my hearing: with a confirmation in the master's looks of a surmise too well justified.

* *Letter III.*

Indeed, my dear, THIS man is not THE man. I have great objections to him. My heart throbs not after him. I glow not, but with indignation against myself for having given room for such an imputation. But you must not, my dearest friend, construe common gratitude into love. I cannot bear that you should. But if ever I should have the misfortune to think it love, I promise you upon my word, which is the same as upon my honour, that I will acquaint you with it.

You bid me to tell you very speedily, and by the new-found expedient, that I am not displeased with you for your agreeable raillery: I dispatch this therefore immediately, postponing to my next the account of the inducements which my friends have to promote with so much earnestness the address of Mr. Solmes.

Be satisfied, my dear, mean time, that I am not displeased with you: indeed I am not. On the contrary, I give you my hearty thanks for your friendly premonitions; and I charge you (as I have often done) that if you observe any thing in me so very faulty as would require from you to others in my behalf the palliation of friendly and partial love, you acquaint me with it: for methinks I would so conduct myself as not to give reason even for an adversary to censure me; and how shall so weak and so young a creature avoid the censure of such, if my friend will not hold a looking-glass before me to let me see my imperfections?

Judge me, then, my dear, as any indifferent person (knowing what you know of me) would do. I may be at first be a little pained; may glow a little perhaps to be found less worthy of your friendship than I wish to be; but assure yourself, that your kind correction will give me reflection that shall amend me. If it do not, you will have a fault to accuse me of, that will be utterly inexcusable: a fault, let me add, that should you not accuse me of it (if in your opinion I am guilty) you will not be so much, so warmly, my friend as I am yours; since I have never spared you on the like occasions.

Here I break off to begin another letter to you, with the assurance, mean time, that I am, and ever will be,

Your equally affectionate and grateful, CL. HARLOWE.

LETTER XII

MISS HOWE, TO MISS CLARISSA HARLOWE THURSDAY MORNING, MARCH 2

Indeed you would not be in love with him for the world!—Your servant, my dear. Nor would I have you. For, I think, with all the advantages of person, fortune, and family, he is not by any means worthy of you. And this opinion I give as well from the reasons you mention (which I cannot but confirm) as from what I have heard of him but a few hours ago from Mrs. Fortescue, a favourite of Lady Betty Lawrance, who knows him well—but let me congratulate you, however, on your being the first of our sex that ever I heard of, who has been able to turn that lion, Love, at her own pleasure, into a lap-dog.

Well but, if you have not the throbs and the glows, you have not: and are not in love; good reason why—because you would not be in love; and there's no more to be said.—Only, my dear, I shall keep a good look-out upon you; and so I hope you will be upon yourself; for it is no manner of argument that because you would not be in love, you therefore are not.—But before I part entirely with this subject, a word in your ear, my charming friend—'tis only by way of caution, and in pursuance of the general observation, that a stander-by is often a better judge of the game than those that play.—May it not be, that you have had, and have, such cross creatures and such odd heads to deal with, as have not allowed you to attend to the throbs?—Or, if you had them a little now and then, whether, having had two accounts to place them to, you have not by mistake put them to the wrong one?

But whether you have a value for Lovelace or not, I know you will be impatient to hear what Mrs. Fortescue has said of him. Nor will I keep you longer in suspense.

An hundred wild stories she tells of him from childhood to manhood: for, as she observed, having never been subject to contradiction, he was always as mischievous as a monkey. But I shall pass over these whole hundred of his puerile rogueries (although indicative ones, as I may say) to take notice as well of some things you are not quite ignorant of, as of others you know not, and to make a few observations upon him and his ways.

Mrs. Fortescue owns, what every body knows, 'that he is notoriously, nay, avowedly, a man of pleasure; yet says, that in any thing he sets his heart upon or undertakes, he is the most industrious and persevering mortal under the sun. He rests it seems not above six hours in the twenty-four—any more than you. He delights in writing. Whether at Lord M.'s, or at Lady Betty's, or Lady Sarah's, he has always a pen in his fingers when he retires. One of his companions (confirming his love of writing) has told her, that his thoughts flow rapidly to his pen:' And you and I, my dear, have observed, on more occasions than one, that though he writes even a fine hand, he is one of the readiest and quickest of writers. He must indeed have had early a very docile genius; since a person of his pleasurable turn and active spirit, could never have submitted to take long or great pains in attaining the qualifications he is master of; qualifications so seldom attained by youth of quality and fortune; by such especially of those of either, who, like him, have never known what it was to be controuled.

'He had once it seems the vanity, upon being complimented on these talents (and on his surprising diligence, for a man of pleasure) to compare himself to Julius Caesar; who performed great actions by day, and wrote them down at night; and valued himself, that he only wanted Caesar's out-setting, to make a figure among his contemporaries.

'He spoke of this indeed, she says, with an air of pleasantry: for she observed, and so have we, that he has the art of acknowledging his vanity with so much humour, that it sets him above the contempt which is due to vanity and self-opinion; and at the same time half persuades those who hear him, that he really deserves the exultation he gives himself.'

But supposing it to be true that all his vacant nightly hours are employed in writing, what can be his subjects? If, like Caesar, his own actions, he must undoubtedly be a very enterprising and very wicked man; since nobody suspects him to have a serious turn; and, decent as he is in his conversation with us, his writings are not probably such as would redound either to his own honour, or to the benefit of others, were they to be read. He must be conscious of this, since Mrs. Fortescue says, 'that in the great correspondence by letters which he holds, he is as secret and as careful as if it were of a treasonable nature;—yet troubles not his head with politics, though nobody knows the interests of princes and courts better than he is said to do.'

That you and I, my dear, should love to write, is no wonder. We have always, from the time each could hold a pen, delighted in epistolary correspondencies. Our employments are domestic and sedentary; and we can scribble upon twenty innocent subjects, and take delight in them because they are innocent; though were they to be seen, they might not much profit or please others. But that such a gay, lively young fellow as this, who rides, hunts, travels, frequents the public entertainments, and has means to pursue his pleasures, should be able to set himself down to write for hours together, as you and I have heard him say he frequently does, that is the strange thing.

Mrs. Fortescue says, 'that he is a complete master of short-hand writing.' By the way, what inducements could a swift writer as he have to learn short-hand!

She says (and we know it as well as she) 'that he has a surprising memory, and a very lively imagination.'

Whatever his other vices are, all the world, as well as Mrs. Fortescue, says, 'he is a sober man. And among all his bad qualities, gaming, that great waster of time as well as fortune, is not his vice:' So that he must have his head as cool, and his reason as clear, as the prime of youth and his natural gaiety will permit; and by his early morning hours, a great portion of time upon his hands to employ in writing, or worse.

Mrs. Fortescue says, 'he has one gentleman who is more his intimate and correspondent than any of the rest.' You remember what his dismissed bailiff said of him and of his associates.* I don't find but that Mrs. Fortescue confirms this part of it, 'that all his relations are afraid of him; and that his pride sets him above owing obligations to them. She believes he is clear of the world; and that he will continue so;' No doubt from the same motive that makes him avoid being obliged to his relations.

* Letter IV.

A person willing to think favourably of him would hope, that a brave, a learned, and a diligent, man, cannot be naturally a bad man.—But if he be better than his enemies say he is (and if worse he is bad indeed) he is guilty of an inexcusable fault in being so careless as he is of his reputation. I think a man can be so but from one of these two reasons: either that he is conscious he deserves the ill spoken of him; or, that he takes a pride in being thought worse than he is. Both very bad and threatening indications; since the first must shew him to be utterly abandoned; and it is but natural to conclude from the other, that what a man is not ashamed to have imputed to him, he will not scruple to be guilty of whenever he has an opportunity.

Upon the whole, and upon all I could gather from Mrs. Fortescue, Mr. Lovelace is a very faulty man. You and I have thought him too gay, too inconsiderate, too rash, too little an hypocrite, to be deep. You see he never would disguise his natural temper (haughty as it certainly is) with respect to your brother's behaviour to him. Where he thinks a contempt due, he pays it to the uttermost. Nor has he complaisance enough to spare your uncles.

But were he deep, and ever so deep, you would soon penetrate him, if they would leave you to yourself. His vanity would be your clue. Never man had more: Yet, as Mrs. Fortescue observed, 'never did man carry it off so happily.' There is a strange mixture in it of humourous vivacity:—Since but for one half of what he says of himself, when he is in the vein, any other man would be insufferable.

Talk of the devil, is an old saying. The lively wretch has made me a visit, and is but just gone away. He is all impatience and resentment at the treatment you meet with, and full of apprehensions too, that they will carry their point with you.

I told him my opinion, that you will never be brought to think of such a man as Solmes; but that it will probably end in a composition, never to have either.

No man, he said, whose fortunes and alliances are so considerable, ever had so little favour from a woman for whose sake he had borne so much.

I told him my mind as freely as I used to do. But whoever was in fault, self being judge? He complained of spies set upon his conduct, and to pry into his life and morals, and this by your brother and uncles.

I told him, that this was very hard upon him; and the more so, as neither his life nor morals perhaps would stand a fair inquiry.

He smiled, and called himself my servant.—The occasion was too fair, he said, for Miss Howe, who never spared him, to let it pass.—But, Lord help the shallow souls of the Harlowes! Would I believe it! they were for turning plotters upon him. They had best take care he did not pay them in their own coin. Their hearts were better turned for such works than their heads.

I asked him, If he valued himself upon having a head better turned than theirs for such works, as he called them?

He drew off: and then ran into the highest professions of reverence and affection for you.

The object so meritorious, who can doubt the reality of his professions?

Adieu, my dearest, my noble friend!—I love and admire you for the generous conclusion of your last more than I can express. Though I began this letter with impertinent raillery, knowing that you always loved to indulge my mad vein; yet never was there a heart that more glowed with friendly love, than that of

Your own ANNA HOWE.

LETTER XIII

MISS CLARISSA HARLOWE, TO MISS HOWE WEDNESDAY, MARCH 1

I now take up my pen to lay before you the inducements and motive which my friends have to espouse so earnestly the address of this Mr. Solmes.

In order to set this matter in a clear light, it is necessary to go a little back, and even perhaps to mention some things which you already know: and so you may look upon what I am going to relate, as a kind of supplement to my letters of the 15th and 20th of January last.*

* Letters IV. and V.

In those letters, of which I have kept memorandums, I gave you an account of my brother's and sister's antipathy to Mr. Lovelace; and the methods they took (so far as they had then come to my knowledge) to ruin him in the opinion of my other friends. And I told you, that after a very cold, yet not a directly affrontive behaviour to him, they all of a sudden* became more violent, and proceeded to personal insults; which brought on at last the unhappy rencounter between my brother and him.

* *See Letter IV.*

Now you must know, that from the last conversation that passed between my aunt and me, it comes out, that this sudden vehemence on my brother's and sister's parts, was owing to stronger reasons than to the college-begun antipathy on his side, or to slighted love on hers; to wit, to an apprehension that my uncles intended to follow my grandfather's example in my favour; at least in a higher degree than they wish they should. An apprehension founded it seems on a conversation between my two uncles and my brother and sister: which my aunt communicated to me in confidence, as an argument to prevail upon me to accept of Mr. Solmes's noble settlements: urging, that such a seasonable compliance, would frustrate my brother's and sister's views, and establish me for ever in the love of my father and uncles.

I will give you the substance of this communicated conversation, after I have made a brief introductory observation or two, which however I hardly need to make to you who are so well acquainted with us all, did not the series or thread of the story require it.

I have more than once mentioned to you the darling view some of us have long had of raising a family, as it is called. A reflection, as I have often thought, upon our own, which is no considerable or upstart one, on either side, on my mother's especially.—A view too frequently it seems entertained by families which, having great substance, cannot be satisfied without rank and title.

My uncles had once extended this view to each of us three children; urging, that as they themselves intended not to marry, we each of us might be so portioned, and so advantageously matched, as that our posterity, if not ourselves, might make a first figure in our country.—While my brother, as the only son, thought the two girls might be very well provided for by ten or fifteen thousand pounds a-piece: and that all the real estates in the family, to wit, my grandfather's, father's, and two uncles', and the remainder of their respective personal estates, together with what he had an expectation of from his godmother, would make such a noble fortune, and give him such an interest, as might entitle him to hope for a peerage. Nothing less would satisfy his ambition.

With this view he gave himself airs very early; 'That his grandfather and uncles were his stewards: that no man ever had better: that daughters were but incumbrances and drawbacks upon a family:' and this low and familiar expression was often in his mouth, and uttered always with the self-complaisance which an imagined happy thought can be supposed to give the speaker; to wit, 'That a man who has sons brings up chickens for his own table,' [though once I made his comparison stagger with him, by asking him, If the sons, to make it hold, were to have their necks wrung off?] 'whereas daughters are chickens brought up for tables of other men.' This, accompanied with the equally polite reflection, 'That, to induce people to take them off their hands, the family-stock must be impaired into the bargain,' used to put my sister out of all patience: and, although she now seems to think a younger sister only can be an incumbrance, she was then often proposing to me to make a party in our own favour against my brother's rapacious views, as she used to call them: while I was for considering the liberties he took of this sort, as the effect of a temporary pleasantry, which, in a young man, not naturally good-humoured, I was glad to see; or as a foible that deserved raillery, but no other notice.

But when my grandfather's will (of the purport of which in my particular favour, until it was opened, I was as ignorant as they) had lopped off one branch of my brother's expectation, he was extremely dissatisfied with me. Nobody indeed was pleased: for although every one loved me, yet being the youngest child, father, uncles, brother, sister, all thought themselves postponed, as to matter of right and power [Who loves not power?]: And my father himself could not bear that I should be made sole, as I may call it, and independent; for such the will, as to that estate and the powers it gave, (unaccountably, as they all said,) made me.

To obviate, therefore, every one's jealousy, I gave up to my father's management, as you know, not only the estate, but the money bequeathed me (which was a moiety of what my grandfather had by him at his death; the other moiety being bequeathed to my sister); contenting myself to take as from his bounty what he was pleased to allow me, without desiring the least addition to my annual stipend. And then I hoped I had laid all envy asleep: but still my brother and sister (jealous, as now is evident, of my two uncles' favour of me, and of the pleasure I had given my father and them by this act of duty) were every now-and-then occasionally doing me covert ill offices: of which, however, I took the less notice, when I was told of them, as I thought I had removed the cause of their envy; and I imputed every thing of that sort to the petulance they are both pretty much noted for.

My brother's acquisition then took place. This made us all very happy; and he went down to take possession of it: and his absence (on so good an account too) made us still happier. Then followed Lord M.'s proposal for my sister: and this was an additional felicity for the time. I have told you how exceedingly good-humoured it made my sister.

You know how that went off: you know what came on in its place.

My brother then returned; and we were all wrong again: and Bella, as I observed in my letters abovementioned, had an opportunity to give herself the credit of having refused Mr. Lovelace, on the score of his reputed faulty morals. This united my brother and sister in one cause. They set themselves on all occasions to depreciate Mr. Lovelace, and his family too (a family which deserves nothing but respect): and this gave rise to the conversation I am leading to, between my uncles and them: of which I now come to give the particulars; after I have observed, that it happened before the rencounter, and soon after the inquiry made into Mr. Lovelace's affairs had come out better than my brother and sister hoped it would.*

* See Letter IV.

They were bitterly inveighing against him, in their usual way, strengthening their invectives with some new stories in his disfavour, when my uncle Antony, having given them a patient hearing, declared, 'That he thought the gentleman behaved like a gentleman; his niece Clary with prudence; and that a more honourable alliance for the family, as he had often told them, could not be wished for: since Mr. Lovelace had a very good paternal estate; and that, by the evidence of an enemy, all clear. Nor did it appear, that he was so bad a man as he had been represented to be: wild indeed; but it was a gay time of life: he was a man of sense: and he was sure that his niece would not have him, if she had not good reason to think him reformed, or that there was a likelihood that she could reform him by her example.'

My uncle then gave one instance, my aunt told me, as a proof of a generosity in Mr. Lovelace's spirit, which convinced him that he was not a bad man in nature; and that he was of a temper, he was pleased to say, like my own; which was, That when he (my uncle) had represented to him, that he might, if he pleased, make three or four hundred pounds a year of his paternal estate, more than he did; he answered, 'That his tenants paid their rents well: that it was a maxim with his family, from which he would by no means depart, Never to rack-rent old tenants, or their descendants; and that it was a pleasure to him, to see all his tenants look fat, sleek, and contented.'

I indeed had once occasionally heard him say something like this; and thought he never looked so well as at that time;—except once; and that was in an instance given by him on the following incident.

An unhappy tenant of my uncle Antony came petitioning to my uncle for forbearance, in Mr. Lovelace's presence. When he had fruitlessly withdrawn, Mr. Lovelace pleaded his cause so well, that the man was called in again, and had his suit granted. And Mr. Lovelace privately followed him out, and gave him two guineas, for present relief; the man having declared, that, at the time, he had not five shilling in the world.

On this occasion, he told my uncle (but without any airs of ostentation), that he had once observed an old tenant and his wife in a very mean habit at church; and questioning them about it the next day, as he knew they had no hard bargain in their farm, the man said, he had done some very foolish things with a good intention, which had put him behind-hand, and he could not have paid his rent, and appear better. He asked him how long it would take him to retrieve the foolish step he acknowledged he had made. He said, Perhaps two or three years. Well then, said he, I will abate you five pounds a year for seven years, provided you will lay it upon your wife and self, that you may make a Sunday-appearance like MY tenants. Mean time, take this (putting his hand in his pocket, and giving him five guineas), to put yourselves in present plight; and let me see you next Sunday at church, hand in hand, like an honest and loving couple; and I bespeak you to dine with me afterwards.

Although this pleased me when I heard it, as giving an instance of generosity and prudence at the same time, not lessening (as my uncle took notice) the yearly value of the farm, yet, my dear, I had no throbs, no glows upon it!—Upon my word, I had not. Nevertheless I own to you, that I could not help saying to myself on the occasion, 'Were it ever to be my lot to have this man, he would not hinder me from pursuing the methods I so much delight to take'—With 'A pity, that such a man were not uniformly good!'

Forgive me this digression.

My uncle went on (as my aunt told me), 'That, besides his paternal estate, he was the immediate heir to very splendid fortunes: that, when he was in treaty for his niece Arabella, Lord M. told him (my uncle) what great things he and his two half-sisters intended to do for him, in order to qualify him for the title, which would be extinct at his Lordship's death, and which they hoped to procure for him, or a still higher, that of those ladies' father, which had been for some time extinct on failure of heirs male: that it was with this view that his relations were all so earnest for his marrying: that as he saw not where Mr. Lovelace could better himself; so, truly, he thought there was wealth enough in their own family to build up three considerable ones: that, therefore, he must needs say, he was the more desirous of this alliance, as there was a great probability, not only from Mr. Lovelace's descent, but from his fortunes, that his niece Clarissa might one day be a peeress of Great Britain:—and, upon that prospect [here was the mortifying stroke], he should, for his own part, think it not wrong to make such dispositions as should contribute to the better support of the dignity.'

My uncle Harlowe, it seems, far from disapproving of what his brother had said, declared, 'That there was but one objection to an alliance with Mr. Lovelace; to wit, his faulty morals: especially as so much could be done for Miss Bella, and for my brother too, by my father; and as my brother was actually possessed of a considerable estate by virtue of the deed of gift and will of his godmother Lovell.'

Had I known this before, I should the less have wondered at many things I have been unable to account for in my brother's and sister's behaviour to me; and been more on my guard than I imagined there was a necessity to be.

You may easily guess how much this conversation affected my brother at the time. He could not, you know, but be very uneasy to hear two of his stewards talk at this rate to his face.

He had from early days, by his violent temper, made himself both feared and courted by the whole family. My father himself, as I have lately mentioned, very often (long before my brother's acquisition had made him still more assuming) gave way to him, as to an only son who was to build up the name, and augment the honour of it. Little inducement, therefore, had my brother to correct a temper which gave him so much consideration with every body.

'See, Sister Bella,' said he, in an indecent passion before my uncles, on this occasion I have mentioned—'See how it is!—You and I ought to look about us!—This little syren is in a fair way to out-uncle, as she has already out-grandfather'd, us both!'

From this time (as I now find it plain upon recollection) did my brother and sister behave to me, as to one who stood in their way; and to each other as having but one interest: and were resolved, therefore, to bend all their force to hinder an alliance from taking effect, which they believed was likely to oblige them to contract their views.

And how was this to be done, after such a declaration from both my uncles?

My brother found out the way. My sister (as I have said) went hand in hand with him. Between them, the family union was broke, and every one was made uneasy. Mr. Lovelace was received more and more coldly by all: but not being to be put out of his course by slights only, personal affronts succeeded; defiances next; then the rencounter: that, as you have heard, did the business. And now, if I do not oblige them, my grandfather's estate is to be litigated with me; and I, who never designed to take advantage of the independency bequeathed me, am to be as dependent upon my father's will, as a daughter ought to be who knows not what is good for herself. This is the language of the family now.

But if I will suffer myself to be prevailed upon, how happy (as they lay it out) shall we all be!—Such presents am I to have, such jewels, and I cannot tell what, from every one in the family! Then Mr. Solmes's fortunes are so great, and his proposals so very advantageous, (no relation whom he values,) that there will be abundant room to raise mine upon them, were the high-intended favours of my own relations to be quite out of the question. Moreover, it is now, with this view, found out, that I have qualifications which of themselves will be a full equivalent to Mr. Solmes for the settlements he is to make; and still leave him under an obligation to me for my compliance. He himself thinks so, I am told—so very poor a creature is he, even in his own eyes, as well as in theirs.

These desirable views answered, how rich, how splendid shall we all three be! And I—what obligations shall I lay upon them all!—And that only by doing an act of duty so suitable to my character, and manner of thinking; if, indeed, I am the generous as well as dutiful creature I have hitherto made them believe I am.

This is the bright side that is turned to my father and uncles, to captivate them: but I am afraid that my brother's and sister's design is to ruin me with them at any rate. Were it otherwise, would they not on my return from you have rather sought to court than frighten me into measures which their hearts are so much bent to carry? A method they have followed ever since.

Mean time, orders are given to all the servants to shew the highest respect to Mr. Solmes; the generous Mr. Solmes is now his character with some of our family! But are not these orders a tacit confession, that they think his own merit will not procure him respect? He is accordingly, in every visit he makes, not only highly caressed by the principals of our family, but obsequiously attended and cringed to by the menials.—And the noble settlements are echoed from every mouth.

Noble is the word used to enforce the offers of a man who is mean enough avowedly to hate, and wicked enough to propose to rob of their just expectations, his own family, (every one of which at the same time stands in too much need of his favour,) in order to settle all he is worth upon me; and if I die without children, and he has none by any other marriage, upon a family which already abounds. Such are his proposals.

But were there no other motive to induce me to despise the upstart man, is not this unjust one to his family enough?—The upstart man, I repeat; for he was not born to the immense riches he is possessed of: riches left by one niggard to another, in injury to the next heir, because that other is a niggard. And should I not be as culpable, do you think, in my acceptance of such unjust settlements, as he is in the offer of them, if I could persuade myself to be a sharer in them, or suffer a reversionary expectation of possessing them to influence my choice?

Indeed, it concerns me not a little, that my friends could be brought to encourage such offers on such motives as I think a person of conscience should not presume to begin the world with.

But this it seems is the only method that can be taken to disappoint Mr. Lovelace; and at the same time to answer all my relations have wish for each of us. And surely I will not stand against such an accession to the family as may happen from marrying Mr. Solmes: since now a possibility is discovered, (which such a grasping mind as my brother's can easily turn into a probability,) that my grandfather's estate will revert to it, with a much more considerable one of the man's own. Instances of estates falling in, in cases far more unlikely than this, are insisted upon; and my sister says, in the words of an old saw, It is good to be related to an estate.

While Solmes, smiling no doubt to himself at a hope so remote, by offers only, obtains all their interests; and doubts not to join to his own the estate I am envied for; which, for the conveniency of its situation between two of his, will it seems be of twice the value to him that it would be of to any other person; and is therefore, I doubt not, a stronger motive with him than the wife.

These, my dear, seem to me the principal inducements of my relations to espouse so vehemently as they do this man's suit. And here, once more, must I deplore the family fault, which gives those inducements such a force as it will be difficult to resist.

And thus far, let matters with regard to Mr. Solmes and me come out as they will, my brother has succeeded in his views; that is to say, he has, in the first place, got my FATHER to make the cause his own, and to insist upon my compliance as an act of duty.

My MOTHER has never thought fit to oppose my father's will, when once he has declared himself determined.

My UNCLES, stiff, unbroken, highly-prosperous bachelors, give me leave to say, (though very worthy persons in the main,) have as high notions of a child's duty, as of a wife's obedience; in the last of which, my mother's meekness has confirmed them, and given them greater reason to expect the first.

My aunt HERVEY (not extremely happy in her own nuptials, and perhaps under some little obligation) is got over, and chuses [sic] not to open her lips in my favour against the wills of a father and uncles so determined.

This passiveness in my mother and in my aunt, in a point so contrary to their own first judgments, is too strong a proof that my father is absolutely resolved.

Their treatment of my worthy MRS. NORTON is a sad confirmation of it: a woman deserving of all consideration for her wisdom, and every body thinking so; but who, not being wealthy enough to have due weight in a point against which she has given her opinion, and which they seem bent upon carrying, is restrained from visiting here, and even from corresponding with me, as I am this very day informed.

Hatred to Lovelace, family aggrandizement, and this great motive paternal authority!—What a force united must they be supposed to have, when singly each consideration is sufficient to carry all before it!

This is the formidable appearance which the address of this disagreeable man wears at present.

My BROTHER and my SISTER triumph.—They have got me down, as Hannah overheard them exult. And so they have (yet I never knew that I was insolently up); for now my brother will either lay me under an obligation to comply to my own unhappiness, and so make me an instrument of his revenge upon Lovelace; or, if I refuse, will throw me into disgrace with my whole family.

Who will wonder at the intrigues and plots carried on by undermining courtiers against one another, when a private family, but three of which can possibly have clashing interests, and one of them (as she presumes to think) above such low motives, cannot be free from them?

What at present most concerns me, is, the peace of my mother's mind! How can the husband of such a wife (a good man too!—But oh! this prerogative of manhood!) be so positive, so unpersuadable, to one who has brought into the family means, which they know so well the value of, that methinks they should value her the more for their sake?

They do indeed value her: but, I am sorry to say, she has purchased that value by her compliances; yet has merit for which she ought to be venerated; prudence which ought of itself to be conformed to in every thing.

But whither roves my pen? How dare a perverse girl take these liberties with relations so very respectable, and whom she highly respects? What an unhappy situation is that which obliges her, in her own defence as it were, to expose their failings?

But you, who know how much I love and reverence my mother, will judge what a difficulty I am under, to be obliged to oppose a scheme which she has engaged in. Yet I must oppose it (to comply is impossible); and must without delay declare my opposition, or my difficulties will increase; since, as I am just now informed, a lawyer has been this very day consulted [Would you have believed it?] in relation to settlements.

Were ours a Roman Catholic family, how much happier for me, that they thought a nunnery would answer all their views!—How happy, had not a certain person slighted somebody! All then would have been probably concluded between them before my brother had arrived to thwart the match: then had I a sister; which now I have not; and two brothers;—both aspiring; possibly both titled: while I should only have valued that in either which is above title, that which is truly noble in both!

But by what a long-reaching selfishness is my brother governed! By what remote, exceedingly remote views! Views, which it is in the power of the slightest accident, of a fever, for instance, (the seeds of which are always vegetating, as I may say, and ready to burst forth, in his own impetuous temper,) or of the provoked weapon of an adversary, to blow up and destroy!

I will break off here. Let me write ever so freely of my friends, I am sure of your kind construction: and I confide in your discretion, that you will avoid reading to or transcribing for others such passages as may have the appearance of treating too freely the parental, or even the fraternal character, or induce others to censure for a supposed failure in duty to the one, or decency to the other,

Your truly affectionate, CL. HARLOWE.

LETTER XIV

MISS CLARISSA HARLOWE, TO MISS HOWE THURSDAY EVENING, MARCH 2

On Hannah's depositing my long letter, (begun yesterday, but by reason of several interruptions not finished till within this hour,) she found and brought me yours of this day. I thank you, my dear, for this kind expedition. These few lines will perhaps be time enough deposited, to be taken away by your servant with the other letter: yet they are only to thank you, and to tell you my increasing apprehensions.

I must take or seek the occasion to apply to my mother for her mediation; for I am in danger of having a day fixed, and antipathy taken for bashfulness.—Should not sisters be sisters to each other? Should not they make a common cause of it, as I may say, a cause of sex, on such occasions as the present? Yet mine, in support of my brother's selfishness, and, no doubt, in concert with him, has been urging in full assembly it seems, (and that with an earnestness peculiar to herself when she sets upon any thing,) that an absolute day be given me; and if I comply not, to be told, that it shall be to the forfeiture of all my fortunes, and of all their love.

She need not be so officious: my brother's interest, without hers, is strong enough; for he has found means to confederate all the family against me. Upon some fresh provocation, or new intelligence concerning Mr. Lovelace, (I know not what it is,) they have bound themselves, or are to bind themselves, by a signed paper, to one another [The Lord bless me, my dear, what shall I do!] to carry their point in favour of Mr. Solmes, in support of my father's authority, as it is called, and against Mr. Lovelace, as a libertine, and an enemy to the family: and if so, I am sure, I may say against me.—How impolitic in them all, to join two people in one interest, whom they wish for ever to keep asunder!

What the discharged steward reported of him is surely bad enough: what Mrs. Fortescue said, not only confirms that bad, but gives room to think him still worse. And yet the something further which my friends have come at, is of so heinous a nature (as Betty Barnes tells Hannah) that it proves him almost to be the worst of men.—But, hang the man, I had almost said—What is he to me? What would he be—were not this Mr. Sol——O my dear, how I hate the man in the light he is proposed to me!

All of them, at the same time, are afraid of Mr. Lovelace; yet not afraid to provoke him!—How am I entangled!—to be obliged to go on corresponding with him for their sakes—Heaven forbid, that their persisted-in violence should so drive me, as to make it necessary for my own!

But surely they will yield—Indeed I cannot.

I believe the gentlest spirits when provoked (causelessly and cruelly provoked) are the most determined. The reason may be, that not taking up resolutions lightly—their very deliberation makes them the more immovable.—And then when a point is clear and self-evident, how can one with patience think of entering into an argument or contention upon it?—

An interruption obliges me to conclude myself, in some hurry, as well as fright, what I must ever be,

Yours more than my own, CLARISSA HARLOWE.

LETTER XV

MISS HOWE, TO MISS CLARISSA HARLOWE FRIDAY, MARCH 3

I have both your letters at once. It is very unhappy, my dear, since your friends will have you marry, that a person of your merit should be addressed by a succession of worthless creatures, who have nothing but their presumption for their excuse.

That these presumers appear not in this very unworthy light to some of your friends, is, because their defects are not so striking to them as to others.—And why? Shall I venture to tell you?—Because they are nearer their own standard—Modesty, after all, perhaps has a concern in it; for how should they think that a niece or sister of theirs [I will not go higher, for fear of incurring your displeasure] should be an angel?

But where indeed is the man to be found (who has the least share of due diffidence) that dares to look up to Miss Clarissa Harlowe with hope, or with any thing but wishes? Thus the bold and forward, not being sensible of their defects, aspire; while the modesty of the really worthy fills them with too much reverence to permit them to explain themselves. Hence your Symmes's, your Byron's, your Mullins's, your Wyerley's (the best of the herd), and your Solmes's, in turn, invade you—Wretches that, looking upon the rest of your family, need not despair of succeeding in an alliance with it—But to you, what an inexcusable presumption!

Yet I am afraid all opposition will be in vain. You must, you will, I doubt, be sacrificed to this odious man. I know your family. There will be no resisting such baits as he has thrown out. O, my dear, my beloved friend! and are such charming qualities, is such exalted merit, to be sunk in such a marriage!—You must not, your uncle tells your mother, dispute their authority. AUTHORITY! what a full word is that in the mouth of a narrow-minded person, who happened to be born thirty years before one!—Of your uncles I speak; for as to the paternal authority, that ought to be sacred.—But should not parents have reason for what they do?

Wonder not, however, at your Bell's unsisterly behaviour in this affair: I have a particular to add to the inducements your insolent brother is governed by, which will account for all her driving. You have already owned, that her outward eye was from the first struck with the figure and address of the man whom she pretends to despise, and who, 'tis certain, thoroughly despises her: but you have not told me, that still she loves him of all men. Bell has a meanness in her very pride; that meanness rises with her pride, and goes hand in hand with it; and no one is so proud as Bell. She has owned her love, her uneasy days, and sleepless nights, and her revenge grafted upon her love, to her favourite Betty Barnes—To lay herself in the power of a servant's tongue! Poor creature!—But LIKE little souls will find one another out, and mingle, as well as LIKE great ones. This, however, she told the wench in strict confidence: and thus, by way of the female round-about, as Lovelace had the sauciness on such another occasion, in ridicule of our sex, to call it, Betty (pleased to be thought worthy of a secret, and to have an opportunity of inveighing against Lovelace's perfidy, as she would have it to be) told it to one of her confidants: that confidant, with like injunctions of secrecy, to Miss Lloyd's Harriot—Harriot to Miss Lloyd—Miss Lloyd to me—I to you—with leave to make what you please of it.

And now you will not wonder to find Miss Bell an implacable rival, rather than an affectionate sister; and will be able to account for the words witchcraft, syren, and such like, thrown out against you; and for her driving on for a fixed day for sacrificing you to Solmes: in short, for her rudeness and violence of every kind.

What a sweet revenge will she take, as well upon Lovelace as upon you, if she can procure her rival sister to be married to the man that sister hates; and so prevent her having the man whom she herself loves (whether she have hope of him or not), and whom she suspects her sister loves!

Poisons and poniard have often been set to work by minds inflamed by disappointed love, and actuated by revenge.—Will you wonder, then, that the ties of relationship in such a case have no force, and that a sister forgets to be a sister?

Now I know this to be her secret motive, (the more grating to her, as her pride is concerned to make her disavow it), and can consider it joined with her former envy, and as strengthened by a brother, who has such an ascendant over the whole family; and whose interest (slave to it as he always was) engaged him to ruin you with every one: both possessed of the ears of all your family, and having it as much in their power as in their will to misrepresent all you say, all you do; such subject also as to the rencounter, and Lovelace's want of morals, to expatiate upon: your whole family likewise avowedly attached to the odious man by means of the captivating proposals he has made them;—when I consider all these things, I am full of apprehensions for you.—O my dear, how will you be able to maintain your ground;—I am sure, (alas! I am too sure) that they will subdue such a fine spirit as yours, unused to opposition; and (tell it not in Gath) you must be Mrs. Solmes!

Mean time, it is now easy, as you will observe, to guess from what quarter the report I mentioned to you in one of my former, came, That the younger sister has robbed the elder of her lover:* for Betty whispered it, at the time she whispered the rest, that neither Lovelace nor you had done honourably by her young mistress.—How cruel, my dear, in you, to rob the poor Bella of the only lover she only had!—At the instant too that she was priding herself, that now at last she should have it in her power not only to gratify her own susceptibilities, but to give an example to the flirts of her sex** (my worship's self in her eye) how to govern their man with a silken rein, and without a curb-bridle!

* *Letter I.*

** *Letter II.*

Upon the whole, I have now no doubt of their persevering in favour of the despicable Solmes; and of their dependence upon the gentleness of your temper, and the regard you have for their favour, and for your own reputation. And now I am more than ever convinced of the propriety of the advice I formerly gave you, to keep in your own hands the estate bequeathed to you by your grandfather.—Had you done so, it would have procured you at least an outward respect from your brother and sister, which would have made them conceal the envy and ill-will that now are bursting upon you from hearts so narrow.

I must harp a little more upon this string—Do not you observe, how much your brother's influence has overtopped yours, since he has got into fortunes so considerable, and since you have given some of them an appetite to continue in themselves the possession of your estate, unless you comply with their terms?

I know your dutiful, your laudable motives; and one would have thought, that you might have trusted to a father who so dearly loved you. But had you been actually in possession of that estate, and living up to it, and upon it, (your youth protected from blighting tongues by the company of your prudent Norton, as you had proposed,) do you think that your brother, grudging it to you at the time as he did, and looking upon it as his right as an only son, would have been practising about it, and aiming at it? I told you some time ago, that I thought your trials but proportioned to your prudence:* but you will be more than woman, if you can extricate yourself with honour, having such violent spirits and sordid minds in some, and such tyrannical and despotic wills in others, to deal with. Indeed, all may be done, and the world be taught further to admire you for your blind duty and will-less resignation, if you can persuade yourself to be Mrs. Solmes.

* *Letter I.*

I am pleased with the instances you give me of Mr. Lovelace's benevolence to his own tenants, and with his little gift to your uncle's. Mrs. Fortescue allows him to be the best of landlords: I might have told you that, had I thought it necessary to put you into some little conceit of him. He has qualities, in short, that may make him a tolerable creature on the other side of fifty: but God help the poor woman to whose lot he shall fall till then! women, I should say, perhaps; since he may break half-a-dozen hearts before that time.—But to the point I was upon—Shall we not have reason to commend the tenant's grateful honesty, if we are told, that with joy the poor man called out your uncle, and on the spot paid him in part of his debt those two guineas?—But what shall we say of that landlord, who, though he knew the poor man to be quite destitute, could take it; and, saying nothing while Mr. Lovelace staid, as soon as he was gone, tell of it in praise of the poor fellow's honesty?—Were this so, and were not that landlord related to my dearest friend, how should I despise such a wretch?—But, perhaps, the story is aggravated. Covetous people have every one's ill word: and so indeed they ought; because they are only solicitous to keep that which they prefer to every one's good one.—Covetous indeed would they be, who deserved neither, yet expected both!

I long for your next letter. Continue to be as particular as possible. I can think of no other subject but what relates to you and to your affairs: for I am, and ever will be, most affectionately,

Your own, ANNA HOWE.

LETTER XVI

MISS CLARISSA HARLOWE, TO MISS HOWE [HER PRECEDING NOT AT THAT TIME RECEIVED.] FRIDAY, MARCH 3

O my dear friend, I have had a sad conflict! Trial upon trial; conference upon conference!—But what law, what ceremony, can give a man a right to a heart which abhors him more than it does any living creature?

I hope my mother will be able to prevail for me.—But I will recount it all, though I sit up the whole night to do it; for I have a vast deal to write, and will be as minute as you wish me to be.

I concluded my last in a fright. It was occasioned by a conversation that passed between my mother and my aunt, part of which Hannah overheard. I need not give you the particulars; since what I have to relate to you from different conversations that have passed between my mother and me, in the space of a very few hours, will include them all. I will begin then.

I went down this morning when breakfast was ready with a very uneasy heart, from what Hannah had informed me of yesterday afternoon; wishing for an opportunity, however, to appeal to my mother, in hopes to engage her interest in my behalf, and purposing to try to find one when she retired to her own apartment after breakfast: but, unluckily, there was the odious Solmes, sitting asquat between my mother and sister, with so much assurance in his looks!—But you know, my dear, that those we love not, cannot do any thing to please us.

Had the wretch kept his seat, it might have been well enough: but the bend and broad-shouldered creature must needs rise, and stalk towards a chair, which was just by that which was set for me.

I removed it to a distance, as if to make way to my own: and down I sat, abruptly I believe; what I had heard all in my head.

But this was not enough to daunt him. The man is a very confident, he is a very bold, staring man!—Indeed, my dear, the man is very confident.

He took the removed chair, and drew it so near mine, squatting in it with his ugly weight, that he pressed upon my hoop.—I was so offended (all I had heard, as I said, in my head) that I removed to another chair. I own

I had too little command of myself. It gave my brother and sister too much advantage. I day say they took it. But I did it involuntarily, I think. I could not help it.—I knew not what I did.

I saw that my father was excessively displeased. When angry, no man's countenance ever shews it so much as my father's. Clarissa Harlowe! said he with a big voice—and there he stopped. Sir! said I, trembling and courtesying (for I had not then sat down again); and put my chair nearer the wretch, and sat down—my face, as I could feel, all in a glow.

Make tea, child, said my kind mamma; sit by me, love, and make tea.

I removed with pleasure to the seat the man had quitted; and being thus indulgently put into employment, soon recovered myself; and in the course of the breakfasting officiously asked two or three questions of Mr. Solmes, which I would not have done, but to make up with my father.—Proud spirits may be brought to! Whisperingly spoke my sister to me, over her shoulder, with an air of triumph and scorn: but I did not mind her.

My mother was all kindness and condescension. I asked her once, if she were pleased with the tea? She said, softly, (and again called me dear,) she was pleased with all I did. I was very proud of this encouraging goodness: and all blew over, as I hoped, between my father and me; for he also spoke kindly to me two or three times.

Small accidents these, my dear, to trouble you with; only as they lead to greater, as you shall hear.

Before the usual breakfast-time was over, my father withdrew with my mother, telling her he wanted to speak with her. Then my sister and next my aunt (who was with us) dropt away.

My brother gave himself some airs of insult, which I understood well enough; but which Mr. Solmes could make nothing of: and at last he arose from his seat—Sister, said he, I have a curiosity to shew you. I will fetch it. And away he went shutting the door close after him.

I saw what all this was for. I arose; the man hemming up for a speech, rising, and beginning to set his splay-feet [indeed, my dear, the man in all his ways is hateful to me] in an approaching posture.—I will save my brother the trouble of bringing to me his curiosity, said I. I courtesied—Your servant, sir—The man cried, Madam, Madam, twice, and looked like a fool.—But away I went—to find my brother, to save my word.—But my brother, indifferent as the weather was, was gone to walk in the garden with my sister. A plain case, that he had left his curiosity with me, and designed to shew me no other.

I had but just got into my own apartment, and began to think of sending Hannah to beg an audience of my mother (the more encouraged by her condescending goodness at breakfast) when Shorey, her woman, brought me her commands to attend me in her closet.

My father, Hannah told me, was just gone out of it with a positive angry countenance. Then I as much dreaded the audience as I had wished for it before.

I went down however; but, apprehending the subject she intended to talk to me upon, approached her trembling, and my heart in visible palpitations.

She saw my concern. Holding out her kind arms, as she sat, Come kiss me, my dear, said she, with a smile like a sun-beam breaking through the cloud that overshadowed her naturally benign aspect—Why flutters my jewel so?

This preparative sweetness, with her goodness just before, confirmed my apprehensions. My mother saw the bitter pill wanted gilding.

O my Mamma! was all I could say; and I clasped my arms round her neck, and my face sunk into her bosom.

My child! my child! restrain, said she, your powers of moving! I dare not else trust myself with you.—And my tears trickled down her bosom, as hers bedewed my neck.

O the words of kindness, all to be expressed in vain, that flowed from her lips!

Lift up your sweet face, my best child, my own Clarissa Harlowe!—O my daughter, best beloved of my heart, lift up a face so ever amiable to me!—Why these sobs?—Is an apprehended duty so affecting a thing, that before I can speak—But I am glad, my love, you can guess at what I have to say to you. I am spared the pains of breaking to you what was a task upon me reluctantly enough undertaken to break to you. Then rising, she drew a chair near her own, and made me sit down by her, overwhelmed as I was with tears of apprehension of what she had to say, and of gratitude for her truly maternal goodness to me—sobs still my only language.

And drawing her chair still nearer to mine, she put her arms round my neck, and my glowing cheek wet with my tears, close to her own: Let me talk to you, my child. Since silence is your choice, hearken to me, and be silent.

You know, my dear, what I every day forego, and undergo, for the sake of peace. Your papa is a very good man, and means well; but he will not be controuled; nor yet persuaded. You have sometimes seemed to pity me, that I am obliged to give up every point. Poor man! his reputation the less for it; mine the greater: yet would I not have this credit, if I could help it, at so dear a rate to him and to myself. You are a dutiful, a prudent, and a wise child, she was pleased to say, in hope, no doubt, to make me so: you would not add, I am sure, to my trouble: you would not wilfully break that peace which costs your mother so much to preserve. Obedience is better than sacrifice. O my Clary Harlowe, rejoice my heart, by telling me that I have apprehended too much!—I see your concern! I see your perplexity! I see your conflict! [loosing her arm, and rising, not willing I should see how much she herself was affected]. I will leave you a moment.—Answer me not—[for I was essaying to speak, and had, as soon as she took her dear cheek from mine, dropt down on my knees, my hands clasped, and lifted up in a supplicating manner]—I am not prepared for your irresistible expostulation, she was pleased to say. I will leave you to recollection: and I charge you, on my blessing, that all this my truly maternal tenderness be not thrown away upon you.

And then she withdrew into the next apartment; wiping her eyes as she went from me; as mine overflowed; my heart taking in the whole compass of her meaning.

She soon returned, having recovered more steadiness.

Still on my knees, I had thrown my face across the chair she had sat in.

Look up to me, my Clary Harlowe—No sullenness, I hope!

No, indeed, my ever-to-be-revered Mamma.—And I arose. I bent my knee.

She raised me. No kneeling to me, but with knees of duty and compliance. Your heart, not your knees, must bend. It is absolutely determined. Prepare yourself therefore to receive your father, when he visits you by-and-by, as he would wish to receive you. But on this one quarter of an hour depends the peace of my future life, the satisfaction of all the family, and your own security from a man of violence: and I charge you besides, on my blessing, that you think of being Mrs. Solmes.

There went the dagger to my heart, and down I sunk: and when I recovered, found myself in the arms of my Hannah, my sister's Betty holding open my reluctantly-opened palm, my laces cut, my linen scented with hartshorn; and my mother gone. Had I been less kindly treated, the hated name still forborne to be mentioned, or mentioned with a little more preparation and reserve, I had stood the horrid sound with less visible emotion—But to be bid, on the blessing of a mother so dearly beloved, so truly reverenced, to think of being MRS. SOLMES—what a denunciation was that!

Shorey came in with a message (delivered in her solemn way): Your mamma, Miss, is concerned for your disorder: she expects you down again in an hour; and bid me say, that she then hopes every thing from your duty.

I made no reply; for what could I say? And leaning upon my Hannah's arm, withdrew to my own apartment. There you will guess how the greatest part of the hour was employed.

Within that time, my mother came up to me.

I love, she was pleased to say, to come into this apartment.—No emotions, child! No flutters!—Am I not your mother?—Do not discompose me by discomposing yourself! Do not occasion me uneasiness, when I would give you nothing but pleasure. Come, my dear, we will go into your closet.

She took my hand, led the way, and made me sit down by her: and after she had inquired how I did, she began in a strain as if she supposed I had made use of the intervening space to overcome all my objections.

She was pleased to tell me, that my father and she, in order to spare my natural modesty, had taken the whole affair upon themselves—

Hear me out; and then speak.—He is not indeed every thing I wish him to be: but he is a man of probity, and has no vices—

No vices, Madam—!

Hear me out, child.—You have not behaved much amiss to him: we have seen with pleasure that you have not—

O Madam, must I not now speak!

I shall have done presently.—A young creature of your virtuous and pious turn, she was pleased to say, cannot surely love a profligate: you love your brother too well, to wish to marry one who had like to have killed him, and who threatened your uncles, and defies us all. You have had your own way six or seven times: we want to secure you against a man so vile. Tell me (I have a right to know) whether you prefer this man to all others?—Yet God forbid that I should know you do; for such a declaration would make us all miserable. Yet tell me, are your affections engaged to this man?

I knew not what the inference would be, if I said they were not.

You hesitate—You answer me not—You cannot answer me.—Rising—Never more will I look upon you with an eye of favour—

O Madam, Madam! Kill me not with your displeasure—I would not, I need not, hesitate one moment, did I not dread the inference, if I answer you as you wish.—Yet be that inference what it will, your threatened displeasure will make me speak. And I declare to you, that I know not my own heart, if it not be absolutely free. And pray, let me ask my dearest Mamma, in what has my conduct been faulty, that, like a giddy creature, I must be forced to marry, to save me from—From what? Let me beseech you, Madam, to be the guardian of my reputation! Let not your Clarissa be precipitated into a state she wishes not to enter into with any man! And this upon a supposition that otherwise she shall marry herself, and disgrace her whole family.

Well then, Clary [passing over the force of my plea] if your heart be free—

O my beloved Mamma, let the usual generosity of your dear heart operate in my favour. Urge not upon me the inference that made me hesitate.

I won't be interrupted, Clary—You have seen in my behaviour to you, on this occasion, a truly maternal tenderness; you have observed that I have undertaken the task with some reluctance, because the man is not every thing; and because I know you carry your notions of perfection in a man too high—

Dearest Madam, this one time excuse me!—Is there then any danger that I should be guilty of an imprudent thing for the man's sake you hint at?

Again interrupted!—Am I to be questioned, and argued with? You know this won't do somewhere else. You know it won't. What reason then, ungenerous girl, can you have for arguing with me thus, but because you think from my indulgence to you, you may?

What can I say? What can I do? What must that cause be that will not bear being argued upon?

Again! Clary Harlowe!

Dearest Madam, forgive me: it was always my pride and my pleasure to obey you. But look upon that man—see but the disagreeableness of his person—

Now, Clary, do I see whose person you have in your eye!—Now is Mr. Solmes, I see, but comparatively disagreeable; disagreeable only as another man has a much more specious person

But, Madam, are not his manners equally so?—Is not his person the true representative of his mind?—That other man is not, shall not be, any thing to me, release me but from this one man, whom my heart, unbidden, resists.

Condition thus with your father. Will he bear, do you think, to be thus dialogued with? Have I not conjured you, as you value my peace—What is it that I do not give up?—This very task, because I apprehended you would not be easily persuaded, is a task indeed upon me. And will you give up nothing? Have you not refused as many as have been offered to you? If you would not have us guess for whom, comply; for comply you must, or be looked upon as in a state of defiance with your whole family.

And saying this, she arose and went from me. But at the chamber-door stopt; and turned back: I will not say below in what a disposition I leave you. Consider of every thing. The matter is resolved upon. As you value your father's blessing and mine, and the satisfaction of all the family, resolve to comply. I will leave you for a few moments. I will come up to you again. See that I find you as I wish to find you; and since your heart is free, let your duty govern it.

In about half an hour, my mother returned. She found me in tears. She took my hand: It is my part evermore, said she, to be of the acknowledging side. I believe I have needlessly exposed myself to your opposition, by the method I have taken with you. I first began as if I expected a denial, and by my indulgence brought it upon myself.

Do not, my dearest Mamma! do not say so!

Were the occasion for this debate, proceeded she, to have risen from myself; were it in my power to dispense with your compliance; you too well know what you can do with me.

Would any body, my dear Miss Howe, wish to marry, who sees a wife of such a temper, and blessed with such an understanding as my mother is noted for, not only deprived of all power, but obliged to be even active in bringing to bear a point of high importance, which she thinks ought not to be insisted upon?

When I came to you a second time, proceeded she, knowing that your opposition would avail you nothing, I refused to hear your reasons: and in this I was wrong too, because a young creature who loves to reason, and used to love to be convinced by reason, ought to have all her objections heard: I now therefore, this third time, see you; and am come resolved to hear all you have to say: and let me, my dear, by my patience engage your gratitude; your generosity, I will call it, because it is to you I speak, who used to have a mind wholly generous.—Let me, if your heart be really free, let me see what it will induce you to do to oblige me: and so as you permit your usual discretion to govern you, I will hear all you have to say; but with this intimation, that say what you will, it will be of no avail elsewhere.

What a dreadful saying is that! But could I engage your pity, Madam, it would be somewhat.

You have as much of my pity as of my love. But what is person, Clary, with one of your prudence, and your heart disengaged?

Should the eye be disgusted, when the heart is to be engaged?—O Madam, who can think of marrying when the heart is shocked at the first appearance, and where the disgust must be confirmed by every conversation afterwards?

This, Clary, is owing to your prepossession. Let me not have cause to regret that noble firmness of mind in so young a creature which I thought your glory, and which was my boast in your character. In this instance it would be obstinacy, and want of duty.—Have you not made objections to several—

That was to their minds, to their principles, Madam.—But this man—

Is an honest man, Clary Harlowe. He has a good mind. He is a virtuous man.

He an honest man? His a good mind, Madam? He a virtuous man?—

Nobody denies these qualities.

Can he be an honest man who offers terms that will rob all his own relations of their just expectations?—Can his mind be good—

You, Clary Harlowe, for whose sake he offers so much, are the last person who should make this observation.

Give me leave to say, Madam, that a person preferring happiness to fortune, as I do; that want not even what I have, and can give up the use of that, as an instance of duty—

No more, no more of your merits!—You know you will be a gainer by that cheerful instance of your duty; not a loser. You know you have but cast your bread upon the waters—so no more of that!—For it is not understood as a merit by every body, I assure you; though I think it a high one; and so did your father and uncles at the time—

At the time, Madam!—How unworthily do my brother and sister, who are afraid that the favour I was so lately in—

I hear nothing against your brother and sister—What family feuds have I in prospect, at a time when I hoped to have most comfort from you all!

God bless my brother and sister in all their worthy views! You shall have no family feuds if I can prevent them. You yourself, Madam, shall tell me what I shall bear from them, and I will bear it: but let my actions, not their misrepresentations (as I am sure by the disgraceful prohibitions I have met with has been the case) speak for me.

Just then, up came my father, with a sternness in his looks that made me tremble.—He took two or three turns about my chamber, though pained by his gout; and then said to my mother, who was silent as soon as she saw him—

My dear, you are long absent.—Dinner is near ready. What you had to say, lay in a very little compass. Surely, you have nothing to do but to declare your will, and my will—But perhaps you may be talking of the preparations—Let us have you soon down—Your daughter in your hand, if worthy of the name.

And down he went, casting his eye upon me with a look so stern, that I was unable to say one word to him, or even for a few minutes to my mother.

Was not this very intimidating, my dear?

My mother, seeing my concern, seemed to pity me. She called me her good child, and kissed me; and told me that my father should not know I had made such opposition. He has kindly furnished us with an excuse for being so long together, said she.—Come, my dear—dinner will be upon table presently—Shall we go down?—And took my hand.

This made me start: What, Madam, go down to let it be supposed we were talking of preparations!—O my beloved Mamma, command me not down upon such a supposition.

You see, child, that to stay longer together, will be owning that you are debating about an absolute duty; and that will not be borne. Did not your father himself some days ago tell you, he would be obeyed? I will a third time leave you. I must say something by way of excuse for you: and that you desire not to go down to dinner—that your modesty on the occasion—

O Madam! say not my modesty on such an occasion: for that will be to give hope—

And design you not to give hope?—Perverse girl!—Rising and flinging from me; take more time for consideration!—Since it is necessary, take more time—and when I see you next, let me know what blame I have to cast upon myself, or to bear from your father, for my indulgence to you.

She made, however, a little stop at the chamber-door; and seemed to expect that I would have besought her to make the gentlest construction for me; for, hesitating, she was pleased to say, I suppose you would not have me make a report—

O Madam, interrupted I, whose favour can I hope for if I lose my mamma's?

To have desired a favourable report, you know, my dear, would have been qualifying upon a point that I was too much determined upon, to give room for any of my friends to think I have the least hesitation about it. And so my mother went down stairs.

I will deposit thus far; and, as I know you will not think me too minute in the relation of particulars so very interesting to one you honour with your love, proceed in the same way. As matters stand, I don't care to have papers, so freely written, about me.

Pray let Robert call every day, if you can spare him, whether I have any thing ready or not.

I should be glad you would not send him empty handed. What a generosity will it be in you, to write as frequently from friendship, as I am forced to do from misfortune! The letters being taken away will be an assurance that you have them. As I shall write and deposit as I have opportunity, the formality of super and sub-scription will be excused. For I need not say how much I am

Your sincere and ever affectionate, CL. HARLOWE.

LETTER XVII

MISS CLARISSA HARLOWE, TO MISS HOWE

My mother, on her return, which was as soon as she had dined, was pleased to inform me, that she told my father, on his questioning her about my cheerul compliance (for, it seems, the cheerful was all that was doubted) that she was willing, on so material a point, to give a child whom she had so much reason to love (as she condescended to acknowledge were her words) liberty to say all that was in her heart to say, that her compliance might be the freer: letting him know, that when he came up, she was attending to my pleas; for that she found I had rather not marry at all.

She told me, that to this my father angrily said, let her take care—let her take care—that she give me not ground to suspect her of a preference somewhere else. But, if it be to ease her heart, and not to dispute my will, you may hear her out.

So, Clary, said my mother, I am returned in a temper accordingly: and I hope you will not again, by your peremptoriness, shew me how I ought to treat you.

Indeed, Madam, you did me justice to say, I have no inclination to marry at all. I have not, I hope, made myself so very unuseful in my papa's family, as—

No more of your merits, Clary! You have been a good child. You have eased me of all the family cares: but do not now give more than ever you relieved me from. You have been amply repaid in the reputation your skill and management have given you: but now there is soon to be a period to all those assistances from you. If you marry, there will be a natural, and, if to please us, a desirable period; because your own family will employ all your talents in that way: if you do not, there will be a period likewise, but not a natural one—you understand me, child.

I wept.

I have made inquiry already after a housekeeper. I would have had your good Norton; but I suppose you will yourself wish to have the worthy woman with you. If you desire it, that shall be agreed upon for you.

But, why, dearest Madam, why am I, the youngest, to be precipitated into a state, that I am very far from wishing to enter into with any body?

You are going to question me, I suppose, why your sister is not thought of for Mr. Solmes?

I hope, Madam, it will not displease you if I were.

I might refer you for an answer to your father.—Mr. Solmes has reasons for preferring you—

And I have reasons, Madam, for disliking him. And why I am—

This quickness upon me, interrupted my mother, is not to be borne! I am gone, and your father comes, if I can do no good with you.

O Madam, I would rather die, than—

She put her hand to my mouth—No peremptoriness, Clary Harlowe: once you declare yourself inflexible, I have done.

I wept for vexation. This is all, all, my brother's doings—his grasping views—

No reflections upon your brother: he has entirely the honour of the family at heart.

I would no more dishonour my family, Madam, than my brother would.

I believe it: but I hope you will allow your father, and me, and your uncles, to judge what will do it honour, what dishonour.

I then offered to live single; never to marry at all; or never but with their full approbation.

If you mean to shew your duty, and your obedience, Clary, you must shew it in our way, not in your own.

I hope, Madam, that I have not so behaved hitherto, as to render such a trial of my obedience necessary.

Yes, Clary, I cannot but say that you have hitherto behaved extremely well: but you have had no trials till now: and I hope, that now you are called to one, you will not fail in it. Parents, proceeded she, when children are young, are pleased with every thing they do. You have been a good child upon the whole: but we have hitherto rather complied with you, than you with us. Now that you are grown up to marriageable years, is the test; especially as your grandfather has made you independent, as we may say, in preference to those who had prior expectations upon that estate.

Madam, my grandfather knew, and expressly mentioned in his will his desire, that my father will more than make it up to my sister. I did nothing but what I thought my duty to procure his favour. It was rather a mark of his affection, than any advantage to me: For, do I either seek or wish to be independent? Were I to be queen of the universe, that dignity should not absolve me from my duty to you and to my father. I would kneel for your blessings, were it in the presence of millions—so that—

I am loth to interrupt you, Clary; though you could more than once break in upon me. You are young and unbroken: but, with all this ostentation of your duty, I desire you to shew a little more deference to me when I am speaking.

I beg your pardon, dear Madam, and your patience with me on such an occasion as this. If I did not speak with earnestness upon it, I should be supposed to have only maidenly objections against a man I never can endure.

Clary Harlowe—!

Dearest, dearest Madam, permit me to speak what I have to say, this once—It is hard, it is very hard, to be forbidden to enter into the cause of all these misunderstandings, because I must not speak disrespectfully of one who supposes me in the way of his ambition, and treats me like a slave—

Whither, whither, Clary—

My dearest Mamma!—My duty will not permit me so far to suppose my father arbitrary, as to make a plea of that arbitrariness to you—

How now, Clary!—O girl!

Your patience, my dearest Mamma:—you were pleased to say, you would hear me with patience.—PERSON in a man is nothing, because I am supposed to be prudent: so my eye is to be disgusted, and my reason not convinced—

Girl, girl!

Thus are my imputed good qualities to be made my punishment; and I am to wedded to a monster—

[Astonishing!—Can this, Clarissa, be from you?

The man, Madam, person and mind, is a monster in my eye.]—And that I may be induced to bear this treatment, I am to be complimented with being indifferent to all men: yet, at other times, and to serve other purposes, be thought prepossessed in favour of a man against whose moral character lie just objections.—Confined, as if, like the giddiest of creatures, I would run away with this man, and disgrace my whole family! O my dearest Mamma! who can be patient under such treatment?

Now, Clary, I suppose you will allow me to speak. I think I have had patience indeed with you.—Could I have thought—but I will put all upon a short issue. Your mother, Clarissa, shall shew you an example of that patience you so boldly claim from her, without having any yourself.

O my dear, how my mother's condescension distressed me at the time!—Infinitely more distressed me, than rigour could have done. But she knew, she was to be sure aware, that she was put upon a harsh, upon an unreasonable service, let me say, or she would not, she could not, have had so much patience with me.

Let me tell you then, proceeded she, that all lies in a small compass, as your father said.—You have been hitherto, as you are pretty ready to plead, a dutiful child. You have indeed had no cause to be otherwise. No child was ever more favoured. Whether you will discredit all your past behaviour; whether, at a time and upon an occasion, that the highest instance of duty is expected from you (an instance that is to crown all); and when you declare that your heart is free—you will give that instance; or whether, having a view to the independence you may claim, (for so, Clary, whatever be your motive, it will be judged,) and which any man you favour, can assert for you against us all; or rather for himself in spite of us—whether, I say, you will break with us all; and stand in defiance of a jealous father, needlessly jealous, I will venture to say, of the prerogatives of his sex, as to me, and still ten times more jealous of the authority of a father;—this is now the point with us. You know your father has made it a point; and did he ever give up one he thought he had a right to carry?

Too true, thought I to myself! And now my brother has engaged my father, his fine scheme will walk alone, without needing his leading-strings; and it is become my father's will that I oppose; not my brother's grasping views.

I was silent. To say the truth, I was just then sullenly silent. My heart was too big. I thought it was hard to be thus given up by my mother; and that she should make a will so uncontroulable as my brother's, her will.—My mother, my dear, though I must not say so, was not obliged to marry against her liking. My mother loved my father.

My silence availed me still less.

I see, my dear, said she, that you are convinced. Now, my good child—now, my Clary, do I love you! It shall not be known, that you have argued with me at all. All shall be imputed to that modesty which has ever so much distinguished you. You shall have the full merit of your resignation.

I wept.

She tenderly wiped the tears from my eyes, and kissed my cheek—Your father expects you down with a cheerful countenance—but I will excuse your going. All your scruples, you see, have met with an indulgence truly maternal from me. I rejoice in the hope that you are convinced. This indeed seems to be a proof of the truth of your agreeable declaration, that your heart is free.

Did not this seem to border upon cruelty, my dear, in so indulgent a mother?—It would be wicked [would it not] to suppose my mother capable of art?—But she is put upon it, and obliged to take methods to which her heart is naturally above stooping; and all intended for my good, because she sees that no arguing will be admitted any where else!

I will go down, proceeded she, and excuse your attendance at afternoon tea, as I did to dinner: for I know you will have some little reluctances to subdue. I will allow you those; and also some little natural shynesses—and so you shall not come down, if you chuse not to come down. Only, my dear, do not disgrace my report when you come to supper. And be sure behave as you used to do to your brother and sister; for your behaviour to them will be one test of your cheerful obedience to us. I advise as a friend, you see, rather than command as a mother—So adieu, my love. And again she kissed me; and was going.

O my dear Mamma, said I, forgive me!—But surely you cannot believe, I can ever think of having that man!

She was very angry, and seemed to be greatly disappointed. She threatened to turn me over to my father and uncles:—she however bid me (generously bid me) consider, what a handle I gave to my brother and sister, if I thought they had views to serve by making my uncles dissatisfied with me.

I, said she, in a milder accent, have early said all that I thought could be said against the present proposal, on a supposition, that you, who have refused several other (whom I own to be preferable as to person) would not approve of it; and could I have succeeded, you, Clary, had never heard of it. But if I could not, how can you expect to prevail? My great ends in the task I have undertaken, are the preservation of the family peace so likely to be overturned; to reinstate you in the affections of your father and uncles: and to preserve you from a man of violence.—Your father, you must needs think will flame out upon your refusal to comply: your uncles are so

thoroughly convinced of the consistency of the measure with their favourite views of aggrandizing the family, that they are as much determined as your father: your aunt Hervey and your uncle Hervey are of the same party. And it is hard, if a father and mother, and uncles, and aunt, all conjoined, cannot be allowed to direct your choice—surely, my dear girl, proceeded she [for I was silent all this time], it cannot be that you are the more averse, because the family views will be promoted by the match—this, I assure you, is what every body must think, if you comply not. Nor, while the man, so obnoxious to us all, remains unmarried, and buzzes about you, will the strongest wishes to live single, be in the least regarded. And well you know, that were Mr. Lovelace an angel, and your father had made it a point that you should not have him, it would be in vain to dispute his will. As to the prohibition laid upon you (much as I will own against my liking), that is owing to the belief that you corresponded by Miss Howe's means with that man; nor do I doubt that you did so.

I answered to every article, in such a manner, as I am sure would have satisfied her, could she have been permitted to judge for herself; and I then inveighed with bitterness against the disgraceful prohibitions laid upon me.

They would serve to shew me, she was pleased to say, how much in earnest my father was. They might be taken off, whenever I thought fit, and no harm done, nor disgrace received. But if I were to be contumacious, I might thank myself for all that would follow.

I sighed. I wept. I was silent.

Shall I, Clary, said she, shall I tell your father that these prohibitions are as unnecessary as I hoped they would be? That you know your duty, and will not offer to controvert his will? What say you, my love?

O Madam, what can I say to questions so indulgently put? I do indeed know my duty: no creature in the world is more willing to practise it: but, pardon me, dearest Madam, if I say, that I must bear these prohibitions, if I am to pay so dear to have them taken off.

Determined and perverse, my dear mamma called me: and after walking twice or thrice in anger about the room, she turned to me: Your heart free, Clarissa! How can you tell me your heart is free? Such extraordinary prepossessions to a particular person must be owing to extraordinary prepossessions in another's favour! Tell me, Clary, and tell me truly—Do you not continue to correspond with Mr. Lovelace?

Dearest Madam, replied I, you know my motives: to prevent mischief, I answered his letters. The reasons for our apprehensions of this sort are not over.

I own to you, Clary, (although now I would not have it known,) that I once thought a little qualifying among such violent spirits was not amiss. I did not know but all things would come round again by the mediation of Lord M. and his two sisters: but as they all three think proper to resent for their nephew; and as their nephew thinks fit to defy us all; and as terms are offered, on the other hand, that could not be asked, which will very probably prevent your grandfather's estate going out of the family, and may be a means to bring still greater into it; I see not, that the continuance of your correspondence with him either can or ought to be permitted. I therefore now forbid it to you, as you value my favour.

Be pleased, Madam, only to advise me how to break it off with safety to my brother and uncles; and it is all I wish for. Would to heaven, the man so hated had not the pretence to make of having been too violently treated, when he meant peace and reconciliation! It would always have been in my own power to have broke with him. His reputed immoralities would have given me a just pretence at any time to do so. But, Madam, as my uncles and my brother will keep no measures; as he has heard what the view is; and his regard for me from resenting their violent treatment of him and his family; what can I do? Would you have me, Madam, make him desperate?

The law will protect us, child! offended magistracy will assert itself—

But, Madam, may not some dreadful mischief first happen?—The law asserts not itself, till it is offended.

You have made offers, Clary, if you might be obliged in the point in question—Are you really in earnest, were you to be complied with, to break off all correspondence with Mr. Lovelace?—Let me know this.

Indeed I am; and I will. You, Madam, shall see all the letters that have passed between us. You shall see I have given him no encouragement independent of my duty. And when you have seen them, you will be better able to direct me how, on the condition I have offered, to break entirely with him.

I take you at your word, Clarissa—Give me his letters; and the copies of yours.

I am sure, Madam, you will keep the knowledge that I write, and what I write—

No conditions with your mother—surely my prudence may be trusted to.

I begged her pardon; and besought her to take the key of the private drawer in my escritoire, where they lay, that she herself might see that I had no reserves to my mother.

She did; and took all his letters, and the copies of mine.—Unconditioned with, she was pleased to say, they shall be yours again, unseen by any body else.

I thanked her; and she withdrew to read them; saying, she would return them, when she had.

You, my dear, have seen all the letters that passed between Mr. Lovelace and me, till my last return from you. You have acknowledged, that he has nothing to boast of from them. Three others I have received since, by the private conveyance I told you of: the last I have not yet answered.

In these three, as in those you have seen, after having besought my favour, and, in the most earnest manner, professed the ardour of his passion for me; and set forth the indignities done him; the defiances my brother throws out against him in all companies; the menaces, and hostile appearance of my uncles wherever they go; and the methods they take to defame him; he declares, 'That neither his own honour, nor the honour of his family, (involved as that is in the undistinguishing reflection cast upon him for an unhappy affair which he would have shunned, but could not) permit him to bear these confirmed indignities: that as my inclinations, if not favourable to him, cannot be, nor are, to such a man as the newly-introduced Solmes, he is interested the more to resent my brother's behaviour; who to every body avows his rancour and malice; and glories in the probability he has, through the address of this Solmes, of mortifying me, and avenging himself on him: that it is impossible he should not think himself concerned to frustrate a measure so directly levelled at him, had he not a still higher motive for hoping to frustrate it: that I must forgive him, if he enter into conference with Solmes upon it. He earnestly insists (upon what he has so often proposed) that I will give him leave, in company with Lord M. to wait upon my uncles, and even upon my father—and he promises patience, if new provocations, absolutely beneath a man to bear, be not given:' which by the way I am far from being able to engage for.

In my answer, I absolutely declare, as I tell him I have often done, 'That he is to expect no favour from me against the approbation of my friends: that I am sure their consents for his visiting any of them will never be obtained: that I will not be either so undutiful, or so indiscreet, as to suffer my interests to be separated from the interests of my family, for any man upon earth: that I do not think myself obliged to him for the forbearance I desire one flaming spirit to have with others: that in this desire I require nothing of him, but what prudence, justice, and the laws of his country require: that if he has any expectations of favour from me, on that account, he deceives himself: that I have no inclination, as I have often told him, to change my condition: that I cannot allow myself to correspond with him any longer in this clandestine manner: it is mean, low, undutiful, I tell him; and has a giddy appearance, which cannot be excused: that therefore he is not to expect that I will continue it.

To this in his last, among other things, he replies, 'That if I am actually determined to break off all correspondence with him, he must conclude, that it is with a view to become the wife of a man, whom no woman of honour and fortune can think tolerable. And in that case, I must excuse him for saying, that he shall neither be able to bear the thoughts of losing for ever a person in whom all his present and all his future hopes are centred; nor support himself with patience under the insolent triumphs of my brother upon it. But that nevertheless he will not threaten either his own life, or that of any other man. He must take his resolutions as such a dreaded event shall impel him at the time. If he shall know that it will have my consent, he must endeavour to resign to his destiny: but if it be brought about by compulsion, he shall not be able to answer for the consequence.'

I will send you these letters for your perusal in a few days. I would enclose them; but that it is possible something may happen, which may make my mother require to re-peruse them. When you see them, you will observe how he endeavours to hold me to this correspondence.

In about an hour my mother returned. Take your letters, Clary: I have nothing, she was pleased to say, to tax your discretion with, as to the wording of yours to him: you have even kept up a proper dignity, as well as observed all the rules of decorum; and you have resented, as you ought to resent, his menacing invectives. In a word, I see not, that he can form the least expectations, from what you have written, that you will encourage the passion he avows for you. But does he not avow his passion? Have you the least doubt about what must be the issue of this correspondence, if continued? And do you yourself think, when you know the avowed hatred of one side, and he declared defiances of the other, that this can be, that it ought to be a match?

By no means it can, Madam; you will be pleased to observed, that I have said as much to him. But now, Madam, that the whole correspondence is before you, I beg your commands what to do in a situation so very disagreeable.

One thing I will tell you, Clary—but I charge you, as you would not have me question the generosity of your spirit, to take no advantage of it, either mentally or verbally; that I am so much pleased with the offer of your keys to me, made in so cheerful and unreserved a manner, and in the prudence you have shewn in your letters, that were it practicable to bring every one, or your father only, into my opinion, I should readily leave all the rest to your discretion, reserving only to myself the direction or approbation of your future letters; and to see, that you broke off the correspondence as soon as possible. But as it is not, and as I know your father would have no patience with you, should it be acknowledged that you correspond with Mr. Lovelace, or that you have corresponded with him since the time he prohibited you to do so; I forbid you to continue such a liberty—Yet, as the case is difficult, let me ask you, What you yourself can propose? Your heart, you say, is free. Your own, that you cannot think, as matters circumstanced, that a match with a man so obnoxious as he now is to us all, is proper to be thought of: What do you propose to do?—What, Clary, are your own thoughts of the matter?

Without hesitation thus I answered—What I humbly propose is this:—'That I will write to Mr. Lovelace (for I have not answered his last) that he has nothing to do between my father and me: that I neither ask his advice nor need it: but that since he thinks he has some pretence for interfering, because of my brother's avowal of the interest of Mr. Solmes in displeasure to him, I will assure him (without giving him any reason to impute the assurance to be in the least favourable to himself) that I will never be that man's.' And if, proceeded I, I may never be permitted to give him this assurance; and Mr. Solmes, in consequence of it, be discouraged from prosecuting his address; let Mr. Lovelace be satisfied or dissatisfied, I will go no farther; nor write another line to him; nor ever see him more, if I can avoid it: and I shall have a good excuse for it, without bringing in any of my family.

Ah! my love!—But what shall we do about the terms Mr. Solmes offers? Those are the inducements with every body. He has even given hopes to your brother that he will make exchanges of estates; or, at least, that he will purchase the northern one; for you know it must be entirely consistent with the family-views, that we increase our interest in this country. Your brother, in short, has given a plan that captivates us all. And a family so rich in all its branches, and that has its views to honour, must be pleased to see a very great probability of taking rank one day among the principal in the kingdom.

And for the sake of these views, for the sake of this plan of my brother's, am I, Madam, to be given in marriage to a man I can never endure!—O my dear Mamma, save me, save me, if you can, from this heavy evil.—I had rather be buried alive, indeed I had, than have that man!

She chid me for my vehemence; but was so good as to tell me, That she would sound my uncle Harlowe, who was then below; and if he encouraged her (or would engage to second her) she would venture to talk to my father herself; and I should hear further in the morning.

She went down to tea, and kindly undertook to excuse my attendance at supper.

But is it not a sad thing, I repeat, to be obliged to stand in opposition to the will of such a mother? Why, as I often say to myself, was such a man as this Solmes fixed upon? The only man in the world, surely, that could offer so much, and deserve so little!

Little indeed does he deserve!—Why, my dear, the man has the most indifferent of characters. Every mouth is opened against him for his sordid ways—A foolish man, to be so base-minded!—When the difference between the obtaining of a fame for generosity, and incurring the censure of being a miser, will not, prudently managed, cost fifty pounds a year.

What a name have you got, at a less expense? And what an opportunity had he of obtaining credit at a very small one, succeeding such a wretched creature as Sir Oliver, in fortunes so vast?—Yet has he so behaved, that the common phrase is applied to him, That Sir Oliver will never be dead while Mr. Solmes lives.

The world, as I have often thought, ill-natured as it is said to be, is generally more just in characters (speaking by what it feels) than is usually apprehended: and those who complain most of its censoriousness, perhaps should look inwardly for the occasion oftener than they do.

My heart is a little at ease, on the hopes that my mother will be able to procure favour for me, and a deliverance from this man; and so I have leisure to moralize. But if I had not, I should not forbear to intermingle occasionally these sorts of remarks, because you command me never to omit them when they occur to my mind: and not to be able to make them, even in a more affecting situation, when one sits down to write, would shew one's self more engaged to self, and to one's own concerns, than attentive to the wishes of a friend. If it be said, that it is natural so to be, what makes that nature, on occasions where a friend may be obliged, or reminded of a piece of instruction, which (writing down) one's self may be the better for, but a fault; which it would set a person above nature to subdue?

LETTER XVIII

MISS CLARISSA HARLOWE, TO MISS HOWE SAT. MAR. 4

Would you not have thought something might have been obtained in my favour, from an offer so reasonable, from an expedient so proper, as I imagine, to put a tolerable end, as from myself, to a correspondence I hardly know how otherwise, with safety to some of my family, to get rid of?—But my brother's plan, (which my mother spoke of, and of which I have in vain endeavoured to procure a copy, with a design to take it to pieces, and expose it, as I question not there is room to do,) joined with my father's impatience of contradiction, are irresistible.

I have not been in bed all night; nor am I in the least drowsy. Expectation, and hope, and doubt, (an uneasy state!) kept me sufficiently wakeful. I stept down at my usual time, that it might not be known I had not been in bed; and gave directions in the family way.

About eight o'clock, Shorey came to me from my mother with orders to attend her in her chamber.

My mother had been weeping, I saw by her eyes: but her aspect seemed to be less tender, and less affectionate, than the day before; and this, as soon as I entered into her presence, struck me with an awe, which gave a great damp to my spirits.

Sit down, Clary Harlowe; I shall talk to you by-and-by: and continued looking into a drawer among laces and linens, in a way neither busy nor unbusy.

I believe it was a quarter of an hour before she spoke to me (my heart throbbing with the suspense all the time); and then she asked me coldly, What directions I had given for the day?

I shewed her the bill of fare for this day, and to-morrow, if, I said, it pleased her to approve of it.

She made a small alteration in it; but with an air so cold and so solemn, as added to my emotions.

Mr. Harlowe talks of dining out to-day, I think, at my brother Antony's—

Mr. Harlowe!—Not my father!—Have I not then a father!—thought I.

Sit down when I bid you.

I sat down.

You look very sullen, Clary.

I hope not, Madam.

If children would always be children—parents—And there she stopt.

She then went to her toilette, and looked into the glass, and gave half a sigh—the other half, as if she would not have sighed if she could have helped it, she gently hem'd away.

I don't love to see the girl look so sullen.

Indeed, Madam, I am not sullen.—And I arose, and, turning from her, drew out my handkerchief; for the tears ran down my cheeks.

I thought, by the glass before me, I saw the mother in her softened eye cast towards me. But her words confirmed not the hoped-for tenderness.

One of the most provoking things in this world is, to have people cry for what they can help!

I wish to heaven I could, Madam!—And I sobbed again.

Tears of penitence and sobs of perverseness are mighty well suited!—You may go up to your chamber. I shall talk with you by-and-by.

I courtesied with reverence.

Mock me not with outward gestures of respect. The heart, Clary, is what I want.

Indeed, Madam, you have it. It is not so much mine as my Mamma's!

Fine talking!—As somebody says, If words were to pass for duty, Clarissa Harlowe would be the dutifulest child breathing.

God bless that somebody!—Be it whom it will, God bless that somebody!—And I courtesied, and, pursuant to her last command, was going.

She seemed struck; but was to be angry with me.

So turning from me, she spoke with quickness, Whither now, Clary Harlowe?

You commanded me, Madam, to go to my chamber.

I see you are very ready to go out of my presence.—Is your compliance the effect of sullenness, or obedience?—You are very ready to leave me.

I could hold no longer; but threw myself at her feet: O my dearest Mamma! Let me know all I am to suffer! Let me know what I am to be!—I will bear it, if I can bear it: but your displeasure I cannot bear!

Leave me, leave me, Clary Harlowe!—No kneeling!—Limbs so supple! Will so stubborn!—Rise, I tell you.

I cannot rise! I will disobey my Mamma, when she bids me leave her without being reconciled to me! No sullens, my Mamma: no perverseness: but, worse than either: this is direct disobedience!—Yet tear not yourself from me! [wrapping my arms about her as I kneeled; she struggling to get from me; my face lifted up to hers, with eyes running over, that spoke not my heart if they were not all humility and reverence] You must not, must not, tear yourself from me! [for still the dear lady struggled, and looked this way and that, all in a sweet disorder, as if she knew not what to do].—I will neither rise, nor leave you, nor let you go, till you say you are not angry with me.

O thou ever-moving child of my heart! [folding her dear arms about my neck, as mine embraced her knees] Why was this task—But leave me!—You have discomposed me beyond expression! Leave me, my dear!—I won't be angry with you—if I can help it—if you'll be good.

I arose trembling, and, hardly knowing what I did, or how I stood or walked, withdrew to my chamber. My Hannah followed me as soon as she heard me quit my mother's presence, and with salts and spring-water just kept me from fainting; and that was as much as she could do. It was near two hours before I could so far recover myself as to take up my pen, to write to you how unhappily my hopes have ended.

My mother went down to breakfast. I was not fit to appear: but if I had been better, I suppose I should not have been sent for; since the permission for my attending her down, was given by my father (when in my chamber) only on condition that she found me worthy of the name of daughter. That, I doubt, I shall never be in his opinion, if he be not brought to change his mind as to this Mr. Solmes.

LETTER XIX

H2rrMISS CLARISSA HARLOWE, TO MISS HOWE [IN ANSWER TO LETTER XV.] SAT. MARCH 4, 12 O'CLOCK

Hannah has just now brought me from the usual place your favour of yesterday. The contents of it have made me very thoughtful; and you will have an answer in my gravest style.—I to have that Mr. Solmes!—No indeed!—I will sooner—But I will write first to those passages in your letter which are less concerning, that I may touch upon this part with more patience.

As to what you mention of my sister's value for Mr. Lovelace, I am not very much surprised at it. She takes such officious pains, and it is so much her subject, to have it thought that she never did, and never could like him, that she gives but too much room to suspect that she does. She never tells the story of their parting, and of her refusal of him, but her colour rises, she looks with disdain upon me, and mingles anger with the airs she gives herself:—anger as well as airs, demonstrating, that she refused a man whom she thought worth accepting: Where else is the reason either for anger or boast?—Poor Bella! She is to be pitied—she cannot either like or dislike with temper! Would to heaven she had been mistress of all her wishes!—Would to heaven she had!

As to what you say of my giving up to my father's controul the estate devised me, my motives at the time, as you acknowledge, were not blamable. Your advice to me on the subject was grounded, as I remember, on your good opinion of me; believing that I should not make a bad use of the power willed me. Neither you nor I, my dear, although you now assume the air of a diviner, [pardon me] could have believed that would have happened which has happened, as to my father's part particularly. You were indeed jealous of my brother's views against me; or rather of his predominant love of himself; but I did not think so hardly of my brother and sister as you always did. You never loved them; and ill-will has eyes ever open to the faulty side; as good-will or love is blind even to real imperfections. I will briefly recollect my motives.

I found jealousies and uneasiness rising in every breast, where all before was unity and love. The honoured testator was reflected upon: a second childhood was attributed to him; and I was censured, as having taken advantage of it. All young creatures, thought I, more or less, covet independency; but those who wish most for it, are seldom the fittest to be trusted either with the government of themselves, or with power over others. This is certainly a very high and unusual devise to so young a creature. We should not aim at all we have power to do. To take all that good-nature, or indulgence, or good opinion confers, shews a want of moderation, and a graspingness that is unworthy of that indulgence; and are bad indications of the use that may be made of the power bequeathed. It is true, thought I, that I have formed agreeable schemes of making others as happy as myself, by the proper discharge of the stewardship intrusted to me. [Are not all estates stewardships, my dear?] But let me examine myself: Is not vanity, or secret love of praise, a principal motive with me at the bottom?—Ought I not to suspect my own heart? If I set up for myself, puffed up with every one's good opinion, may I not be left to myself?—Every one's eyes are upon the conduct, upon the visits, upon the visiters, of a young creature of our sex, made independent: And are not such subjected, more than any others, to the attempts of enterprisers and fortune-seekers?—And then, left to myself, should I take a wrong step, though with ever so good an intention, how many should I have to triumph over me, how few to pity me!—The more of the one, and the fewer of the other, for having aimed at excelling.

These were some of my reflections at the time: and I have no doubt, but that in the same situation I should do the very same thing; and that upon the maturest deliberation. Who can command or foresee events? To act up to our best judgments at the time, is all we can do. If I have erred, 'tis to worldly wisdom only that I have erred. If we suffer by an act of duty, or even by an act of generosity, is it not pleasurable on reflection, that the fault is in others, rather than in ourselves?—I had much rather have reason to think others unkind, than that they should have any to think me undutiful.

And so, my dear, I am sure had you.

And now for the most concerning part of your letter.

You think I must of necessity, as matters are circumstanced, be Solmes's wife. I will not be very rash, my dear, in protesting to the contrary: but I think it never can, and, what is still more, never ought to be!—My temper, I know, is depended upon. But I have heretofore said,* that I have something in me of my father's family, as well as of my mother's. And have I any encouragement to follow too implicitly the example which my mother sets of meekness, and resignedness to the wills of others? Is she not for ever obliged (as she was pleased to hint to me) to be of the forbearing side? In my mother's case, your observation I must own is verified, that those who will bear much, shall have much to bear.** What is it, as she says, that she has not sacrificed to peace?—Yet, has she by her sacrifices always found the peace she has deserved to find? Indeed, no!—I am afraid the very contrary. And often and often have I had reason (on her account) to reflect, that we poor mortals, by our over-solicitude to preserve undisturbed the qualities we are constitutionally fond of, frequently lose the benefits we propose to ourselves from them: since the designing and encroaching (finding out what we most fear to forfeit) direct their batteries against these our weaker places, and, making an artillery (if I may so phrase it) of our hopes and fears, play upon us at their pleasure.

* *See Letter IX.*

** *See Letter X.*

Steadiness of mind, (a quality which the ill-bred and censorious deny to any of our sex) when we are absolutely convinced of being in the right [otherwise it is not steadiness, but obstinacy] and when it is exerted in material cases, is a quality, which, as my good Dr. Lewen was wont to say, brings great credit to the possessor of it; at the same time that it usually, when tried and known, raises such above the attempts of the meanly machinating. He used therefore to inculcate upon me this steadiness, upon laudable convictions. And why may I not think that I am now put upon a proper exercise of it?

I said above, that I never can be, that I never ought to be, Mrs. Solmes.—I repeat, that I ought not: for surely, my dear, I should not give up to my brother's ambition the happiness of my future life. Surely I ought not to be the instrument of depriving Mr. Solmes's relations of their natural rights and reversionary prospects, for the sake of further aggrandizing a family (although that I am of) which already lives in great affluence and splendour; and which might be as justly dissatisfied, were all that some of it aim at to be obtained, that they were not princes, as now they are that they are not peers [For when ever was an ambitious mind, as you observe in the case of avarice,* satisfied by acquisition?]. The less, surely, ought I to give into these grasping views of my brother, as I myself heartily despise the end aimed at;

as I wish not either to change my state, or better my fortunes; and as I am fully persuaded, that happiness and riches are two things, and very seldom meet together.

* *See Letter X.*

Yet I dread, I exceedingly dread, the conflicts I know I must encounter with. It is possible, that I may be more unhappy from the due observation of the good doctor's general precept, than were I to yield the point; since what I call steadiness is deemed stubbornness, obstinacy, prepossession, by those who have a right to put what interpretation they please upon my conduct.

So, my dear, were we perfect (which no one can be) we could not be happy in this life, unless those with whom we have to deal (those more especially who have any controul upon us) were governed by the same principles. But then does not the good Doctor's conclusion recur,—That we have nothing to do, but to chuse what is right; to be steady in the pursuit of it; and to leave the issue to Providence?

This, if you approve of my motives, (and if you don't, pray inform me) must be my aim in the present case.

But what then can I plead for a palliation to myself of my mother's sufferings on my account? Perhaps this consideration will carry some force with it—That her difficulties cannot last long; only till this great struggle shall be one way or other determined—Whereas my unhappiness, if I comply, will (from an aversion not to be overcome) be for life. To which let me add, That as I have reason to think that the present measures are not entered upon with her own natural liking, she will have the less pain, should they want the success which I think in my heart they ought to want.

I have run a great length in a very little time. The subject touched me to the quick. My reflections upon it will give you reason to expect from me a perhaps too steady behaviour in a new conference, which, I find, I must have with my mother. My father and brother, as she was pleased to tell me, dine at my uncle Antony's; and that, as I have reason to believe, on purpose to give an opportunity for it.

Hannah informs me, that she heard my father high and angry with my mother, at taking leave of her: I suppose for being to favourable to me; for Hannah heard her say, as in tears, 'Indeed, Mr. Harlowe, you greatly distress me!—The poor girl does not deserve—' Hannah heard no more, but that he said, he would break somebody's heart—Mine, I suppose—Not my mother's, I hope.

As only my sister dines with my mother, I thought I should have been commanded down: but she sent me up a plate from her table. I continued my writing. I could not touch a morsel. I ordered Hannah however to eat of it, that I might not be thought sullen.

Before I conclude this, I will see whether any thing offers from either of my private correspondencies, that will make it proper to add to it; and will take a turn in the wood-yard and garden for that purpose.

I am stopped. Hannah shall deposit this. She was ordered by my mother (who asked where I was) to tell me, that she would come up and talk with me in my own closet.—She is coming! Adieu, my dear.

LETTER XX

MISS CLARISSA HARLOWE, TO MISS HOWE SAT. AFTERNOON

The expected conference is over: but my difficulties are increased. This, as my mother was pleased to tell me, being the last persuasory effort that is to be attempted, I will be particular in the account of it as my head and my heart will allow it to be.

I have made, said she, as she entered my room, a short as well as early dinner, on purpose to confer with you: and I do assure you, that it will be the last conference I shall either be permitted or inclined to hold with you on the subject, if you should prove as refractory as it is imagined you will prove by some, who are of opinion, that I have not the weight with you which my indulgence deserves. But I hope you will convince as well them as me of the contrary.

Your father both dines and sups at your uncle's, on purpose to give us this opportunity; and, according to the report I shall make on his return, (which I have promised shall be a very faithful one,) he will take his measures with you.

I was offering to speak—Hear, Clarissa, what I have to tell you, said she, before you speak, unless what you have to say will signify to me your compliance—Say—Will it?—If it will, you may speak.

I was silent.

She looked with concern and anger upon me—No compliance, I find!—Such a dutiful young creature hitherto!—Will you not, can you not, speak as I would have you speak?—Then [rejecting me as it were with her hand] continue silent.—I, no more than your father, will bear your avowed contradiction.

She paused, with a look of expectation, as if she waited for my consenting answer.

I was still silent; looking down; the tears in my eyes.

O thou determined girl!—But say—Speak out—Are you resolved to stand in opposition to us all, in a point our hearts are set upon?

May I, Madam, be permitted to expostulate?—

To what purpose expostulate with me, Clarissa? Your father is determined. Have I not told you there is no receding; that the honour as well as the interest of the family is concerned? Be ingenuous: you used to be so, even occasionally against yourself:—Who at the long run must submit—all of us to you; or you to all of us?—If you intend to yield at last if you find you cannot conquer, yield now, and with a grace—for yield you must, or be none of our child.

I wept. I knew not what to say; or rather how to express what I had to say.

Take notice, that there are flaws in your grandfather's will: not a shilling of that estate will be yours, if you do not yield. Your grandfather left it to you, as a reward of your duty to him and to us—You will justly forfeit it, if—

Permit me, good Madam, to say, that, if it were unjustly bequeathed me, I ought not to wish to have it. But I hope Mr. Solmes will be apprised of these flaws.

This is very pertly said, Clarissa: but reflect, that the forfeiture of that estate, through your opposition, will be attended with the total loss of your father's favour: and then how destitute must you be; how unable to support yourself; and how many benevolent designs and good actions must you give up!

I must accommodate myself, Madam, in the latter case, to my circumstance: much only is required where much is given. It becomes me to be thankful for what I have had. I have reason to bless you, Madam, and my good Mrs. Norton, for bringing me up to be satisfied with little; with much less, I will venture to say, than my father's indulgence annually confers upon me.—And then I thought of the old Roman and his lentils.

What perverseness! said my mother.—But if you depend upon the favour of either or both of your uncles, vain will be that dependence: they will give you up, I do assure you, if your father does, and absolutely renounce you.

I am sorry, Madam, that I have had so little merit as to have made no deeper impressions of favour for me in their hearts: but I will love and honour them as long as I live.

All this, Clarissa, makes your prepossession in a certain man's favour the more evident. Indeed, your brother and sister cannot go any where, but they hear of these prepossessions.

It is a great grief to me, Madam, to be made the subject of the public talk: but I hope you will have the goodness to excuse me for observing, that the authors of my disgrace within doors, the talkers of my prepossession without, and the reporters of it from abroad, are originally the same persons.

She severely chid me for this.

I received her rebukes in silence.

You are sullen, Clarissa: I see you are sullen.—And she walked about the room in anger. Then turning to me—You can bear the imputation of sullenness I see!—You have no concern to clear yourself of it. I was afraid of telling you all I was enjoined to tell you, in case you were to be unpersuadable: but I find that I had a greater opinion of your delicacy, of your gentleness, than I needed to have—it cannot discompose so steady, so inflexible a young creature, to be told, as I now tell you, that the settlements are actually drawn; and that you will be called down in a very few days to hear them read, and to sign them: for it is impossible, if your heart be free, that you can make the least objection to them; except it will be an objection with you, that they are so much in your favour, and in the favour of all our family.

I was speechless, absolutely speechless. Although my heart was ready to burst, yet could I neither weep nor speak.

I am sorry, said she, for your averseness to this match: [match she was pleased to call it!] but there is no help. The honour and interest of the family, as your aunt has told you, and as I have told you, are concerned; and you must comply.

I was still speechless.

She folded the warm statue, as she was pleased to call me, in her arms; and entreated me, for heaven's sake, to comply.

Speech and tears were lent me at the same time.—You have given me life, Madam, said I, clasping my uplifted hands together, and falling on one knee; a happy one, till now, has your goodness, and my papa's, made it! O do not, do not, make all the remainder of it miserable!

Your father, replied she, is resolved not to see you, till he sees you as obedient a child as you used to be. You have never been put to a test till now, that deserved to be called a test. This is, this must be, my last effort with you. Give me hope, my dear child: my peace is concerned: I will compound with you but for hope: and yet your father will not be satisfied without an implicit, and even a cheerful obedience—Give me but hope, child!

To give you hope, my dearest, my most indulgent Mamma, is to give you every thing. Can I be honest, if I give a hope that I cannot confirm?

She was very angry. She again called me perverse: she upbraided me with regarding only my own prepossessions, and respecting not either her peace of mind or my own duty:—'It is a grating thing, said she, for the parents of a child, who delighted in her in all the time of her helpless infancy, and throughout every stage of her childhood; and in every part of her education to womanhood, because of the promises she gave of proving the most grateful and dutiful of children; to find, just when the time arrived which should crown their wishes, that child stand in the way of her own happiness, and her parents' comfort,and, refusing an excellent offer and noble settlements, give suspicions to her anxious friends, that she would become the property of a vile rake and libertine, who (be the occasion what it will) defies her family, and has actually embrued his hands in her brother's blood.

'I have had a very hard time of it, said she, between your father and you; for, seeing your dislike, I have more than once pleaded for you: but all to no purpose. I am only treated as a too fond mother, who, from motives of a blamable indulgence, encourage a child to stand in opposition to a father's will. I am charged with dividing the family into two parts; I and my youngest daughter standing against my husband, his two brothers, my son, my eldest daughter, and my sister Hervey. I have been told, that I must be convinced of the fitness as well as advantage to the whole (your brother and Mr. Lovelace out of the question) of carrying the contract with Mr. Solmes, on which so many contracts depend, into execution.

'Your father's heart, I tell you once more, is in it: he has declared, that he had rather have no daughter in you, than one he cannot dispose of for your own good: especially if you have owned, that your heart is free; and as the general good of his whole family is to be promoted by your obedience. He has pleaded, poor man! that his frequent gouty paroxysms (every fit more threatening than the former) give him no extraordinary prospects, either of worldly happiness, or of long days: and he hopes, that you, who have been supposed to have contributed to the lengthening of your grandfather's life, will not, by your disobedience, shorten your father's.'

This was a most affecting plea, my dear. I wept in silence upon it. I could not speak to it. And my mother proceeded: 'What therefore can be his motives, Clary Harlowe, in the earnest desire he has to see this treaty perfected, but the welfare and aggrandizement of his family; which already having fortunes to become the highest condition, cannot but aspire to greater distinctions? However slight such views as these may appear to you, Clary, you know, that they are not slight ones to any other of the family: and your father will be his own judge of what is and what is not likely to promote the good of his children. Your abstractedness, child, (affectation of abstractedness, some call it,) savours, let me tell you, of greater particularity, than we aim to carry. Modesty and humility, therefore, will oblige you rather to mistrust yourself of peculiarity, than censure views which all the world pursues, as opportunity offers.'

I was still silent; and she proceeded—'It is owing to the good opinion, Clary, which your father has of you, and of your prudence, duty, and gratitude, that he engaged for your compliance, in your absence (before you returned from Miss Howe); and that he built and finished contracts upon it, which cannot be made void, or cancelled.'

But why then, thought I, did they receive me, on my return from Miss Howe, with so much intimidating solemnity?—To be sure, my dear, this argument, as well as the rest, was obtruded upon my mother.

She went on, 'Your father has declared, that your unexpected opposition, [unexpected she was pleased to call it,] and Mr. Lovelace's continued menaces and insults, more and more convince him, that a short day is necessary in order to put an end to all that man's hopes, and to his own apprehensions resulting from the disobedience of a child so favoured. He has therefore actually ordered patterns of the richest silks to be sent for from London—'

I started—I was out of breath—I gasped, at this frightful precipitance—I was going to open with warmth against it. I knew whose the happy expedient must be: female minds, I once heard my brother say, that could but be brought to balance on the change of their state, might easily be determined by the glare and splendour of the nuptial preparations, and the pride of becoming the mistress of a family.—But she was pleased to hurry on, that I might not have time to express my disgusts at such a communication—to this effect: 'Your father therefore, my Clary, cannot, either for your sake, or his own, labour under a suspense so affecting to his repose. He has even thought fit to acquaint me, on my pleading for you, that it becomes me, as I value my own peace, [how harsh to such a wife!] and as I wish, that he does not suspect that I secretly favour the address of a vile rake, (a character which all the sex, he is pleased to say, virtuous and vicious, are but too fond of!) to exert my authority over you: and that this I may the less scrupulously do, as you have owned [the old string!] that your heart is free.'

Unworthy reflection in my mother's case, surely, this of our sex's valuing a libertine; since she made choice of my father in preference to several suitors of equal fortune, because they were of inferior reputation for morals!

'Your father, added she, at his going out, told me what he expected from me, in case I found out that I had not the requisite influence upon you—It was this—That I should directly separate myself from you, and leave you singly to take the consequence of your double disobedience—I therefore entreat you, my dear Clarissa, concluded she, and that in the most earnest and condescending manner, to signify to your father, on his return, your ready obedience; and this as well for my sake as your own.'

Affected by my mother's goodness to me, and by that part of her argument which related to her own peace, and to the suspicions they had of her secretly inclining to prefer the man so hated by them, to the man so much my aversion, I could not but wish it were possible for me to obey, I therefore paused, hesitated, considered, and was silent for some time. I could see, that my mother hoped that the result of this hesitation would be favourable to her arguments. But then recollecting, that all was owing to the instigations of a brother and sister, wholly actuated by selfish and envious views; that I had not deserved the treatment I had of late met with; that my disgrace was already become the public talk; that the man was Mr. Solmes; and that my aversion to him was too generally known, to make my compliance either creditable to myself or to them: that it would give my brother and sister a triumph over me, and over Mr. Lovelace, which they would not fail to glory in; and which, although it concerned me but little to regard on his account, yet might be attended with fatal mischiefs—And then Mr. Solmes's disagreeable person; his still more disagreeable manners; his low understanding—Understanding! the glory of a man, so little to be dispensed with in the head and director of a family, in order to preserve to him that respect which a good wife (and that for the justification of her own choice) should pay him herself, and wish every body to pay him.—And as Mr. Solmes's inferiority in this respectable faculty of the human mind [I must be allowed to say this to you, and no great self assumption neither] would proclaim to all future, as well as to all present observers, what must have been my mean inducement. All these reflections crowding upon my remembrance; I would, Madam, said I, folding my hands, with an earnestness in which my whole heart was engaged, bear the cruelest tortures, bear loss of limb, and even of life, to give you peace. But this man, every moment I would, at you command, think of him with favour, is the more my aversion. You cannot, indeed you cannot, think, how my whole soul resists him!—And to talk of contracts concluded upon; of patterns; of a short day!—Save me, save me, O my dearest Mamma, save your child, from this heavy, from this insupportable evil—!

Never was there a countenance that expressed so significantly, as my mother's did, an anguish, which she struggled to hide, under an anger she was compelled to assume—till the latter overcoming the former, she turned from me with an uplifted eye, and stamping—Strange perverseness! were the only words I heard of a sentence that she angrily pronounced; and was going. I then, half-frantically I believe, laid hold of her gown—Have patience with me, dearest Madam! said I—Do not you renounce me totally!—If you must separate yourself from your child, let it not be with absolute reprobation on your own part!—My uncles may be hard-hearted—my father may be immovable—I may suffer from my brother's ambition, and from my sister's envy!—But let me not lose my Mamma's love; at least, her pity.

She turned to me with benigner rays—You have my love! You have my pity! But, O my dearest girl—I have not yours.

Indeed, indeed, Madam, you have: and all my reverence, all my gratitude, you have!—But in this one point—Cannot I be this once obliged?—Will no expedient be accepted? Have I not made a very fair proposal as to Mr. Lovelace?

I wish, for both our sakes, my dear unpersuadable girl, that the decision of this point lay with me. But why, when you know it does not, why should you thus perplex and urge me?—To renounce Mr. Lovelace is now but half what is aimed at. Nor will any body else believe you in earnest in the offer, if I would. While you remain single, Mr. Lovelace will have hopes—and you, in the opinion of others, inclinations.

Permit me, dearest Madam, to say, that your goodness to me, your patience, your peace, weigh more with me, than all the rest put together: for although I am to be treated by my brother, and, through his instigations, by my father, as a slave in this point, and not as a daughter, yet my mind is not that of a slave. You have not brought me up to be mean.

So, Clary! you are already at defiance with your father! I have had too much cause before to apprehend as much—What will this come to?—I, and then my dear mamma sighed—I, am forced to put up with many humours—

That you are, my ever-honoured Mamma, is my grief. And can it be thought, that this very consideration, and the apprehension of what may result from a much worse-tempered man, (a man who has not half the sense of my father,) has not made an impression upon me, to the disadvantage of the married life? Yet 'tis something of an alleviation, if one must bear undue controul, to bear it from a man of sense. My father, I have heard you say, Madam, was for years a very good-humoured gentleman—unobjectionable in person and manners—but the man proposed to me—

Forbear reflecting upon your father: [Did I, my dear, in what I have repeated, and I think they are the very words, reflect upon my father?] it is not possible, I must say again, and again, were all men equally indifferent to you, that you should be thus sturdy in your will. I am tired out with your obstinacy—The most unpersuadable girl—You forget, that I must separate myself from you, if you will not comply. You do not remember that you father will take you up, where I leave you. Once more, however, I will put it to you,—Are you determined to brave your father's displeasure?—Are you determined to defy your uncles?—Do you choose to break with us all, rather than encourage Mr. Solmes?—Rather than give me hope?

Dreadful alternative—But is not my sincerity, is not the integrity of my heart, concerned in the answer? May not my everlasting happiness be the sacrifice? Will not the least shadow of the hope you just now demanded from me, be driven into absolute and sudden certainty? Is it not sought to ensnare, to entangle me in my own desire of obeying, if I could give answers that might be construed into hope?—Forgive me, Madam: bear with your child's boldness in such a cause as this!—Settlements drawn!—Patterns sent for!—An early day!—Dear, dear Madam, how can I give hope, and not intend to be this man's?

Ah, girl, never say your heart is free! You deceive yourself if you think it is.

Thus to be driven [and I wrung my hands through impatience] by the instigations of a designing, an ambitious brother, and by a sister, that—

How often, Clary, must I forbid your unsisterly reflections?—Does not your father, do not your uncles, does not every body, patronize Mr. Solmes? And let me tell you, ungrateful girl, and unmovable as ungrateful, let me repeatedly tell you, that it is evident to me, that nothing but a love unworthy of your prudence can make you a creature late so dutiful, now so sturdy. You may guess what your father's first question on his return will be. He must know, that I can do nothing with you. I have done my part. Seek me, if your mind change before he comes back: you have yet a little more time, as he stays supper. I will no more seek you, nor to you.—And away she flung.

What could I do but weep?

I am extremely affected on my mother's account—more, I must needs say, than on my own. And indeed, all things considered, and especially, that the measure she is engaged in, is (as I dare say it is) against her own judgment, she deserves more compassion than myself.—Excellent woman! What pity, that meekness and condescension should not be attended with the due rewards of those charming graces!—Yet had she not let violent spirits (as I have elsewhere observed with no small regret) find their power over hers, it could not have been thus.

But here, run away with my pen, I suffer my mother to be angry with me on her own account. She hinted to me, indeed, that I must seek her, if my mind changed; which is a condition that amounts to a prohibition of attending her: but, as she left me in displeasure, will it not have a very obstinate appearance, and look like a kind of renunciation of her mediation in my favour, if I go not down before my father returns, to supplicate her pity, and her kind report to him?

I will attend her. I had rather all the world should be angry with me than my mamma!

Mean time, to clear my hands from papers of such a nature, Hannah shall deposit this. If two or three letters reach you together, they will but express from one period to another, the anxieties and difficulties which the mind of your unhappy but ever affectionate friend labours under.

CL. H.

LETTER XXI

MISS CLARISSA HARLOWE, TO MISS HOWE SAT. NIGHT

I have been down. I am to be unlucky in all I do, I think, be my intentions ever so good. I have made matters worse instead of better: as I shall now tell you.

I found my mother and sister together in my sister's parlour. My mother, I fear, by the glow of her fine face, (and as the browner, sullener glow in her sister's confirmed,) had been expressing herself with warmth, against her unhappier child: perhaps giving such an account of what had passed, as should clear herself, and convince Bella, and, through her, my brother and uncles, of the sincere pains she had taken with me.

I entered like a dejected criminal; and besought the favour of a private audience. My mother's return, both looks and words, gave but too much reason for my above surmise.

You have, said she [looking at me with a sternness that never sits well on her sweet features] rather a requesting than a conceding countenance, Clarissa Harlowe: if I am mistaken, tell me so; and I will withdraw with you wherever you will.—Yet whether so, or not, you may say what you have to say before your sister.

My mother, I thought, might have withdrawn with me, as she knows that I have not a friend in my sister.

I come down, Madam, said I, to beg of you to forgive me for any thing you may have taken amiss in what passed above respecting your honoured self; and that you will be pleased to use your endeavours to soften my papa's displeasure against me, on his return.

Such aggravating looks; such lifting up of hands and eyes; such a furrowed forehead, in my sister!

My mother was angry enough without all that; and asked me to what purpose I came down, if I were still so intractable.

She had hardly spoken the words, when Shorey came in to tell her, that Mr. Solmes was in the hall, and desired admittance.

Ugly creature! What, at the close of day, quite dark, brought him hither?—But, on second thoughts, I believe it was contrived, that he should be here at supper, to know the result of the conference between my mother and me, and that my father, on his return, might find us together.

I was hurrying away, but my mother commanded me (since I had come down only, as she said, to mock her) not to stir; and at the same time see if I could behave so to Mr. Solmes, as might encourage her to make the favourable report to my father which I had besought her to make.

My sister triumphed. I was vexed to be so caught, and to have such an angry and cutting rebuke given me, with an aspect much more like the taunting sister than the indulgent mother, if I may presume to say so: for she herself seemed to enjoy the surprise upon me.

The man stalked in. His usual walk is by pauses, as if (from the same vacuity of thought which made Dryden's clown whistle) he was telling his steps: and first paid his clumsy respects to my mother; then to my sister; next to me, as if I was already his wife, and therefore to be last in his notice; and sitting down by me, told us in general what weather it was. Very cold he made it; but I was warm enough. Then addressing himself to me: And how do you find it, Miss? was his question; and would have taken my hand.

I withdrew it, I believe with disdain enough. My mother frowned. My sister bit her lip.

I could not contain myself: I was never so bold in my life; for I went on with my plea, as if Mr. Solmes had not been there.

My mother coloured, and looked at him, at my sister, and at me. My sister's eyes were opener and bigger than ever I saw them before.

The man understood me. He hemmed, and removed from one chair to another.

I went on, supplicating for my mother's favourable report: Nothing but invincible dislike, said I—

What would the girl be at, interrupted my mother? Why, Clary! Is this a subject!—Is this!—Is this!—Is this a time—And again she looked upon Mr. Solmes.

I am sorry, on reflection, that I put my mamma into so much confusion—To be sure it was very saucy in me.

I beg pardon, Madam, said I. But my papa will soon return. And since I am not permitted to withdraw, it is not necessary, I humbly presume, that Mr. Solmes's presence should deprive me of this opportunity to implore your favourable report; and at the same time, if he still visit on my account [looking at him] to convince him, that it cannot possibly be to any purpose—

Is the girl mad? said my mother, interrupting me.

My sister, with the affectation of a whisper to my mother—This is—This is spite, Madam, [very spitefully she spoke the word,] because you commanded her to stay.

I only looked at her, and turning to my mother, Permit me, Madam, said I, to repeat my request. I have no brother, no sister!—If I ever lose my mamma's favour, I am lost for ever!

Mr. Solmes removed to his first seat, and fell to gnawing the head of his hazel; a carved head, almost as ugly as his own—I did not think the man was so sensible.

My sister rose, with a face all over scarlet; and stepping to the table, where lay a fan, she took it up, and, although Mr. Solmes had observed that the weather was cold, fanned herself very violently.

My mother came to me, and angrily taking my hand, led me out of that parlour into my own; which, you know, is next to it—Is not this behaviour very bold, very provoking, think you, Clary?

I beg your pardon, Madam, if it has that appearance to you. But indeed, my dear Mamma, there seem to be snares laying in wait for me. Too well I know my brother's drift. With a good word he shall have my consent for all he wishes to worm me out of—neither he, nor my sister, shall need to take half this pains—

My mother was about to leave me in high displeasure.

I besought her to stay: One favour, but one favour, dearest Madam, said I, give me leave to beg of you—

What would the girl?

I see how every thing is working about.—I never, never can think of Mr. Solmes. My papa will be in tumults when he is told that I cannot. They will judge of the tenderness of your heart to a poor child who seems devoted by every one else, from the willingness you have already shewn to hearken to my prayers. There will be endeavours used to confine me, and keep me out of your presence, and out of the presence of every one who used to love me [this, my dear Miss Howe, is threatened]. If this be effected; if it be put out of my power to plead my own cause, and to appeal to you, and to my uncle Harlowe, of whom only I have hope; then will every ear be opened against me, and every tale encouraged—It is, therefore, my humble request, that, added to the disgraceful prohibitions I now suffer under, you will not, if you can help it, give way to my being denied your ear.

Your listening Hannah has given you this intelligence, as she does many others.

My Hannah, Madam, listens not—My Hannah—

No more in Hannah's behalf—Hannah is known to make mischief—Hannah is known—But no more of that bold intermeddler—'Tis true your father threatened to confine you to your chamber, if you complied not, in order the more assuredly to deprive you of the opportunity of corresponding with those who harden your heart against his will. He bid me tell you so, when he went out, if I found you refractory. But I was loth to deliver so harsh a declaration; being still in hope that you would come down to us in a compliant temper. Hannah has overheard this, I suppose; and has told you of it; as also, that he declared he would break your heart, rather than you should break his. And I now assure you, that you will be confined, and prohibited making teasing appeals to any of us: and we shall see who is to submit, you to us, or every body to you.

Again I offered to clear Hannah, and to lay the latter part of the intelligence to my sister's echo, Betty Barnes, who had boasted of it to another servant: but I was again bid to be silent on that head. I should soon find, my mother was pleased to say, that others could be as determined as I was obstinate: and once for all would add, that since she saw that I built upon her indulgence, and was indifferent about involving her in contentions with my father, she would now assure me, that she was as much determined against Mr. Lovelace, and for Mr. Solmes and the family schemes, as any body; and would not refuse her consent to any measures that should be thought necessary to reduce a stubborn child to her duty.

I was ready to sink. She was so good as to lend me her arm to support me.

And this, said I, is all I have to hope for from my Mamma?

It is. But, Clary, this one further opportunity I give you—Go in again to Mr. Solmes, and behave discreetly to him; and let your father find you together, upon civil terms at least.

My feet moved [of themselves, I think] farther from the parlour where he was, and towards the stairs; and there I stopped and paused.

If, proceeded she, you are determined to stand in defiance of us all—then indeed you may go up to your chamber (as you are ready to do)—And God help you!

God help me, indeed! for I cannot give hope of what I cannot intend—But let me have your prayers, my dear Mamma!—Those shall have mine, who have brought me into all this distress.

I was moving to go up—

And will you go up, Clary?

I turned my face to her: my officious tears would needs plead for me: I could not just then speak, and stood still.

Good girl, distress me not thus!—Dear, good girl, do not thus distress me! holding out her hand; but standing still likewise.

What can I do, Madam?—What can I do?

Go in again, my child—Go in again, my dear child!—repeated she; and let your father find you together.

What, Madam, to give him hope?—To give hope to Mr. Solmes?

Obstinate, perverse, undutiful Clarissa! with a rejecting hand, and angry aspect; then take your own way, and go up!—But stir not down again, I charge you, without leave, or till your father's pleasure be known concerning you.

She flung away from me with high indignation: and I went up with a very heavy heart; and feet as slow as my heart was heavy.

My father is come home, and my brother with him. Late as it is, they are all shut up together. Not a door opens; not a soul stirs. Hannah, as she moves up and down, is shunned as a person infected.

The angry assembly is broken up. My two uncles and my aunt Hervey are sent for, it seems, to be here in the morning to breakfast. I shall then, I suppose, know my doom. 'Tis past eleven, and I am ordered not to go to bed.

TWELVE O'CLOCK.

This moment the keys of every thing are taken from me. It was proposed to send for me down: but my father said, he could not bear to look upon me.—Strange alteration in a few weeks!—Shorey was the messenger. The tears stood in her eyes when she delivered her message.

You, my dear, are happy—May you always be so—and then I can never be wholly miserable. Adieu, my beloved friend!

CL. HARLOWE.

LETTER XXII

MISS CLARISSA HARLOWE, TO MISS HOWE SUNDAY MORNING, MARCH 5

Hannah has just brought me from the private place in the garden-wall, a letter from Mr. Lovelace, deposited last night, signed also by Lord M.

He tells me in it, 'That Mr. Solmes makes it his boast, that he is to be married in a few days to one of the shyest women in England: that my brother explains his meaning: This shy creature, he says, is me; and he assures every one, that his younger sister is very soon to be Mr. Solmes's wife. He tells me of the patterns bespoken which my mother mentioned to me.'

Not one thing escapes him that is done or said in this house.

'My sister, he says, reports the same things; and that with such particular aggravations of insult upon him, that he cannot but be extremely piqued, as well at the manner, as from the occasion; and expresses himself with great violence upon it.

'He knows not, he says, what my relations' inducements can be to prefer such a man as Solmes to him. If advantageous settlements be the motive, Solmes shall not offer what he will refuse to comply with.

'As to his estate and family; the first cannot be excepted against: and for the second, he will not disgrace himself by a comparison so odious. He appeals to Lord M. for the regularity of his life and manners ever since he has made his addresses to me, or had hope of my favour.'

I suppose he would have his Lordship's signing to this letter to be taken as a voucher for him.

'He desires my leave (in company with my Lord), in a pacific manner, to attend my father and uncles, in order to make proposals that must be accepted, if they will see him, and hear what they are: and tells me, that he will submit to any measures that I shall prescribe, in order to bring about a reconciliation.'

He presumes to be very earnest with me, 'to give him a private meeting some night, in my father's garden, attended by whom I please.'

Really, my dear, were you to see his letter, you would think I had given him great encouragement, and that I am in direct treaty with him; or that he is sure that my friends will drive me into a foreign protection; for he has the boldness to offer, in my Lord's name, an asylum to me, should I be tyrannically treated in Solmes's behalf.

I suppose it is the way of this sex to endeavour to entangle the thoughtless of ours by bold supposals and offers, in hopes that we shall be too complaisant or bashful to quarrel with them; and, if not checked, to reckon upon our silence, as assents voluntarily given, or concessions made in their favour.

There are other particulars in this letter which I ought to mention to you: but I will take an opportunity to send you the letter itself, or a copy of it.

For my own part, I am very uneasy to think how I have been drawn on one hand, and driven on the other, into a clandestine, in short, into a mere loverlike correspondence, which my heart condemns.

It is easy to see, if I do not break it off, that Mr. Lovelace's advantages, by reason of my unhappy situation, will every day increase, and I shall be more and more entangled. Yet if I do put an end to it, without making it a condition of being freed from Mr. Solmes's address—May I, my dear, is it best to continue it a little longer, in order to extricate myself out of the other difficulty, by giving up all thoughts of Mr. Lovelace?—Whose advice can I now ask but yours.

All my relations are met. They are at breakfast together. Mr. Solmes is expected. I am excessively uneasy. I must lay down my pen.

They are all going to church together. Grievously disordered they appear to be, as Hannah tells me. She believes something is resolved upon.

SUNDAY NOON.

What a cruel thing is suspense!—I will ask leave to go to church this afternoon. I expect to be denied. But, if I do not ask, they may allege, that my not going is owing to myself.

I desired to speak with Shorey. Shorey came. I directed her to carry to my mother my request for permission to go to church this afternoon. What think you was the return? Tell her, that she must direct herself to her brother for any favour she has to ask.—So, my dear, I am to be delivered up to my brother!

I was resolved, however, to ask of him this favour. Accordingly, when they sent me up my solitary dinner, I gave the messenger a billet, in which I made it my humble request through him to my father, to be permitted to go to church this afternoon.

This was the contemptuous answer: 'Tell her, that her request will be taken into consideration to-morrow.'

Patience will be the fittest return I can make to such an insult. But this method will not do with me; indeed it will not! And yet it is but the beginning, I suppose, of what I am to expect from my brother, now I am delivered up to him.

On recollection, I thought it best to renew my request. I did. The following is a copy of what I wrote, and what follows that, of the answer sent me.

SIR,

I know not what to make of the answer brought to my request of being permitted to go to church this afternoon. If you designed to shew your pleasantry by it, I hope that will continue; and then my request will be granted.

You know, that I never absented myself, when well, and at home, till the two last Sundays; when I was advised not to go. My present situation is such, that I never more wanted the benefit of the public prayers.

I will solemnly engage only to go thither, and back again.

I hope it cannot be thought that I would do otherwise.

My dejection of spirits will give a too just excuse on the score of indisposition for avoiding visits. Nor will I, but by distant civilities, return the compliments of any of my acquaintances. My disgraces, if they are to have an end, need not be proclaimed to the whole world. I ask this favour, therefore, for my reputation's sake, that I may be able to hold up my head in the neighbourhood, if I live to see an end of the unmerited severities which seem to be designed for

Your unhappy sister, CL. HARLOWE.

TO MISS CLARISSA HARLOWE

For a girl to lay so much stress upon going to church, and yet resolve to defy her parents, in an article of the greatest consequence to them, and to the whole family, is an absurdity. You are recommended, Miss, to the practice of your private devotions. May they be efficacious upon the mind of one of the most pervicacious young creatures that ever was heard of! The intention is, I tell you plainly, to mortify you into a sense of your duty. The neighbours you are so solicitous to appear well with, already know, that you defy that. So, Miss, if you have a real value for your reputation, shew it as you ought. It is yet in your own power to establish or impair it.

JA. HARLOWE.

Thus, my dear Miss Howe, has my brother got me into his snares; and I, like a poor silly bird, the more I struggle, am the more entangled.

LETTER XXIII

MISS CLARISSA HARLOWE, TO MISS HOWE MONDAY MORNING, MARCH 6

They are resolved to break my heart. My poor Hannah is discharged—disgracefully discharged!—Thus it was.

Within half an hour after I had sent the poor girl down for my breakfast, that bold creature Betty Barnes, my sister's confidant and servant, (if a favourite maid and confidant can be deemed a servant,) came up.

What, Miss, will you please to have for breakfast?

I was surprised. What will I have for breakfast, Betty!—How!—What!—How comes it!—Then I named Hannah. I could not tell what to say.

Don't be surprised, Miss:—but you'll see Hannah no more in this house.

God forbid!—Is any harm come to Hannah?—What! What is the matter with Hannah?

Why, Miss, the short and the long is this: Your papa and mamma think Hannah has staid long enough in the house to do mischief; and so she is ordered to troop [that was the confident creature's word]; and I am directed to wait upon you in her stead.

I burst into tears. I have no service for you, Betty Barnes; none at all. But where is Hannah? Cannot I speak with the poor girl? I owe her half a year's wages. May I not see the honest creature, and pay her her wages? I may never see her again perhaps; for they are resolved to break my heart.

And they think you are resolved to break theirs: so tit for tat, Miss.

Impertinent I called her; and asked her, if it were upon such confident terms that her service was to begin.

I was so very earnest to see the poor maid, that (to oblige me, as she said) she went down with my request.

The worthy creature was as earnest to see me; and the favour was granted in presence of Shorey and Betty.

I thanked her, when she came up, for her past service to me.

Her heart was ready to break. And she began to vindicate her fidelity and love; and disclaimed any mischief she had ever made.

I told her, that those who occasioned her being turned out of my service, made no question of her integrity: that her dismission was intended for an indignity to me: that I was very sorry to be obliged to part with her, and hoped she would meet with as good a service.

Never, never, wringing her hands, should she meet with a mistress she loved so well. And the poor creature ran on in my praises, and in professions of love to me.

We are all apt, you know, my dear, to praise our benefactors, because they are our benefactors; as if every body did right or wrong, as they obliged or disobliged us. But this good creature deserved to be kindly treated; so I could have no merit in favouring one whom it would have been ungrateful not to distinguish.

I gave her a little linen, some laces, and other odd things; and instead of four pounds which were due to her, ten guineas: and said, if ever I were again allowed to be my own mistress, I would think of her in the first place.

Betty enviously whispered Shorey upon it.

Hannah told me, before their faces, having no other opportunity, that she had been examined about letters to me, and from me: and that she had given her pockets to Miss Harlowe, who looked into them, and put her fingers in her stays, to satisfy herself that she had not any.

She gave me an account of the number of my pheasants and bantams; and I said, they should be my own care twice or thrice a day.

We wept over each other at parting. The girl prayed for all the family.

To have so good a servant so disgracefully dismissed, is very cruel: and I could not help saying that these methods might break my heart, but not any other way answer the end of the authors of my disgraces.

Betty, with a very saucy fleer, said to Shorey, There would be a trial of skill about that she fancied. But I took no notice of it. If this wench thinks that I have robbed her young mistress of a lover, as you say she has given out, she may believe that it is some degree of merit in herself to be impertinent to me.

Thus have I been forced to part with my faithful Hannah. If you can command the good creature to a place worthy of her, pray do for my sake.

LETTER XXIV

MISS CLARISSA HARLOWE, TO MISS HOWE MONDAY, NEAR 12 O'CLOCK

The enclosed letter was just now delivered to me. My brother has carried all his points.

I send you also the copy of my answer. No more at this time can I write—!

MONDAY, MAR. 6. MISS CLARY,

By command of your father and mother I write expressly to forbid you to come into their presence, or into the garden when they are there: nor when they are not there, but with Betty Banes to attend you; except by particular license or command.

On their blessings, you are forbidden likewise to correspond with the vile Lovelace; as it is well known you did by means of your sly Hannah. Whence her sudden discharge. As was fit.

Neither are you to correspond with Miss Howe; who has given herself high airs of late; and might possibly help on your correspondence with that detested libertine. Nor, in short, with any body without leave.

You are not to enter into the presence of either of your uncles, without their leave first obtained. It is a mercy to you, after such a behaviour to your mother, that your father refuses to see you.

You are not to be seen in any apartment of the house you so lately governed as you pleased, unless you are commanded down.

In short, you are strictly to confine yourself to your chamber, except now and then, in Betty Barnes's sight (as aforesaid) you take a morning or evening turn in the garden: and then you are to go directly, and without stopping at any apartment in the way, up or down the back stairs, that the sight of so perverse a young creature may not add to the pain you have given every body.

The hourly threatenings of your fine fellow, as well as your own unheard-of obstinacy, will account to you for all this. What a hand has the best and most indulgent of mothers had with you, who so long pleaded for you, and undertook for you; even when others, from the manner of your setting out, despaired of moving you!—What must your perverseness have been, that such a mother can give you up! She thinks it right so to do: nor will take you to favour, unless you make the first steps, by a compliance with your duty.

As for myself, whom perhaps you think hardly of [in very good company, if you do, that is my sole consolation]; I have advised, that you may be permitted to pursue your own inclinations, (some people need no greater punishment than such a permission,) and not to have the house encumbered by one who must give them the more pain for the necessity she has laid them under of avoiding the sight of her, although in it.

If any thing I have written appear severe or harsh, it is still in your power (but perhaps will not always be so) to remedy it; and that by a single word.

Betty Barnes has orders to obey you in all points consistent with her duty to those whom you owe it, as well as she.

JA. HARLOWE. TO JAMES HARLOWE, JUNIOR, ESQ. SIR,

I will only say, That you may congratulate yourself on having so far succeeded in all your views, that you may report what you please of me, and I can no more defend myself, than if I were dead. Yet one favour, nevertheless, I will beg of you. It is this—That you will not occasion more severities, more disgraces, that are necessary for carrying into execution your further designs, whatever they be, against

Your unhappy sister, CLARISSA HARLOWE.

LETTER XXV

MISS CLARISSA HARLOWE, TO MISS HOWE TUESDAY, MARCH 7

By my last deposit, you will see how I am driven, and what a poor prisoner I am.—No regard had to my reputation. The whole matter is now before you. Can such measures be supposed to soften?—But surely they can only mean to try and frighten me into my brother's views!—All my hope is, to be able to weather this point till my cousin Morden comes from Florence; and he is soon expected: yet, if they are determined upon a short day, I doubt he will not be here in time enough to save me.

It is plain by my brother's letter, that my mother has not spared me, in the report she was pleased to make of the conference between herself and me: yet she was pleased to hint to me, that my brother had views which she would have had me try to disappoint. But indeed she had engaged to give a faithful account of what was to pass between herself and me: and it was, doubtless, much more eligible to give up a daughter, than to disoblige a husband, and every other person of the family.

They think they have done every thing by turning away my poor Hannah: but as long as the liberty of the garden, and my poultry-visits, are allowed me, they will be mistaken.

I asked Mrs. Betty, if she had any orders to watch or attend me; or whether I was to ask her leave whenever I should be disposed to walk in the garden, or to go feed my bantams?—Lord bless her! what could I mean by such a question! Yet she owned, that she had heard, that I was not to go into the garden, when my father, mother, or uncles were there.

However, as it behoved me to be assured on this head, I went down directly, and staid an hour, without question or impediment; and yet a good part of the time, I walked under and in sight, as I may say, of my brother's study window, where both he and my sister happened to be. And I am sure they saw me, by the loud mirth they affected, by way of insult, as I suppose.

So this part of my restraint was doubtless a stretch of the authority given him. The enforcing of that may perhaps come next. But I hope not.

TUESDAY NIGHT.

Since I wrote the above, I ventured to send a letter by Shorey to my mother. I desired her to give it into her own hand, when nobody was by.

I shall enclose a copy of it. You will see that I would have it thought, that now Hannah is gone, I have no way to correspond out of the house. I am far from thinking all I do right. I am afraid this is a little piece of art, that is not so. But this is an afterthought. The letter went first.

HONOURED MADAM,

Having acknowledged to you, that I had received letters from Mr. Lovelace full of resentment, and that I answered them purely to prevent further mischief, and having shewn you copies of my answers, which you did not disapprove of, although you thought fit, after you had read them, to forbid me any further correspondence with him, I think it my duty to acquaint you, that another letter from him has since come to my hand, in which he is very earnest with me to permit him to wait on my papa, or you, or my two uncles, in a pacific way, accompanied by Lord M.: on which I beg your commands.

I own to you, Madam, that had not the prohibition been renewed, and had not Hannah been so suddenly dismissed my service, I should have made the less scruple to have written an answer, and to have commanded her to convey it to him, with all speed, in order to dissuade him from these visits, lest any thing should happen on the occasion that my heart aches but to think of.

And here I cannot but express my grief, that I should have all the punishment and all the blame, who, as I have reason to think, have prevented great mischief, and have not been the occasion of any. For, Madam, could I be supposed to govern the passions of either of the gentlemen?—Over the one indeed I have had some little influence, without giving him hitherto any reason to think he has fastened an obligation upon me for it.—Over the other, Who, Madam, has any?—I am grieved at heart, to be obliged to lay so great a blame at my brother's door, although my reputation and my liberty are both to be sacrificed to his resentment and ambition. May not, however, so deep a sufferer be permitted to speak out?

This communication being as voluntarily made, as dutifully intended, I humbly presume to hope, that I shall not be required to produce the letter itself. I cannot either in honour or prudence do that, because of the vehemence of his style; for having heard [not, I assure you, by my means, or through Hannah's] of some part of the harsh treatment I have met with; he thinks himself entitled to place it to his own account, by reason of speeches thrown out by some of my relations, equally vehement.

If I do not answer him, he will be made desperate, and think himself justified (thought I shall not think him so) in resenting the treatment he complains of: if I do, and if, in compliment to me, he forbears to resent what he thinks himself entitled to resent; be pleased, Madam, to consider the obligation he will suppose he lays me under.

If I were as strongly prepossessed in his favour as is supposed, I should not have wished this to be considered by you. And permit me, as a still further proof that I am not prepossessed, to beg of you to consider, Whether, upon the whole, the proposal I made, of declaring for the single life (which I will religiously adhere to) is not the best way to get rid of his pretensions with honour. To renounce him, and not be allowed to aver, that I will never be the other man's, will make him conclude (driven as I am driven) that I am determined in that other man's favour.

If this has not its due weight, my brother's strange schemes must be tried, and I will resign myself to my destiny with all the acquiescence that shall be granted to my prayers. And so leaving the whole to your own wisdom, and whether you choose to consult my papa and uncles upon this humble application, or not; or whether I shall be allowed to write an answer to Mr. Lovelace, or not [and if allowed to do so, I beg your direction by whom to send it]; I remain,

Honoured Madam, Your unhappy, but ever dutiful daughter, CL. HARLOWE.

WEDNESDAY MORNING.

I have just received an answer to the enclosed letter. My mother, you will observe, has ordered me to burn it: but, as you will have it in your safekeeping, and nobody else will see it, her end will be equally answered, as if it were burnt. It has neither date nor superscription.

CLARISSA,

Say not all the blame and all the punishment is yours. I am as much blamed, and as much punished, as you are; yet am more innocent. When your obstinacy is equal to any other person's passion, blame not your brother. We judged right, that Hannah carried on your correspondencies. Now she is gone, and you cannot write [we think you cannot] to Miss Howe, nor she to you, without our knowledge, one cause of uneasiness and jealousy is over.

I had no dislike of Hannah. I did not tell her so; because somebody was within hearing when she desired to pay her duty to me at going. I gave her a caution, in a raised voice, To take care, wherever she went to live next, if there were any young ladies, how she made parties, and assisted in clandestine correspondencies. But I slid two guineas into her hand: nor was I angry to hear that you were still more bountiful to her. So much for Hannah.

I don't know what to write, about your answering that man of violence. What can you think of it, that such a family as ours, should have such a rod held over it?—For my part, I have not owned that I know you have corresponded. By your last boldness to me [an astonishing one it was, to pursue before Mr. Solmes the subject I was forced to break from above-stairs!] you may, as far as I know, plead, that you had my countenance for your correspondence with him; and so add to the uneasiness between your father and me. You were once my comfort, Clarissa; you made all my hardships tolerable:—But now!—However, nothing, it is plain, can move you; and I will say no more on that head: for you are under your father's discipline now; and he will neither be prescribed to, nor entreated.

I should have been glad to see the letter you tell me of, as I saw the rest. You say, both honour and prudence forbid you to shew it to me.—O Clarissa! what think you of receiving letters that honour and prudence forbid you to shew to a mother!—But it is not for me to see it, if you would choose to shew it me. I will not be in your secret. I will not know that you did correspond. And, as to an answer, take your own methods. But let him know it will be the last you will write. And, if you do write, I won't see it: so seal it up (if you do) and give it to Shorey; and she—Yet do not think I give you license to write.

We will be upon no conditions with him, nor will you be allowed to be upon any. Your father and uncles would have no patience were he to come. What have you to do to oblige him with your refusal of Mr. Solmes?—Will not that refusal be to give him hope? And while he has any, can we be easy or free from his insults? Were even your brother in fault, as that fault cannot be conquered, is a sister to carry on a correspondence that shall endanger her brother? But your father has given his sanction to your brother's dislikes, your uncles', and every body's!—No matter to whom owing.

As to the rest, you have by your obstinacy put it out of my power to do any thing for you. Your father takes it upon himself to be answerable for all consequences. You must not therefore apply to me for favour. I shall endeavour to be only an observer: Happy, if I could be an unconcerned one!—While I had power, you would not let me use it as I would have used it. Your aunt has been forced to engage not to interfere but by your father's direction. You'll have severe trials. If you have any favour to hope for, it must be from the mediation of your uncles. And yet, I believe, they are equally determined: for they make it a principle, [alas! they never had children!] that that child, who in marriage is not governed by her parents, is to be given up as a lost creature!

I charge you, let not this letter be found. Burn it. There is too much of the mother in it, to a daughter so unaccountably obstinate.

Write not another letter to me. I can do nothing for you. But you can do every thing for yourself.

Now, my dear, to proceed with my melancholy narrative.

After this letter, you will believe, that I could have very little hopes, that an application directly to my father would stand me in any stead: but I thought it became me to write, were it but to acquit myself to myself, that I have left nothing unattempted that has the least likelihood to restore me to his favour. Accordingly I wrote to the following effect:

I presume not, I say, to argue with my Papa; I only beg his mercy and indulgence in this one point, on which depends my present, and perhaps my future, happiness; and beseech him not to reprobate his child for an aversion which it is not in her power to conquer. I beg, that I may not be sacrificed to projects, and remote contingencies. I complain of the disgraces I suffer in this banishment from his presence, and in being confined to my chamber. In every thing but this one point, I promise implicit duty and resignation to his will. I repeat my offers of a single life; and appeal to him, whether I have ever given him cause to doubt my word. I beg to be admitted to his, and to my mamma's, presence, and that my conduct may be under their own eye: and this with the more earnestness, as I have too much reason to believe that snares are laid for me; and tauntings and revilings used on purpose to make a handle of my words against me, when I am not permitted to speak in my own defence. I conclude with hoping, that my brother's instigations may not rob an unhappy child of her father.

This is the answer, sent without superscription, and unsealed, although by Betty Barnes, who delivered it with an air, as if she knew the contents.

WEDNESDAY.

I write, perverse girl; but with all the indignation that your disobedience deserves. To desire to be forgiven a fault you own, and yet resolve to persevere in, is a boldness, no more to be equaled, than passed over. It is my authority you defy. Your reflections upon a brother, that is an honour to us all, deserve my utmost resentment. I see how light all relationship sits upon you. The cause I guess at, too. I cannot bear the reflections that naturally arise from this consideration. Your behaviour to your too-indulgent and too-fond mother— —But, I have no patience—Continue banished from my presence, undutiful as you are, till you know how to conform to my will. Ingrateful creature! Your letter but upbraid me for my past indulgence. Write no more to me, till you can distinguish better; and till you are convinced of your duty to

A JUSTLY INCENSED FATHER. ***

This angry letter was accompanied by one from my mother, unsealed, and unsuperscribed also. Those who take so much pains to confederate every one against me, I make no doubt, obliged her to bear her testimony against the poor girl.

My mother's letter being a repetition of some of the severe things that passed between herself and me, of which I have already informed you, I shall not need to give you the contents—only thus far, that she also praises my brother, and blames me for my freedoms with him.

LETTER XXVI

MISS CLARISSA HARLOWE, TO MISS HOWE THURSDAY MORN., MARCH 9

I have another letter from Mr. Lovelace, although I had not answered his former.

This man, somehow or other, knows every thing that passes in our family. My confinement; Hanna's dismission; and more of the resentments and resolutions of my father, uncles, and brother, than I can possibly know, and almost as soon as the things happen, which he tells me of. He cannot come at these intelligencies fairly.

He is excessively uneasy upon what he hears; and his expressions, both of love to me, and resentment to them, are very fervent. He solicits me, 'To engage my honour to him never to have Mr. Solmes.'

I think I may fairly promise him that I will not.

He begs, 'That I will not think he is endeavouring to make to himself a merit at any man's expense, since he hopes to obtain my favour on the foot of his own; nor that he seeks to intimidate me into a consideration for him. But declares, that the treatment he meets with from my family is of such a nature, that he is perpetually reproached for not resenting it; and that as well by Lord M. and Lady Sarah, and Lady Betty, as by all his other friends: and if he must have no hope from me, he cannot answer for what his despair will make him do.'

Indeed, he says, 'his relations, the ladies particularly, advise him to have recourse to a legal remedy: But how, he asks, can a man of honour go to law for verbal abuses given by people entitled to wear swords?'

You see, my dear, that my mother seems as apprehensive of mischief as myself; and has indirectly offered to let Shorey carry my answer to the letter he sent me before.

He is full of the favours of the ladies of his family to me: to whom, nevertheless, I am personally a stranger; except, that I once saw Miss Patty Montague at Mrs. Knolly's.

It is natural, I believe, for a person to be the more desirous of making new friends, in proportion as she loses the favour of old ones. Yet had I rather appear amiable in the eyes of my own relations, and in your eyes, than in those of all the world besides—but these four ladies of his family have such excellent characters, that one cannot but wish to be thought well of by them. Cannot there be a way to find out, by Mrs. Fortescue's means, or by Mr. Hickman, who has some knowledge of Lord M. [covertly, however,] what their opinions are of the present situation of things in our family; and of the little likelihood there is, that ever the alliance once approved of by them, can take effect?

I cannot, for my own part, think so well of myself, as to imagine, that they can wish their kinsman to persevere in his views with regard to me, through such contempts and discouragements.—Not that it would concern me, should they advise him to the contrary. By my Lord's signing Mr. Lovelace's former letter; by Mr. Lovelace's assurances of the continued favour of all his relations; and by the report of others; I seem still to stand high in their favour. But, methinks, I should be glad to have this confirmed to me, as from themselves, by the lips of an indifferent person; and the rather, because of their fortunes and family; and take it amiss (as they have reason) to be included by ours in the contempt thrown upon their kinsman.

Curiosity at present is all my motive: nor will there ever, I hope, be a stronger, notwithstanding your questionable throbs—even were the merits of Mr. Lovelace much greater than they are.

I have answered his letters. If he takes me at my word, I shall need to be less solicitous for the opinions of his relations in my favour: and yet one would be glad to be well thought of by the worthy.

This is the substance of my letter:

'I express my surprise at his knowing (and so early) all that passes here.'

I assure him, 'That were there not such a man in the world as himself, I would not have Mr. Solmes.'

I tell him, 'That to return, as I understand he does, defiances for defiances, to my relations, is far from being a proof with me, either of his politeness, or of the consideration he pretends to have for me.

'That the moment I hear he visits any of my friends without their consent, I will make a resolution never to see him more, if I can help it.'

I apprize him, 'That I am connived at in sending this letter (although no one has seen the contents) provided it shall be the last I will ever write to him: that I had more than once told him, that the single life was my choice; and this before Mr. Solmes was introduced as a visitor in our family: that Mr. Wyerley, and other gentlemen, knew it to be my choice, before himself was acquainted with any of us: that I had never been induced to receive a line from him on the subject, but that I thought he had not acted ungenerously by my brother; and yet had not been so handsomely treated by my friends, as he might have expected: but that had he even my friends on his side, I should have very great objections to him, were I to get over my choice of a single life, so really preferable to me as it is; and that I should have declared as much to him, had I not regarded him as more than a common visiter. On all these accounts, I desire, that the one more letter, which I will allow him to deposit in the usual place, may be the very last; and that only, to acquaint me with his acquiescence that it shall be so; at least till happier times.'

This last I put in that he may not be quite desperate. But, if he take me at my word, I shall be rid of one of my tormentors.

I have promised to lay before you all his letters, and my answers: I repeat that promise: and am the less solicitous, for that reason, to amplify upon the contents of either. But I cannot too often express my vexation, to be driven to such streights and difficulties, here at home, as oblige me to answer letters, (from a man I had not absolutely intended to encourage, and to whom I had really great objections,) filled as his are with such warm protestations, and written to me with a spirit of expectation.

For, my dear, you never knew so bold a supposer. As commentators find beauties in an author, to which the author perhaps was a stranger; so he sometimes compliments me in high strains of gratitude for favours, and for a consideration, which I never designed him; insomuch that I am frequently under a necessity of explaining away the attributed goodness to him, which, if I shewed, I should have the less opinion of myself.

In short, my dear, like a restiff horse, (as I have heard described by sportsmen,) he pains one's hands, and half disjoints one's arms, to rein him in. And, when you see his letters, you must form no judgment upon them, till you have read my answers. If you do, you will indeed think you have cause to attribute self-deceit, and throbs, and glows, to your friend: and yet, at other times, the contradictory nature complains, that I shew him as little favour, and my friends as much inveteracy, as if, in the rencontre betwixt my brother and him, he had been the aggressor; and as if the catastrophe had been as fatal, as it might have been.

If he has a design by this conduct (sometimes complaining of my shyness, at others exalting in my imaginary favours) to induce me at one time to acquiesce with his compliments; at another to be more complaisant for his complaints; and if the contradiction be not the effect of his inattention and giddiness; I shall think him as deep and as artful (too probably, as practised) a creature, as ever lived; and were I to be sure of it, should hate him, if possible, worse than I do Solmes.

But enough for the present of a creature so very various.

LETTER XXVII

MISS HOWE, TO MISS CLARISSA HARLOWE THURSDAY NIGHT, MARCH 9

I have not patience with any of the people you are with. I know not what to advise you to do. How do you know that you are not punishable for being the cause, though to your own loss, that the will of your grandfather is not complied with?—Wills are sacred things, child. You see, that they, even they, think so, who imagine they suffer by a will, through the distinction paid you in it.

I allow of all your noble reasonings for what you did at the time: But, since such a charming, such a generous instance of filial duty is to go thus unrewarded, why should you not resume?

Your grandfather knew the family-failing. He knew what a noble spirit you had to do good. He himself, perhaps, [excuse me, my dear,] had done too little in his life-time; and therefore he put it in your power to make up for the defects of the whole family. Were it to me, I would resume it. Indeed I would.

You will say, you cannot do it, while you are with them. I don't know that. Do you think they can use you worse than they do? And is it not your right? And do they not make use of your own generosity to oppress you? Your uncle Harlowe is one trustee; your cousin Morden is the other: insist upon your right to your uncle; and write to your cousin Morden about it. This, I dare say, will make them alter their behaviour to you.

Your insolent brother—what has he to do to controul you?—Were it me [I wish it were for one month, and no more] I'd shew him the difference. I would be in my own mansion, pursuing my charming schemes, and making all around me happy. I would set up my own chariot. I would visit them when they deserved it. But when my brother and sister gave themselves airs, I would let them know, that I was their sister, and not their servant: and, if that did not do, I would shut my gates against them; and bid them go and be company for each other.

It must be confessed, however, that this brother and sister of yours, judging as such narrow spirits will ever judge, have some reason for treating you as they do. It must have long been a mortification to them (set disappointed love on her side, and avarice on his, out of the question) to be so much eclipsed by a younger sister. Such a sun in a family, where there are none but faint twinklers, how could they bear it! Why, my dear, they must look upon you as a prodigy among them: and prodigies, you know, though they obtain our admiration, never attract our love. The distance between you and them is immense. Their eyes ache to look up at you. What shades does your full day of merit cast upon them! Can you wonder, then, that they should embrace the first opportunity that offered, to endeavour to bring you down to their level?

Depend upon it, my dear, you will have more of it, and more still, as you bear it.

As to this odious Solmes, I wonder not at your aversion to him. It is needless to say any thing to you, who have so sincere any antipathy to him, to strengthen your dislike: Yet, who can resist her own talents? One of mine, as I have heretofore said, is to give an ugly likeness. Shall I indulge it?—I will. And the rather, as, in doing so, you will have my opinion in justification of your aversion to him, and in approbation of a steadiness that I ever admired, and must for ever approve of, in your temper.

'I was twice in this wretch's company. At one of the times your Lovelace was there. I need not mention to you, who have such a pretty curiosity, (though at present, only a curiosity, you know,) the unspeakable difference.

'Lovelace entertained the company in his lively gay way, and made every body laugh at one of his stories. It was before this creature was thought of for you. Solmes laughed too. It was, however, his laugh: for his first three years, at least, I imagine, must have been one continual fit of crying; and his muscles have never yet been able to recover a risible tone. His very smile [you never saw him smile, I believe; never at least gave him cause to smile] is so little natural to his features, that it appears to him as hideous as the grin of a man in malice.

'I took great notice of him, as I do of all the noble lords of the creation, in their peculiarities; and was disgusted, nay, shocked at him, even then. I was glad, I remember, on that particular occasion, to see his strange features recovering their natural gloominess; though they did this but slowly, as if the muscles which contributed to his distortions, had turned upon rusty springs.

'What a dreadful thing must even the love of such a husband be! For my part, were I his wife! (But what have I done to myself, to make such a supposition?) I should never have comfort but in his absence, or when I was quarreling with him. A splenetic woman, who must have somebody to find fault with, might indeed be brought to endure such a wretch: the sight of him would always furnish out the occasion, and all her servants, for that reason, and for that only, would have cause to blame their master. But how grievous and apprehensive a thing it must be for his wife, had she the least degree of delicacy, to catch herself in having done something to oblige him?

'So much for his person. As to the other half of him, he is said to be an insinuating, creeping mortal to any body he hopes to be a gainer by: an insolent, overbearing one, where he has no such views: And is not this the genuine spirit of meanness? He is reported to be spiteful and malicious, even to the whole family of any single person who has once disobliged him; and to his own relations most of all. I am told, that they are none of them such wretches as himself. This may be one reason why he is for disinheriting them.

'My Kitty, from one of his domestics, tells me, that his tenants hate him: and that he never had a servant who spoke well of him. Vilely suspicious of their wronging him (probably from the badness of his own heart) he is always changing.

'His pockets, they say, are continually crammed with keys: so that, when he would treat a guest, (a friend he has not out of your family), he is half as long puzzling which is which, as his niggardly treat might be concluded in. And if it be wine, he always fetches it himself. Nor has he much trouble in doing so; for he has very few visiters—only those, whom business or necessity brings: for a gentleman who can help it, would rather be benighted, than put up at his house.'

Yet this is the man they have found out (for considerations as sordid as those he is governed by) for a husband, that is to say, for a lord and master, for Miss Clarissa Harlowe!

But, perhaps, he may not be quite so miserable as he is represented. Characters extremely good, or extremely bad, are seldom justly given. Favour for a person will exalt the one, as disfavour will sink the other. But your uncle Antony has told my mother, who objected to his covetousness, that it was intended to tie him up, as he called it, to your own terms; which would be with a hempen, rather than a matrimonial, cord, I dare say. But, is not this a plain indication, that even his own recommenders think him a mean creature; and that he must be articled with—perhaps for necessaries? But enough, and too much, of such a wretch as this!—You must not have him, my dear,—that I am clear in—though not so clear, how you will be able to avoid it, except you assert the independence to which your estate gives you a title.

Here my mother broke in upon me. She wanted to see what I had written. I was silly enough to read Solmes's character to her.

She owned, that the man was not the most desirable of men; and that he had not the happiest appearance: But what, said she, is person in a man? And I was chidden for setting you against complying with your father's will. Then followed a lecture on the preference to be given in favour of a man who took care to discharge all his obligations to the world, and to keep all together, in opposition to a spendthrift or profligate. A fruitful subject you know, whether any particular person be meant by it, or not.

Why will these wise parents, by saying too much against the persons they dislike, put one upon defending them? Lovelace is not a spendthrift; owes not obligations to the world; though, I doubt not, profligate enough. Then, putting one upon doing such but common justice, we must needs be prepossessed, truly!—And so perhaps we are put upon curiosities first, that is to say, how such a one or his friends may think of one: and then, but too probably, comes in a distinguishing preference, or something that looks exceedingly like it.

My mother charged me at last, to write that side over again.—But excuse me, my good Mamma! I would not have the character lost upon any consideration; since my vein ran freely into it: and I never wrote to please myself, but I pleased you. A very good reason why—we have but one mind between us—only, that sometimes you are a little too grave, methinks; I, no doubt, a little too flippant in your opinion.

This difference in our tempers, however, is probably the reason that we love one another so well, that in the words of Norris, no third love can come in betwixt. Since each, in the other's eye, having something amiss, and each loving the other well enough to bear being told of it (and the rather perhaps as neither wishes to mend it); this takes off a good deal from that rivalry which might encourage a little (if not a great deal) of that latent spleen, which in time might rise into envy, and that into ill-will. So, my dear, if this be the case, let each keep her fault, and much good may do her with it: and what an hero or heroine must he or she be, who can conquer a constitutional fault? Let it be avarice, as in some I dare not name: let it be gravity, as in my best friend: or let it be flippancy, as in—I need not say whom.

It is proper to acquaint you, that I was obliged to comply with my mother's curiosity, [my mother has her share, her full share, of curiosity, my dear,] and to let her see here-and-there some passages in your letters—

I am broken in upon—but I will tell you by-and-by what passed between my mother and me on this occasion—and the rather, as she had her GIRL, her favourite HICKMAN, and your LOVELACE, all at once in her eye, in her part of the conversation.

Thus it was.

'I cannot but think, Nancy, said she, after all, that there is a little hardship in Miss Harlowe's case: and yet (as her mother says) it is a grating thing to have a child, who was always noted for her duty in smaller points, to stand in opposition to her parents' will in the greater; yea, in the greatest of all. And now, to middle the matter between both, it is pity, that the man they favour has not that sort of merit which a person of a mind so delicate as that of Miss Harlowe might reasonably expect in a husband.—But then, this man is surely preferable to a libertine: to a libertine too, who has had a duel with her own brother; fathers and mothers must think so, were it not for that circumstance—and it is strange if they do not know best.'

And so they must, thought I, from their experience, if no little dirty views give them also that prepossession in one man's favour, which they are so apt to censure their daughters for having in another's—and if, as I may add in your case, they have no creeping, old, musty uncle Antonys to strengthen their prepossessions, as he does my mother's. Poor, creeping, positive soul, what has such an old bachelor as he to do, to prate about the duties of children to parents; unless he had a notion that parents owe some to their children? But your mother, by her indolent meekness, let me call it, has spoiled all the three brothers.

'But you see, child, proceeded my mother, what a different behaviour MINE is to YOU. I recommend to you one of the soberest, yet politest, men in England—'

I think little of my mother's politest, my dear. She judges of honest Hickman for her daughter, as she would have done, I suppose, twenty years ago, for herself.

'Of a good family, continued my mother; a fine, clear, and improving estate [a prime consideration with my mother, as well as with some other folks, whom you know]: and I beg and I pray you to encourage him: at least not to use him the worse, for his being so obsequious to you.'

Yes, indeed! To use him kindly, that he may treat me familiarly—but distance to the men-wretches is best—I say.

'Yet all will hardly prevail upon you to do as I would have you. What would you say, were I to treat you as Miss Harlowe's father and mother treat her?

'What would I say, Madam!—That's easily answered. I would say nothing. Can you think such usage, and to such a young lady, is to be borne?

'Come, come, Nancy, be not so hasty: you have heard but one side; and that there is more to be said is plain, by your reading to me but parts of her letters. They are her parents. They must know best. Miss Harlowe, as fine a child as she is, must have done something, must have said something, (you know how they loved her,) to make them treat her thus.

'But if she should be blameless, Madam, how does your own supposition condemn them?'

Then came up Solmes's great estate; his good management of it—'A little too NEAR indeed,' was the word!—[O how money-lovers, thought I, will palliate! Yet my mother is a princess in spirit to this Solmes!] 'What strange effects, added she, have prepossession and love upon young ladies!'

I don't know how it is, my dear; but people take high delight in finding out folks in love. Curiosity begets curiosity. I believe that's the thing.

She proceeded to praise Mr. Lovelace's person, and his qualifications natural and acquired. But then she would judge as mothers will judge, and as daughters are very loth to judge: but could say nothing in answer to your offer of living single; and breaking with him—if—if—[three or four if's she made of one good one, if] that could be depended on.

But still obedience without reserve, reason what I will, is the burden of my mother's song: and this, for my sake, as well as for yours.

I must needs say, that I think duty to parents is a very meritorious excellence. But I bless God I have not your trials. We can all be good when we have no temptation nor provocation to the contrary: but few young persons (who can help themselves too as you can) would bear what you bear.

I will now mention all that is upon my mind, in relation to the behaviour of your father and uncles, and the rest of them, because I would not offend you: but I have now a higher opinion of my own sagacity, than ever I had, in that I could never cordially love any one of your family but yourself. I am not born to like them. But it is my duty to be sincere to my friend: and this will excuse her Anna Howe to Miss Clarissa Harlowe.

I ought indeed to have excepted your mother; a lady to be reverenced: and now to be pitied. What must have been her treatment, to be thus subjugated, as I may call it? Little did the good old viscount think, when he married his darling, his only daughter, to so well-appearing a gentleman, and to her own liking too, that she would have been so much kept down.

Another would call your father a tyrant, if I must not: all the world that know him, do call him so; and if you love your mother, you should not be very angry at the world for taking that liberty.

Yet, after all, I cannot help thinking, that she is the less to be pitied, as she may be said (be the gout, or what will, the occasion of his moroseness) to have long behaved unworthy of her birth and fine qualities, in yielding so much as she yields to encroaching spirits [you may confine the reflection to your brother, if it will pain you to extend it]; and this for the sake of preserving a temporary peace to herself; which was the less worth endeavouring to preserve, as it always produced a strength in the will of others, which subjected her to an arbitrariness that of course grew, and became established, upon her patience.—And now to give up the most deserving of her children (against her judgment) a sacrifice to the ambition and selfishness of the least deserving!—But I fly from this subject—having I fear, said too much to be forgiven—and yet much less than is in my heart to say upon the over-meek subject.

Mr. Hickman is expected from London this evening. I have desired him to inquire after Lovelace's life and conversation in town. If he has not inquired, I shall be very angry with him. Don't expect a very good account of either. He is certainly an intriguing wretch, and full of inventions.

Upon my word, I most heartily despise that sex! I wish they would let our fathers and mothers alone; teasing them to tease us with their golden promises, and protestations and settlements, and the rest of their ostentatious nonsense. How charmingly might you and I live together, and despise them all!—But to be cajoled, wire-drawn, and ensnared, like silly birds, into a state of bondage, or vile subordination; to be courted as princesses for a few weeks, in order to be treated as slaves for the rest of our lives. Indeed, my dear, as you say of Solmes, I cannot endure them!—But for your relations [friends no more will I call them, unworthy as they are even of the other name!] to take such a wretch's price as that; and to the cutting off of all reversions from his own family:—How must a mind but commonly just resist such a measure!

Mr. Hickman shall sound Lord M. upon the subject you recommend. But beforehand, I can tell you what he and what his sisters will say, when they are sounded. Who would not be proud of such a relation as Miss Clarissa Harlowe?—Mrs. Fortescue told me, that they are all your very great admirers.

If I have not been clear enough in my advice about what you shall do, let me say, that I can give it in one word: it is only by re-urging you to RESUME. If you do, all the rest will follow.

We are told here, that Mrs. Norton, as well as your aunt Hervey, has given her opinion on the implicit side of the question. If she can think, that the part she has had in your education, and your own admirable talents and acquirements, are to be thrown away upon such a worthless creature as Solmes, I could heartily quarrel with her. You may think I say this to lessen your regard for the good woman. And perhaps not wholly without cause, if you do. For, to own the truth, methinks, I don't love her so well as I should do, did you love her so apparently less, that I could be out of doubt, that you love me better.

Your mother tells you, 'That you will have great trials: that you are under your father's discipline.'—The word is enough for me to despise them who give occasion for its use.—'That it is out of her power to help you!' And again: 'That if you have any favour to hope for, it must be by the mediation of your uncles.' I suppose you will write to the oddities, since you are forbid to see them. But can it be, that such a lady, such a sister, such a wife, such a mother, has no influence in her own family? Who, indeed, as you say, if this be so, would marry, that can live single? My choler is again beginning to rise. RESUME, my dear: and that is all I will give myself time to say further, lest I offend you when I cannot serve you—only this, that I am

Your truly affectionate friend and servant, ANNA HOWE.

LETTER XXVIII

MISS CLARISSA HARLOWE, TO MISS HOWE FRIDAY, MARCH 10

You will permit me, my dear, to touch upon a few passages in your last letter, that affect me sensibly.

In the first place, you must allow me to say, low as I am in spirits, that I am very angry with you, for your reflections on my relations, particularly on my father and mother, and on the memory of my grandfather. Nor, my dear, does your own mother always escape the keen edge of your vivacity. One cannot one's self forbear to write or speak freely of those we love and honour, when grief from imagined hard treatment wrings the heart: but it goes against one to hear any body else take the same liberties. Then you have so very strong a manner of expression where you take a distaste, that when passion has subdued, and I come (upon reflection) to see by your severity what I have given occasion for, I cannot help condemning myself.

But least of all can I bear that you should reflect upon my mother. What, my dear, if her meekness should not be rewarded? Is the want of reward, or the want even of a grateful acknowledgement, a reason for us to dispense with what we think our duty? They were my father's lively spirits that first made him an interest in her gentle bosom. They were the same spirits turned inward, as I have heretofore observed,* that made him so impatient when the cruel malady seized him. He always loved my mother: And would not LOVE and PITY excusably, nay laudably, make a good wife (who was an hourly witness of his pangs, when labouring under a paroxysm, and his paroxysms becoming more and more frequent, as well as more and more severe) give up her own will, her own likings, to oblige a husband, thus afflicted, whose love for her was unquestionable?—And if so, was it not too natural [human nature is not perfect, my dear] that the husband thus humoured by the wife, should be unable to bear controul from any body else, much less contradiction from his children?

* *See Letter V.*

If then you would avoid my highest displeasure, you must spare my mother: and, surely, you will allow me, with her, to pity, as well as to love and honour my father.

I have no friend but you to whom I can appeal, to whom I dare complain. Unhappily circumstanced as I am, it is but too probable that I shall complain, because it is but too probably that I shall have more and more cause given me for complaint. But be it your part, if I do, to sooth my angry passions, and to soften my resentments; and this the rather, as you know what an influence your advice has upon me; and as you must also know, that the freedoms you take with my friends, can have no other tendency, but to weaken the sense of my duty to them, without answering any good end to myself.

I cannot help owning, however, that I am pleased to have you join with me in opinion of the contempt which Mr. Solmes deserves from me. But yet, permit me to say, that he is not quite so horrible a creature as you make him: as to his person, I mean; for with regard to his mind, by all I have heard, you have done him but justice: but you have such a talent at an ugly likeness, and such a vivacity, that they sometimes carry you out of verisimilitude. In short, my dear, I have known you, in more instances than one, sit down resolved to write all that wit, rather than strict justice, could suggest upon the given occasion. Perhaps it may be thought, that I should say the less on this particular subject, because your dislike of him arises from love to me: But should it not be our aim to judge of ourselves, and of every thing that affects us, as we may reasonably imagine other people would judge of us and of our actions?

As to the advice you give, to resume my estate, I am determined not to litigate with my father, let what will be the consequence to myself. I may give you, at another time, a more particular answer to your reasonings on this subject: but, at present, will only observe, that it is in my opinion, that Lovelace himself would hardly think me worth addressing, were he to know this would be my resolution. These men, my dear, with all their flatteries, look forward to the PERMANENT. Indeed, it is fit they should. For love must be a very foolish thing to look back upon, when it has brought persons born to affluence into indigence, and laid a generous mind under obligation and dependence.

You very ingeniously account for the love we bear to one another, from the difference in our tempers. I own, I should not have thought of that. There may possibly be something in it: but whether there be or not, whenever I am cool, and give myself time to reflect, I will love you the better for the correction you give, be as severe as you will upon me. Spare me not, therefore, my dear friend, whenever you think me in the least faulty. I love your agreeable raillery: you know I always did: nor, however over-serious you think me, did I ever think you flippant, as you harshly call it. One of the first conditions of our mutual friendship was, each should say or write to the other whatever was upon her mind, without any offence to be taken: a condition, that is indeed indispensable in friendship.

I knew your mother would be for implicit obedience in a child. I am sorry my case is so circumstanced, that I cannot comply. It would be my duty to do so, if I could. You are indeed very happy, that you have nothing but your own agreeable, yet whimsical, humours to contend with, in the choice she invites you to make of Mr. Hickman. How happy I should be, to be treated with so much lenity!—I should blush to have my mother say, that she begged and prayed me, and all in vain, to encourage a man so unexceptionable as Mr. Hickman.

Indeed, my beloved Miss Howe, I am ashamed to have your mother say, with ME in her view, 'What strange effects have prepossession and love upon young creatures of our sex!' This touches me the more sensibly, because you yourself, my dear, are so ready to persuade me into it.

I should be very blamable to endeavour to hide any the least bias upon my mind, from you: and I cannot but say—that this man—this Lovelace—is a man that might be liked well enough, if he bore such a character as Mr. Hickman bears; and even if there were hopes of reclaiming him. And further still I will acknowledge, that I believe it possible that one might be driven, by violent measures, step by step, as it were, into something that might be called—I don't know what to call it—a conditional kind of liking, or so. But as to the word LOVE—justifiable and charming as it is in some cases, (that is to say, in all the relative, in all the social, and, what is still beyond both, in all our superior duties, in which it may be properly called divine;) it has, methinks, in the narrow, circumscribed, selfish, peculiar sense, in which you apply it to me, (the man too so little to be approved of for his morals, if all that report says of him be true,) no pretty sound with it. Treat me as freely as you will in all other respects, I will love you, as I have said, the better for your friendly freedom. But, methinks, I could be glad that you would not let this imputation pass so glibly from your pen, or your lips, as attributable to one of your own sex, whether I be the person or not: since the other must have a double triumph, when a person of your delicacy (armed with such contempts of them all, as you would have one think) can give up a friend, with an exultation over her weakness, as a silly, love-sick creature.

I could make some other observations upon the contents of your last two letters; but my mind is not free enough at present. The occasion for the above stuck with me; and I could not help taking the earliest notice of them.

Having written to the end of my second sheet, I will close this letter, and in my next, acquaint you with all that has happened here since my last.

LETTER XXIX

MISS CLARISSA HARLOWE, TO MISS HOWE SATURDAY, MARCH 11

I have had such taunting messages, and such repeated avowals of ill offices, brought me from my brother and sister, if I do no comply with their wills, (delivered, too, with provoking sauciness by Betty Barnes,) that I have thought it proper, before I entered upon my intended address to my uncles, in pursuance of the hint given me in my mother's letter, to expostulate a little with them. But I have done it in such a manner, as will give you (if you please to take it as you have done some parts of my former letters) great advantage over me. In short, you will have more cause than ever, to declare me far gone in love, if my reasons for the change of my style in these letters, with regard to Mr. Lovelace, do not engage your more favourable opinion.—For I have thought proper to give them their own way: and, since they will have it, that I have a preferable regard for Mr. Lovelace, I give them cause rather to confirm their opinion than doubt it.

These are my reasons in brief, for the alteration of my style.

In the first place, they have grounded their principal argument for my compliance with their will, upon my acknowledgement that my heart is free; and so, supposing I give up no preferable person, my opposition has the look of downright obstinacy in their eyes; and they argue, that at worst, my aversion to Solmes is an aversion that may be easily surmounted, and ought to be surmounted in duty to my father, and for the promotion of family views.

Next, although they build upon this argument in order to silence me, they seem not to believe me, but treat me as disgracefully, as if I were in love with one of my father's footmen: so that my conditional willingness to give up Mr. Lovelace has procured me no favour.

In the next place, I cannot but think, that my brother's antipathy to Mr. Lovelace is far from being well grounded: the man's inordinate passion for the sex is the crime that is always rung in my ears: and a very great one it is: But, does my brother recriminate upon him thus in love to me?—No—his whole behaviour shews me, that that is not his principal motive, and that he thinks me rather in his way than otherwise.

It is then the call of justice, as I may say, to speak a little in favour of a man, who, although provoked by my brother, did not do him all the mischief he could have done him, and which my brother had endeavoured to do him. It might not be amiss therefore, I thought, to alarm them a little with apprehension, that the methods they are taking with me are the very reverse of those they should take to answer the end they design by them. And after all, what is the compliment I make Mr. Lovelace, if I allow it to be thought that I do really prefer him to such a man as him they terrify me with? Then, my Miss Howe [concluded I] accuses me of a tameness which subject me to insults from my brother: I will keep that dear friend in my eye; and for all these considerations, try what a little of her spirit will do—sit it ever so awkwardly upon me.

In this way of thinking, I wrote to my brother and sister. This is my letter to him.

TREATED as I am, and, in a great measure, if not wholly, by your instigations, Brother, you must permit me to expostulate with you upon the occasion. It is not my intention to displease you in what I am going to write: and yet I must deal freely with you: the occasion calls for it.

And permit me, in the first place, to remind you, that I am your sister; and not your servant; and that, therefore, the bitter revilings and passionate language brought me from you, upon an occasion in which you have no reason to prescribe to me, are neither worthy of my character to bear, nor of yours to offer.

Put the case, that I were to marry the man you dislike: and that he were not to make a polite or tender husband, Is that a reason for you to be an unpolite and disobliging brother?—Why must you, Sir, anticipate my misfortunes, were such a case to happen?—Let me tell you plainly, that the man who could treat me as a wife, worse than you of late have treated me as a sister, must be a barbarous man indeed.

Ask yourself, I pray you, Sir, if you would thus have treated your sister Bella, had she thought fit to receive the addresses of the man so much hated by you?—If not, let me caution you, my Brother, not to take your measures by what you think will be borne, but rather by what ought to be offered.

How would you take it, if you had a brother, who, in a like case, were to act by you, as you do by me?—You cannot but remember what a laconic answer you gave even to my father, who recommended to you Miss Nelly

D'Oily—You did not like her, were your words: and that was thought sufficient.

You must needs think, that I cannot but know to whom to attribute my disgraces, when I recollect my father's indulgence to me, permitting me to decline several offers; and to whom, that a common cause is endeavoured to be made, in favour of a man whose person and manners are more exceptional than those of any of the gentlemen I have been permitted to refuse.

I offer not to compare the two men together: nor is there indeed the least comparison to be made between them. All the difference to the one's disadvantage, if I did, is but one point—of the greatest importance, indeed—But to whom of most importance?—To myself, surely, were I to encourage his application: of the least to you. Nevertheless, if you do not, by your strange politics, unite that man and me as joint sufferers in one cause, you shall find me as much resolved to renounce him, as I am to refuse the other. I have made an overture to this purpose: I hope you will not give me reason to confirm my apprehensions, that it will be owing to you if it be not accepted.

It is a sad thing to have it to say, without being conscious of ever having given you cause of offence, that I have in you a brother, but not a friend.

Perhaps you will not condescend to enter into the reasons of your late and present conduct with a foolish sister. But if politeness, if civility, be not due to that character, and to my sex, justice is.

Let me take the liberty further to observe, that the principal end of a young man's education at the university, is, to learn him to reason justly, and to subdue the violence of his passions. I hope, Brother, that you will not give room for any body who knows us both, to conclude, that the toilette has taught the one more of the latter doctrine, than the university has taught the other. I am truly sorry to have cause to say, that I have heard it often remarked, that your uncontrouled passions are not a credit to your liberal education.

I hope, Sir, that you will excuse the freedom I have taken with you: you have given me too much reason for it, and you have taken much greater with me, without reason:—so, if you are offended, ought to look at the cause, and not at the effect:—then examining yourself, that cause will cease, and there will not be any where a more accomplished gentleman than my brother.

Sisterly affection, I do assure you, Sir, (unkindly as you have used me,) and not the pertness which of late you have been so apt to impute to me, is my motive in this hint. Let me invoke your returning kindness, my only brother! And give me cause, I beseech you, to call you my compassionating friend. For I am, and ever will be,

Your affectionate sister, CLARISSA HARLOWE.

This is my brother's answer.

TO MISS CLARISSA HARLOWE

I KNOW there will be no end of your impertinent scribble, if I don't write to you. I write therefore: but, without entering into argument with such a conceited and pert preacher and questioner, it is, to forbid you to plague me with your quaint nonsense. I know not what wit in a woman is good for, but to make her overvalue herself, and despise every other person. Yours, Miss Pert, has set you above your duty, and above being taught or prescribed to, either by parents, or any body else. But go on, Miss: your mortification will be the greater; that's all, child. It shall, I assure you, if I can make it so, so long as you prefer that villainous Lovelace, (who is justly hated by all your family) to every body. We see by your letter now (what we too justly suspected before), most evidently we see, the hold he has got of your forward heart. But the stronger the hold, the greater must be the force (and you shall have enough of that) to tear such a miscreant from it. In me, notwithstanding your saucy lecturing, and your saucy reflections before, you are sure of a friend, as well as of a brother, if it be not your own fault. But if you will still think of such a wretch as that Lovelace, never expect either friend or brother in

JA. HARLOWE. ***

I will now give you a copy of my letter to my sister; with her answer.

IN what, my dear Sister, have I offended you, that instead of endeavouring to soften my father's anger against me, (as I am sure I should have done for you, had my unhappy case been yours,) you should, in so hard-hearted a manner, join to aggravate not only his displeasure, but my mother's against me. Make but my case your own, my dear Bella; and suppose you were commanded to marry Mr. Lovelace, (to whom you are believed to have such an antipathy,) would you not think it a very grievous injunction?—Yet cannot your dislike to Mr. Lovelace be greater than mine is to Mr. Solmes. Nor are love and hatred voluntary passions.

My brother may perhaps think it a proof of a manly spirit, to shew himself an utter stranger to the gentle passions. We have both heard him boast, that he never loved with distinction: and, having predominating passions, and checked in his first attempt, perhaps he never will. It is the less wonder, then, raw from the college, so lately himself the tutored, that he should set up for a tutor, a prescriber to our gentler sex, whose tastes and manners are differently formed: for what, according to his account, are colleges, but classes of tyrants, from the upper students over the lower, and from them to the tutor?—That he, with such masculine passions should endeavour to controul and bear down an unhappy sister, in a case where his antipathy, and, give me leave to say, his ambition [once you would have allowed the latter to be his fault] can be gratified by so doing, may not be quite so much to be wondered at—but that a sister should give up the cause of a sister, and join with him to set her father and mother against her, in a case that might have been her own—indeed, my Bella, this is not pretty in you.

There was a time that Mr. Lovelace was thought reclaimable, and when it was far from being deemed a censurable view to hope to bring back to the paths of virtue and honour, a man of his sense and understanding. I am far from wishing to make the experiment: but nevertheless will say, that if I have not a regard for him, the disgraceful methods taken to compel me to receive the addresses of such a man as Mr. Solmes are enough to induce it.

Do you, my Sister, for one moment, lay aside all prejudice, and compare the two men in their births, their educations, their persons, their understandings, their manners, their air, and their whole deportments; and in their fortunes too, taking in reversions; and then judge of both; yet, as I have frequently offered, I will live single with all my heart, if that will do.

I cannot thus live in displeasure and disgrace. I would, if I could, oblige all my friends. But will it be just, will it be honest, to marry a man I cannot endure? If I have not been used to oppose the will of my father, but have always delighted to oblige and obey, judge of the strength of my antipathy, by the painful opposition I am obliged to make, and cannot help it.

Pity then, my dearest Bella, my sister, my friend, my companion, my adviser, as you used to be when I was happy, and plead for

Your ever-affectionate, CL. HARLOWE.

*** TO MISS CLARY HARLOWE

Let it be pretty or not pretty, in your wise opinion, I shall speak my mind, I will assure you, both of you and your conduct in relation to this detested Lovelace. You are a fond foolish girl with all your wisdom. Your letter shews that enough in twenty places. And as to your cant of living single, nobody will believe you. This is one of your fetches to avoid complying with your duty, and the will of the most indulgent parents in the world, as yours have been to you, I am sure—though now they see themselves finely requited for it.

We all, indeed, once thought your temper soft and amiable: but why was it? You never were contradicted before: you had always your own way. But no sooner do you meet with opposition in your wishes to throw yourself away upon a vile rake, but you shew what you are. You cannot love Mr. Solmes! that's the pretence; but Sister, Sister, let me tell you, that is because Lovelace has got into your fond heart:—a wretch hated, justly hated, by us all; and who has dipped his hands in the blood of your brother: yet him you would make our relation, would you?

I have no patience with you, but for putting the case of my liking such a vile wretch as him. As to the encouragement you pretend he received formerly from all our family, it was before we knew him to be so vile: and the proofs that had such force upon us, ought to have had some upon you:—and would, had you not been a foolish forward girl; as on this occasion every body sees you are.

O how you run out in favour of the wretch!—His birth, his education, his person, his understanding, his manners, his air, his fortune—reversions too taken in to augment the surfeiting catalogue! What a fond string of lovesick praises is here! And yet you would live single—Yes, I warrant!—when so many imaginary perfections dance before your dazzled eye!—But no more—I only desire, that you will not, while you seem to have such an opinion of your wit, think every one else a fool; and that you can at pleasure, by your whining flourishes, make us all dance after your lead.

Write as often as you will, this shall be the last answer or notice you shall have upon this subject from

ARABELLA HARLOWE. ***

I had in readiness a letter for each of my uncles; and meeting in the garden a servant of my uncle Harlowe, I gave him to deliver according to their respective directions. If I am to form a judgment by the answers I have received from my brother and sister, as above, I must not, I doubt, expect any good from those letters. But when I have tried every expedient, I shall have the less to blame myself for, if any thing unhappy should fall out. I will send you copies of both, when I shall see what notice they will be thought worthy of, if of any.

LETTER XXX

MISS CLARISSA HARLOWE, TO MISS HOWE SUNDAY NIGHT, MARCH 12

This man, this Lovelace, gives me great uneasiness. He is extremely bold and rash. He was this afternoon at our church—in hopes to see me, I suppose: and yet, if he had such hopes, his usual intelligence must have failed him.

Shorey was at church; and a principal part of her observation was upon his haughty and proud behaviour when he turned round in the pew where he sat to our family-pew. My father and both my uncles were there; so were my mother and sister. My brother happily was not.—They all came home in disorder. Nor did the congregation mind any body but him; it being his first appearance there since the unhappy rencounter.

What did the man come for, if he intended to look challenge and defiance, as Shorey says he did, and as others, it seems, thought he did, as well as she? Did he come for my sake; and, by behaving in such a manner to those present of my family, imagine he was doing me either service or pleasure?—He knows how they hate him: nor will he take pains, would pains do, to obviate their hatred.

You and I, my dear, have often taken notice of his pride; and you have rallied him upon it; and instead of exculpating himself, he has owned it: and by owning it he has thought he has done enough.

For my own part, I thought pride in his case an improper subject for raillery.—People of birth and fortune to be proud, is so needless, so mean a vice!—If they deserve respect, they will have it, without requiring it. In other words, for persons to endeavour to gain respect by a haughty behaviour, is to give a proof that they mistrust their own merit: To make confession that they know that their actions will not attract it.—Distinction or quality may be prided in by those to whom distinction or quality is a new thing. And then the reflection and contempt which such bring upon themselves by it, is a counter-balance.

Such added advantages, too, as this man has in his person and mien: learned also, as they say he is: Such a man to be haughty, to be imperious!—The lines of his own face at the same time condemning him—how wholly inexcusable!—Proud of what? Not of doing well: the only justifiable pride.—Proud of exterior advantages!—Must not one be led by such a stop-short pride, as I may call it, in him or her who has it, to mistrust the interior? Some people may indeed be afraid, that if they did not assume, they would be trampled upon. A very narrow fear, however, since they trample upon themselves, who can fear this. But this man must be secure that humility would be an ornament to him.

He has talents indeed: but those talents and his personal advantages have been snares to him. It is plain they have. And this shews, that, weighed in an equal balance, he would be found greatly wanting.

Had my friends confided as they did at first, in that discretion which they do not accuse me of being defective in, I dare say I should have found him out: and then should have been as resolute to dismiss him, as I was to dismiss others, and as I am never to have Mr. Solmes. O that they did but know my heart!—It shall sooner burst, than voluntarily, uncompelled, undriven, dictate a measure that shall cast a slur either upon them, or upon my sex.

Excuse me, my dear friend, for these grave soliloquies, as I may call them. How have I run from reflection to reflection!—But the occasion is recent—They are all in commotion below upon it.

Shorey says, that Mr. Lovelace watched my mother's eye, and bowed to her: and she returned the compliment. He always admired my mother. She would not, I believe, have hated him, had she not been bid to hate him: and had it not been for the rencounter between him and her only son.

Dr. Lewen was at church; and observing, as every one else did, the disorder into which Mr. Lovelace's appearance* had put all our family, was so good as to engage him in conversation, when the service was over, till they were all gone to their coaches.

** See Letter XXXI, for Mr. Lovelace's account of his*

behaviour and intentions in his appearance at church.

My uncles had my letters in the morning. They, as well as my father, are more and more incensed against me, it seems. Their answers, if they vouchsafe to answer me, will demonstrate, I doubt not, the unseasonableness of this rash man's presence at our church.

They are angry also, as I understand, with my mother, for returning his compliment. What an enemy is hatred, even to the common forms of civility! which, however, more distinguish the payer of a compliment, than the receiver. But they all see, they say, that there is but one way to put an end to his insults. So I shall suffer: And in what will the rash man have benefited himself, or mended his prospects?

I am extremely apprehensive that this worse than ghost-like appearance of his, bodes some still bolder step. If he come hither (and very desirous he is of my leave to come) I am afraid there will be murder. To avoid that, if there were no other way, I would most willingly be buried alive.

They are all in consultation—upon my letters, I suppose—so they were in the morning; which occasioned my uncles to be at our church. I will send you the copies of those letters, as I promised in my last, when I see whether I can give you their answers with them. This letter is all—I cannot tell what—the effect of apprehension and displeasure at the man who has occasioned my apprehensions. Six lines would have contained all that is in it to the purpose of my story.

CL. H.

LETTER XXXI

MR. LOVELACE, TO JOHN BELFORD, ESQ. MONDAY, MARCH 13

In vain dost thou* and thy compeers press me to go to town, while I am in such an uncertainty as I am in at present with this proud beauty. All the ground I have hitherto gained with her is entirely owing to her concern for the safety of people whom I have reason to hate.

> **These gentlemen affected what they called the Roman style (to wit, the thee and the thou) in their letters: and it was an agreed rule with them, to take in good part whatever freedoms they treated each other with, if the passages were written in that style.*

Write then, thou biddest me, if I will not come. That, indeed, I can do; and as well without a subject, as with one. And what follows shall be a proof of it.

The lady's malevolent brother has now, as I told thee at M. Hall, introduced another man; the most unpromising in his person and qualities, the most formidable in his offers, that has yet appeared.

This man has by his proposals captivated every soul of the Harlowes—Soul! did I say—There is not a soul among them but my charmer's: and she, withstanding them all, is actually confined, and otherwise maltreated by a father the most gloomy and positive; at the instigation of a brother the most arrogant and selfish. But thou knowest their characters; and I will not therefore sully my paper with them.

But is it not a confounded thing to be in love with one, who is the daughter, the sister, the niece, of a family, I must eternally despise? And, the devil of it, that love increasing with her—what shall I call it?—'Tis not scorn:—'Tis not pride:—'Tis not the insolence of an adored beauty:—But 'tis to virtue, it seems, that my difficulties are owin; and I pay for not being a sly sinner, an hypocrite; for being regardless of my reputation; for permittin slander to open its mouth against me. But is it necessary for such a one as I, who have been used to carry all before me, upon my own terms—I, who never inspired a fear, that had not a discernibly-predominant mixture of love in it, to be a hypocrite?—Well says the poet:

He who seems virtuous does but act a part;
And shews not his own nature, but his art.

Well, but it seems I must practise for this art, if it would succeed with this truly-admirable creature; but why practise for it?—Cannot I indeed reform?—I have but one vice;—Have I, Jack?—Thou knowest my heart, if any man living does. As far as I know it myself, thou knowest it. But 'tis a cursed deceiver; for it has many a time imposed upon its master—Master, did I say? That I am not now; nor have I been from the moment I beheld this angel of a woman. Prepared indeed as I was by her character before I saw her: For what a mind must that be, which, though not virtuous itself, admires not virtue in another?—My visit to Arabella, owing to a mistake of the sister, into which, as thou hast heard me say, I was led by the blundering uncle; who was to introduce me (but lately come from abroad) to the divinity, as I thought; but, instead of her, carried me to a mere mortal. And much difficulty had I, so fond and forward my lady! to get off without forfeiting all with a family I intended should give me a goddess.

I have boasted that I was once in love before:—and indeed I thought I was. It was in my early manhood—with that quality jilt, whose infidelity I have vowed to revenge upon as many of the sex as shall come into my power. I believe, in different climes, I have already sacrificed an hecatomb to my Nemesis, in pursuance of this vow. But upon recollecting what I was then, and comparing it with what I find myself now, I cannot say that I was ever in love before.

What was it then, dost thou ask me, since the disappointment had such effects upon me, when I found myself jilted, that I was hardly kept in my senses?—Why, I'll grant thee what, as near as I can remember; for it was a great while ago:—It was—Egad, Jack, I can hardly tell what it was—but a vehement aspiration after a novelty, I think. Those confounded poets, with their terrenely-celestial descriptions, did as much with me as the lady: they fired my imagination, and set me upon a desire to become a goddess-maker. I must needs try my new-fledged pinions in sonnet, elogy, and madrigal. I must have a Cynthia, a Stella, a Sacharissa, as well as the best of them: darts and flames, and the devil knows what, must I give to my cupid. I must create beauty, and place it where nobody else could find it: and many a time have I been at a loss for a subject, when my new-created goddess has been kinder than it was proper for my plaintive sonnet that she should be.

Then I found I had a vanity of another sort in my passion: I found myself well received among the women in general; and I thought it a pretty lady-like tyranny [I was then very young, and very vain!] to single out some one of the sex, to make half a score jealous. And I can tell thee, it had its effect: for many an eye have I made to sparkle with rival indignation: many a cheek glow; and even many a fan have I caused to be snapped at a sister-beauty; accompanied with a reflection perhaps at being seen alone with a wild young fellow who could not be in private with both at once.

In short, Jack, it was more pride than love, as I now find it, that put me upon making such a confounded rout about losing that noble varletess. I thought she loved me at least as well as I believed I loved her: nay, I had the vanity to suppose she could not help it. My friends were pleased with my choice. They wanted me to be shackled: for early did they doubt my morals, as to the sex. They saw, that the dancing, the singing, the musical ladies were all fond of my company: For who [I am in a humour to be vain, I think!]—for who danced, who sung, who touched the string, whatever the instrument, with a better grace than thy friend?

I have no notion of playing the hypocrite so egregiously, as to pretend to be blind to qualifications which every one sees and acknowledges. Such praise-begetting hypocrisy! Such affectedly disclaimed attributes! Such contemptible praise-traps!—But yet, shall my vanity extend only to personals, such as the gracefulness of dress, my debonnaire, and my assurance?—Self-taught, self-acquired, these!—For my parts, I value not myself upon them. Thou wilt say, I have no cause.—Perhaps not. But if I had any thing valuable as to intellectuals, those are not my own; and to be proud of what a man is answerable for the abuse of, and has no merit in the right use of, is to strut, like the jay, in borrowed plumage.

But to return to my fair jilt. I could not bear, that a woman, who was the first that had bound me in silken fetters [they were not iron ones, like those I now wear] should prefer a coronet to me: and when the bird was flown, I set more value upon it, that when I had it safe in my cage, and could visit in when I pleased.

But now am I indeed in love. I can think of nothing, of nobody, but the divine Clarissa Harlowe—Harlowe!—How that hated word sticks in my throat—But I shall give her for it the name of Love.*

* Lovelace.

CLARISSA! O there's music in the name,
That, soft'ning me to infant tenderness,
Makes my heart spring like the first leaps of life!

But couldst thou have believed that I, who think it possible for me to favour as much as I can be favoured; that I, who for this charming creature think of foregoing the life of honour for the life of shackles; could adopt these over-tender lines of Otway?

I checked myself, and leaving the first three lines of the following of Dryden to the family of whiners, find the workings of the passion in my stormy soul better expressed by the three last:

Love various minds does variously inspire:
He stirs in gentle natures gentle fires;
Like that of incense on the alter laid.

But raging flames tempestuous souls invade:
A fire which ev'ry windy passion blows;
With pride it mounts, and with revenge it glows.

And with REVENGE it shall glow!—For, dost thou think, that if it were not from the hope, that this stupid family are all combined to do my work for me, I would bear their insults?—Is it possible to imagine, that I would be braved as I am braved, threatened as I am threatened, by those who are afraid to see me; and by this brutal brother, too, to whom I gave a life; [a life, indeed, not worth my taking!] had I not a greater pride in knowing that by means of his very spy upon me, I am playing him off as I please; cooling or inflaming his violent passions as may best suit my purposes; permitting so much to be revealed of my life and actions, and intentions, as may give him such a confidence in his double-faced agent, as shall enable me to dance his employer upon my own wires?

This it is that makes my pride mount above my resentment. By this engine, whose springs I am continually oiling, I play them all off. The busy old tarpaulin uncle I make but my ambassador to Queen Anabella Howe, to engage her (for example-sake to her princessly daughter) to join in their cause, and to assert an authority they are resolved, right or wrong, (or I could do nothing,) to maintain.

And what my motive, dost thou ask? No less than this, That my beloved shall find no protection out of my family; for, if I know hers, fly she must, or have the man she hates. This, therefore, if I take my measures right, and my familiar fail me not, will secure her mine, in spite of them all; in spite of her own inflexible heart: mine, without condition; without reformation-promises; without the necessity of a siege of years, perhaps; and to be even then, after wearing the guise of merit-doubting hypocrisy, at an uncertainty, upon a probation unapproved of. Then shall I have all the rascals and rascalesses of the family come creeping to me: I prescribing to them; and bringing that sordidly imperious brother to kneel at the footstool of my throne.

All my fear arises from the little hold I have in the heart of this charming frost-piece: such a constant glow upon her lovely features: eyes so sparkling: limbs so divinely turned: health so florid: youth so blooming: air so animated—to have an heart so impenetrable: and I, the hitherto successful Lovelace, the addresser—How can it be? Yet there are people, and I have talked with some of them, who remember that she was born. Her nurse Norton boasts of her maternal offices in her earliest infancy; and in her education gradatim. So there is full proof, that she came not from above all at once an angel! How then can she be so impenetrable?

But here's her mistake; nor will she be cured of it—She takes the man she calls her father [her mother had been faultless, had she not been her father's wife]; she takes the men she calls her uncles; the fellow she calls her brother; and the poor contemptible she calls her sister; to be her father, to be her uncles, her brother, her sister; and that, as such, she owes to some of them reverence, to others respect, let them treat her ever so cruelly!—Sordid ties!—Mere cradle prejudices!—For had they not been imposed upon her by Nature, when she was in a perverse humour, or could she have chosen her relations, would any of these have been among them?

How my heart rises at her preference of them to me, when she is convinced of their injustice to me! Convinced, that the alliance would do honour to them all—herself excepted; to whom every one owes honour; and from whom the most princely family might receive it. But how much more will my heart rise with indignation against her, if I find she hesitates but one moment (however persecuted) about preferring me to the man she avowedly hates! But she cannot surely be so mean as to purchase her peace with them at so dear a rate. She cannot give a sanction to projects formed in malice, and founded in a selfishness (and that at her own expense) which she has spirit enough to despise in others; and ought to disavow, that we may not think her a Harlowe.

By this incoherent ramble thou wilt gather, that I am not likely to come up in haste; since I must endeavour first to obtain some assurance from the beloved of my soul, that I shall not be sacrificed to such a wretch as Solmes! Woe be to the fair one, if ever she be driven into my power (for I despair of a voluntary impulse in my favour) and I find a difficulty in obtaining this security.

That her indifference to me is not owing to the superior liking she has for any other, is what rivets my chains. But take care, fair one; take care, O thou most exalted of female minds, and loveliest of persons, how thou debasest thyself by encouraging such a competition as thy sordid relations have set on foot in mere malice to me!—Thou wilt say I rave. And so I do:

Perdition catch my soul, but I do love her.

Else, could I hear the perpetual revilings of her implacable family?—Else, could I basely creep about—not her proud father's house—but his paddock and garden walls?—Yet (a quarter of a mile distance between us) not hoping to behold the least glimpse of her shadow?—Else, should I think myself repaid, amply repaid, if the fourth, fifth, or sixth midnight stroll, through unfrequented paths, and over briery enclosures, affords me a few cold lines; the even expected purport only to let me know, that she values the most worthless person of her very worthless family, more than she values me; and that she would not write at all, but to induce me to bear insults, which unman me to bear?—My lodging in the intermediate way at a wretched alehouse; disguised like an inmate of it: accommodations equally vile, as those I met with in my Westphalian journey. 'Tis well, that the necessity for all this arise not from scorn and tyranny! but is first imposed upon herself!

But was ever hero in romance (fighting with giants and dragons excepted) called upon to harder trials?—Fortune and family, and reversionary grandeur on my side! Such a wretched fellow my competitor!—Must I not be deplorably in love, that can go through these difficulties, encounter these contempts?—By my soul, I am half ashamed of myself: I, who am perjured too, by priority of obligation, if I am faithful to any woman in the world?

And yet, why say I, I am half ashamed?—Is it not a glory to love her whom every one who sees her either loves, or reveres, or both? Dryden says,

The cause of love can never be assign'd:
'Tis in no face;—but in the lover's mind.
—And Cowley thus addresses beauty as a mere imaginary:

Beauty! thou wild fantastic ape,
Who dost in ev'ry country change thy shape:
Here black; there brown; here tawny; and there white!
Thou flatt'rer, who comply'st with ev'ry sight!
Who hast no certain what, nor where.

But both these, had they been her contemporaries, and known her, would have confessed themselves mistaken: and, taking together person, mind, and behaviour, would have acknowledged the justice of the universal voice in her favour.

—Full many a lady

I've ey'd with best regard; and many a time
Th' harmony of their tongues hath into bondage
Brought my too-diligent ear. For sev'ral virtues
Have I liked several women. Never any
With so full a soul, but some defect in her
Did quarrel with the noblest grace she ow'd,
And put it to the foil. But SHE!—O SHE!
So perfect and so peerless is created,
Of ev'ry creature's best.

SHAKESP.

Thou art curious to know, if I have not started a new game? If it be possible for so universal a lover to be confined so long to one object?—Thou knowest nothing of this charming creature, that thou canst put such questions to me; or thinkest thou knowest me better than thou dost. All that's excellent in her sex is this lady!—Until by MATRIMONIAL or EQUAL intimacies, I have found her less than angel, it is impossible to think of any other. Then there are so many stimulatives to such a spirit as mine in this affair, besides love: such a field of stratagem and contrivance, which thou knowest to be the delight of my heart. Then the rewarding end of all!—To carry off such a girl as this, in spite of all her watchful and implacable friends; and in spite of a prudence and reserve that I never met with in any of the sex;—what a triumph!—What a triumph over the whole sex!—And then such a revenge to gratify; which is only at present politically reined in, eventually to break forth with greater fury—Is it possible, thinkest thou, that there can be room for a thought that is not of her, and devoted to her?

By the devices I have this moment received, I have reason to think, that I shall have occasion for thee here. Hold thyself in readiness to come down upon the first summons.

Let Belton, and Mowbray, and Tourville, likewise prepare themselves. I have a great mind to contrive a method to send James Harlowe to travel for improvement. Never was there a booby 'squire that more wanted it. Contrive it, did I say? I have already contrived it; could I but put it in execution without being suspected to have a hand in it. This I am resolved upon; if I have not his sister, I will have him.

But be this as it may, there is a present likelihood of room for glorious mischief. A confederacy had been for some time formed against me; but the uncles and the nephew are now to be double-servanted [single-servanted they were before]; and those servants are to be double armed when they attend their masters abroad. This indicates their resolute enmity to me, and as resolute favour to Solmes.

The reinforced orders for this hostile apparatus are owing it seems to a visit I made yesterday to their church.—A good place I thought to begin a reconciliation in; supposing the heads of the family to be christians, and that they meant something by their prayers. My hopes were to have an invitation (or, at least, to gain a pretence) to accompany home the gloomy sire; and so get an opportunity to see my goddess: for I believed they durst not but be civil to me, at least. But they were filled with terror it seems at my entrance; a terror they could not get over. I saw it indeed in their countenances; and that they all expected something extraordinary to follow.—And so it should have done, had I been more sure than I am of their daughter's favour. Yet not a hair of any of their stupid heads do I intend to hurt.

You shall all have your directions in writing, if there be occasion. But after all, I dare say there will be no need but to shew your faces in my company.

Such faces never could four men shew—Mowbray's so fierce and so fighting: Belton's so pert and so pimply: Tourville's so fair and so foppish: thine so rough and so resolute: and I your leader!—What hearts, although meditating hostility, must those be which we shall not appall?—Each man occasionally attended by a servant or two, long ago chosen for qualities resembling those of his master.

Thus, Jack, as thou desirest, have I written.—Written upon something; upon nothing; upon REVENGE, which I love; upon LOVE, which I hate, heartily hate, because 'tis my master: and upon the devil knows what besides: for looking back, I am amazed at the length of it. Thou mayest read it: I would not for a king's ransom. But so as I do but write, thou sayest thou wilt be pleased.

Be pleased then. I command thee to be pleased: if not for the writer's or written sake, for thy word's sake. And so in the royal style (for am I not likely to be thy king and thy emperor in the great affair before us?) I bid thee very heartily

Farewell.

LETTER XXXII

MISS CLARISSA HARLOWE, TO MISS HOWE TUESDAY, MARCH 14

I now send you copies of my letters to my uncles: with their answers. Be pleased to return the latter by the first deposit. I leave them for you to make remarks upon. I shall make none.

TO JOHN HARLOWE, ESQ. SAT. MARCH 11.

Allow me, my honoured second Papa, as in my happy days you taught me to call you, to implore your interest with my Papa, to engage him to dispense with a command, which, if insisted upon, will deprive me of my free-will, and make me miserable for my whole life.

For my whole life! let me repeat: Is that a small point, my dear Uncle, to give up? Am not I to live with the man? Is any body else? Shall I not therefore be allowed to judge for myself, whether I can, or cannot, live happily with him?

Should it be ever so unhappily, will it be prudence to complain or appeal? If it were, to whom could I appeal with effect against a husband? And would not the invincible and avowed dislike I have for him at setting out, seem to justify any ill usage from him, in that state, were I to be ever so observant of him? And if I were to be at all observant of him, it must be from fear, not love.

Once more, let me repeat, That this is not a small point to give up: and that it is for life. Why, I pray you, good Sir, should I be made miserable for life? Why should I be deprived of all comfort, but that which the hope that it would be a very short one, would afford me?

Marriage is a very solemn engagement, enough to make a young creature's heart ache, with the best prospects, when she thinks seriously of it!—To be given up to a strange man; to be engrafted into a strange family; to give up her very name, as a mark of her becoming his absolute and dependent property; to be obliged to prefer this strange man to father, mother—to every body:—and his humours to all her own—or to contend, perhaps, in breach of avowed duty, for every innocent instance of free-will.

To go no where; to make acquaintance; to give up acquaintance; to renounce even the strictest friendships, perhaps; all at his pleasure, whether she thinks it reasonable to do so or not. Surely, Sir, a young creature ought not to be obliged to make all these sacrifices but for such a man as she can love. If she be, how sad must be the case! How miserable the life, if it can be called life!

I wish I could obey you all. What a pleasure would it be to me, if I could!—Marry first, and love will come after, was said by one of my dearest friends! But this is a shocking assertion. A thousand thing may happen to make that state but barely tolerable, where it is entered into with mutual affections: What must it then be, where the husband can have no confidence in the love of his wife: but has reason rather to question it, from the preference he himself believes she would have given to somebody else, had she had her own option? What doubts, what jealousies, what want of tenderness, what unfavourable prepossessions, will there be, in a matrimony thus circumstanced! How will every look, every action, even the most innocent, be liable to misconstruction!—While, on the other hand, an indifference, a carelessness to oblige, may take place; and fear only can constrain even an appearance of what ought to be the effect of undisguised love!

Think seriously of these things, dear, good Sir, and represent them to my father in that strong light which the subject will bear; but in which my sex, and my tender years and inexperience, will not permit me to paint it; and use your powerful interest, that your poor niece may not be consigned to a misery so durable.

I offered to engage not to marry at all, if that condition may be accepted. What a disgrace is it to me to be thus sequestered from company, thus banished my papa's and mamma's presence; thus slighted and deserted by you, Sir, and my other kind uncle! And to be hindered from attending at that public worship, which, were I out of the way of my duty, would be most likely to reduce me into the right path again!—Is this the way, Sir; can this be thought to be the way to be taken with a free and open spirit? May not this strange method rather harden than convince? I cannot bear to live in disgrace thus. The very servants so lately permitted to be under my own direction, hardly daring to speak to me; my own servant discarded with high marks of undeserved suspicion and displeasure, and my sister's maid set over me.

The matter may be too far pushed.—Indeed it may.—And then, perhaps, every one will be sorry for their parts in it.

May I be permitted to mention an expedient?—'If I am to be watched, banished, and confined; suppose, Sir, it were to be at your house?'—Then the neighbouring gentry will the less wonder, that the person of whom they used to think so favourably, appear not at church here; and that she received not their visits.

I hope there can be no objection to this. You used to love to have me with you, Sir, when all went happily with me: And will you not now permit me, in my troubles, the favour of your house, till all this displeasure is overblown?—Upon my word, Sir, I will not stir out of doors, if you require the contrary of me: nor will I see any body, but whom you will allow me to see; provided Mr. Solmes be not brought to persecute me there.

Procure, then, this favour for me; if you cannot procure the still greater, that of a happy reconciliation (which nevertheless I presume to hope for, if you will be so good as to plead for me); and you will then add to those favours and to that indulgence, which have bound me, and will for ever bind me to be

Your dutiful and obliged niece, CLARISSA HARLOWE.

THE ANSWER SUNDAY NIGHT. MY DEAR NIECE,

It grieves me to be forced to deny you any thing you ask. Yet it must be so; for unless you can bring your mind to oblige us in this one point, in which our promises and honour were engaged before we believed there could be so sturdy an opposition, you must never expect to be what you have been to us all.

In short, Niece, we are in an embattled phalanx. Your reading makes you a stranger to nothing but what you should be most acquainted with. So you will see by that expression, that we are not to be pierced by your persuasions, and invincible persistence. We have agreed all to be moved, or none; and not to comply without one another. So you know your destiny; and have nothing to do but to yield to it.

Let me tell you, the virtue of obedience lies not in obliging when you can be obliged again. But give up an inclination, and there is some merit in that.

As to your expedient; you shall not come to my house, Miss Clary; though this is a prayer I little thought I ever should have denied you: for were you to keep your word as to seeing nobody but whom we please, yet can you write to somebody else, and receive letters from him. This we too well know you can, and have done—more is the shame and the pity!

You offer to live single, Miss—we wished you married: but because you may not have the man your heart is set upon, why, truly, you will have nobody we shall recommend: and as we know, that somehow or other you correspond with him, or at least did as long as you could; and as he defies us all, and would not dare to do so, if he were not sure of you in spite of us all, (which is not a little vexatious to us, you must think,) we are resolved to frustrate him, and triumph over him, rather than that he should triumph over us: that's one word for all. So expect not any advocateship from me: I will not plead for you; and that's enough. From

Your displeased uncle, JOHN HARLOWE.

P.S. For the rest I refer to my brother Antony.

*** TO ANTONY HARLOWE, ESQ. SATURDAY, MARCH 11. HONOURED SIR,

As you have thought fit to favour Mr. Solmes with your particular recommendation, and was very earnest in his behalf, ranking him (as you told me, upon introducing him to me) among your select friends; and expecting my regards to him accordingly; I beg your patience, while I offer a few things, out of many that I could offer, to your serious consideration, on occasion of his address to me, if I am to use that word.

I am charged with prepossession in another person's favour. You will be pleased, Sir, to remember, that till my brother returned from Scotland, that other person was not absolutely discouraged, nor was I forbid to receive his visits. I believe it will not be pretended, that in birth, education, or personal endowments, a comparison can be made between the two. And only let me ask you, Sir, if the one would have been thought of for me, had he not made such offers, as, upon my word, I think, I ought not in justice to accept of, nor he to propose: offers, which if he had not made, I dare say, my papa would not have required them of him.

But the one, it seems, has many faults:—Is the other faultless?—The principal thing objected to Mr. Lovelace (and a very inexcusable one) is that he is immoral in his loves—Is not the other in his hatreds?—Nay, as I may say, in his loves too (the object only differing) if the love of money be the root of all evil.

But, Sir, if I am prepossessed, what has Mr. Solmes to hope for?—Why should he persevere? What must I think of the man who would wish me to be his wife against my inclination?—And is it not a very harsh thing for my friends to desire to see me married to one I cannot love, when they will not be persuaded but that there is one whom I do love?

Treated as I am, now is the time for me to speak out or never.—Let me review what it is Mr. Solmes depends upon on this occasion. Does he believe, that the disgrace which I supper on his account, will give him a merit with me? Does he think to win my esteem, through my uncles' sternness to me; by my brother's contemptuous usage; by my sister's unkindness; by being denied to visit, or be visited; and to correspond with my chosen friend, although a person of unexceptionable honour and prudence, and of my own sex; my servant to be torn from me, and another servant set over me; to be confined, like a prisoner, to narrow and disgraceful limits, in order avowedly to mortify me, and to break my spirit; to be turned out of that family-management which I loved, and had the greater pleasure in it, because it was an ease, as I thought, to my mamma, and what my sister chose not; and yet, though time hangs heavy upon my hands, to be so put out of my course, that I have as little inclination as liberty to pursue any of my choice delights?—Are these steps necessary to reduce me to a level so low, as to make me a fit wife for this man?—Yet these are all he can have to trust to. And if his reliance is on these measures, I would have him to know, that he mistakes meekness and gentleness of disposition for servility and baseness of heart.

I beseech you, Sir, to let the natural turn and bent of his mind and my mind be considered: What are his qualities, by which he would hope to win my esteem?—Dear, dear Sir, if I am to be compelled, let it be in favour of a man that can read and write—that can teach me something: For what a husband must that man make, who can do nothing but command; and needs himself the instruction he should be qualified to give?

I may be conceited, Sir; I may be vain of my little reading; of my writing; as of late I have more than once been told I am. But, Sir, the more unequal the proposed match, if so: the better opinion I have of myself, the worse I must have of him; and the more unfit are we for each other.

Indeed, Sir, I must say, I thought my friends had put a higher value upon me. My brother pretended once, that it was owing to such value, that Mr. Lovelace's address was prohibited.—Can this be; and such a man as Mr. Solmes be intended for me?

As to his proposed settlements, I hope I shall not incur your great displeasure, if I say, what all who know me have reason to think (and some have upbraided me for), that I despise those motives. Dear, dear Sir, what are settlements to one who has as much of her own as she wishes for?—Who has more in her own power, as a single person, than it is probable she would be permitted to have at her disposal, as a wife?—Whose expenses and ambition are moderate; and who, if she had superfluities, would rather dispense them to the necessitous, than lay them by her useless? If then such narrow motives have so little weight with me for my own benefit, shall the remote and uncertain view of family-aggrandizements, and that in the person of my brother and his descendents, be thought sufficient to influence me?

Has the behaviour of that brother to me of late, or his consideration for the family (which had so little weight with him, that he could choose to hazard a life so justly precious as an only son's, rather than not ratify passions which he is above attempting to subdue, and, give me leave to say, has been too much indulged in, either with regard to his own good, or the peace of any body related to him;) Has his behaviour, I say, deserved of me in particular, that I should make a sacrifice of my temporal (and, who knows? of my eternal) happiness, to promote a plan formed upon chimerical, at least upon unlikely, contingencies; as I will undertake to demonstrate, if I may be permitted to examine it?

I am afraid you will condemn my warmth: But does not the occasion require it? To the want of a greater degree of earnestness in my opposition, it seems, it is owing, that such advances have been made, as have been made. Then, dear Sir, allow something, I beseech you, for a spirit raised and embittered by disgraces, which (knowing my own heart) I am confident to say, are unmerited.

But why have I said so much, in answer to the supposed charge of prepossession, when I have declared to my mamma, as now, Sir, I do to you, that if it be not insisted upon that I shall marry any other person, particularly this Mr. Solmes, I will enter into any engagements never to have the other, nor any man else, without their consents; that is to say, without the consents of my father and my mother, and of you my uncle, and my elder uncle, and my cousin Morden, as he is one of the trustees for my grandfather's bounty to me?—As to my brother indeed, I cannot say, that his treatment of me has been of late so brotherly, as to entitle him to more than civility from me: and for this, give me leave to add, he would be very much my debtor.

If I have not been explicit enough in declaring my dislike to Mr. Solmes (that the prepossession which is charged upon me may not be supposed to influence me against him) I do absolutely declare, That were there no such man as Mr. Lovelace in the world, I would not have Mr. Solmes. It is necessary, in some one of my letters to my dear friends, that I should write so clearly as to put this matter out of all doubt: and to whom can I better address myself with an explicitness that can admit of no mistake, than to that uncle who professes the highest regard for plain-dealing and sincerity?

Let me, for these reasons, be still more particular in some of my exceptions to him.

Mr. Solmes appears to me (to all the world, indeed) to have a very narrow mind, and no great capacity: he is coarse and indelicate; as rough in his manners as in his person: he is not only narrow, but covetous: being possessed of great wealth, he enjoys it not; nor has the spirit to communicate to a distress of any kind. Does not his own sister live unhappily, for want of a little of his superfluities? And suffers not he his aged uncle, the brother of his own mother, to owe to the generosity of strangers the poor subsistence he picks up from half-a-dozen families?—You know, Sir, my open, free, communicative temper: how unhappy must I be, circumscribed in his narrow, selfish circle! out of which being with-held by this diabolical parsimony, he dare no more stir, than a conjurer out of his; nor would let me.

Such a man, as this, love!—Yes, perhaps he may, my grandfather's estate; which he has told several persons (and could not resist hinting the same thing tome, with that sort of pleasure which a low mind takes, when it intimates its own interest as a sufficient motive for it to expect another's favour) lies so extremely convenient for him, that it would double the value of a considerable part of his own. That estate, and an alliance which would do credit to his obscurity and narrowness, they make him think he can love, and induce him to believe he does: but at most, he is but a second-place love. Riches were, are, and always will be, his predominant passion. His were left him by a miser, on this very account: and I must be obliged to forego all the choice delights of my life, and be as mean as he, or else be quite unhappy. Pardon, Sir, this severity of expression—one is apt to say more than one would of a person one dislikes, when more is said in his favour than he can possibly deserve; and when he is urged to my acceptance with so much vehemence, that there is no choice left me.

Whether these things be perfectly so, or not, while I think they are, it is impossible I should ever look upon Mr. Solmes in the light he is offered to me. Nay, were he to be proved ten times better than I have represented him, and sincerely think him; yet would he be still ten times more disagreeable to me than any other man I know in the world. Let me therefore beseech you, Sir, to become an advocate for your niece, that she may not be made a victim to a man so highly disgustful to her.

You and my other uncle can do a great deal for me, if you please, with my papa. Be persuaded, Sir, that I am not governed by obstinacy in this case; but by aversion; an aversion I cannot overcome: for, if I have but endeavoured to reason with myself, (out of regard to the duty I owe to my father's will,) my heart has recoiled, and I have been averse to myself, for offering but to argue with myself, in behalf of a man who, in the light he appears to me, has no one merit; and who, knowing this aversion, could not persevere as he does, if he had the spirit of a man.

If, Sir, you can think of the contents of this letter reasonable, I beseech you to support them with your interest. If not—I shall be most unhappy!—Nevertheless, it is but just in me so to write, as that Mr. Solmes may know what he has to trust to.

Forgive, dear Sir, this tedious letter; and suffer it to have weight with you; and you will for ever oblige

Your dutiful and affectionate niece,

CL. HARLOWE. *** MR. ANTONY HARLOWE, TO MISS CL. HARLOWE NIECE CLARY,

You had better not write to us, or to any of us. To me, particularly, you had better never to have set pen to paper, on the subject whereon you have written. He that is first in his own cause, saith the wise man, seemeth just: but his neighbour cometh and searcheth him. And so, in this respect, I will be your neighbour: for I will search your heart to the bottom; that is to say, if your letter be written from your heart. Yet do I know what a task I have undertaken, because of the knack you are noted for at writing. But in defence of a father's authority, in behalf of the good, and honour, and prosperity of the family one comes of, what a hard thing it would be, if one could not beat down all the arguments a rebel child (how loth I am to write down that word of Miss Clary Harlowe!) can bring, in behalf of her obstinacy!

In the first place, don't you declare (and that contrary to your declarations to your mother, remember that, girl!) that you prefer the man we all hate, and who hates us as bad!—Then what a character have you given of a worthy man! I wonder you dare write so freely of one we all respect—but possibly it may be for that very reason.

How you begin your letter!—Because I value Mr. Solmes as my friend, you treat him the worse—That's the plain dunstable of the matter, Miss!—I am not such a fool but I can see that.—And so a noted whoremonger is to be chosen before a man who is a money-lover!—Let me tell you, Niece, this little becomes so nice a one as you have been always reckoned. Who, think you, does more injustice, a prodigal man or a saving man?—The one saves his own money; the other spends other people's. But your favourite is a sinner in grain, and upon record.

The devil's in your sex! God forgive me for saying so—the nicest of them will prefer a vile rake and wh—— I suppose I must not repeat the word:—the word will offend, when the vicious denominated by that word will be chosen!—I had not been a bachelor to this time, if I had not seen such a mass of contradictions in you all.—Such gnat-strainers and camel-swallowers, as venerable Holy Writ has it.

What names will perverseness call things by!—A prudent man, who intends to be just to every body, is a covetous man!—While a vile, profligate rake is christened with the appellation of a gallant man; and a polite man, I'll warrant you!

It is my firm opinion, Lovelace would not have so much regard for you as he professes, but for two reasons. And what are these?—Why, out of spite to all of us—one of them. The other, because of your independent fortune. I wish your good grandfather had not left what he did so much in your own power, as I may say. But little did he imagine his beloved grand-daughter would have turned upon all her friends as she has done!

What has Mr. Solmes to hope for, if you are prepossessed! Hey-day! Is this you, cousin Clary!—Has he then nothing to hope for from your father's, and mother's, and our recommendations?—No, nothing at all, it seems!—O brave!—I should think that this, with a dutiful child, as we took you to be, was enough. Depending on this your duty, we proceeded: and now there is no help for it: for we will not be balked: neither shall our friend Mr. Solmes, I can tell you that.

If your estate is convenient for him, what then? Does that (pert cousin) make it out that he does not love you? He had need to expect some good with you, that has so little good to hope for from you; mind that. But pray, is not this estate our estate, as we may say? Have we not all an interest in it, and a prior right, if right were to have taken place? And was it not more than a good old man's dotage, God rest his soul! that gave it you before us all?—Well then, ought we not to have a choice who shall have it in marriage with you? and would you have the conscience to wish us to let a vile fellow, who hates us all, run away with it?—You bid me weigh what you write: do you weigh this, Girl: and it will appear we have more to say for ourselves than you was aware of.

As to your hard treatment, as you call it, thank yourself for that. It may be over when you will: so I reckon nothing upon that. You was not banished and confined till all entreaty and fair speeches were tried with you: mind that. And Mr. Solmes can't help your obstinacy: let that be observed too.

As to being visited, and visiting; you never was fond of either: so that's a grievance put into the scale to make weight.—As to disgrace, that's as bad to us as to you: so fine a young creature! So much as we used to brag of you too!—And besides, this is all in your power, as the rest.

But your heart recoils, when you would persuade yourself to obey your parent—Finely described, is it not!—Too truly described, I own, as you go on. I know that you may love him if you will. I had a good mind to bid you hate him; then, perhaps, you would like him the better: for I have always found a most horrid romantic perverseness in your sex.—To do and to love what you should not, is meat, drink, and vesture, to you all.

I am absolutely of your brother's mind, That reading and writing, though not too much for the wits of you young girls, are too much for your judgments.—You say, you may be conceited, Cousin; you may be vain!—And so you are, to despise this gentleman as you do. He can read and write as well as most gentlemen, I can tell you that. Who told you Mr. Solmes cannot read and write? But you must have a husband who can learn you something!—I wish you knew but your duty as well as you do your talents—that, Niece, you have of late days to learn; and Mr. Solmes will therefore find something to instruct you in. I will not shew him this letter of yours, though you seem to desire it, lest it should provoke him to be too severe a schoolmaster, when you are his'n.

But now I think of it, suppose you are the reader at your pen than he—You will make the more useful wife to him; won't you? For who so good an economist as you?—And you may keep all of his accounts, and save yourselves a steward.—And, let me tell you, this is a fine advantage in a family: for those stewards are often sad dogs, and creep into a man's estate before he knows where he is; and not seldom is he forced to pay them interest for his own money.

I know not why a good wife should be above these things. It is better than lying a-bed half the day, and junketing and card-playing all the night, and making yourselves wholly useless to every good purpose in your own families, as is now the fashion among ye. The duce take you all that do so, say I!—Only that, thank my stars, I am a bachelor.

Then this is a province you are admirably versed in: you grieve that it is taken from you here, you know. So here, Miss, with Mr. Solmes you will have something to keep account of, for the sake of you and your children: with the other, perhaps you will have an account to keep, too—but an account of what will go over the left shoulder; only of what he squanders, what he borrows, and what he owes, and never will pay. Come, come, Cousin, you know nothing of the world; a man's a man; and you may have many partners in a handsome man, and costly ones too, who may lavish away all you save. Mr. Solmes therefore for my money, and I hope for yours.

But Mr. Solmes is a coarse man. He is not delicate enough for your niceness; because I suppose he dresses not like a fop and a coxcomb, and because he lays not himself out in complimental nonsense, the poison of female minds. He is a man of sense, that I can tell you. No man talks more to the purpose to us: but you fly him so, that he has no opportunity given him, to express it to you: and a man who loves, if he have ever so much sense, looks a fool; especially when he is despised, and treated as you treated him the last time he was in your company.

As to his sister; she threw herself away (as you want to do) against his full warning: for he told her what she had to trust to, if she married where she did marry. And he was as good as his word; and so an honest man ought: offences against warning ought to be smarted for. Take care this be not your case: mind that.

His uncle deserves no favour from him; for he would have circumvented Mr. Solmes, and got Sir Oliver to leave to himself the estate he had always designed for him his nephew, and brought him up in the hope of it. Too ready forgiveness does but encourage offences: that's your good father's maxim: and there would not be so many headstrong daughters as there are, if this maxim were kept in mind.—Punishments are of service to offenders; rewards should be only to the meriting: and I think the former are to be dealt out rigourously, in willful cases.

As to his love; he shews it but too much for your deservings, as they have been of late; let me tell you that: and this is his misfortune; and may in time perhaps be yours.

As to his parsimony, which you wickedly call diabolical, [a very free word in your mouth, let me tell ye], little reason have you of all people for this, on whom he proposes, of his own accord, to settle all he has in the world: a proof, let him love riches as he will, that he loves you better. But that you may be without excuse on this score, we will tie him up to your own terms, and oblige him by the marriage-articles to allow you a very handsome quarterly sum to do what you please with. And this has been told you before; and I have said it to Mrs. Howe (that good and worthy lady) before her proud daughter, that you might hear of it again.

To contradict the charge of prepossession to Lovelace, you offer never to have him without our consents: and what is this saying, but that you will hope on for our consents, and to wheedle and tire us out? Then he will always be in expectation while you are single: and we are to live on at this rate (are we?) vexed by you, and continually watchful about you; and as continually exposed to his insolence and threats. Remember last Sunday, Girl!—What might have happened, had your brother and he met?—Moreover, you cannot do with such a spirit as his, as you can with worthy Mr. Solmes: the one you make tremble; the other will make you quake: mind that—and you will not be able to help yourself. And remember, that if there should be any misunderstanding between one of them and you, we should all interpose; and with effect, no doubt: but with the other, it would be self-do, self-have; and who would either care or dare to put in a word for you? Nor let the supposition of matrimonial differences frighten you: honey-moon lasts not now-a-days above a fortnight; and Dunmow flitch, as I have been informed, was never claimed; though some say once it was. Marriage is a queer state, Child, whether paired by the parties or by their friends. Out of three brothers of us, you know, there was but one had courage to marry. And why was it, do you think? We were wise by other people's experience.

Don't despise money so much: you may come to know the value of it: that is a piece of instruction that you are to learn; and which, according to your own notions, Mr. Solmes will be able to teach you.

I do indeed condemn your warmth. I will not allow for disgraces you bring upon yourself. If I thought them unmerited, I would be your advocate. But it was always my notion, that children should not dispute their parents' authority. When your grandfather left his estate to you, though his three sons, and a grandson, and your elder sister, were in being, we all acquiesced: and why? Because it was our father's doing. Do you imitate that example: if you will not, those who set it you have the more reason to hold you inexcusable: mind that, Cousin.

You mention your brother too scornfully: and, in your letter to him, are very disrespectful; and so indeed you are to your sister, in the letter you wrote to her. Your brother, Madam, is your brother; and third older than yourself, and a man: and pray be so good as not to forget what is due to a brother, who (next to us three brothers) is the head of the family, and on whom the name depends—as upon your dutiful compliance laid down for the honour of the family you are come of. And pray now let me ask you, If the honour of that will not be an honour to you?—If you don't think so, the more unworthy you. You shall see the plan, if you promise not to be prejudiced against it right or wrong. If you are not besotted to that man, I am sure you will like it. If you are, were Mr. Solmes an angel, it would signify nothing: for the devil is love, and love is the devil, when it gets into any of your heads. Many examples have I seen of that.

If there were no such man as Lovelace in the world, you would not have Mr. Solmes.—You would not, Miss!—Very pretty, truly!—We see how your spirit is embittered indeed.—Wonder not, since it is come to your will not's, that those who have authority over you, say, You shall have the other. And I am one: mind that. And if it behoves YOU to speak out, Miss, it behoves US not to speak in. What's sauce for the goose is sauce for the gander: take that in your thought too.

I humbly apprehend, that Mr. Solmes has the spirit of a man, and a gentleman. I would admonish you therefore not to provoke it. He pities you as much as he loves you. He says, he will convince you of his love by deeds, since he is not permitted by you to express it by words. And all his dependence is upon your generosity hereafter. We hope he may depend upon that: we encourage him to think he may. And this heartens him up. So that you may lay his constancy at your parents' and your uncles' doors; and this will be another mark of your duty, you know.

You must be sensible, that you reflect upon your parents, and all of us, when you tell me you cannot in justice accept of the settlements proposed to you. This reflection we should have wondered at from you once; but now we don't.

There are many other very censurable passages in this free letter of yours; but we must place them to the account of your embittered spirit. I am glad you mentioned that word, because we should have been at a loss what to have called it.—I should much rather nevertheless have had reason to give it a better name.

I love you dearly still, Miss. I think you, though my niece, one of the finest young gentlewomen I ever saw. But, upon my conscience, I think you ought to obey your parents, and oblige me and my brother John: for you know very well, that we have nothing but your good at heart: consistently indeed with the good and honour of all of us. What must we think of any one of it, who would not promote the good of the whole? and who would set one part of it against another?—Which God forbid, say I!—You see I am for the good of all. What shall I get by it, let things go as they will? Do I want any thing of any body for my own sake?—Does my brother John?—Well, then, Cousin Clary, what would you be at, as I may say?

O but you can't love Mr. Solmes!—But, I say, you know not what you can do. You encourage yourself in your dislike. You permit your heart (little did I think it was such a froward one) to recoil. Take it to task, Niece; drive it on as fast as it recoils, [we do so in all our sea-fights, and land-fights too, by our sailors and soldiers, or we should not conquer]; and we are all sure you will overcome it. And why? Because you ought. So we think, whatever you think: and whose thoughts are to be preferred? You may be wittier than we; but, if you were wiser, we have lived some of us, let me tell you, to very little purpose, thirty or forty years longer than you.

I have written as long a letter as yours. I may not write in so lively, or so polite a style as my Niece: but I think I have all the argument on my side: and you will vastly oblige me, if you will shew me, by your compliance with all our desires, that you think so too. If you do not, you must not expect an advocate, or even a friend, in me, dearly as I love you. For then I shall be sorry to be called

Your uncle, ANT. HARLOWE.

TUESDAY, TWO IN THE MORNING. POSTSCRIPT.

You must send me no more letters: but a compliable one you may send. But I need not have forbid you; for I am sure this, by fair argument, is unanswerable—I know it is. I have written day and night, I may say, ever since Sunday morning, only church-time, or the like of that: but this is the last, I can tell you, from

ANT. H.

LETTER XXXIII

MISS CLARISSA HARLOWE, TO MISS HOWE THURSDAY, MARCH 16

Having met with such bad success in my application to my relations, I have taken a step that will surprise you. It is no other than writing a letter to Mr. Solmes himself. I sent it, and have his answer. He had certainly help in it. For I have seen a letter of his, and indifferently worded, as poorly spelt. Yet the superscription is of his dictating, I dare say, for he is a formal wretch. With these, I shall enclose one from my brother to me, on occasion of mine to Mr. Solmes. I did think that it was possible to discourage the man from proceeding; and if I could have done that, it would have answered all my wishes. It was worth the trial. But you'll see nothing will do. My brother has taken his measures too securely.

TO ROGER SOLMES, ESQ. WEDNESDAY, MARCH 15. SIR,

You will wonder to receive a letter from me; and more still at the uncommon subject of it. But the necessity of the case will justify me, at least in my own apprehension; and I shall therefore make no other apology for it.

When you first came acquainted with our family, you found the writer of this one of the happiest creatures in the world; beloved by the best and most indulgent of parents; and rejoicing in the kind favour of two affectionate uncles, and in the esteem of every one.

But how is this scene now changed!—You was pleased to cast a favourable eye upon me. You addressed yourself to my friends: your proposals were approved of by them—approved of without consulting me; as if my choice and happiness were of the least signification. Those who had a right to all reasonable obedience from me, insisted upon it without reserve. I had not the felicity to think as they did; almost the first time my sentiments differed from theirs. I besought them to indulge me in a point so important to my future happiness: but, alas, in vain! And then (for I thought it was but honest) I told you my mind; and even that my affections were engaged. But, to my mortification and surprise, you persisted, and still persist.

The consequence of all is too grievous for me to repeat: you, who have such free access to the rest of the family, know it too well—too well you know it, either for the credit of your own generosity, or for my reputation. I am used, on your account, as I never before was used, and never before was thought to deserve to be used; and this was the hard, the impossible, condition of their returning favour, that I must prefer a man to all others, that of all others I cannot prefer.

Thus distressed, and made unhappy, and all to your sake, and through your cruel perseverance, I write, Sir, to demand of you the peace of mind you have robbed me of: to demand of you the love of so many dear friends, of which you have deprived me; and, if you have the generosity that should distinguish a man, and a gentleman, to adjure you not to continue an address that has been attended with such cruel effects to the creature you profess to esteem.

If you really value me, as my friends would make me believe, and as you have declared you do, must it not be a mean and selfish value? A value that can have no merit with the unhappy object of it, because it is attended with effects so grievous to her? It must be for your own sake only, not for mine. And even in this point you must be mistaken: For, would a prudent man wish to marry one who has not a heart to give? Who cannot esteem him? Who therefore must prove a bad wife!—And how cruel would it be to make a poor creature a bad wife, whose pride it would be to make a good one!

If I am capable of judging, our tempers and inclinations are vastly different. Any other of my sex will make you happier than I can. The treatment I meet with, and the obstinacy, as it is called, with which I support myself under it, ought to convince you of this; were I not able to give so good a reason for this my supposed perverseness, as that I cannot consent to marry a man whom I cannot value.

But if, Sir, you have not so much generosity in your value for me, as to desist for my own sake, let me conjure you, by the regard due to yourself, and to your own future happiness, to discontinue your suit, and place your affections on a worthier object: for why should you make me miserable, and yourself not happy? By this means you will do all that is now in your power to restore to me the affection of my friends; and, if that can be, it will leave me in as happy a state as you found me in. You need only to say, that you see there are no HOPES, as you will perhaps complaisantly call it, of succeeding with me [and indeed, Sir, there cannot be a greater truth]; and that you will therefore no more think of me, but turn your thoughts another way.

Your compliance with this request will lay me under the highest obligation to your generosity, and make me ever

Your well-wisher, and humble servant, CLARISSA HARLOWE.

TO MISS CLARISSA HARLOWE These most humbly present.

DEAREST MISS,

Your letter has had a very contrary effect upon me, to what you seem to have expected from it. It has doubly convinced me of the excellency of your mind, and of the honour of your disposition. Call it selfish, or what you please, I must persist in my suit; and happy shall I be, if by patience and perseverance, and a steady and unalterable devoir, I may at last overcome the difficulty laid in my way.

As your good parents, your uncles, and other friends, are absolutely determined you shall never have Mr. Lovelace, if they can help it; and as I presume no other person is in the way, I will contentedly wait the issue of this matter. And forgive me, dearest Miss, but a person should sooner persuade me to give up to him my estate, as an instance of my generosity, because he could not be happy without it, than I would a much more valuable treasure, to promote the felicity of another, and make his way easier to circumvent myself.

Pardon me, dear Miss; but I must persevere, though I am sorry you suffer on my account, as you are pleased to think; for I never before saw the woman I could love: and while there is any hope, and that you remain undisposed of to some happier man, I must and will be

Your faithful and obsequious admirer, ROGER SOLMES.

MARCH 16. *** MR. JAMES HARLOWE, TO MISS CL. HARLOWE MARCH 16.

What a fine whim you took into your head, to write a letter to Mr. Solmes, to persuade him to give up his pretensions to you!—Of all the pretty romantic flights you have delighted in, this was certainly one of the most extraordinary. But to say nothing of what fires us all with indignation against you (your owning your prepossession in a villain's favour, and your impertinence to me, and your sister, and your uncles; one of which has given it you home, child), how can you lay at Mr. Solmes's door the usage you so bitterly complain of?—You know, little fool as you are, that it is your fondness for Lovelace that has brought upon you all these things;

and which would have happened, whether Mr. Solmes had honoured you with his addresses or not.

As you must needs know this to be true, consider, pretty witty Miss, if your fond, love-sick heart can let you consider, what a fine figure all your expostulations with us, and charges upon Mr. Solmes, make!—With what propriety do you demand of him to restore to you your former happiness (as you call it, and merely call it; for if you thought our favour so, you would restore it to yourself), since it is yet in your own power to do so? Therefore, Miss Pert, none of your pathetics, except in the right place. Depend upon it, whether you have Mr. Solmes, or not, you shall never have your heart's delight, the vile rake Lovelace, if our parents, if our uncles, if I, can hinder it. No! you fallen angel, you shall not give your father and mother such a son, nor me such a brother, in giving yourself that profligate wretch for a husband. And so set your heart at rest, and lay aside all thoughts of him, if ever you expect forgiveness, reconciliation, or a kind opinion, from any of your family; but especially from him, who, at present, styles himself

Your brother, JAMES HARLOWE.

P.S. I know your knack at letter-writing. If you send me an answer for this, I will return it unopened; for I will not argue with your perverseness in so plain a case—Only once for all, I was willing to put you right as to Mr. Solmes; whom I think to blame to trouble his head about you.

LETTER XXXIV

MR. LOVELACE, TO JOHN BELFORD, ESQ. FRIDAY, MARCH 17

I receive, with great pleasure, the early and cheerful assurances of your loyalty and love. And let our principal and most trusty friends named in my last know that I do.

I would have thee, Jack, come down, as soon as thou canst. I believe I shall not want the others so soon. Yet they may come down to Lord M.'s. I will be there, if not to receive them, to satisfy my lord, that there is no new mischief in hand, which will require his second intervention.

For thyself, thou must be constantly with me: not for my security: the family dare do nothing but bully: they bark only at a distance: but for my entertainment: that thou mayest, from the Latin and the English classics, keep my lovesick soul from drooping.

Thou hadst best come to me here, in thy old corporal's coat: thy servant out of livery; and to be upon a familiar footing with me, as a distant relation, to be provided for by thy interest above—I mean not in Heaven, thou mayest be sure. Thou wilt find me at a little alehouse, they call it an inn; the White Hart, most terribly wounded, (but by the weather only,) the sign: in a sorry village, within five miles from Harlowe-place. Every body knows Harlowe-place, for, like Versailles, it is sprung up from a dunghill, within every elderly person's remembrance. Every poor body, particularly, knows it: but that only for a few years past, since a certain angel has appeared there among the sons and daughters of men.

The people here at the Hart are poor, but honest; and have gotten it into their heads, that I am a man of quality in disguise; and there is no reining-in their officious respect. Here is a pretty little smirking daughter, seventeen six days ago. I call her my Rose-bud. Her grandmother (for there is no mother), a good neat old woman, as ever filled a wicker chair in a chimney-corner, has besought me to be merciful to her.

This is the right way with me. Many and many a pretty rogue had I spared, whom I did not spare, had my power been acknowledged, and my mercy in time implored. But the debellare superbos should be my motto, were I to have a new one.

This simple chit (for there is a simplicity in her thou wouldst be highly pleased with: all humble; all officious; all innocent—I love her for her humility, her officiousness, and even for her innocence) will be pretty amusement to thee; while I combat with the weather, and dodge and creep about the walls and purlieus of Harlowe-place. Thou wilt see in her mind, all that her superiors have been taught to conceal, in order to render themselves less natural, and of consequence less pleasing.

But I charge thee, that thou do not (what I would not permit myself to do for the world—I charge thee, that thou do not) crop my Rose-bud. She is the only flower of fragrance, that has blown in this vicinage for ten years past, or will for ten years to come: for I have looked backward to the have-been's, and forward to the will-be's; having but too much leisure upon my hands in my present waiting.

I never was so honest for so long together since my matriculation. It behoves me so to be—some way or other, my recess at this little inn may be found out; and it will then be thought that my Rose-bud has attracted me. A report in my favour, from simplicities so amiable, may establish me; for the grandmother's relation to my Rose-bud may be sworn to: and the father is an honest, poor man; has no joy, but in his Rose-bud.—O Jack! spare thou, therefore, (for I shall leave thee often alone with her, spare thou) my Rose-bud!—Let the rule I never departed from, but it cost me a long regret, be observed to my Rose-bud!—never to ruin a poor girl, whose simplicity and innocence were all she had to trust to; and whose fortunes were too low to save her from the rude contempts of worse minds than her own, and from an indigence extreme: such a one will only pine in secret; and at last, perhaps, in order to refuge herself from slanderous tongues and virulence, be induced to tempt some guilty stream, or seek her end in the knee-encircling garter, that peradventure, was the first attempt of abandoned love.—No defiances will my Rose-bud breathe; no self-dependent, thee-doubting watchfulness (indirectly challenging thy inventive machinations to do their worst) will she assume. Unsuspicious of her danger, the lamb's throat will hardly shun thy knife!—O be not thou the butcher of my lambkin!

The less thou be so, for the reason I am going to give thee—The gentle heart is touched by love: her soft bosom heaves with a passion she has not yet found a name for. I once caught her eye following a young carpenter, a widow neighbour's son, living [to speak in her dialect] at the little white house over the way. A gentle youth he also seems to be, about three years older than herself: playmates from infancy, till his eighteenth and her fifteenth year furnished a reason for a greater distance in shew, while their hearts gave a better for their being nearer than ever—for I soon perceived the love reciprocal. A scrape and a bow at first seeing his pretty mistress; turning often to salute her following eye; and, when a winding lane was to deprive him of her sight, his whole body turned round, his hat more reverently doffed than before. This answered (for, unseen, I was behind her) by a low courtesy, and a sigh, that Johnny was too far off to hear!—Happy whelp! said I to myself.—I withdrew; and in tript my Rose-bud, as if satisfied with the dumb shew, and wishing nothing beyond it.

I have examined the little heart. She has made me her confidant. She owns, she could love Johnny Barton very well: and Johnny Barton has told her, he could love her better than any maiden he ever saw—but, alas! it must not be thought of. Why not be thought of!—She don't know!—And then she sighed: But Johnny has an aunt, who will give him an hundred pounds, when his time is out; and her father cannot give her but a few things, or so, to set her out with: and though Johnny's mother says, she knows not where Johnny would have a prettier, or notabler wife, yet—And then she sighed again—What signifies talking?—I would not have Johnny be unhappy and poor for me!—For what good would that do me, you know, Sir!

What would I give [by my soul, my angel will indeed reform me, if her friends' implacable folly ruin us not both!—What would I give] to have so innocent and so good a heart, as either my Rose-bud's, or Johnny's!

I have a confounded mischievous one—by nature too, I think!—A good motion now-and-then rises from it: but it dies away presently—a love of intrigue—an invention for mischief—a triumph in subduing—fortune encouraging and supporting—and a constitution—What signifies palliating? But I believe I had been a rogue, had I been a plough-boy.

But the devil's in this sex! Eternal misguiders. Who, that has once trespassed with them, ever recovered his virtue? And yet where there is not virtue, which nevertheless we freelivers are continually plotting to destroy, what is there even in the ultimate of our wishes with them?—Preparation and expectation are in a manner every thing: reflection indeed may be something, if the mind be hardened above feeling the guilt of a past trespass: but the fruition, what is there in that? And yet that being the end, nature will not be satisfied without it.

See what grave reflections an innocent subject will produce! It gives me some pleasure to think, that it is not out of my power to reform: but then, Jack, I am afraid I must keep better company than I do at present—for we certainly harden one another. But be not cast down, my boy; there will be time enough to give the whole fraternity warning to choose another leader: and I fancy thou wilt be the man.

Mean time, as I make it my rule, whenever I have committed a very capital enormity, to do some good by way of atonement; and as I believe I am a pretty deal indebted on that score, I intend, before I leave these parts (successfully shall I leave them I hope, or I shall be tempted to double the mischief by way of revenge, though not to my Rose-bud any) to join an hundred pounds to Johnny's aunt's hundred pounds, to make one innocent couple happy.—I repeat therefore, and for half a dozen more therefores, spare thou my Rose-bud.

An interruption—another letter anon; and both shall go together.

LETTER XXXV

MR. LOVELACE, TO JOHN BELFORD, ESQ

I have found out by my watchful spy almost as many of my charmer's motions, as those of the rest of her relations. It delights me to think how the rascal is caressed by the uncles and nephew; and let into their secrets; yet it proceeds all the time by my line of direction. I have charged him, however, on forfeiture of his present weekly stipend, and my future favour, to take care, that neither my beloved, nor any of the family suspect him: I have told him that he may indeed watch her egresses and regresses; but that only keep off other servants from her paths; yet not to be seen by her himself.

The dear creature has tempted him, he told them, with a bribe [which she never offered] to convey a letter [which she never wrote] to Miss Howe; he believes, with one enclosed (perhaps to me): but he declined it: and he begged they would take notice of it to her. This brought him a stingy shilling; great applause; and an injunction followed it to all the servants, for the strictest look-out, lest she should contrive some way to send it—and, above an hour after, an order was given him to throw himself in her way; and (expressing his concern for denying her request) to tender his service to her, and to bring them her letter: which it will be proper for him to report that she has refused to give him.

Now seest thou not, how many good ends this contrivance answers?

In the first place, the lady is secured by it, against her own knowledge, in the liberty allowed her of taking her private walks in the garden: for this attempt has confirmed them in their belief, that now they have turned off her maid, she has no way to send a letter out of the house: if she had, she would not have run the risque of tempting a fellow who had not been in her secret—so that she can prosecute unsuspectedly her correspondence with me and Miss Howe.

In the next place, it will perhaps afford me an opportunity of a private interview with her, which I am meditating, let her take it as she will; having found out by my spy (who can keep off every body else) that she goes every morning and evening to a wood-house remote from the dwelling-house, under pretence of visiting and feeding a set of bantam-poultry, which were produced from a breed that was her grandfather's, and of which for that reason she is very fond; as also of some other curious fowls brought from the same place. I have an account of all her motions here. And as she has owned to me in one of her letters that she corresponds privately with Miss Howe, I presume it is by this way.

The interview I am meditating, will produce her consent, I hope, to other favours of the like kind: for, should she not choose the place in which I am expecting to see her, I can attend her any where in the rambling Dutch-taste garden, whenever she will permit me that honour: for my implement, high Joseph Leman, has procured me the opportunity of getting two keys made to the garden-door (one of which I have given him for reasons good); which door opens to the haunted coppice, as tradition has made the servants think it; a man having been found hanging in it about twenty years ago: and Joseph, upon proper notice, will leave it unbolted.

But I was obliged previously to give him my honour, that no mischief should happen to any of my adversaries, from this liberty: for the fellow tells me, that he loves all his masters: and, only that he knows I am a man of honour; and that my alliance will do credit to the family; and after prejudices are overcome, every body will think so; or he would not for the world act the part he does.

There never was a rogue, who had not a salvo to himself for being so.—What a praise to honesty, that every man pretends to it, even at the instant that he knows he is pursuing the methods that will perhaps prove him a knave to the whole world, as well as to his own conscience!

But what this stupid family can mean, to make all this necessary, I cannot imagine. My REVENGE and my LOVE are uppermost by turns. If the latter succeed not, the gratifying of the former will be my only consolation: and, by all that's good, they shall feel it; although for it I become an exile from my native country for ever.

I will throw myself into my charmer's presence. I have twice already attempted it in vain. I shall then see what I may depend upon from her favour. If I thought I had no prospect of that, I should be tempted to carry her off. That would be a rape worthy of Jupiter!

But all gentle shall be my movements: all respectful, even to reverence, my address to her—her hand shall be the only witness to the pressure of my lip—my trembling lip: I know it will tremble, if I do not bid it tremble. As soft my sighs, as the sighs of my gentle Rose-bud. By my humility will I invite her confidence: the loneliness of the place shall give me no advantage: to dissipate her fears, and engage her reliance upon my honour for the future, shall be my whole endeavour: but little will I complain of, not at all will I threaten, those who are continually threatening me: but yet with a view to act the part of Dryden's lion; to secure my love, or to let loose my vengeance upon my hunters.

What tho' his mighty soul his grief contains?
He meditates revenge who least complains:
And like a lion slumb'ring in his way,
Or sleep dissembling, while he waits his prey,
His fearless foes within his distance draws,
Constrains his roaring, and contracts his paws:
Till at the last, his time for fury found,
He shoots with sudden vengeance from the ground:
The prostrate vulgar passes o'er, and spares,
But, with a lordly rage, his hunter tears.

LETTER XXXVI

MISS CLARISSA HARLOWE, TO MISS HOWE SATURDAY, MARCH 18

I have been frighted out of my wits—still am in a manner out of breath—thus occasioned—I went down, under the usual pretence, in hopes to find something from you. Concerned at my disappointment, I was returning from the wood-house, when I heard a rustling as of somebody behind a stack of wood. I was extremely surprised: but still more, to behold a man coming from behind the furthermost stack. Oh! thought I, at that moment, the sin of a prohibited correspondence!

In the same point of time that I saw him, he besought me not to be frighted: and, still nearer approaching me, threw open a horseman's coat: And who should it be but Mr. Lovelace!—I could not scream out (yet attempted to scream, the moment I saw a man; and again, when I saw who it was); for I had no voice: and had I not caught hold of a prop which supported the old roof, I should have sunk.

I had hitherto, as you know, kept him at a distance: And now, as I recovered myself, judge of my first emotions, when I recollected his character from every mouth of my family; his enterprising temper; and found myself alone with him, in a place so near a bye-lane, and so remote from the house.

But his respectful behaviour soon dissipated these fears, and gave me others; lest we should be seen together, and information of it given to my brother: the consequences of which, I could readily think, would be, if not further mischief, an imputed assignation, a stricter confinement, a forfeited correspondence with you, my beloved friend, and a pretence for the most violent compulsion: and neither the one set of reflections, nor the other, acquitted him to me for his bold intrusion.

As soon therefore as I could speak, I expressed with the greatest warmth my displeasure; and told him, that he cared not how much he exposed me to the resentment of all my friends, provided he could gratify his own impetuous humour. I then commanded him to leave the place that moment; and was hurrying from him, when he threw himself in the way at my feet, beseeching my stay for one moment; declaring, that he suffered himself to be guilty of this rashness, as I thought it, to avoid one much greater:—for, in short, he could not bear the hourly insults he received from my family, with the thoughts of having so little interest in my favour, that he could not promise himself that his patience and forbearance would be attended with any other issue than to lose me for ever, and be triumphed over and insulted upon it.

This man, you know, has very ready knees. You have said, that he ought, in small points, frequently to offend, on purpose to shew what an address he is master of.

He ran on, expressing his apprehensions that a temper so gentle and obliging, as he said mine was, to every body but him, (and a dutifulness so exemplary inclined me to do my part to others, whether they did theirs or not by me,) would be wrought upon in favour of a man set up in part to be revenged upon myself, for my grandfather's envied distinction of me; and in part to be revenged upon him, for having given life to one, who would have taken his; and now sought to deprive him of hopes dearer to him than life.

I told him, he might be assured, that the severity and ill-usage I met with would be far from effecting the proposed end: that although I could, with great sincerity, declare for a single life (which had always been my choice); and particularly, that if ever I married, if they would not insist upon the man I had an aversion to, it should not be with the man they disliked—

He interrupted me here: He hoped I would forgive him for it; but he could not help expressing his great concern, that, after so many instances of his passionate and obsequious devotion—

And pray, Sir, said I, let me interrupt you in my turn;—Why don't you assert, in still plainer words, the obligation you have laid me under by this your boasted devotion? Why don't you let me know, in terms as high as your implication, that a perseverance I have not wished for, which has set all my relations at variance with me, is a merit that throws upon me the guilt of ingratitude for not having answered it as you seem to expect?

I must forgive him, he said, if he, who pretended only to a comparative merit, (and otherwise thought no man living could deserve me,) had presumed to hope for a greater share in my favour, than he had hitherto met with, when such men as Mr. Symmes, Mr. Wyerley, and now, lastly, so vile a reptile as this Solmes, however discouraged by myself, were made his competitors. As to the perseverance I mentioned, it was impossible for him not to persevere: but I must needs know, that were he not in being, the terms Solmes had proposed were such, as would have involved me in the same difficulties with my relations that I now laboured under. He therefore took the liberty to say, that my favour to him, far from increasing those difficulties, would be the readiest way to extricate me from them. They had made it impossible [he told me, with too much truth] to oblige them any way, but by sacrificing myself to Solmes. They were well apprized besides of the difference between the two; one, whom they hoped to manage as they pleased; the other, who could and would protect me from every insult; and who had natural prospects much superior to my brother's foolish views of a title.

How comes this man to know so well all our foibles? But I more wonder, how he came to have a notion of meeting me in this place?

I was very uneasy to be gone; and the more as the night came on apace. But there was no getting from him, till I had heard a great deal more of what he had to say.

As he hoped, that I would one day make him the happiest man in the world, he assured me, that he had so much regard for my fame, that he would be as far from advising any step that was likely to cast a shade upon my reputation, (although that step was to be ever so much in his own favour,) as I would be to follow such advice. But since I was not to be permitted to live single, he would submit it to my consideration, whether I had any way but one to avoid the intended violence to my inclinations—my father so jealous of his authority: both my uncles in my father's way of thinking: my cousin Morden at a distance: my uncle and aunt Hervey awed into insignificance, was his word: my brother and sister inflaming every one: Solmes's offers captivating: Miss Howe's mother rather of a party with them, for motives respecting example to her own daughter.

And then he asked me, if I would receive a letter from Lady Betty Lawrance, on this occasion: for Lady Sarah Sadleir, he said, having lately lost her only child, hardly looked into the world, or thought of it farther than to wish him married, and, preferably to all the women in the world, with me.

To be sure, my dear, there is a great deal in what the man said—I may be allowed to say this, without an imputed glow or throb. But I told him nevertheless, that although I had great honour for the ladies he was related to, yet I should not choose to receive a letter on a subject that had a tendency to promote an end I was far from intending to promote: that it became me, ill as I was treated at present, to hope every thing, to bear every thing, and to try ever thing: when my father saw my steadfastness, and that I would die rather than have Mr. Solmes, he would perhaps recede—

Interrupting me, he represented the unlikelihood there was of that, from the courses they had entered upon; which he thus enumerated:—

Their engaging Mrs. Howe against me, in the first place, as a person I might have thought to fly to, if pushed to desperation—my brother continually buzzing in my father's ears, that my cousin Morden would soon arrive, and then would insist upon giving me possession of my grandfather's estate, in pursuance of the will; which would render me independent of my father—their disgraceful confinement of me—their dismissing so suddenly my servant, and setting my sister's over me—their engaging my mother, contrary to her own judgment, against me: these, he said, were all so many flagrant proofs that they would stick at nothing to carry their point; and were what made him inexpressibly uneasy.

He appealed to me, whether ever I knew my father recede from any resolution he had once fixed; especially, if he thought either his prerogative, or his authority concerned in the question. His acquaintance with our family, he said, enabled him to give several instances (but they would be too grating to me) of an arbitrariness that had few examples even in the families of princes: an arbitrariness, which the most excellent of women, my mother, too severely experienced. He was proceeding, as I thought, with reflections of this sort; and I angrily told him, I would not permit my father to be reflected upon; adding, that his severity to me, however unmerited, was not a warrant for me to dispense with my duty to him.

He had no pleasure, he said, in urging any thing that could be so construed; for, however well warranted he was to make such reflections from the provocations they were continually giving him, he knew how offensive to me any liberties of this sort would be. And yet he must own, that it was painful to him, who had youth and passions to be allowed for, as well as others, and who had always valued himself under speaking his mind, to curb himself, under such treatment. Nevertheless, his consideration for me would make him confine himself, in his observations, to facts that were too flagrant, and too openly avowed, to be disputed. It could not therefore justly displease, he would venture to say, if he made this natural inference from the premises, That if such were my father's behaviour to a wife, who disputed not the imaginary prerogatives he was so unprecedently fond of asserting, what room had a daughter to hope, that he would depart from an authority he was so earnest, and so much more concerned, to maintain?—Family-interests at the same time engaging; an aversion, however causelessly conceived, stimulating my brother's and sister's resentments and selfish views cooperating; and my banishment from their presence depriving me of all personal plea or entreaty in my own favour.

How unhappy, my dear, that there is but too much reason for these observations, and for this inference; made, likewise, with more coolness and respect to my family than one would have apprehended from a man so much provoked, and of passions so high, and generally thought uncontroulable!

Will you not question me about throbs and glows, if from such instances of a command over his fiery temper, for my sake, I am ready to infer, that were my friends capable of a reconciliation with him, he might be affected by arguments apparently calculated for his present and future good! Nor is it a very bad indication, that he has such moderate notions of that very high prerogative in husbands, of which we in our family have been accustomed to hear so much.

He represented to me, that my present disgraceful confinement was known to all the world: that neither my sister nor my brother scrupled to represent me as an obliged and favoured child in a state of actual rebellion. That, nevertheless, every body who knew me was ready to justify me for an aversion to a man whom every body thought utterly unworthy of me, and more fit for my sister: that unhappy as he was, in not having been able to make any greater impression upon me in his favour, all the world gave me to him. Nor was there but one objection made to him by his very enemies (his birth, his prospects all very unexceptionable, and the latter splendid); and that objection, he thanked God, and my example, was in a fair way of being removed for ever: since he had seen his error, and was heartily sick of the courses he had followed; which, however, were far less enormous than malice and envy had represented them to be. But of this he should say the less, as it were much better to justify himself by his actions, than by the most solemn asseverations and promises. And then, complimenting my person, he assured me (for that he always loved virtue, although he had not followed its rules as he ought) that he was still more captivated with the graces of my mind: and would frankly own, that till he had the honour to know me, he had never met with an inducement sufficient to enable him to overcome an unhappy kind of prejudice to matrimony; which had made him before impenetrable to the wishes and recommendations of all his relations.

You see, my dear, he scruples not to speak of himself, as his enemies speak of him. I can't say, but his openness in these particulars gives a credit to his other professions. I should easily, I think, detect an hypocrite: and this man particularly, who is said to have allowed himself in great liberties, were he to pretend to instantaneous lights and convictions—at this time of life too. Habits, I am sensible, are not so easily changed. You have always joined with me in remarking, that he will speak his mind with freedom, even to a degree of unpoliteness sometimes; and that his very treatment of my family is a proof that he cannot make a mean court to any body for interest sake—What pity, where there are such laudable traces, that they should have been so mired, and choaked up, as I may say!—We have heard, that the man's head is better than his heart: But do you really think Mr. Lovelace can have a very bad heart? Why should not there be something in blood in the human creature, as well as in the ignobler animals? None of his family are exceptionable—but himself, indeed. The characters of the ladies are admirable. But I shall incur the imputation I wish to avoid. Yet what a look of censoriousness does it carry in an unsparing friend, to take one to task for doing that justice, and making those which one ought without scruple to do, and to make, in the behalf of any other man living?

He then again pressed me to receive a letter of offered protection from Lady Betty. He said, that people of birth stood a little too much upon punctilio; as people of value also did (but indeed birth, worthily lived up to, was virtue: virtue, birth; the inducements to a decent punctilio the same; the origin of both one): [how came this notion from him!] else, Lady Betty would write to me: but she would be willing to be first apprized that her offer will be well received—as it would have the appearance of being made against the liking of one part of my family; and which nothing would induce her to make, but the degree of unworthy persecution which I actually laboured under, and had reason further to apprehend.

I told him, that, however greatly I thought myself obliged to Lady Betty Lawrance, if this offer came from herself; yet it was easy to see to what it led. It might look like vanity in me perhaps to say, that this urgency in him, on this occasion, wore the face of art, in order to engage me into measures from which I might not easily extricate myself. I said, that I should not be affected by the splendour of even a royal title. Goodness, I thought, was greatness. That the excellent characters of the ladies of his family weighed more with me, than the consideration that they were half-sisters to Lord M. and daughters of an earl: that he would not have found encouragement from me, had my friends been consenting to his address, if he had only a mere relative merit to those ladies: since, in that case, the very reasons that made me admire them, would have been so many objections to their kinsman.

I then assured him, that it was with infinite concern, that I had found myself drawn into an epistolary correspondence with him; especially since that correspondence had been prohibited: and the only agreeable use I could think of making of this unexpected and undesired interview, was, to let him know, that I should from henceforth think myself obliged to discontinue it. And I hoped, that he would not have the thought of engaging me to carry it on by menacing my relations.

There was light enough to distinguish, that he looked very grave upon this. He so much valued my free choice, he said, and my unbiassed favour, (scorning to set himself upon a footing with Solmes in the compulsory methods used in that man's behalf,) that he should hate himself, were he capable of a view of intimidating me by so very poor a method. But, nevertheless, there were two things to be considered: First, that the continual outrages he was treated with; the spies set over him, one of which he had detected; the indignities all his family were likewise treated with;—as also, myself; avowedly in malice to him, or he should not presume to take upon himself to resent for me, without my leave [the artful wretch saw he would have lain open here, had he not thus guarded]—all these considerations called upon him to shew a proper resentment: and he would leave it to me to judge, whether it would be reasonable for him, as a man of spirit, to bear such insults, if it were not for my sake. I would be pleased to consider, in the next place, whether the situation I was in, (a prisoner in my father's house, and my whole family determined to compel me to marry a man unworthy of me, and that speedily, and whether I consented or not,) admitted of delay in the preventive measures he was desirous to put me upon, in the last resort only. Nor was there a necessity, he said, if I were actually in Lady Betty's protection, that I should be his, if, afterwards, I should see any thing objectionable in his conduct.

But what would the world conclude would be the end, I demanded, were I, in the last resort, as he proposed, to throw myself into the protection of his friends, but that it was with such a view?

And what less did the world think of me now, he asked, than that I was confined that I might not? You are to consider, Madam, you have not now an option; and to whom is it owing that you have not; and that you are in the power of those (parents, why should I call them?) who are determined, that you shall not have an option. All I propose is, that you will embrace such a protection—but not till you have tried every way, to avoid the necessity for it.

And give me leave to say, proceeded he, that if a correspondence, on which I have founded all my hopes, is, at this critical conjuncture, to be broken off; and if you are resolved not to be provided against the worst; it must be plain to me, that you will at last yield to that worst—worst to me only—it cannot be to you—and then! [and he put his hand clenched to his forehead] How shall I bear this supposition?—Then will you be that Solmes's!—But, by all that's sacred, neither he, nor your brother, nor your uncles, shall enjoy their triumph—Perdition seize my soul, if they shall!

The man's vehemence frightened me: yet, in resentment, I would have left him; but, throwing himself at my feet again, Leave me not thus—I beseech you, dearest Madam, leave me not thus, in despair! I kneel not, repenting of what I have vowed in such a case as that I have supposed. I re-vow it, at your feet!—and so he did. But think not it is by way of menace, or to intimidate you to favour me. If your heart inclines you [and then he arose] to obey your father (your brother rather) and to have Solmes; although I shall avenge myself on those who have insulted me, for their insults to myself and family, yet will I tear out my heart from this bosom (if possible with my own hands) were it to scruple to give up its ardours to a woman capable of such a preference.

I told him, that he talked to me in very high language; but he might assure himself that I never would have Mr. Solmes, (yet that this I said not in favour to him,) and I had declared as much to my relations, were there not such a man as himself in the world.

Would I declare, that I would still honour him with my correspondence?—He could not bear, that, hoping to obtain greater instances of my favour, he should forfeit the only one he had to boast of.

I bid him forbear rashness or resentment to any of my family, and I would, for some time at least, till I saw what issue my present trials were likely to have, proceed with a correspondence, which, nevertheless, my heart condemned—

And his spirit him, the impatient creature said, interrupting me, for bearing what he did; when he considered, that the necessity of it was imposed upon him, not by my will, (for then he would bear it cheerfully, and a thousand times more,) but by creatures—And there he stopt.

I told him plainly that he might thank himself (whose indifferent character, as to morals, had given such a handle against him) for all. It was but just, that a man should be spoken evil of, who set no value upon his reputation.

He offered to vindicate himself. But I told him, I would judge him by his own rule—by his actions, not by his professions.

Were not his enemies, he said, so powerful, and so determined; and had they not already shewn their intentions in such high acts of even cruel compulsion; but would leave me to my choice, or to my desire of living single; he would have been content to undergo a twelvemonth's probation, or more: but he was confident, that one month would either complete all their purposes, or render them abortive: and I best knew what hopes I had of my father's receding—he did not know him, if I had any.

I said, I would try every method, that either my duty or my influence upon any of them should suggest, before I would put myself into any other protection: and, if nothing else would do, would resign the envied estate; and that I dared to say would.

He was contented, he said, to abide that issue. He should be far from wishing me to embrace any other protection, but, as he had frequently said, in the last necessity. But dearest creature, said he, catching my hand with ardour, and pressing it to his lips, if the yielding up of that estate will do—resign it—and be mine—and I will corroborate, with all my soul, your resignation!

This was not ungenerously said: But what will not these men say to obtain belief, and a power over one?

I made many efforts to go; and now it was so dark, that I began to have great apprehensions. I cannot say from his behaviour: indeed, he has a good deal raised himself in my opinion by the personal respect, even to reverence, which he paid me during the whole conference: for, although he flamed out once, upon a supposition that Solmes might succeed, it was upon a supposition that would excuse passion, if any thing could, you know, in a man pretending to love with fervour; although it was so levelled, that I could not avoid resenting it.

He recommended himself to my favour at parting, with great earnestness, yet with as great submission; not offering to condition any thing with me; although he hinted his wishes for another meeting: which I forbad him ever attempting again in the same place. And I will own to you, from whom I should be really blamable to conceal any thing, that his arguments (drawn from the disgraceful treatment I meet with) of what I am to expect, make me begin to apprehend that I shall be under an obligation to be either the one man's or the other's—and, if so, I fancy I shall not incur your blame, were I to say which of the two it must be: you have said, which it must not be. But, O my dear, the single life is by far the most eligible to me: indeed it is. And I hope yet to be permitted to make that option.

I got back without observation; but the apprehension that I should not, gave me great uneasiness; and made me begin a letter in a greater flutter than he gave me cause to be in, except at the first seeing him; for then indeed my spirits failed me; and it was a particular felicity, that, in such a place, in such a fright, and alone with him, I fainted not away.

I should add, that having reproached him with his behaviour the last Sunday at church, he solemnly assured me, that it was not what had been represented to me: that he did not expect to see me there: but hoped to have an opportunity to address himself to my father, and to be permitted to attend him home. But that the good Dr. Lewen had persuaded him not to attempt speaking to any of the family, at that time; observing to him the emotions into which his presence had put every body. He intended no pride, or haughtiness of behaviour, he assured me; and that the attributing such to him was the effect of that ill-will which he had the mortification to find insuperable: adding, that when he bowed to my mother, it was a compliment he intended generally to every one in the pew, as well as to her, whom he sincerely venerated.

If he may be believed, (and I should think he would not have come purposely to defy my family, yet expect favour from me,) one may see, my dear, the force of hatred, which misrepresents all things. Yet why should Shorey (except officiously to please her principals) make a report in his disfavour? He told me, that he would appeal to Dr. Lewen for his justification on this head; adding, that the whole conversation between the Doctor and him turned upon his desire to attempt to reconcile himself to us all, in the face of the church; and upon the Doctor's endeavouring to dissuade him from making such a public overture, till he knew how it would be accepted. But to what purpose his appeal, when I am debarred from seeing that good man, or any one who would advise me what to do in my present difficult situation!

I fancy, my dear, however, that there would hardly be a guilty person in the world, were each suspected or accused person to tell his or her own story, and be allowed any degree of credit.

I have written a very long letter.

To be so particular as you require in subjects of conversation, it is impossible to be short.

I will add to it only the assurance, That I am, and ever will be,

Your affectionate and faithful friend and servant, CLARISSA HARLOWE.

You'll be so good, my dear, as to remember, that the date of your last letter to me was the 9th.

LETTER XXXVII

MISS HOWE, TO MISS CLARISSA HARLOWE. SUNDAY, MARCH 19

I beg your pardon, my dearest friend, for having given you occasion to remind me of the date of my last. I was willing to have before me as much of the workings of your wise relations as possible; being verily persuaded, that one side or the other would have yielded by this time: and then I should have had some degree of certainty to found my observations upon. And indeed what can I write that I have not already written?—You know, that I can do nothing but rave at your stupid persecutors: and that you don't like. I have advised you to resume your own estate: that you won't do. You cannot bear the thoughts of having their Solmes: and Lovelace is resolved you shall be his, let who will say to the contrary. I think you must be either the one man's or the other's. Let us see what their next step will be.

As to Lovelace, while he tells his own story (having also behaved so handsomely on his intrusion in the wood-house, and intended so well at church) who can say, that the man is in the least blameworthy?—Wicked people! to combine against so innocent a man!—But, as I said, let us see what their next step will be, and what course you will take upon it; and then we may be the more enlightened.

As to your change of style to your uncles, and brother and sister, since they were so fond of attributing to you a regard for Lovelace, and would not be persuaded to the contrary; and since you only strengthened their arguments against yourself by denying it; you did but just as I would have done, in giving way to their suspicions, and trying what that would do—But if—but if—Pray, my dear, indulge me a little—you yourself think it was necessary to apologize to me for that change of style to them—and till you will speak out like a friend to her unquestionable friend, I must tease you a little—let it run therefore; for it will run—

If, then, there be not a reason for this change of style, which you have not thought fit to give me, be so good as to watch, as I once before advised you, how the cause for it will come on—Why should it be permitted to steal upon you, and you know nothing of the matter?

When we get a great cold, we are apt to puzzle ourselves to find out when it began, or how we got it; and when that is accounted for, down we sit contented, and let it have its course; or, if it be very troublesome, take a sweat, or use other means to get rid of it. So my dear, before the malady you wot of, yet wot not of, grows so importunate, as that you must be obliged to sweat it out, let me advise you to mind how it comes on. For I am persuaded, as surely as that I am now writing to you, that the indiscreet violence of your friends on the one hand, and the insinuating address of Lovelace on the other, (if the man be not a greater fool than any body thinks him,) will effectually bring it to this, and do all his work for him.

But let it—if it must be Lovelace or Solmes, the choice cannot admit of debate. Yet if all be true that is reported, I should prefer almost any of your other lovers to either; unworthy as they also are. But who can be worthy of a Clarissa?

I wish you are not indeed angry with me for harping so much on one string. I must own, that I should think myself inexcusable so to do, (the rather, as I am bold enough to imagine it a point out of all doubt from fifty places in your letters, were I to labour the proof,) if you would ingenuously own—

Own what? you'll say. Why, my Anna Howe, I hope you don't think that I am already in love—!

No, to be sure! How can your Anna Howe have such a thought?—What then shall we call it? You might have helped me to a phrase—A conditional kind of liking!—that's it.—O my friend! did I not know how much you despise prudery; and that you are too young, and too lovely, to be a prude—

But, avoiding such hard names, let me tell you one thing, my dear (which nevertheless I have told you before); and that is this: that I shall think I have reason to be highly displeased with you, if, when you write to me, you endeavour to keep from me any secret of your heart.

Let me add, that if you would clearly and explicitly tell me, how far Lovelace has, or has not, a hold in your affections, I could better advise you what to do, than at present I can. You, who are so famed for prescience, as I may call it; and than whom no young lady ever had stronger pretensions to a share of it; have had, no doubt, reasonings in your heart about him, supposing you were to be one day his: [no doubt but you have had the same in Solmes's case: whence the ground for the hatred of the one; and for the conditional liking of the other.] Will you tell me, my dear, what you have thought of Lovelace's best and of his worst?—How far eligible for the first; how far rejectable for the last?—Then weighing both parts in opposite scales, we shall see which is likely to preponderate; or rather which does preponderate. Nothing less than the knowledge of the inmost recesses of your heart, can satisfy my love and my friendship. Surely, you are not afraid to trust yourself with a secret of this nature: if you are, then you may the more allowably doubt me. But, I dare say, you will not own either—nor is there, I hope, cause for either.

Be pleased to observe one thing, my dear, that whenever I have given myself any of those airs of raillery, which have seemed to make you look about you, (when, likewise, your case may call for a more serious turn from a sympathizing friend,) it has not been upon those passages which are written, though, perhaps not intended, with such explicitness [don't be alarmed, my dear!] as leaves little cause of doubt: but only when you affect reserve; when you give new words for common things; when you come with your curiosities, with your conditional likings, and with your PRUDE-encies [mind how I spell the word] in a case that with every other person defies all prudence—over-acts of treason all these, against the sovereign friendship we have avowed to each other.

Remember, that you found me out in a moment. You challenged me. I owned directly, that there was only my pride between the man and me; for I could not endure, I told you, to think of any fellow living to give me a moment's uneasiness. And then my man, as I have elsewhere said, was not such a one as yours: so I had reason to impute full as much as to my own inconsideration, as to his power over me: nay, more: but still more to yours. For you reasoned me out of the curiosity first; and when the liking was brought to be conditional—why then, you know, I throbbed no more about him.

O! pray now, as you say, now I have mentioned that my fellow was not such a charming fellow as yours, let Miss Biddulph, Miss Lloyd, Miss Campion, and me, have your opinion, how far figure ought to engage us: with a view to your own case, however—mind that—as Mr. Tony says—and whether at all, if the man be vain of it; since, as you observe in a former, that vanity is a stop-short pride in such a one, that would make one justly doubt the worthiness of his interior. You, our pattern, so lovely in feature, so graceful in person, have none of it; and have therefore with the best grace always held, that it is not excusable even in a woman.

You must know, that this subject was warmly debated among us in our last conversation: and Miss Lloyd wished me to write to you upon it for your opinion; to which, in every debated case, we always paid the greatest deference. I hope you will not be so much engrossed by your weighty cares, as not to have freedom of spirits enough to enter upon the task. You know how much we all admire your opinion on such topics; which ever produces something new and instructive, as you handle the subjects. And pray tell us, to what you think it owing, that your man seems so careful to adorn that self-adorned person of his! yet so manages, that one cannot for one's heart think him a coxcomb?—Let this question, and the above tasks, divert, and not displease you, my dear. One subject, though ever so important, could never yet engross your capacious mind. If they should displease you, you must recollect the many instances of my impertinence which you have forgiven, and then say, 'This is a mad girl: but yet I love her!—And she is my own'

ANNA HOWE.

LETTER XXXVIII

MISS CLARISSA HARLOWE, TO MISS HOWE MONDAY, MARCH 20

Your last so sensibly affects me, that I must postpone every other consideration, however weighty, to reply to it: and this I will do very distinctly, and with all the openness of heart which our mutual friendship demands.

But let me observe, in the first place, gratefully observe, that if I have in fifty passages of my letters given you such undoubted proofs of my value for Mr. Lovelace, that you have spared me for the sake of my explicitness, it is acting by me with a generosity worthy of yourself.

But lives the man, think you, who is so very bad, that he does not give even a doubting mind reason at one time to be better pleased with him than at another? And when that reason offers, is it not just to express one's self accordingly? I would do the man who addresses me as much justice, as if he did not address me: it has such a look of tyranny, it appears so ungenerous, methinks, in our sex, to use a man worse for his respect to us, (no other cause for disrespect occurring,) that I would not by any means be that person who should do so.

But, although I may intend no more than justice, it will perhaps be difficult to hinder those who know the man's views, from construing it as a partial favour: and especially if the eager-eyed observer has been formerly touched herself, and would triumph that her friend had been no more able to escape than she. Noble minds, emulative of perfection, (and yet the passion properly directed, I do not take to be an imperfection neither,) may be allowed a little generous envy, I think.

If I meant by this a reflection, by way of revenge, it is but a revenge, my dear, in the soft sense of the word. I love, as I have told you, your pleasantry. Although at the time your reproof may pain me a little; yet, on recollection, when I find it more of the cautioning friend than of the satirizing observer, I shall be all gratitude upon it. All the business will be this; I shall be sensible of the pain in the present letter perhaps; but I shall thank you in the next, and ever after.

In this way, I hope, my dear, you will account for a little of that sensibility which you find above, and perhaps still more, as I proceed.—You frequently remind me, by an excellent example, your own to me, that I must not spare you!

I am not conscious, that I have written any thing of this man, that has not been more in his dispraise than in his favour. Such is the man, that I think I must have been faulty, and ought to take myself to account, if I had not. But you think otherwise, I will not put you upon labouring the proof, as you call it. My conduct must then have a faulty appearance at least, and I will endeavour to rectify it. But of this I assure you, that whatever interpretation my words were capable of, I intended not any reserve to you. I wrote my heart at the time: if I had had thought of disguising it, or been conscious that there was reason for doing so, perhaps I had not given you the opportunity of remarking upon my curiosity after his relations' esteem for me; nor upon my conditional liking, and such-like. All I intended by the first, I believe, I honestly told you at the time. To that letter I therefore refer, whether it make for me, or against me: and by the other, that I might bear in mind, what it became a person of my sex and character to be and to do, in such an unhappy situation, where the imputed love is thought an undutiful, and therefore a criminal passion; and where the supported object of it is a man of faulty morals too. And I am sure you will excuse my desire of appearing at those times the person I ought to be; had I no other view in it but to merit the continuance of your good opinion.

But that I may acquit myself of having reserves—O, my dear, I must here break off—!

LETTER XXXIX

MISS CLARISSA HARLOWE, TO MISS HOWE MONDAY, MARCH 12

This letter will account to you, my dear, for my abrupt breaking off in the answer I was writing to yours of yesterday; and which, possibly, I shall not be able to finish and send you till to-morrow or next day; having a great deal to say to the subjects you put to me in it. What I am now to give you are the particulars of another effort made by my friends, through the good Mrs. Norton.

It seems they had sent to her yesterday, to be here this day, to take their instructions, and to try what she could do with me. It would, at least, I suppose they thought, have this effect; to render me inexcusable with her; or to let her see, that there was no room for the expostulations she had often wanted to make in my favour to my mother.

The declaration, that my heart was free, afforded them an argument to prove obstinacy and perverseness upon me; since it could be nothing else that governed me in my opposition to their wills, if I had no particular esteem for another man. And now, that I have given them reason (in order to obviate this argument) to suppose that I have a preference to another, they are resolved to carry their schemes into execution as soon as possible. And in order to do this, they sent for this good woman, for whom they know I have even a filial regard.

She found assembled my father and mother, my brother and sister, my two uncles, and my aunt Hervey.

My brother acquainted her with all that had passed since she was last permitted to see me; with the contents of my letters avowing my regard for Mr. Lovelace (as they all interpreted them); with the substance of their answers to them; and with their resolutions.

My mother spoke next; and delivered herself to this effect, as the good woman told me.

After reciting how many times I had been indulged in my refusals of different men, and the pains she had taken with me, to induce me to oblige my whole family in one instance out of five or six, and my obstinacy upon it; 'O my good Mrs. Norton, said the dear lady, could you have thought, that my Clarissa and your Clarissa was capable of so determined an opposition to the will of parents so indulgent to her? But see what you can do with her. The matter is gone too far to be receded from on our parts. Her father had concluded every thing with Mr. Solmes, not doubting her compliance. Such noble settlements, Mrs. Norton, and such advantages to the whole family!—In short, she has it in her power to lay an obligation upon us all. Mr. Solmes, knowing she has good principles, and hoping by his patience now, and good treatment hereafter, to engage her gratitude, and by degrees her love, is willing to overlook all!—'

[Overlook all, my dear! Mr. Solmes to overlook all! There's a word!]

'So, Mrs. Norton, if you are convinced, that it is a child's duty to submit to her parents' authority, in the most important point as well as in the least, I beg you will try your influence over her: I have none: her father has none: her uncles neither: although it is her apparent interest to oblige us all; for, on that condition, her grandfather's estate is not half of what, living and dying, is purposed to be done for her. If any body can prevail with her, it is you; and I hope you will heartily enter upon this task.'

The good woman asked, Whether she was permitted to expostulate with them upon the occasion, before she came up to me?

My arrogant brother told her, she was sent for to expostulate with his sister, and not with them. And this, Goody Norton [she is always Goody with him!] you may tell her, that the treaty with Mr. Solmes is concluded: that nothing but her compliance with her duty is wanting; of consequence, that there is no room for your expostulation, or hers either.

Be assured of this, Mrs. Norton, said my father, in an angry tone, that we will not be baffled by her. We will not appear like fools in this matter, and as if we have no authority over our own daughter. We will not, in short, be bullied out of our child by a cursed rake, who had like to have killed our only son!—And so she had better make a merit of her obedience; for comply she shall, if I live; independent as she thinks my father's indiscreet bounty has made her of me, her father. Indeed, since that, she has never been like she was before. An unjust bequest!—And it is likely to prosper accordingly!—But if she marry that vile rake Lovelace, I will litigate every shilling with her: tell her so; and that the will may be set aside, and shall.

My uncles joined, with equal heat.

My brother was violent in his declarations.

My sister put in with vehemence, on the same side.

My aunt Hervey was pleased to say, there was no article so proper for parents to govern in, as this of marriage: and it was very fit mine should be obliged.

Thus instructed, the good woman came up to me. She told me all that had passed, and was very earnest with me to comply; and so much justice did she to the task imposed upon her, that I more than once thought, that her own opinion went with theirs. But when she saw what an immovable aversion I had to the man, she lamented with me their determined resolution: and then examined into the sincerity of my declaration, that I would gladly compound with them by living single. Of this being satisfied, she was so convinced that this offer, which, carried into execution, would exclude Lovelace effectually, ought to be accepted, that she would go down (although I told her, it was what I had tendered over-and-over to no purpose) and undertake to be guaranty for me on that score.

She went accordingly; but soon returned in tears; being used harshly for urging this alternative:—They had a right to my obedience upon their own terms, they said: my proposal was an artifice, only to gain time: nothing but marrying Mr. Solmes should do: they had told me so before: they should not be at rest till it was done; for they knew what an interest Lovelace had in my heart: I had as good as owned it in my letters to my uncles, and brother and sister, although I had most disingenuously declared otherwise to my mother. I depended, they said, upon their indulgence, and my own power over them: they would not have banished me from their presence, if they had not known that their consideration for me was greater than mine for them. And they would be obeyed, or I never should be restored to their favour, let the consequence be what it would.

My brother thought fit to tell the good woman, that her whining nonsense did but harden me. There was a perverseness, he said, in female minds, a tragedy-pride, that would make a romantic young creature, such a one as me, risque any thing to obtain pity. I was of an age, and a turn [the insolent said] to be fond of a lover-like distress: and my grief (which she pleaded) would never break my heart: I should sooner break that of the best and most indulgent of mothers. He added, that she might once more go up to me: but that, if she prevailed not, he should suspect, that the man they all hated had found a way to attach her to his interest.

Every body blamed him for this unworthy reflection; which greatly affected the good woman. But nevertheless he said, and nobody contradicted him, that if she could not prevail upon her sweet child, [as it seems she had fondly called me,] she had best draw to her own home, and there tarry till she was sent for; and so leave her sweet child to her father's management.

Sure nobody had ever so insolent, so hard-hearted a brother, as I have! So much resignation to be expected from me! So much arrogance, and to so good a woman, and of so fine an understanding, to be allowed in him.

She nevertheless told him, that however she might be ridiculed for speaking of the sweetness of my disposition, she must take upon herself to say, that there never was a sweeter in the sex: and that she had ever found, that my mild methods, and gentleness, I might at any time be prevailed upon, even in points against my own judgment and opinion.

My aunt Hervey hereupon said, It was worth while to consider what Mrs. Norton said: and that she had sometimes allowed herself to doubt, whether I had been begun with by such methods as generous tempers are only to be influenced by, in cases where their hearts are supposed to be opposite to the will of their friends.

She had both my brother and sister upon her for this: who referred to my mother, whether she had not treated me with an indulgence that had hardly any example?

My mother said, she must own, that no indulgence had been wanting from her: but she must needs say, and had often said it, that the reception I met with on my return from Miss Howe, and the manner in which the proposal of Mr. Solmes was made to me, (which was such as left nothing to my choice,) and before I had an opportunity to converse with him, were not what she had by any means approved of.

She was silenced, you will guess by whom,—with, My dear!—my dear!—You have ever something to say, something to palliate, for this rebel of a girl!—Remember her treatment of you, of me!—Remember, that the wretch, whom we so justly hate, would not dare persist in his purposes, but for her encouragement of him, and obstinacy to us.—Mrs. Norton, [angrily to her,] go up to her once more—and if you think gentleness will do, you have a commission to be gentle—if it will not, never make use of that plea again.

Ay, my good woman, said my mother, try your force with her. My sister Hervey and I will go up to her, and bring her down in our hands, to receive her father's blessing, and assurances of every body's love, if she will be prevailed upon: and, in that case, we will all love you the better for your good offices.

She came up to me, and repeated all these passages with tears. But I told her, that after what had passed between us, she could not hope to prevail upon me to comply with measures so wholly my brother's, and so much to my aversion. And then folding me to her maternal bosom, I leave you, my dearest Miss, said she—I leave you, because I must!—But let me beseech you to do nothing rashly; nothing unbecoming your character. If all be true that is said, Mr. Lovelace cannot deserve you. If you can comply, remember it is your duty to comply. They take not, I own, the right method with so generous a spirit. But remember, that there would not be any merit in your compliance, if it were not to be against your own liking. Remember also, what is expected from a character so extraordinary as yours: remember, it is in your power to unite or disunite your whole family for ever. Although it should at present be disagreeable to you to be thus compelled, your prudence, I dare say, when you consider the matter seriously, will enable you to get over all prejudices against the one, and all prepossessions in favour of the other: and then the obligation you will lay all your family under, will be not only meritorious in you, with regard to them, but in a few months, very probably, highly satisfactory, as well as reputable, to yourself.

Consider, my dear Mrs. Norton, said I, only consider, that it is not a small thing that is insisted upon; not for a short duration; it is for my life: consider too, that all this is owing to an overbearing brother, who governs every body. Consider how desirous I am to oblige them, if a single life, and breaking all correspondence with the man they hate, because my brother hates him, will do it.

I consider every thing, my dearest Miss: and, added to what I have said, do you only consider, that if, by pursuing your own will, and rejecting theirs, you should be unhappy, you will be deprived of all that consolation which those have, who have been directed by their parents, although the event prove not answerable to their wishes.

I must go, repeated she: your brother will say [and she wept] that I harden you by my whining nonsense. 'Tis indeed hard, that so much regard should be paid to the humours of one child, and so little to the inclination of another. But let me repeat, that it is your duty to acquiesce, if you can acquiesce: your father has given your brother's schemes his sanction, and they are now his. Mr. Lovelace, I doubt, is not a man that will justify your choice so much as he will their dislike. It is easy to see that your brother has a view in discrediting you with all your friends, with your uncles in particular: but for that very reason, you should comply, if possible, in order to disconcert his ungenerous measures. I will pray for you; and that is all I can do for you. I must now go down, and make a report, that you are resolved never to have Mr. Solmes—Must I?—Consider, my dear Miss Clary—Must I?

Indeed you must!—But of this I do assure you, that I will do nothing to disgrace the part you have had in my education. I will bear every thing that shall be short of forcing my hand into his who never can have any share in my heart. I will try by patient duty, by humility, to overcome them. But death will I choose, in any shape, rather than that man.

I dread to go down, said she, with so determined an answer: they will have no patience with me.—But let me leave you with one observation, which I beg of you always to bear in mind:—

'That persons of prudence, and distinguished talents, like yours, seem to be sprinkled through the world, to give credit, by their example, to religion and virtue. When such persons wilfully err, how great must be the fault! How ungrateful to that God, who blessed them with such talents! What a loss likewise to the world! What a wound to virtue!—But this, I hope, will never be to be said of Miss Clarissa Harlowe!'

I could give her no answer, but by my tears. And I thought, when she went away, the better half of my heart went with her.

I listened to hear what reception she would meet with below; and found it was just such a one as she had apprehended.

Will she, or will she not, be Mrs. Solmes? None of your whining circumlocutions, Mrs. Norton!—[You may guess who said this] Will she, or will she not, comply with her parents' will?

This cut short all she was going to say.

If I must speak so briefly, Miss will sooner die, than have—

Any body but Lovelace! interrupted my brother.—This, Madam, this, Sir, is your meek daughter! This is Mrs. Norton's sweet child!—Well, Goody, you may return to your own habitation. I am empowered to forbid you to have any correspondence with this perverse girl for a month to come, as you value the favour of our whole family, or of any individual of it.

And saying this, uncontradicted by any body, he himself shewed her to the door,—no doubt, with all that air of cruel insult, which the haughty rich can put on to the unhappy low, who have not pleased them.

So here, my dear Miss Howe, am I deprived of the advice of one of the most prudent and conscientious women in the world, were I to have ever so much occasion for it.

I might indeed write (as I presume, under your cover) and receive her answers to what I should write. But should such a correspondence be charged upon her, I know she would not be guilty of a falsehood for the world, nor even of an equivocation: and should she own it after this prohibition, she would forfeit my mother's favour for ever. And in my dangerous fever, some time ago, I engaged my mother to promise me, that, if I died before I could do any thing for the good woman, she would set her above want for the rest of her life, should her eyes fail her, or sickness befall her, and she could not provide for herself, as she now so prettily does by her fine needle-works.

What measures will they fall upon next?—Will they not recede when they find that it must be a rooted antipathy, and nothing else, that could make a temper, not naturally inflexible, so sturdy?

Adieu, my dear. Be you happy!—To know that it is in your power to be so, is all that seems wanting to make you so.

CL. HARLOWE.

LETTER XL

MISS CLARISSA HARLOWE, TO MISS HOWE [In continuation of the subject in Letter XXXVIII]

I will now, though midnight (for I have no sleep in my eyes) resume the subject I was forced so abruptly to quit, and will obey yours, Miss Lloyd's, Miss Campion's, and Miss Biddulph's call, with as much temper as my divided thought will admit. The dead stillness of this solemn hour will, I hope, contribute to calm my disturbed mind.

In order to acquit myself of so heavy a charge as that of having reserves to so dear a friend, I will acknowledge (and I thought I had over-and-over) that it is owing to my particular situation, if Mr. Lovelace appears to me in a tolerable light: and I take upon me to say, that had they opposed to him a man of sense, of virtue, of generosity; one who enjoyed his fortune with credit, who had a tenderness in his nature for the calamities of others, which would have given a moral assurance, that he would have been still less wanting in grateful returns to an obliging spirit:—had they opposed such a man as this to Mr. Lovelace, and been as earnest to have me married, as now they are, I do not know myself, if they would have had reason to tax me with that invincible obstinacy which they lay to my charge: and this whatever had been the figure of the man; since the heart is what we women should judge by in the choice we make, as the best security for the party's good behaviour in every relation of life.

But, situated as I am, thus persecuted and driven, I own to you, that I have now-and-then had a little more difficulty than I wished for, in passing by Mr. Lovelace's tolerable qualities, to keep up my dislike to him for his others.

You say, I must have argued with myself in his favour, and in his disfavour, on a supposition, that I might possibly be one day his. I own that I have: and thus called upon by my dearest friend, I will set before you both parts of the argument.

And first, what occurred to me in his favour.

At his introduction into our family, his negative virtues were insisted upon:—He was no gamester; no horse-racer; no fox-hunter; no drinker: my poor aunt Hervey had, in confidence, given us to apprehend much disagreeable evil (especially to a wife of the least delicacy) from a wine-lover: and common sense instructed us, that sobriety in a man is no small point to be secured, when so many mischiefs happen daily from excess. I remember, that my sister made the most of this favourable circumstance in his character while she had any hopes of him.

He was never thought to be a niggard; not even ungenerous: nor when his conduct came to be inquired into, an extravagant, a squanderer: his pride [so far was it a laudable pride] secured him from that. Then he was ever ready to own his errors. He was no jester upon sacred things: poor Mr. Wyerley's fault; who seemed to think there was wit in saying bold things, which would shock a serious mind. His conversation with us was always unexceptionable, even chastely so; which, be his actions what they would, shewed him capable of being influenced by decent company; and that he might probably therefore be a led man, rather than a leader, in other company. And one late instance, so late as last Saturday evening, has raised him not a little in my opinion, with regard to this point of good (and at the same time, of manly) behaviour.

As to the advantage of birth, that is of his side, above any man who has been found out for me. If we may judge by that expression of his, which you were pleased with at the time; 'That upon true quality, and hereditary distinction, if good sense were not wanting, humour sat as easy as his glove;' that, with as familiar an air, was his familiar expression; 'while none but the prosperous upstart, MUSHROOMED into rank, (another of his peculiars,) was arrogantly proud of it.'—If, I say, we may judge of him by this, we shall conclude in his favour, that he knows what sort of behaviour is to be expected from persons of birth, whether he act up to it or not. Conviction is half way to amendment.

His fortunes in possession are handsome; in expectation, splendid: so nothing need be said on that subject.

But it is impossible, say some, that he should make a tender or kind husband. Those who are for imposing upon me such a man as Mr. Solmes, and by methods so violent, are not entitled to make this objection. But now, on this subject, let me tell you how I have argued with myself—for still you must remember, that I am upon the extenuating part of his character.

A great deal of the treatment a wife may expect from him, will possibly depend upon herself. Perhaps she must practise as well as promise obedience, to a man so little used to controul; and must be careful to oblige. And what husband expects not this?—The more perhaps if he had not reason to assure himself of the preferable love of his wife before she became such. And how much easier and pleasanter to obey the man of her choice, if he should be even more unreasonable sometimes, than one she would not have had, could she have avoided it? Then, I think, as the men were the framers of the matrimonial office, and made obedience a part of the woman's vow, she ought not, even in policy, to shew him, that she can break through her part of the contract, (however lightly she may think of the instance,) lest he should take it into his head (himself is judge) to think as lightly of other points, which she may hold more important—but, indeed, no point so solemnly vowed can be slight.

Thus principled, and acting accordingly, what a wretch must that husband be, who could treat such a wife brutally!—Will Lovelace's wife be the only person to whom he will not pay the grateful debt of civility and good manners? He is allowed to be brave: Who ever knew a brave man, if a brave man of sense, an universally base man? And how much the gentleness of our sex, and the manner of our training up and education, make us need the protection of the brave, and the countenance of the generous, let the general approbation, which we are all so naturally inclined to give to men of that character, testify.

At worst, will he confine me prisoner to my chamber? Will he deny me the visits of my dearest friend, and forbid me to correspond with her? Will he take from me the mistressly management, which I had not faultily discharged? Will he set a servant over me, with license to insult me? Will he, as he has not a sister, permit his cousins Montague, or would either of those ladies accept of a permission, to insult and tyrannize over me?—It cannot be.—Why then, think I often, do you tempt me, O my cruel friends, to try the difference?

And then has the secret pleasure intruded itself, to be able to reclaim such a man to the paths of virtue and honour: to be a secondary means, if I were to be his, of saving him, and preventing the mischiefs so enterprising a creature might otherwise be guilty of, if he be such a one.

When I have thought of him in these lights, (and that as a man of sense he will sooner see his errors, than another,) I own to you, that I have had some difficulty to avoid taking the path they so violently endeavour to make me shun: and all that command of my passions which has been attributed to me as my greatest praise, and, in so young a creature, as my distinction, has hardly been sufficient for me.

And let me add, that the favour of his relations (all but himself unexceptionable) has made a good deal of additional weight, thrown in the same scale.

But now, in his disfavour. When I have reflected upon the prohibition of my parents; the giddy appearance, disgraceful to our sex, that such a preference would have: that there is no manner of likelihood, enflamed by the rencounter, and upheld by art and ambition on my brother's side, that ever the animosity will be got over: that I must therefore be at perpetual variance with all my own family: that I must go to him, and to his, as an obliged and half-fortuned person: that his aversion to them all is as strong as theirs to him: that his whole family are hated for his sake; they hating ours in return: that he has a very immoral character as to women: that knowing this, it is a high degree of impurity to think of joining in wedlock with such a man: that he is young, unbroken, his passions unsubdued: that he is violent in his temper, yet artful; I am afraid vindictive too: that such a husband might unsettle me in all my own principles, and hazard my future hopes: that his own relations, two excellent aunts, and an uncle, from whom he has such large expectations, have no influence upon him: that what tolerable qualities he has, are founded more in pride than in virtue: that allowing, as he does, the excellency of moral precepts, and believing the doctrine of future rewards and punishments, he can live as if he despised the one, and defied the other: the probability that the taint arising from such free principles, may go down into the manners of posterity: that I knowing these things, and the importance of them, should be more inexcusable than one who knows them not; since an error against judgment is worse, infinitely worse, than an error in judgment. Reflecting upon these things, I cannot help conjuring you, my dear, to pray with me, and to pray for me, that I may not be pushed upon such indiscreet measures, as will render me inexcusable to myself: for that is the test, after all. The world's opinion ought to be but a secondary consideration.

I have said in his praise, that he is extremely ready to own his errors: but I have sometimes made a great drawback upon this article, in his disfavour; having been ready to apprehend, that this ingenuousness may possibly be attributable to two causes, neither of them, by any means, creditable to him. The one, that his vices are so much his masters, that he attempts not to conquer them; the other, that he may think it policy, to give up one half of his character to save the other, when the whole may be blamable: by this means, silencing by acknowledgment the objections he cannot answer; which may give him the praise of ingenuousness, when he can obtain no other, and when the challenged proof might bring out, upon discussion, other evils. These, you will allow, are severe constructions; but every thing his enemies say of him cannot be false.

I will proceed by-and-by.

Sometimes we have both thought him one of the most undesigning merely witty men we ever knew; at other times one of the deepest creatures we ever conversed with. So that when in one visit we have imagined we fathomed him, in the next he has made us ready to give him up as impenetrable. This impenetrableness, my dear, is to be put among the shades in his character. Yet, upon the whole, you have been so far of his party, that you have contested that his principal fault is over-frankness, and too much regardlessness of appearances, and that he is too giddy to be very artful: you would have it, that at the time he says any thing good, he means what he speaks; that his variableness and levity are constitutional, owing to sound health, and to a soul and body [that was your observation] fitted for and pleased with each other. And hence you concluded, that could this consentaneousness [as you call it] of corporal and animal faculties be pointed by discretion; that is to say, could his vivacity be confined within the pale of but moral obligations, he would be far from being rejectable as a companion for life.

But I used then to say, and I still am of opinion, that he wants a heart: and if he does, he wants every thing. A wrong head may be convinced, may have a right turn given it: but who is able to give a heart, if a heart be wanting? Divine Grace, working a miracle, or next to a miracle, can only change a bad heart. Should not one fly the man who is but suspected of such a one? What, O what, do parents do, when they endeavour to force a child's inclination, but make her think better than otherwise she would think of a man obnoxious to themselves, and perhaps whose character will not stand examination?

I have said, that I think Mr. Lovelace a vindictive man: upon my word, I have sometimes doubted, whether his perseverance in his addresses to me has not been the more obstinate, since he has found himself so disagreeable to my friends. From that time I verily think he has been the more fervent in them; yet courts them not, but sets them at defiance. For this indeed he pleads disinterestedness [I am sure he cannot politeness]; and the more plausibly, as he is apprized of the ability they have to make it worth his while to court them. 'Tis true he has declared, and with too much reason, (or there would be no bearing him,) that the lowest submissions on his part would not be accepted; and to oblige me, has offered to seek a reconciliation with them, if I would give him hope of success.

As to his behaviour at church, the Sunday before last, I lay no stress upon that, because I doubt there was too much outward pride in his intentional humility, or Shorey, who is not his enemy, could not have mistaken it.

I do not think him so deeply learned in human nature, or in ethics, as some have thought him. Don't you remember how he stared at the following trite observations, which every moralist could have furnished him with? Complaining as he did, in a half-menacing strain, of the obloquies raised against him—'That if he were innocent, he should despise the obloquy: if not, revenge would not wipe off his guilt.' 'That nobody ever thought of turning a sword into a sponge!' 'That it was in his own power by reformation of an error laid to his charge by an enemy, to make that enemy one of his best friends; and (which was the noblest revenge in the world) against his will; since an enemy would not wish him to be without the faults he taxed him with.'

But the intention, he said, was the wound.

How so, I asked him, when that cannot wound without the application? 'That the adversary only held the sword: he himself pointed it to his breast:—And why should he mortally resent that malice, which he might be the better for as long as he lived?'—What could be the reading he has been said to be master of, to wonder, as he did, at these observations?

But, indeed, he must take pleasure in revenge; and yet holds others to be inexcusable for the same fault. He is not, however, the only one who can see how truly blamable those errors are in another, which they hardly think such in themselves.

From these considerations, from these over-balances, it was, that I said, in a former, that I would not be in love with this man for the world: and it was going further than prudence would warrant, when I was for compounding with you, by the words conditional liking, which you so humourously rally.

Well but, methinks you say, what is all this to the purpose? This is still but reasoning: but, if you are in love, you are: and love, like the vapours, is the deeper rooted for having no sufficient cause assignable for its hold. And so you call upon me again to have no reserves, and so-forth.

Why then, my dear, if you will have it, I think, that, with all his preponderating faults, I like him better than I ever thought I should like him; and, those faults considered, better perhaps than I ought to like him. And I believe, it is possible for the persecution I labour under to induce me to like him still more—especially while I can recollect to his advantage our last interview, and as every day produces stronger instances of tyranny, I will call it, on the other side.—In a word, I will frankly own (since you cannot think any thing I say too explicit) that were he now but a moral man, I would prefer him to all the men I ever saw.

So that this is but conditional liking still, you'll say: nor, I hope, is it more. I never was in love as it is called; and whether this be it, or not, I must submit to you. But will venture to think it, if it be, no such mighty monarch, no such unconquerable power, as I have heard it represented; and it must have met with greater encouragement than I think I have given it, to be absolutely unconquerable—since I am persuaded, that I could yet, without a throb, most willingly give up the one man to get rid of the other.

But now to be a little more serious with you: if, my dear, my particularly-unhappy situation had driven (or led me, if you please) into a liking of the man; and if that liking had, in your opinion, inclined me to love him, should you, whose mind is susceptible of the most friendly impressions, who have such high notions of the delicacy which ought to be observed by our sex in these matters, and who actually do enter so deeply into the distresses of one you love—should you have pushed so far that unhappy friend on so very nice a subject?—Especially, when I aimed not (as you could prove by fifty instances, it seems) to guard against being found out. Had you rallied me by word of mouth in the manner you do, it might have been more in character; especially, if your friend's distresses had been surmounted, and if she had affected prudish airs in revolving the subject: but to sit down to write it, as methinks I see you, with a gladdened eye, and with all the archness of exultation—indeed, my dear, (and I take notice of it, rather for the sake of your own generosity, than for my sake, for, as I have said, I love your raillery,) it is not so very pretty; the delicacy of the subject, and the delicacy of your own mind, considered.

I lay down my pen here, that you may consider of it a little, if you please.

I resume, to give you my opinion of the force which figure or person ought to have upon our sex: and this I shall do both generally as to the other sex, and particularly as to this man; whence you will be able to collect how far my friends are in the right, or in the wrong, when they attribute a good deal of prejudice in favour of one man, and in disfavour of the other, on the score of figure. But, first, let me observe, that they see abundant reason, on comparing Mr. Lovelace and Mr. Solmes together, to believe that this may be a consideration with me; and therefore they believe it is.

There is certainly something very plausible and attractive, as well as creditable to a woman's choice, in figure. It gives a favourable impression at first sight, in which we wish to be confirmed: and if, upon further acquaintance, we find reason to be so, we are pleased with our judgment, and like the person the better, for having given us cause to compliment our own sagacity, in our first-sighted impressions. But, nevertheless, it has been generally a rule with me, to suspect a fine figure, both in man and woman; and I have had a good deal of reason to approve my rule;—with regard to men especially, who ought to value themselves rather upon their intellectual than personal qualities. For, as to our sex, if a fine woman should be led by the opinion of the world, to be vain and conceited upon her form and features; and that to such a degree, as to have neglected the more material and more durable recommendations, the world will be ready to excuse her; since a pretty fool, in all she says, and in all she does, will please, we know not why.

But who would grudge this pretty fool her short day! Since, with her summer's sun, when her butterfly flutters are over, and the winter of age and furrows arrives, she will feel the just effects of having neglected to cultivate her better faculties: for then, lie another Helen, she will be unable to bear the reflection even of her own glass, and being sunk into the insignificance of a mere old woman, she will be entitled to the contempts which follow that character. While the discreet matron, who carries up [we will not, in such a one's case, say down] into advanced life, the ever-amiable character of virtuous prudence and useful experience, finds solid veneration take place of airy admiration, and more than supply the want of it.

But for a man to be vain of his person, how effeminate! If such a one happens to have genius, it seldom strikes deep into intellectual subjects. His outside usually runs away with him. To adorn, and perhaps, intending to adorn, to render ridiculous that person, takes up all his attention. All he does is personal; that is to say, for himself: all he admires, is himself: and in spite of the correction of the stage, which so often and so justly exposes a coxcomb, he usually dwindles down, and sinks into that character; and, of consequence, becomes the scorn of one sex, and the jest of the other.

This is generally the case of your fine figures of men, and of those who value themselves on dress and outward appearance: whence it is, that I repeat, that mere person in a man is a despicable consideration. But if a man, besides figure, has learning, and such talents as would have distinguished him, whatever were his form, then indeed person is an addition: and if he has not run too egregiously into self-admiration, and if he has preserved his morals, he is truly a valuable being.

Mr. Lovelace has certainly taste; and, as far as I am able to determine, he has judgment in most of the politer arts. But although he has a humourous way of carrying it off, yet one may see that he values himself not a little, both on his person and his parts, and even upon his dress; and yet he has so happy an ease in the latter, that it seems to be the least part of his study.

And as to the former, I should hold myself inexcusable, if I were to add to his vanity by shewing the least regard for what is too evidently so much his.

And now, my dear, let me ask you, Have I come up to your expectation? If I have not, when my mind is more at ease, I will endeavour to please you better. For, methinks, my sentences drag, my style creeps, my imagination is sunk, my spirits serve me not, only to tell you, that whether I have more or less, I am wholly devoted to the commands of my dear Miss Howe.

P.S. The insolent Betty Barnes has just now fired me anew, by reporting to me the following expressions of the hideous creature, Solmes—'That he is sure of the coy girl; and that with little labour to himself. That be I ever so averse to him beforehand, he can depend upon my principles; and it will be a pleasure to him to see by what pretty degrees I shall come to.' [Horrid wretch!] 'That it was Sir Oliver's observation, who knew the world perfectly well, that fear was a better security than love, for a woman's good behaviour to her husband; although, for his part, to such a fine creature [truly] he would try what love would do, for a few weeks at least; being unwilling to believe what the old knight used to aver, that fondness spoils more wives than it makes good.'

What think you, my dear, of such a wretch as this! tutored, too, by that old surly misogynist, as he was deemed, Sir Oliver?—

LETTER XLI

MISS CLARISSA HARLOWE, TO MISS HOWE TUESDAY, MARCH 21

How willingly would my dear mother shew kindness to me, were she permitted! None of this persecution should I labour under, I am sure, if that regard were paid to her prudence and fine understanding, which they so well deserve. Whether owing to her, or to my aunt, or to both, that a new trial was to be made upon me, I cannot tell, but this morning her Shorey delivered into my hand the following condescending letter.

MY DEAR GIRL,

For so I must still call you; since dear you may be to me, in every sense of the word—we have taken into particular consideration some hints that fell yesterday from your good Norton, as if we had not, at Mr. Solmes's first application, treated you with that condescension, wherewith we have in all other instances treated you. If it even had been so, my dear, you were not excusable to be wanting in your part, and to set yourself to oppose your father's will in a point which he had entered too far, to recede with honour. But all yet may be well. On your single will, my child, depends all our happiness.

Your father permits me to tell you, that if you now at last comply with his expectations, all past disobligations shall be buried in oblivion, as if they had never been: but withal, that this is the last time that that grace will be offered you.

I hinted to you, you must remember,* that patterns of the richest silks were sent for. They are come. And as they are come, your father, to shew how much he is determined, will have me send them up to you. I could have wished they might not have accompanied this letter, but there is not great matter in that. I must tell you, that your delicacy is not quite so much regarded as I had once thought it deserved to be.

* *See Letter XX.*

These are the newest, as well as richest, that we could procure; answerable to our situation in the world; answerable to the fortune, additional to your grandfather's estate, designed you; and to the noble settlements agreed upon.

Your father intends you six suits (three of them dressed suits) at his own expense. You have an entire new suit; and one besides, which I think you never wore but twice. As the new suit is rich, if you choose to make that one of the six, your father will present you with an hundred guineas in lieu.

Mr. Solmes intends to present you with a set of jewels. As you have your grandmother's and your own, if you choose to have the former new set, and to make them serve, his present will be made in money; a very round sum—which will be given in full property to yourself; besides a fine annual allowance for pin-money, as it is called. So that your objection against the spirit of a man you think worse of than it deserves, will have no weight; but you will be more independent than a wife of less discretion than we attribute to you, perhaps ought to be. You know full well, that I, who first and last brought a still larger fortune into the family than you will carry to Mr. Solmes, had not a provision made me of near this that we have made for you.—Where people marry to their liking, terms are the least things stood upon—yet should I be sorry if you cannot (to oblige us all) overcome a dislike.

Wonder not, Clary, that I write to you thus plainly and freely upon this subject. Your behaviour hitherto has been such, that we have had no opportunity of entering minutely into the subject with you. Yet, after all that has passed between you and me in conversation, and between you and your uncles by letter, you have no room to doubt what is to be the consequence.—Either, child, we must give up our authority, or you your humour. You cannot expect the one. We have all the reason in the world to expect the other. You know I have told you more than once, that you must resolve to have Mr. Solmes, or never to be looked upon as our child.

The draught of the settlement you may see whenever you will. We think there can be no room for objection to any of the articles. There is still more in them in our family's favour, than was stipulated at first, when your aunt talked of them to you. More so, indeed, than we could have asked. If, upon perusal of them, you think any alteration necessary, it shall be made.—Do, my dear girl, send to me within this day or two, or rather ask me, for the perusal of them.

As a certain person's appearance at church so lately, and what he gives out every where, makes us extremely uneasy, and as that uneasiness will continue while you are single, you must not wonder that a short day is intended. This day fortnight we design it to be, if you have no objection to make that I shall approve of. But if you determine as we would have you, and signify it to us, we shall not stand with you for a week or so.

Your sightlines of person may perhaps make some think this alliance disparaging. But I hope you will not put such a personal value upon yourself: if you do, it will indeed be the less wonder that person should weigh with you (however weak the consideration!) in another man.

Thus we parents, in justice, ought to judge: that our two daughters are equally dear and valuable to us: if so, why should Clarissa think that a disparagement, which Arabella would not (nor we for her) have thought any, had the address been made to her?—You will know what I mean by this, without my explaining myself farther.

Signify to us, now, therefore, your compliance with our wishes. And then there is an end of your confinement. An act of oblivion, as I may call it, shall pass upon all your former refractoriness: and you will once more make us happy in you, and in one another. You may, in this case, directly come down to your father and me, in his study; where we will give you our opinions of the patterns, with our hearty forgiveness and blessings.

Come, be a good child, as you used to be, my Clarissa. I have (notwithstanding your past behaviour, and the hopelessness which some have expressed in your compliance) undertaken this one time more for you. Discredit not my hopes, my dear girl. I have promised never more to interfere between your father and you, if this my most earnest application succeed not. I expect you down, love. Your father expects you down. But be sure don't let him see any thing uncheerful in your compliance. If you come, I will clasp you to my fond heart, with as much pleasure as ever I pressed you to it in my whole life. You don't know what I have suffered within these few weeks past; nor ever will be able to guess, till you come to be in my situation; which is that of a fond and indulgent mother, praying night and day, and struggling to preserve, against the attempts of more ungovernable spirits, the peace and union of her family.

But you know the terms. Come not near us, if you have resolve to be undutiful: but this, after what I have written, I hope you cannot be.

If you come directly, and, as I have said, cheerfully, as if your heart were in your duty, (and you told me it was free, you know,) I shall then, as I said, give you the most tender proofs how much I am

Your truly affectionate Mother.

Think for me, my dearest friend, how I must be affected by this letter; the contents of it is so surprisingly terrifying, yet so sweetly urged!—O why, cried I to myself, am I obliged to undergo this severe conflict between a command that I cannot obey, and language so condescendingly moving!—Could I have been sure of being struck dead at the alter before the ceremony had given the man I hate a title to my vows, I think I could have submitted to having been led to it. But to think of living with and living for a man one abhors, what a sad thing is that!

And then, how could the glare of habit and ornament be supposed any inducement to one, who has always held, that the principal view of a good wife in the adorning of her person, ought to be, to preserve the affection of her husband, and to do credit to his choice; and that she should be even fearful of attracting the eyes of others?—In this view, must not the very richness of the patterns add to my disgusts?—Great encouragement, indeed, to think of adorning one's self to be the wife of Mr. Solmes!

Upon the whole, it was not possible for me to go down upon the prescribed condition. Do you think it was?—And to write, if my letter would have been read, what could I write that would be admitted, and after what I had written and said to so little effect?

I walked backward and forward. I threw down with disdain the patterns. Now to my closet retired I; then quitting it, threw myself upon the settee; then upon this chair, then upon that; then into one window, then into another—I knew not what to do!—And while I was in this suspense, having again taken up the letter to re-peruse it, Betty came in, reminding me, by order, that my papa and mamma waited for me in my father's study.

Tell my mamma, said I, that I beg the favour of seeing her here for one moment, or to permit me to attend her any where by herself.

I listened at the stairs-head—You see, my dear, how it is, cried my father, very angrily: all your condescension (as your indulgence heretofore) is thrown away. You blame your son's violence, as you call it [I had some pleasure in hearing this]; but nothing else will do with her. You shall not see her alone. Is my presence an exception to the bold creature?

Tell her, said my mother to Betty, she knows upon what terms she may come down to us. Nor will I see her upon any other.

The maid brought me this answer. I had recourse to my pen and ink; but I trembled so, that I could not write, nor knew what to say, had I steadier fingers. At last Betty brought me these lines from my father.

UNDUTIFUL AND PERVERSE CLARISSA,

No condescension, I see, will move you. Your mother shall not see you; nor will I. Prepare however to obey. You know our pleasure. Your uncle Antony, your brother, and your sister, and your favourite Mrs. Norton, shall see the ceremony performed privately at your uncle's chapel. And when Mr. Solmes can introduce you to us, in the temper we wish to behold you in, we may perhaps forgive his wife, although we never can, in any other character, our perverse daughter. As it will be so privately performed, clothes and equipage may be provided for afterwards. So prepare to go to your uncle's for an early day in next week. We will not see you till all is over: and we will have it over the sooner, in order to shorten the time of your deserved confinement, and our own trouble in contending with such a rebel, as you have been of late. I will hear no pleas, I will receive no letter, nor expostulation. Nor shall you hear from me any more till you have changed your name to my liking. This from

Your incensed Father.

If this resolution be adhered to, then will my father never see me more!—For I will never be the wife of that Solmes—I will die first—!

TUESDAY EVENING.

He, this Solmes, came hither soon after I had received my father's letter. He sent up to beg leave to wait upon me—I wonder at his assurance—!

I said to Betty, who brought me this message, let him restore an unhappy creature to her father and mother, and then I may hear what he has to say. But, if my friends will not see me on his account, I will not see him upon his own.

I hope, Miss, said Betty, you will not send me down with this answer. He is with you papa and mamma.

I am driven to despair, said I. I cannot be used worse. I will not see him.

Down she went with my answer. She pretended, it seems, to be loth to repeat it: so was commanded out of her affected reserves, and gave it in its full force.

O how I heard my father storm!

They were altogether, it seems, in his study. My brother was for having me turned out of the house that moment, to Lovelace, and my evil destiny. My mother was pleased to put in a gentle word for me: I know not what it was: but thus she was answered—My dear, this is the most provoking thing in the world in a woman of your good sense!—To love a rebel, as well as if she were dutiful. What encouragement for duty is this?—Have I not loved her as well as ever you did? And why am I changed! Would to the Lord, your sex knew how to distinguish! It is plain, that she relies upon her power over you. The fond mother ever made a hardened child!

She was pleased, however, to blame Betty, as the wench owned, for giving my answer its full force. But my father praised her for it.

The wench says, that he would have come up in his wrath, at my refusing to see Mr. Solmes, had not my brother and sister prevailed upon him to the contrary.

I wish he had!—And, were it not for his own sake, that he had killed me!

Mr. Solmes condescended [I am mightily obliged to him truly!] to plead for me.

They are all in tumults! How it will end, I know not—I am quite weary of life—So happy, till within these few weeks!—So miserable now!

Well, indeed, might my mother say, that I should have severe trials.*

* See Letter XXV.

P.S. The idiot [such a one am I treated like!] is begged, as I may say, by my brother and sister. They have desired, that I may be consigned over entirely to their management. If it be granted, [it is granted, on my father's part, I understand, but not yet on my mother's,] what cruelty may I not expect from their envy, jealousy, and ill-will!—I shall soon see, by its effects, if I am to be so consigned. This is a written intimation privately dropt in my wood-house walk, by my cousin Dolly Hervey. The dear girl longs to see me, she tells me: but is forbidden till she see me as Mrs. Solmes, or as consenting to be his. I will take example by their perseverance!—Indeed I will—!

LETTER XLII

MISS CLARISSA HARLOWE, TO MISS HOWE

An angry dialogue, a scolding-bout rather, has passed between my sister and me. Did you think I could scold, my dear?

She was sent up to me, upon my refusal to see Mr. Solmes—let loose upon me, I think!—No intention on their parts to conciliate! It seems evident that I am given up to my brother and her, by general consent.

I will do justice to every thing she said against me, which carried any force with it. As I ask for your approbation or disapprobation of my conduct, upon the facts I lay before you, I should think it the sign of a very bad cause, if I endeavoured to mislead my judge.

She began with representing to me the danger I had been in, had my father come up, as he would have done had he not been hindered—by Mr. Solmes, among the rest. She reflected upon my Norton, as if she encouraged me in my perverseness. She ridiculed me for my supposed esteem for Mr. Lovelace—was surprised that the witty, the prudent, nay, the dutiful and pi—ous [so she sneeringly pronounced the word] Clarissa Harlowe, should be so strangely fond of a profligate man, that her parents were forced to lock her up, in order to hinder her from running into his arms. 'Let me ask you, my dear, said she, how you now keep your account of the disposition of your time? How many hours in the twenty-four do you devote to your needle? How many to your prayers? How many to letter-writing? And how many to love?—I doubt, I doubt, my little dear, was her arch expression, the latter article is like Aaron's rod, and swallows up the rest!—Tell me; is it not so?'

To these I answered, That it was a double mortification to me to owe my safety from the effects of my father's indignation to a man I could never thank for any thing. I vindicated the good Mrs. Norton with a warmth that was due to her merit. With equal warmth I resented her reflections upon me on Mr. Lovelace's account. As to the disposition of my time in the twenty-four hours, I told her it would better have become her to pity a sister in distress, than to exult over her—especially, when I could too justly attribute to the disposition of some of her wakeful hours no small part of that distress.

She raved extremely at this last hint: but reminded me of the gentle treatment of all my friends, my mother's in particular, before it came to this. She said, that I had discovered a spirit they never had expected: that, if they had thought me such a championess, they would hardly have ventured to engage with me: but that now, the short and the long of it was, that the matter had gone too far to be given up: that it was become a contention between duty and willfulness; whether a parent's authority were to yield to a daughter's obstinacy, or the contrary: that I must therefore bend or break, that was all, child.

I told her, that I wished the subject were of such a nature, that I could return her pleasantry with equal lightness of heart: but that, if Mr. Solmes had such merit in every body's eyes, in hers, particularly, why might he not be a brother to me, rather than a husband?

O child, says she, methinks you are as pleasant to the full as I am: I begin to have some hopes of you now. But do you think I will rob my sister of her humble servant? Had he first addressed himself to me, proceeded she, something might have been said: but to take my younger sister's refusal! No, no, child; it is not come to that neither! Besides, that would be to leave the door open in your heart for you know who, child; and we would fain bar him out, if possible. In short [and then she changed both her tone and her looks] had I been as forward as somebody, to throw myself into the arms of one of the greatest profligates in England, who had endeavoured to support his claim to me through the blood of my brother, then might all my family join together to save me from such a wretch, and to marry me as fast as they could, to some worthy man, who might opportunely offer himself. And now, Clary, all's out, and make the most of it.

Did not this deserve a severe return? Do, say it did, to justify my reply.—Alas! for my poor sister! said I—The man was not always so great a profligate. How true is the observation, That unrequited love turns to deepest hate!

I thought she would beat me. But I proceeded—I have heard often of my brother's danger, and my brother's murderer. When so little ceremony is made with me, why should I not speak out?—Did he not seek to kill the other, if he could have done it? Would my brother have given Lovelace his life, had it been in his power?—The aggressor should not complain.—And, as to opportune offers, would to Heaven some one had offered opportunely to somebody! It is not my fault, Bella, the opportune gentleman don't come!

Could you, my dear, have shewn more spirit? I expected to feel the weight of her hand. She did come up to me, with it held up: then, speechless with passion, ran half way down the stairs, and came up again.

When she could speak—God give me patience with you!

Amen, said I: but you see, Bella, how ill you bear the retort you provoke. Will you forgive me; and let me find a sister in you, as I am sorry, if you had reason to think me unsisterly in what I have said?

Then did she pour upon me, with greater violence; considering my gentleness as a triumph of temper over her. She was resolved, she said, to let every body know how I took the wicked Lovelace's part against my brother.

I wished, I told her, I could make the plea for myself, which she might for herself; to wit, that my anger was more inexcusable than my judgment. But I presumed she had some other view in coming to me, than she had hitherto acquainted me with. Let me, said I, but know (after all that has passed) if you have any thing to propose that I can comply with; any thing that can make my only sister once more my friend?

I had before, upon hearing her ridiculing me on my supposed character of meekness, said, that, although I wished to be thought meek, I would not be abject; although humble not mean: and here, in a sneering way, she cautioned me on that head.

I replied, that her pleasantry was much more agreeable than her anger. But I wished she would let me know the end of a visit that had hitherto (between us) been so unsisterly.

She desired to be informed, in the name of every body, was her word, what I was determined upon? And whether to comply or not?—One word for all: My friends were not to have patience with so perverse a creature for ever.

This then I told her I would do: Absolutely break with the man they were all so determined against: upon condition, however, that neither Mr. Solmes, nor any other, were urged upon me with the force of a command.

And what was this, more than I had offered before? What, but ringing my changes upon the same bells, and neither receding nor advancing one tittle?

If I knew what other proposals I could make, I told her, that would be acceptable to them all, and free me from the address of a man so disagreeable to me, I would make them. I had indeed before offered, never to marry without my father's consent—

She interrupted me, That was because I depended upon my whining tricks to bring my father and mother to what I pleased.

A poor dependence! I said:—She knew those who would make that dependence vain—

And I should have brought them to my own beck, very probably, and my uncle Harlowe too, as also my aunt Hervey, had I not been forbidden from their sight, and thereby hindered from playing my pug's tricks before them.

At least, Bella, said I, you have hinted to me to whom I am obliged, that my father and mother, and every body else, treat me thus harshly. But surely you make them all very weak. Indifferent persons, judging of us two from what you say, would either think me a very artful creature, or you a very spiteful one—

You are indeed a very artful one, for that matter, interrupted she in a passion: one of the artfullest I ever knew! And then followed an accusation so low! so unsisterly!—That I half-bewitched people by my insinuating address: that nobody could be valued or respected, but must stand like ciphers wherever I came. How often, said she, have I and my brother been talking upon a subject, and had every body's attention, till you came in, with your bewitching meek pride, and humble significance? And then have we either been stopped by references to Miss Clary's opinion, forsooth; or been forced to stop ourselves, or must have talked on unattended to by every body.

She paused. Dear Bella, proceed!

She indeed seemed only gathering breath.

And so I will, said she—Did you not bewitch my grandfather? Could any thing be pleasing to him, that you did not say or do? How did he use to hang, till he slabbered again, poor doting old man! on your silver tongue! Yet what did you say, that we could not have said? What did you do, that we did not endeavour to do?—And what was all this for? Why, truly, his last will shewed what effect your smooth obligingness had upon him!—To leave the acquired part of his estate from the next heirs, his own sons, to a grandchild; to his youngest grandchild! A daughter too!—To leave the family-pictures from his sons to you, because you could tiddle about them, and, though you now neglect their examples, could wipe and clean them with your dainty hands! The family-plate too, in such quantities, of two or three generations standing, must not be changed, because his precious child,* humouring his old fal-lal taste, admired it, to make it all her own.

** Alluding to his words in the preamble to the clauses in his will. See Letter IV.*

This was too low to move me: O my poor sister! said I: not to be able, or at least willing, to distinguish between art and nature! If I did oblige, I was happy in it: I looked for no further reward: my mind is above art, from the dirty motives you mention. I wish with all my heart my grandfather had not thus distinguished me; he saw my brother likely to be amply provided for out of the family, as well as in it: he desired that you might have the greater share of my father's favour for it; and no doubt but you both have. You know, Bella, that the estate my grandfather bequeathed me was not half the real estate he left.

What's all that to an estate in possession, and left you with such distinctions, as gave you a reputation of greater value than the estate itself?

Hence my misfortune, Bella, in your envy, I doubt!—But have I not given up that possession in the best manner I could—

Yes, interrupting me, she hated me for that best manner. Specious little witch! she called me: your best manner, so full of art and design, had never been seen through, if you, with your blandishing ways, have not been put out of sight, and reduced to positive declarations!—Hindered from playing your little declarations!—Hindered from playing your little whining tricks! curling, like a serpent about your mamma; and making her cry to deny you any thing your little obstinate heart was set upon—!

Obstinate heart, Bella!

Yes, obstinate heart! For did you ever give up any thing? Had you not the art to make them think all was right you asked, though my brother and I were frequently refused favours of no greater import!

I know not, Bella, that I ever asked any thing unfit to be granted. I seldom asked favours for myself, but for others.

I was a reflecting creature for this.

All you speak of, Bella, was a long time ago. I cannot go so far back into our childish follies. Little did I think of how long standing your late-shewn antipathy is.

I was a reflector again! Such a saucy meekness; such a best manner; and such venom in words!—O Clary! Clary! Thou wert always a two-faced girl!

Nobody thought I had two faces, when I gave up all into my father's management; taking from his bounty, as before, all my little pocket-money, without a shilling addition to my stipend, or desiring it—

Yes, cunning creature!—And that was another of your fetches!—For did it not engage my fond father (as no doubt you thought it would) to tell you, that since you had done so grateful and dutiful a thing, he would keep entire, for your use, all the produce of the estate left you, and be but your steward in it; and that you should be entitled to the same allowances as before? Another of your hook-in's, Clary!—So that all your extravagancies have been supported gratis.

My extravagancies, Bella!—But did my father ever give me any thing he did not give you?

Yes, indeed; I got more by that means, than I should have had the conscience to ask. But I have still the greater part to shew! But you! What have you to shew?—I dare say, not fifty pieces in the world!

Indeed I have not!

I believe you!—Your mamma Norton, I suppose—But mum for that—!

Unworthy Bella! The good woman, although low in circumstance, is great in mind! Much greater than those who would impute meanness to a soul incapable of it.

What then have you done with the sums given you from infancy to squander?—Let me ask you [affecting archness], Has, has, has Lovelace, has your rake, put it out at interest for you?

O that my sister would not make me blush for her! It is, however, out at interest!—And I hope it will bring me interest upon interest!—Better than to lie useless in my cabinet.

She understood me, she said. Were I a man, she should suppose I was aiming to carry the county—Popularity! A crowd to follow me with their blessings as I went to and from church, and nobody else to be regarded, were agreeable things. House-top-proclamations! I hid not my light under a bushel, she would say that for me. But was it not a little hard upon me, to be kept from blazing on a Sunday?—And to be hindered from my charitable ostentations?

This, indeed, Bella, is cruel in you, who have so largely contributed to my confinement.—But go on. You'll be out of breath by-and-by. I cannot wish to be able to return this usage.—Poor Bella! And I believe I smiled a little too contemptuously for a sister to a sister.

None of your saucy contempts [rising in her voice]: None of your poor Bella's, with that air of superiority in a younger sister!

Well then, rich Bella! courtesying—that will please you better—and it is due likewise to the hoards you boast of.

Look ye, Clary, holding up her hand, if you are not a little more abject in your meekness, a little more mean in your humility, and treat me with the respect due to an elder sister—you shall find—

Not that you will treat me worse than you have done, Bella!—That cannot be; unless you were to let fall your uplifted hand upon me—and that would less become you to do, than me to bear.

Good, meek creature:—But you were upon your overtures just now!—I shall surprise every body by tarrying so long. They will think some good may be done with you—and supper will be ready.

A tear would stray down my cheek—How happy have I been, said I, sighing, in the supper-time conversations, with all my dear friends in my eye round their hospitable board.

I met only with insult for this—Bella has not a feeling heart. The highest joy in this life she is not capable of: but then she saves herself many griefs, by her impenetrableness—yet, for ten times the pain that such a sensibility is attended with, would I not part with the pleasure it brings with it.

She asked me, upon my turning from her, if she should not say any thing below of my compliances?

You may say, that I will do every thing they would have me do, if they will free me from Mr. Solmes's address.

This is all you desire at present, creeper on! insinuator! [What words she has!] But will not t'other man flame out, and roar most horribly, upon the snatching from his paws a prey he thought himself sure of?

I must let you talk in your own way, or we shall never come to a point. I shall not matter in his roaring, as you call it. I will promise him, that, if I ever marry any other man, it shall not be till he is married. And if he be not satisfied with such a condescension, I shall think he ought: and I will give any assurances, that I will neither correspond with him, nor see him. Surely this will do.

But I suppose then you will have no objection to see and converse, on a civil footing, with Mr. Solmes—as your father's friend, or so?

No! I must be permitted to retire to my apartment whenever he comes. I would no more converse with the one, than correspond with the other. That would be to make Mr. Lovelace guilty of some rashness, on a belief, that I broke with him, to have Mr. Solmes.

And so, that wicked wretch is to be allowed such a controul over you, that you are not to be civil to your father's friends, at his own house, for fear of incensing him!—When this comes to be represented, be so good as to tell me, what is it you expect from it!

Every thing, I said, or nothing, as she was pleased to represent it.—Be so good as to give it your interest, Bella, and say, further, 'That I will by any means I can, in the law or otherwise, make over to my father, to my uncles, or even to my brother, all I am entitled to by my grandfather's will, as a security for the performance of my promises. And as I shall have no reason to expect any favour from my father, if I break them, I shall not be worth any body's having. And further still, unkindly as my brother has used me, I will go down to Scotland privately, as his housekeeper [I now see I may be spared here] if he will promise to treat me no worse than he would do an hired one.—Or I will go to Florence, to my cousin Morden, if his stay in Italy will admit of it. In either case, it may be given out, that I am gone to the other; or to the world's end. I care not whither it is said I am gone, or do go.'

Let me ask you, child, if you will give your pretty proposal in writing?

Yes, with all my heart. And I stepped to my closet, and wrote to the purpose I have mentioned; and moreover, the following lines to my brother.

> MY DEAR BROTHER,
>
> I hope I have made such proposals to my sister as will be accepted. I am sure they will, if you please to give them your sanction. Let me beg of you, for God's sake, that you will. I think myself very unhappy in having incurred your displeasure. No sister can love a brother better than I love you. Pray do not put the worst but the best constructions upon my proposals, when you have them reported to you. Indeed I mean the best. I have no subterfuges, no arts, no intentions, but to keep to the letter of them. You shall yourself draw up every thing into writing, as strong as you can, and I will sign it: and what the law will not do to enforce it, my resolution and my will shall: so that I shall be worth nobody's address, that has not my papa's consent: nor shall any person, nor any consideration, induce me to revoke it. You can do more than any body to reconcile my parents and uncles to me. Let me owe this desirable favour to your brotherly interposition, and you will for ever oblige
>
> Your afflicted Sister, CL. HARLOWE.

And how do you think Bella employed herself while I was writing?—Why, playing gently upon my harpsichord; and humming to it, to shew her unconcernedness.

When I approached her with what I had written, she arose with an air of levity—Why, love, you have not written already!—You have, I protest!—O what a ready penwoman!—And may I read it?

If you please. And let me beseech you, my dear Bella, to back these proposals with your good offices: and [folding my uplifted hands; tears, I believe, standing in my eyes] I will love you as never sister loved another.

Thou art a strange creature, said she; there is no withstanding thee.

She took the proposals and letter; and having read them, burst into an affected laugh: How wise ones may be taken in!—Then you did not know, that I was jesting with you all this time!—And so you would have me carry down this pretty piece of nonsense?

Don't let me be surprised at your seeming unsisterliness, Bella. I hope it is but seeming. There can be no wit in such jesting as this.

The folly of the creature!—How natural is it for people, when they set their hearts upon any thing, to think every body must see with their eyes!—Pray, dear child, what becomes of your father's authority here?—Who stoops here, the parent, or the child?—How does this square with engagements actually agreed upon between your father and Mr. Solmes? What security, that your rake will not follow you to the world's end?—Nevertheless, that you may not think that I stand in the way of a reconciliation on such fine terms as these, I will be your messenger this once, and hear what my papa will say to it; although beforehand I can tell you, these proposals will not answer the principal end.

So down she went. But, it seems, my aunt Hervey and my uncle Harlowe were not gone away: and as they have all engaged to act in concert, messengers were dispatched to my uncle and aunt to desire them to be there to breakfast in the morning.

MONDAY NIGHT, ELEVEN O'CLOCK.

I am afraid I shall not be thought worthy—

Just as I began to fear I should not be thought worthy of an answer, Betty rapped at my door, and said, if I were not in bed, she had a letter for me. I had but just done writing the above dialogue, and stept to the door with the pen in my hand—Always writing, Miss! said the bold wench: it is admirable how you can get away what you write—but the fairies, they say, are always at hand to help lovers.—She retired in so much haste, that, had I been disposed, I could not take the notice of this insolence which it deserved.

I enclose my brother's letter. He was resolved to let me see, that I should have nothing to expect from his kindness. But surely he will not be permitted to carry every point. The assembling of my friends to-morrow is a good sign: and I will hope something from that, and from proposals so reasonable. And now I will try if any repose will fall to my lot for the remainder of this night.

TO MISS CLARY HARLOWE [ENCLOSED IN THE PRECEDING.]

Your proposals will be considered by your father and mother, and all your friends, to-morrow morning. What trouble does your shameful forwardness give us all! I wonder you have the courage to write to me, upon whom you are so continually emptying your whole female quiver. I have no patience with you, for reflecting upon me as the aggressor in a quarrel which owed its beginning to my consideration for you.

You have made such confessions in a villain's favour, as ought to cause all your relations to renounce you for ever. For my part, I will not believe any woman in the world, who promises against her avowed inclination. To put it out of your power to ruin yourself is the only way left to prevent your ruin. I did not intend to write; but your too-kind sister has prevailed upon me. As to your going to Scotland, that day of grace is over.—Nor would I advise, that you should go to grandfather-up your cousin Morden. Besides, that worthy gentleman might be involved in some fatal dispute, upon your account; and then be called the aggressor.

A fine situation you have brought yourself to, to propose to hide yourself from your rake, and to have falsehoods told, to conceal you!—Your confinement, at this rate, is the happiest thing that could befal you. Your bravo's behaviour at church, looking out for you, is a sufficient indication of his power over you, had you not so shamelessly acknowledged it.

One word for all—Your parents and uncles may do as they will: but if, for the honour of the family, I cannot carry this point, I will retire to Scotland, and never see the face of any one of it more.

JAMES HARLOWE. ***

There's a brother!—There's flaming duty to a father, and mother, and uncles!—But he sees himself valued, and made of consequence; and he gives himself airs accordingly!—Nevertheless, as I said above, I will hope better things from those who have not the interest my brother has to keep open these unhappy differences.

LETTER XLIII

MISS CLARISSA HARLOWE, TO MISS HOWE TUESDAY, MARCH 21

Would you not have thought, my dear Miss Howe, as well as I, that my proposal must have been accepted: and that my brother, by the last article of his unbrotherly letter (where he threatens to go to Scotland if it should be hearkened to) was of opinion that it would.

For my part, after I had read the unkind letter over and over, I concluded, upon the whole, that a reconciliation upon terms so disadvantageous to myself, as hardly any other person in my case, I dare say, would have proposed, must be the result of this morning's conference. And in that belief I had begun to give myself new trouble in thinking (this difficulty over) how I should be able to pacify Lovelace on that part of my engagement, by which I undertook to break off all correspondence with him, unless my friends should be brought, by the interposition of his powerful friends, and any offers they might make, (which it was rather his part to suggest, than mine to intimate,) to change their minds.

Thus was I employed, not very agreeably, you may believe, because of the vehemence of the tempers I had to conflict with; when breakfasting-time approached, and my judges began to arrive.

And oh! how my heart fluttered on hearing the chariot of the one, and then of the other, rattle through the court-yard, and the hollow-sounding foot-step giving notice of each person's stepping out, to take his place on the awful bench which my fancy had formed for them and my other judges!

That, thought I, is my aunt Hervey's! That my uncle Harlowe's! Now comes my uncle Antony! And my imagination made a fourth chariot for the odious Solmes, although it happened he was not there.

And now, thought I, are they all assembled: and now my brother calls upon my sister to make her report! Now the hard-hearted Bella interlards her speech with invective! Now has she concluded her report! Now they debate upon it!—Now does my brother flame! Now threaten to go to Scotland! Now is he chidden, and now soothed!

And then I ran through the whole conference in my imagination, forming speeches for this person and that, pro and con, till all concluded, as I flattered myself, in an acceptance of my conditions, and in giving directions to have an instrument drawn to tie me up to my good behaviour; while I supposed all agreed to give Solmes a wife every way more worthy of him, and with her the promise of my grandfather's estate, in case of my forfeiture, or dying unmarried, on the righteous condition he proposes to entitle himself to it with me.

And now, thought I, am I to be ordered down to recognize my own proposals. And how shall I look upon my awful judges? How shall I stand the questions of some, the set surliness of others, the returning love of one or two? How greatly shall I be affected!

Then I wept: then I dried my eyes: then I practised at my glass for a look more cheerful than my heart.

And now [as any thing stirred] is my sister coming to declare the issue of all! Tears gushing again, my heart fluttering as a bird against its wires; drying my eyes again and again to no purpose.

And thus, my Nancy, [excuse the fanciful prolixity,] was I employed, and such were my thoughts and imaginations, when I found a very different result from the hopeful conference.

For about ten o'clock up came my sister, with an air of cruel triumph, waving her hand with a light flourish—

Obedience without reserve is required of you, Clary. My papa is justly incensed, that you should presume to dispute his will, and to make conditions with him. He knows what is best for you: and as you own matters are gone a great way between this hated Lovelace and you, they will believe nothing you say; except you will give the one only instance, that will put them out of doubt of the sincerity of your promises.

What, child, are you surprised?—Cannot you speak?—Then, it seems, you had expected a different issue, had you?—Strange that you could!—With all your acknowledgements and confessions, so creditable to your noted prudence—!

I was indeed speechless for some time: my eyes were even fixed, and ceased to flow. But upon the hard-hearted Bella's proceeding with her airs of insult, Indeed I was mistaken, said I; indeed I was!——For in you, Bella, I expected, I hoped for, a sister—

What! interrupted she, with all your mannerly flings, and your despising airs, did you expect that I was capable of telling stories for you?—

Did you think, that when I was asked my own opinion of the sincerity of your declarations, I could not tell tem, how far matters had gone between you and your fellow?—When the intention is to bend that stubborn will of yours to your duty, do you think I would deceive them?—Do you think I would encourage them to call you down, to contradict all that I should have invented in your favour?

Well, well, Bella; I am the less obliged to you; that's all. I was willing to think that I had still a brother and sister. But I find I am mistaken.

Pretty mopsy-eyed soul!—was her expression!—And was it willing to think it had still a brother and sister? And why don't you go on, Clary? [mocking my half-weeping accent] I thought I had a father, and mother, two uncles, and an aunt: but I am mis—taken, that's all—come, Clary, say this, and it will in part be true, because you have thrown off all their authority, and because you respect one vile wretch more than them all.

How have I deserved this at your hands, Sister?—But I will only say, I pity you.

And with that disdainful air too, Clary!—None of that bridled neck! none of your scornful pity, girl!—I beseech you!

This sort of behaviour is natural to you, surely, Bella!—What new talents does it discover in you!—But proceed—If it be a pleasure to you, proceed, Bella. And since I must not pity you, I will pity myself: for nobody else will.

Because you don't, said she—

Hush, Bella, interrupting her, because I don't deserve it—I know you were going to say so. I will say as you say in every thing; and that's the way to please you.

Then say, Lovelace is a villain.

So I will, when I think him so.

Then you don't think him so?

Indeed I don't. You did not always, Bella.

And what, Clary, mean you by that? [bristling up to me]—Tell me what you mean by that reflection?

Tell me why you call it a reflection?—What did I say?

Thou art a provoking creature—But what say you to two or three duels of that wretch's?

I can't tell what to say, unless I knew the occasions.

Do you justify duelling at all?

I do not: neither can I help his duelling.

Will you go down, and humble that stubborn spirit of yours to your mamma?

I said nothing.

Shall I conduct your Ladyship down? [offering to take my declined hand].

What! not vouchsafe to answer me?

I turned from her in silence.

What! turn your back upon me too!—Shall I bring up your mamma to you, love? [following me, and taking my struggling hand] What? not speak yet! Come, my sullen, silent dear, speak one word to me—you must say two very soon to Mr. Solmes, I can tell you that.

Then [gushing into tears, which I could not hold in longer] they shall be the last words I will ever speak.

Well, well, [insultingly wiping my averted face with her handkerchief, while her other hand held mine, in a ridiculing tone,] I am glad any thing will make thee speak: then you think you may be brought to speak the two words—only they are to be the last!—How like a gentle lovyer from its tender bleeding heart was that!

Ridiculous Bella!

Saucy Clary! [changing her sneering tone to an imperious one] But do you think you can humble yourself to go down to your mamma?

I am tired of such stuff as this. Tell me, Bella, if my mamma will condescend to see me?

Yes, if you can be dutiful at last.

I can. I will.

But what call you dutiful?

To give up my own inclinations—That's something more for you to tell of—in obedience to my parents' commands; and to beg that I may not be made miserable with a man that is fitter for any body than for me.

For me, do you mean, Clary?

Why not? since you have put the question. You have a better opinion of him than I have. My friends, I hope, would not think him too good for me, and not good enough for you. But cannot you tell me, Bella, what is to become of me, without insulting over me thus?—If I must be thus treated, remember, that if I am guilty of any rashness, the usage I meet with will justify it.

So, Clary, you are contriving an excuse, I find, for somewhat that we have not doubted has been in your head a great while.

If it were so, you seem resolved, for your part, and so does my brother for his, that I shall not want one.—But indeed, Bella, I can bear no longer this repetition of the worst part of yesterday's conversation: I desire I may throw myself at my father's and mother's feet, and hear from them what their sentence is. I shall at least avoid, by that means, the unsisterly insults I meet with from you.

Hey-day! What, is this you? Is it you, my meek sister Clary?

Yes, it is I, Bella; and I will claim the protection due to a child of the family, or to know why I am to be thus treated, when I offer only to preserve to myself the liberty of refusal, which belongs to my sex; and, to please my parents, would give up my choice. I have contented myself till now to take second-hand messengers, and first-hand insults: you are but my sister: my brother is not my sovereign. And while I have a father and mother living, I will not be thus treated by a brother and sister, and their servants, all setting upon me, as it should seem, to make me desperate, and do a rash thing.—I will know, in short, sister Bella, why I am to be constrained thus?—What is intended by it?—And whether I am to be considered as a child or a slave?

She stood aghast all this time, partly with real, partly with affected, surprise.

And is it you? Is it indeed you?—Well, Clary, you amaze me! But since you are so desirous to refer yourself to your father and mother, I will go down, and tell them what you say. Your friends are not yet gone, I believe: they shall assemble again; and then you may come down, and plead your own cause in person.

Let me then. But let my brother and you be absent. You have made yourselves too much parties against me, to sit as my judges. And I desire to have none of yours or his interpositions. I am sure you could not have represented what I proposed fairly: I am sure you could not. Nor is it possible you should be commissioned to treat me thus.

Well, well, I'll call up my brother to you.—I will indeed.—He shall justify himself, as well as me.

I desire not to see my brother, except he will come as a brother, laying aside the authority he has unjustly assumed over me.

And so, Clary, it is nothing to him, or to me, is it, that our sister shall disgrace her whole family?

As how, Bella, disgrace it?—The man whom you thus freely treat, is a man of birth and fortune: he is a man of parts, and nobly allied.—He was once thought worthy of you: and I wish to Heaven you had had him. I am sure it was not thus my fault you had not, although you treat me thus.

This set her into a flame: I wish I had forborne it. O how the poor Bella raved! I thought she would have beat me once or twice: and she vowed her fingers itched to do so—but I was not worth her anger: yet she flamed on.

We were heard to be high.—And Betty came up from my mother to command my sister to attend her.—She went down accordingly, threatening me with letting every one know what a violent creature I had shewn myself to be.

TUESDAY NOON, MARCH 21

I have as yet heard no more of my sister: and have not courage enough to insist upon throwing myself at the feet of my father and mother, as I thought in my heat of temper I should be able to do. And I am now grown as calm as ever; and were Bella to come up again, as fit to be played upon as before.

I am indeed sorry that I sent her from me in such disorder. But my papa's letter threatening me with my uncle Antony's house and chapel, terrifies me strangely; and by their silence I'm afraid some new storm is gathering.

But what shall I do with this Lovelace? I have just now, but the unsuspected hole in the wall (that I told you of in my letter by Hannah) got a letter from him—so uneasy is he for fear I should be prevailed upon in Solmes's favour; so full of menaces, if I am; so resenting the usage I receive [for, how I cannot tell, but he has undoubtedly intelligence of all that is done in the family]; such protestations of inviolable faith and honour; such vows of reformation; such pressing arguments to escape from this disgraceful confinement—O my Nancy, what shall I do with this Lovelace?—

LETTER XLIV

MISS CLARISSA HARLOWE, TO MISS HOWE WENESDAY MORNING, NINE O'CLOCK

My aunt Hervey lay here last night, and is but just gone from me. She came up to me with my sister. They would not trust my aunt without this ill-natured witness. When she entered my chamber, I told her, that this visit was a high favour to a poor prisoner, in her hard confinement. I kissed her hand. She, kindly saluting me, said, Why this distance to your aunt, my dear, who loves you so well?

She owned, that she came to expostulate with me, for the peace-sake of the family: for that she could not believe it possible, if I did not conceive myself unkindly treated, that I, who had ever shewn such a sweetness of temper, as well as manners, should be thus resolute, in a point so very near to my father, and all my friends. My mother and she were both willing to impute my resolution to the manner I had been begun with; and to my supposing that my brother had originally more of a hand in the proposals made by Mr. Solmes, than my father or other friends. In short, fain would my aunt have furnished me with an excuse to come off my opposition; Bell all the while humming a tune, and opening this book and that, without meaning; but saying nothing.

After having shewed me, that my opposition could not be of signification, my father's honour being engaged, my aunt concluded with enforcing upon me my duty, in stronger terms than I believe she would have done, (the circumstances of the case considered), had not my sister been present.

It would be repeating what I have so often mentioned, to give you the arguments that passed on both sides.—So I will only recite what she was pleased to say, that carried with it a new face.

When she found me inflexible, as she was pleased to call it, she said, For her part, she could not but say, that if I were not to have either Mr. Solmes or Mr. Lovelace, and yet, to make my friends easy, must marry, she should not think amiss of Mr. Wyerley. What did I think of Mr. Wyerley?

Ay, Clary, put in my sister, what say you to Mr. Wyerley?

I saw through this immediately. It was said on purpose, I doubted not, to have an argument against me of absolute prepossession in Mr. Lovelace's favour: since Mr. Wyerley every where avows his value, even to veneration, for me; and is far less exceptionable both in person and mind, than Mr. Solmes: and I was willing to turn the tables, by trying how far Mr. Solmes's terms might be dispensed with; since the same terms could not be expected from Mr. Wyerley.

I therefore desired to know, whether my answer, if it should be in favour of Mr. Wyerley, would release me from Mr. Solmes?—For I owned, that I had not the aversion to him, that I had to the other.

Nay, she had no commission to propose such a thing. She only knew, that my father and mother would not be easy till Mr. Lovelace's hopes were entirely defeated.

Cunning creature! said my sister.

And this, and her joining in the question before, convinced me, that it was a designed snare for me.

Don't you, dear Madam, said I, put questions that can answer no end, but to support my brother's schemes against me.—But are there any hopes of an end to my sufferings and disgrace, without having this hated man imposed upon me? Will not what I have offered be accepted? I am sure it ought—I will venture to say that.

Why, Niece, if there be not any such hopes, I presume you don't think yourself absolved from the duty due from a child to her parents?

Yes, said my sister, I do not doubt but it is Miss Clary's aim, if she does not fly to her Lovelace, to get her estate into her own hands, and go to live at The Grove, in that independence upon which she builds all her perverseness. And, dear heart! my little love, how will you then blaze away! Your mamma Norton, your oracle, with your poor at your gates, mingling so proudly and so meanly with the ragged herd! Reflecting, by your ostentation, upon all the ladies in the county, who do not as you do. This is known to be your scheme! and the poor without-doors, and Lovelace within, with one hand building up a name, pulling it down with the other!—O what a charming scheme is this!—But let me tell you, my pretty little flighty one, that your father's living will shall controul your grandfather's dead one; and that estate will be disposed of as your fond grandfather would have disposed of it, had he lived to see such a change in his favourite. In a word, Miss, it will be kept out of your hands, till my father sees you discreet enough to have the management of it, or till you can dutifully, by law, tear it from him.

Fie, Miss Harlowe! said my aunt: this is not pretty to your sister.

O Madam, let her go on. This is nothing to what I have borne from Miss Harlowe. She is either commissioned to treat me ill by her envy, or by an higher authority, to which I must submit.—As to revoking the estate, what hinders, if I pleased? I know my power; but have not the least thought of exerting it. Be pleased to let my father know, that, whatever be the consequence to myself, were he to turn me out of doors, (which I should rather he would do, than to be confined and insulted as I am), and were I to be reduced to indigence and want, I would seek no relief that should be contrary to his will.

For that matter, child, said my aunt, were you to marry, you must do as your husband will have you. If that husband be Mr. Lovelace, he will be glad of any opportunity of further embroiling the families. And, let me tell you, Niece, if he had the respect for you which he pretends to have, he would not throw out defiances as he does. He is known to be a very revengeful man; and were I you, Miss Clary, I should be afraid he would wreak upon me that vengeance, though I had not offended him, which he is continually threatening to pour upon the family.

Mr. Lovelace's threatened vengeance is in return for threatened vengeance. It is not every body will bear insult, as, of late, I have been forced to bear it.

O how my sister's face shone with passion!

But Mr. Lovelace, proceeded I, as I have said twenty and twenty times, would be quite out of question with me, were I to be generously treated!

My sister said something with great vehemence: but only raising my voice, to be heard, without minding her, Pray, Madam, (provokingly interrogated I), was he not known to have been as wild a man, when he was at first introduced into our family, as he now is said to be? Yet then, the common phrases of wild oats, and black oxen, and such-like, were qualifiers; and marriage, and the wife's discretion, were to perform wonders—but (turning to my sister) I find I have said too much.

O thou wicked reflecter!—And what made me abhor him, think you, but the proof of those villainous freedoms that ought to have had the same effect upon you, were you but half so good a creature as you pretend to be?

Proof, did you say, Bella! I thought you had not proof?—But you know best.

Was not this very spiteful, my dear?

Now, Clary, said she, would I give a thousand pounds to know all that is in thy little rancorous and reflecting heart at this moment.

I might let you know for a much less sum, and not be afraid of being worse treated than I have been.

Well, young ladies, I am sorry to see passion run so high between you. You know, Niece, (to me,) you had not been confined thus to your apartment, could your mother by condescension, or your father by authority, have been able to move you. But how can you expect, when there must be a concession on one side, that it should be on theirs? If my Dolly, who has not the hundredth part of your understanding, were thus to set herself up in absolute contradiction to my will, in a point so material, I should not take it well of her—indeed I should not.

I believe not, Madam: and if Miss Hervey had just such a brother, and just such a sister [you may look, Bella!] and if both were to aggravate her parents, as my brother and sister do mine—then, perhaps, you might use her as I am used: and if she hated the man you proposed to her, and with as much reason as I do Mr. Solmes—

And loved a rake and libertine, Miss, as you do Lovelace, said my sister—

Then might she [continued I, not minding her,] beg to be excused from obeying. Yet if she did, and would give you the most solemn assurances, and security besides, that she would never have the man you disliked, against your consent—I dare say, Miss Hervey's father and mother would sit down satisfied, and not endeavour to force her inclinations.

So!—[said my sister, with uplifted hands] father and mother now come in for their share!

But if, child, replied my aunt, I knew she loved a rake, and suspected that she sought only to gain time, in order to wire-draw me into a consent—

I beg pardon, Madam, for interrupting you; but if Miss Hervey could obtain your consent, what further would be said?

True, child; but she never should.

Then, Madam, it would never be.

That I doubt, Niece.

If you do, Madam, can you think confinement and ill usage is the way to prevent the apprehended rashness?

My dear, this sort of intimation would make one but too apprehensive, that there is no trusting to yourself, when one knows your inclination.

That apprehension, Madam, seems to have been conceived before this intimation, or the least cause for it, was given. Why else the disgraceful confinement I have been laid under?—Let me venture to say, that my sufferings seem to be rather owing to a concerted design to intimidate me [Bella held up her hands], (knowing there were too good grounds for my opposition,) than to a doubt of my conduct; for, when they were inflicted first, I had given no cause of doubt: nor should there now be room for any, if my discretion might be trusted to.

My aunt, after a little hesitation, said, But, consider, my dear, what confusion will be perpetuated in your family, if you marry this hated Lovelace!

And let it be considered, what misery to me, Madam, if I marry that hated Solmes!

Many a young creature has thought she could not love a man, with whom she has afterwards been very happy. Few women, child, marry their first loves.

That may be the reason there are so few happy marriages.

But there are few first impressions fit to be encouraged.

I am afraid so too, Madam. I have a very indifferent opinion of light and first impressions. But, as I have often said, all I wish for is, to have leave to live single.

Indeed you must not, Miss. Your father and mother will be unhappy till they see you married, and out of Lovelace's reach. I am told that you propose to condition with him (so far are matters gone between you) never to have any man, if you have not him.

I know no better way to prevent mischief on all sides, I freely own it—and there is not, if he be out of the question, another man in the world I can think favourably of. Nevertheless, I would give all I have in the world, that he were married to some other person—indeed I would, Bella, for all you put on that smile of incredulity.

May be so, Clary: but I will smile for all that.

If he be out of the question! repeated my aunt—So, Miss Clary, I see how it is—I will go down—[Miss Harlowe, shall I follow you?]—And I will endeavour to persuade your father to let my sister herself come up: and a happier event may then result.

Depend upon it, Madam, said my sister, this will be the case: my mother and she will both be in tears; but with this different effect: my mother will come down softened, and cut to the heart; but will leave her favourite hardened, from the advantages she will think she has over my mother's tenderness—why, Madam, it is for this very reason the girl is not admitted into her presence.

Thus she ran on, as she went downstairs.